Gary Wright joined Kent Police at the age of eighteen and worked in a variety of uniformed roles. At the age of twenty-nine, and completely out of the blue, he suffered two cardiac arrests that led to the diagnosis of a life-limiting and incurable disease of the heart. Following the implantation of an internal defibrillator into his heart, he was unable to continue policing and retired at the age of thirty. He bought a coffee shop in Ramsgate Harbour, and spent years looking out over the sea and dreaming up stories. He now writes full time, committing those very stories to paper.

PART ONE

Before the Storm

Prologue

Thirty-five Years Before

'MUMMY!'

The rip dragged him away, but not under. Not yet. It was playing a game, toying with the little boy it held in its grip. It pounded and crushed him, tearing the air from his lungs as the safety of the shore grew distant.

His arms burned as his muscles fought against the Goliath that was trying to seize him, to claim him. His legs trod just like he'd learned. Primeval instinct, perhaps. Intuition. Survival, come what may. But still, he couldn't find any traction.

'MUMMY, MUMMY!'

More energy used, and the sea didn't like it, pummelling him with bigger waves. Punishment. That'll teach him for trying to escape.

'ANDREW!'

He opened his mouth to shout back, but nothing came. Instead, sea brine kissed his lips. He could taste it. Salt, like when he sweated. Salt, like on his dinner. He knew the taste but, just like his mummy's voice, in the grip of the sea and the lap of the Gods, it was wildly different.

'ANDREW! SOMEONE, HELP!'

The shore was getting further and further away. His eyes burned as the waves struck his face, licking him with acidic verve. Blinking didn't work. Instead, he screwed his eyes shut, closing out the beast. All he wanted was his mummy.

'MU—'

It was one wave too many and it flooded his open mouth, squeezing every last breath from him.

He went under.

His fingers reached for the surface but there was nothing to grab. No purchase. No toehold, no footing. Nothing to cling on to as he clawed for something. Anything. It was just a thin dividing line between above and below.

The violence above contrasted with the calm just inches underneath. The crashing of the waves was replaced with a melodic thudding. He knew he needed to breathe, to fight, to overcome, but it was too hard. He was exhausted, his reserves empty. Now, he didn't feel pain. Now, he wasn't scared.

It was almost peaceful.

Almost.

His eyes stayed shut as darkness consumed him.

Chapter 1

ANDREW

One Day Before

Saturday brought sunshine. Warmth. Andrew stared from the kitchen window and, as far as his eyes could see, the sky above was a uniform, strikingly blue canvas.

'Brekkie, kids,' Sophie shouted upstairs.

'Alright, Mum!' Maria shouted back. Sophie was no longer Mummy, and Andrew no longer Daddy. Their little girl had trimmed their names long before any child should. Six going on sixteen, they had said. Both parents missed it, though they'd never say it out loud. The difference two letters made was profound. It was just one syllable, but was yet another sign that their baby was growing up so much faster than they wanted her to.

It wasn't a light pitter-patter of feet on the stairs that announced their imminent arrival, more a herd of elephants on the rampage. Maria barged through the kitchen door with Joe following close behind. Though they were just best friends, they may as well have been brother and sister. He was there often enough, after all. They wore wide smiles on sun-kissed cheeks. The innocence of youth abounded from every sinew, overflowing from every pore as they glowed with excitement.

'Alright, bud?' Andrew said to Joe, their knuckles meeting in a fist bump.

'Yeah, Ange!' Joe replied.

Ange. It was Joe's nickname for him, and Joe's alone.

'Ready for it?' Andrew asked, as he ruffled Joe's thick blond hair.

Joe might have been Maria's best friend, but the bond between man and boy was a powerful one. In the absence of a son of his and Sophie's own, Joe was a more than worthy void-filler. Joe smiled, and nodded until his head looked like it might separate from his shoulders.

'Ready...' Andrew said, offering his hand in the air at just the right height for Joe to slap it three times.

'One, two, three.' Their hands met.

'Four, five, six,' Joe continued as their fingers gripped each other's, and rose and fell in perfect harmony.

'Seven,' Joe said, as the handshake turned into another high-five.

'Eight, nine, ten,' he concluded, as the high-five evolved into three more fist bumps.

It was their secret handshake, their special greeting, their moment, each time they saw one another.

'Again!'

Andrew met the boy's smile with one of his own. How could he say no to a grin as broad as that?

'One second,' he said, as his phone vibrated in his pocket. He pulled it out, and fumbled to unlock it. Andrew might have only been up for an hour or so, but Chris had been at work since the sun had begun its slow ascent across the horizon. 9 a.m. was a safe time to check in.

Morning mate, hope you're all alright? Let me know what you're up to, and give Joe a big squeeze from me x

Morning, all good here. Do I really need to tell you where we're going…? Surely it's obvious on a day like today X

Was it a rhetorical question? Maybe. Probably. Of course it was.

Andrew looked beyond the kitchen and into the garden through the bifold doors that led onto the patio. The sun bore down, its rays shining a spotlight on everything they touched. His eyes diverted to the neat row of begonias that Sophie had spent so much time and care sowing, and were now blooming in the midst of summer. The flowers positively glowed, their colours radiating as if given new life by a little bit of vitamin D. And yet, as he took in the majesty of the images his eyes sent to his brain, he still looked for the shaded areas, for the shadows.

'Alright, love?' Sophie asked, nudging Andrew as she brushed past him.

'Course, sweetheart,' he replied, nodding his head a little too vigorously.

'Working out a plan?'

He knew what she was talking about. His eyes darted to the patio itself. Bluntly, it was a state. In a garden where everything else was prim and proper, it stood out like a Vespa at a Harley convention.

'I told you I'd do it,' he replied. 'You haven't got to ask me every six months.'

It wasn't a nudge that greeted him this time, more a firm dig in the ribs. Sophie smiled as their hands came together and their fingers interlocked.

'Bloody builders,' she said. 'You can never rely on them.'

'I'll get on it soon.'

'Soon,' Sophie replied, raising her hands and using two fingers on each to make speech marks in the air.

Andrew turned away, suppressing a laugh. He grafted all week long. No way was he giving up a weekend to do yet more work at home. His body was honed from all those years on the tools and the gym, but that didn't mean he didn't get tired. Time waited for no man, and he could feel it creeping up on him day by day, week by week, month by month. Then, a brainwave.

'Unless you're alright to take the kids on your own sometime?' he said, turning back to face his wife.

Her face was granite.

'Okay, okay,' he said, resigned to his fate.

Their beach hut occupied a prime spot on the promenade that sat a few feet above Beachbrook main sands. Beachbrook was a typical tourist town; packed to the rafters with holiday makers in the summer, but deserted and left to the locals in the winter. Local businesses prospered in the warm months but were shuttered in the cold.

In those summer months, though, the town lived and breathed as if she was alive. She was beautiful, her vistas and horizons postcard perfect. Her perfume was vinegar from the chippy and sugar-dusted doughnuts. She played a melody of seagulls squawking and excited children running on her golden sands while, behind them, the drum of the breaking waves thumped just like a beating heart.

Today, those drumbeats were quiet. They couldn't really

be called waves, more a ripple as they steadily enveloped the feet of the kids who frolicked at her shoreline. Today, she was tired. Today, she was holding back. Today, Andrew could breathe.

He assumed his usual position on a fold-out chair outside the beach hut, tapping his feet on the ground. The concrete nestled into the soles of his trainers like an old friend. Those four metres of promenade that separated the hut from the sands had been the clincher when Sophie had looked at him with doughy eyes all those years ago when they'd talked about acquiring a base on the beach. It was a four-metre barrier in his mind, a safety net protecting him from what had befallen him all those years before.

He might have been dressed flamboyantly, but he hadn't put swimmers on. He never did. His gaze went to Maria and Joe as they raced down the three-stepped ladder that Andrew had propped from the promenade down onto the beach, and chased across the sand, footsteps in tandem as grains of golden dust were kicked up in their wake.

'Alright, love?' Sophie asked.

'Yeah, fine,' he replied. He didn't look at her, keeping his focus entirely on Maria and Joe. Though the two kids were only about twenty metres away from him, it took a knowing eye to be able to differentiate them.

Both blonde and with matching orange wetsuits, a passer-by would probably assume they were related and, in truth, they were just like twins.

They ran to a pool of water that was set a good fifteen metres away from the sea in a direct line with the beach hut. It was a permanent, natural feature of Beachbrook main sands, and filled every time the tide washed over it, but was disconnected from the sea itself. They'd christened it the 'little sea', way back when Maria had barely been able to waddle on the sand and, as Andrew watched, he knew what they wanted to do. Call it a father's intuition. Even from a distance, he could sense their eyes twitching as, around them, parents tended to toddlers and babies, giving some of them their first experience of toes in water. He watched as Maria and Joe whispered to each other, their conspiring now obvious. He knew what they'd be saying. This is the baby pool. We're not babies. So predictable, he thought and, just as he stood up, they began to edge away from the little sea.

Andrew walked to the edge of the promenade and jumped onto the sand below, ignoring the ladder and instantly regretting his choice. It may have only been a three-foot gap separating above from below, but his joints ached when he landed. Old football injuries coming back to haunt him, or simply a body getting old? He'd go with the former, but he knew it was more than likely the latter. Though the sand was dry and powdery underfoot, it felt heavy. It always did with shoes on. Barefoot, it'd form and mould around the skin but not with trainers. He looked up and quickened his pace, feeling his heart rate spiking. The kids shared mischievous grins as they edged backwards. As Andrew reached them, their feet were being swallowed by the trickling waves of his old enemy.

'Maria, what have we said about going in the sea without me or your mum being here?'

'You are here,' she replied. 'You were watching us, weren't you?' Typical Maria, Andrew thought. Even at the age of six she had, somehow, turned his questions into an interrogation of her own.

'Of course I was watching you, princess,' Andrew said, trying but failing to prevent his eyes from rolling back into his head. The truth was that he'd been wrapped around her little finger since the first day he had laid eyes on her. 'One of us has got to be here by the water if you want to go in. You know that.'

'Okay, Dad,' she said.

She turned away from him to look at Joe, and the cracks of her lips rose upwards. She'd won, and she knew it. Joe didn't say anything. Confrontation just wasn't his bag, particularly where Andrew was involved. Andrew and Joe were the best of mates, and these mates didn't argue.

Andrew watched, his gaze never diverting from the target of his focus. Maria didn't go past her knees. Though she loved to push boundaries, she knew that there was a firm line in the sand. To everyone in the water around them, and to the parents who formed a line adjacent to Andrew, watching their kids frolic and splash to their hearts' content, it was utopia. The sun blazed. The birds sang. The sea sent glittering shards of light reflecting in a million different directions as it eased in and out on the tide.

Yet, to Andrew, it was anything but easy. The sea was wearing a mask, constrained by a leash. When it broke free, it was an entity that simply couldn't be contained. He knew it, and the twenty minutes the kids spent splashing and playing in the shallows felt like an hour to him. When they came out, Maria ran straight past him and back to Sophie who was waiting for her with an open towel.

Andrew's shoulders finally relaxed as Joe's hand slipped into his and he forced a weary smile. Another day had passed without incident. They made their way back towards the beach hut, Joe's bare feet growing heavy as dry sand clung to his wet skin, and Andrew's trainers leaving deep craters behind them.

He heard gentle waves trickling into the shore behind him,

and turned to face the sea one last time before they packed up and headed home. Today, it had behaved, and he nodded towards it. It wasn't reverential, and it wasn't respect. No, it was just a sense of acknowledgement. It had been those waves and that tide all those years before that had tried to claim him. Today, it had toed the line.

As Andrew trudged back to the beach hut, he climbed the ladder and kicked his trainers together, knocking clumps of sand from his soles as he felt welcome, solid ground underfoot. Maria was already in the hut, and he took a second to look at the two women in his life. He didn't like the beach, that much was a given. Still, it was worth it if they were happy. Sophie was busy drying Maria off and he could hear familiar protestations coming from his daughter.

'I can do it myself, Mum.' Maria took the towel from her mum and was swallowed up in it.

'You've got to get the sand off,' Sophie said.

'I WILL!' Maria shouted.

Sophie held her hands up and walked away towards Andrew, knowing better than to try to help her anymore. He put his arm around her as they watched Maria wrestle with the towel. Andrew stroked Sophie's stomach with his spare hand.

'You'll be easier to manage than your big sister, right?' he asked, with a smile.

'For a few years, maybe,' Sophie replied.

Andrew looked down as a football came to rest against his heel. He turned around; Joe was standing a few yards away, bare-chested and with his wetsuit tied at the waist. He was wearing the goalkeeping gloves that he took everywhere with him. One day, he said, he was going to be between the sticks for England. In Joe, Andrew had a kindred spirit.

Though well past his prime, the feel of a ball at his feet still evoked happy memories. All of a sudden, his joints didn't feel quite so sore.

With the flick of a foot and a touch of experience, the light foam ball floated on the breeze back towards Joe, who caught it with steady hands. It had taken months of practice, but they'd got there. The boy was coming on leaps and bounds. Joe threw the ball back, and it landed perfectly at Andrew's feet.

'Cantona takes it down,' Andrew said, pivoting one way before swivelling the other.

'Who?' Joe asked, dropping his hands to his side.

Andrew shook his head ever so slightly.

'Lays it off to Scholes, takes it up the centre,' he continued, flicking the ball from one foot to the other as he dribbled it across the promenade.

'Who?' Joe repeated.

'Ronaldoooooooo,' Andrew shouted, digging the ball out from under his feet and lifting it towards Joe.

Game on. Joe knew that name. The ball swerved in the air, but, with the spring of youth in his step, he dived onto the ground, and deflected it with the very tips of his fingers.

'Joe!' Andrew shouted, his face contorting as the boy's body scraped along the concrete.

'RAMSDALE,' Joe shouted leaping to his feet and running rings around Andrew. The graze on his side didn't matter. Not to Joe, anyway. Nothing mattered. He'd made the save. He'd won.

Andrew grabbed hold of him, bringing his victory lap to a halt. He looked at Joe's side, at where the skin had been scraped and grazed, and winced. It was going to be a sore one, alright.

'You alright?' he asked, setting Joe back down on the concrete.

'I won,' Joe replied, continuing his victory parade.

Andrew smiled. Momentarily, he could forget the sea. For a few, fleeting seconds, he could live in the moment, alive in the present, basking in Joe's exuberance. It was moments like that which made the beach tolerable.

The sun had passed its peak and was on a slow descent towards the horizon. Home time. For Andrew, the best time. They packed up their beach hut and, as the shadows of late afternoon crept across the sand and began to encroach upon the promenade, made their way up the slope that took them to the top of the white cliffs. Those chalky summits surrounded the beach and gave it that picture-perfect finish. Andrew looked all around him. Was it really that bad, he wondered?

As he drove, Andrew tried to listen as Maria and Joe spoke in hushed, excited voices in the back. He couldn't make out what they were saying, but whatever it was, it sounded like mischief was afoot. Home was a mere five minutes away, and they arrived to find Chris and Linda waiting for them in the garden, drinks prepared and barbeque lit. Linda had even donned the marigolds and done the washing up that had been left on the side.

'See, this is why we gave you a key!' Sophie said, hugging Linda. Sophie glowed with the sheen of an expectant mother who didn't have to work, who had everything under control and who was enjoying her pregnancy.

'You know me,' Linda replied, 'OCD with the cleaning!'

Joe charged up to his parents and cuddled them both.

'Daddy, Daddy!' he shouted. 'You should've seen my save today!'

Chris scooped his boy into his arms.

'Ball's the wrong shape,' Chris replied, blowing a raspberry on Joe's cheek.

'Bloody egg chasers,' Andrew said. In the world of sport, there were football lovers and rugby worshippers. Andrew and Chris were deeply entrenched in their own camps and, to Chris' eternal chagrin, Joe was drifting towards Andrew's way of thinking.

'Good day?' Linda asked, stealing Joe from her husband and gripping him in an embrace of her own. She licked her finger and wiped Joe's salt-stained cheek.

'Best EVER!' Joe replied.

'What, ever ever?' Linda asked.

'EVER EVER,' Joe replied, as he nuzzled his nose against his mummy's. Linda tickled him on his side, but he recoiled, wincing as he did.

'What's up?' she asked, setting Joe down and lifting his t-shirt, revealing an angry-looking graze on his side.

'You should've seen my save, Mummy,' he said.

Linda wasn't listening. Andrew could sense that the paramedic in her had taken over.

'How did you do that?' she asked, moving in closer for inspection.

'Andrew was shooting and I saved it,' he replied. 'OUCH!'

'Sorry, love,' she whispered, pulling her prodding fingers away. She looked up, and caught Andrew's gaze. Her eyes had begun to fill with tears. He'd been making his excuses in his head, but her weary look of displeasure had caught him off guard.

'It was a great save,' he mumbled. It's all he had managed to come up with. He turned around, and with a face turning to a shade of puce, walked back to Chris.

The two husbands stood and watched as their respective wives sat on the plumply cushioned rattan sofa that hugged the edges of the patio, bookended by pot plants that were blooming in all the colours of summer. If the house was a work of art, then so was the garden. It was just one of those evenings, where everything was perfect. Everything, that is, except the patio. Sophie and Linda spoke in hushed tones, but Andrew knew what the topic of conversation was. They were staring at the ground, and Sophie was pointing at the deep cracks and broken edges that stood out in glorious technicolour.

'I told you, I'll do it,' Andrew called across to his wife. Sophie rolled her eyes in response. 'Soon,' he added, but it didn't placate her.

While the ladies sat, with their conversation quiet, Andrew turned to Chris. The chat was easy. It always had been.

'Nice shirt,' Chris said, smirking.

'Sod off,' Andrew shot back, as they clinked glasses.

'Tourist,' Chris said.

'Just blending in,' Andrew replied.

'If I had your guns, I'd have them out all the time,' Chris said.

Andrew looked down at his biceps. The building game lent itself to acquiring a certain physique.

'You can always come and lay some bricks with me,' he said, knowing exactly what the answer would be.

'On your bike,' came the response, as it had done a thousand times before. 'Although, if it means I get a house like this...'

'You can have the mortgage as well, if you like,' Andrew replied, laughing. 'You cooking then?'

'No chance, day from hell,' Chris replied. 'It's all yours.'

'Every day's a day from hell, isn't it?' Andrew said, smiling. 'I've known you, what, six years, and I can't remember you having a good one.'

'You don't want to know,' Chris replied.

'Try me,' Andrew said.

'Alright then,' Chris said. 'So I'm out single crewed, and I get the duff car with knackered air con. I mean, it's not like the old bill to have many perks, but these uniforms are hideous enough in the heat.'

Andrew smirked, and waved his hand over his nose.

'Sod off,' Chris said, smiling. 'Anyway, I get asked to go and back up one of the younger lads at a sudden death. Easy job, you know, old person died in their sleep, neighbour called it in, not been seen for a while, yadda yadda yadda. Anyway, the probationer is already there, key in the key safe, door open, ambulance called to confirm life extinct, undertaker called to collect body, but the copper is new so the skipper asked me to check it all out.'

'Right...' Andrew said.

'So I get there,' Chris continued, 'I check the paperwork, all good. I check they've searched for meds and that, all good. Then I ask whether they've checked the body.' Chris took a deep breath, shook his head and had a deep gulp of beer.

'Go on...' Andrew said.

'Well no, apparently he's never touched a dead body before,' Chris said, rolling his eyes. 'I mean, fair enough, right? Fair enough. But still, it's part of the job. So we go into the bedroom...'

'And?' Andrew asks.

'And,' Chris said, 'I tell matey boy to gently take down the covers, I mean, I've got a real thing about us respecting the dead, you know. We'll all be there one day. But anyway, he gently pulls down the covers, and…'

'Aaaaaaaand?!' Andrew was dying to know what happened.

'Old bloke opened his eyes and asked us what the hell we were doing in his house,' Chris muttered.

'You're kidding,' Andrew giggled.

'On my life,' Chris said. 'Obviously pretty funny in hindsight, but you should have seen the mountain of paperwork I had to fill in.'

He dropped his warrant card and keys on the table next to his beer.

'Hilarious,' Linda smirked, hearing Chris' appraisal of his day. 'You think your day was bad, I had someone collapse at the top of a block of flats, and the lift was broken. Had to get the fire brigade in to help get them down.'

'You chose the green uniform…' Chris said, baiting his wife. The banter between the police and the ambulance service didn't just stop when they clocked off.

'We can't all be heroes,' Linda said, smiling.

Andrew sat down, waiting for the coals of the barbeque to smoulder. He closed his eyes, savouring his beer and drinking in the peace around him. His mind transported him far away and, in that moment, he could've been sitting on a veranda in the Mediterranean without a care in the world.

Andrew's moment of serenity was brought to an abrupt end as whoops of laughter pierced the air. In an instant, his cheeks were slapped with a burst of water. He opened his eyes. Maria and Joe had Super Soakers in their hands and malevolence written all over their faces.

'Little shits,' Andrew said under his breath, provoking an 'Oi!' from his wife.

The kids didn't stand a chance. Andrew and Chris sprang into action and wrestled the weapons from their children's hands, making them regret picking a fight they couldn't win. The two adults looked smugly at each other as the kids skulked away to the back of the garden, soaking wet and beaten. The mums looked at each other with a knowing glance. Once kids, always kids. Their husbands sat down next to them, each basking in the glory of a water fight well won.

'So, what's the plan tomorrow then?' Linda asked.

'Not sure yet,' Sophie replied.

'You know how much we appreciate you having Joe, right?' Linda said. Her voice was quiet, her words reserved and uttered with delicate awareness of the burden she was sure she was placing upon Sophie and Andrew.

Andrew opened his mouth to speak, but Sophie beat him to the punch.

'We love having him!' she replied, smiling and stroking Linda's arm, putting her at ease. 'Besides, someone's got to keep us all safe, right?'

Linda smiled but Andrew could tell it was laced with doubt. She'd told him before, that if they could afford it then she'd give up work in a heartbeat. This was another whole weekend that she wouldn't be able to spend with her son. Andrew knew how he'd feel if he wasn't able to spend time with Maria often enough. Time was precious, he knew, but Linda and Chris' situation was different. They couldn't afford not to work.

Joe appeared next to his mum and sat on her lap. He was still soaked wet through, but Linda wasn't giving up the chance of a cuddle.

'My boy,' Linda said, as she held her cheek to Joe's.

Six years since the kids were born had passed by in the blink of an eye. Nursery had been and gone and, now, another school year was nearly over.

Andrew watched, sensing Linda's misgivings. 'What do you fancy doing tomorrow, Joe?'

'BEACH!' Maria shouted, appearing as if from nowhere.

'Oi, miss, I was talking to Joe,' Andrew said.

'Whatever Maria wants,' Joe said. 'Beach sounds good.'

Again, Andrew opened his mouth to speak but, once more, Sophie got in there first.

'We'll see,' Sophie said. 'Weather is supposed to be on the turn tonight.'

Andrew caught Chris' eye. Instinctively, they each knew what the other was thinking. Jets of water filled the air as the two men jumped to their feet, armed with childish weaponry. It was an ambush.

As Sophie spoke, water sprayed across her cheeks and straight into Maria's chest.

'GOT HER!' Andrew shouted.

The kids ran as quickly as they could, almost snorting with laughter and hotly pursued by their dads. Sophie and Linda again looked at each other, each wearing half a smile and gently shaking their heads.

'They'll never grow up, will they?' Linda said.

Sophie turned to watch as, once again, Andrew and Chris pinned down their kids and soaked them from head to toe.

'Never,' she replied.

Chapter 2

LINDA

Seven Hours Before

'Mummy! Mummy!'

Linda picked up her phone and the light of Joe's smiling face on the screen broke the darkness. 2.02 a.m. She lay there for a while, keeping her eyes shut. *Go to sleep. Go to sleep.* She knew how this scenario was likely to play out. It had only been a couple of hours since she'd finally managed to prise herself away from his clutches. She couldn't remember the last time that Chris had put him to bed. It was always her. Always.

'Mummy! Mummy!' Joe shouted, louder this time. Linda rolled over and looked at Chris who was lying asleep next to her, snoring. Either he hadn't heard Joe, or he was a bloody good actor. Either way he never got up and, deep down, it really rankled with her. Sure, he worked a full-time shift pattern, but so did she. The constant jet lag was bad enough at the best of times. Add a sleepless child into the mix and the result was a mummy who was getting close to the end of her tether.

Linda got out of bed and heard the wind howling outside.

She made no attempt to hide her irritation from Chris, opening and closing the bedroom door with enough force to make him stir, but it didn't rouse him from his slumber. She shuffled across the landing to Joe's bedroom where she found her boy sitting up on his bed, wide awake and with a whistling draught coming in through his window. Chris was meant to fix it, but it had always been a job for another day. She sighed and pushed a blanket against the frame. A temporary fix, but good enough.

'Mummy,' he said with a smile on his face.

'What's going on, Joe?' Linda asked, rubbing her gritty eyes. 'It's the middle of the night, you should be asleep.'

He pointed at the window, gesturing to the wind that was picking up pace outside.

'Can we play?' he asked.

'How about we read a book and get you back to sleep?' she said. His wide eyes and cheeky grin told her that this was going to take a while.

'Story time!' Joe said excitedly.

'Go and choose one then,' Linda said as she lay down on his bed. Her eyes hung heavy as she tried to keep them open. She'd pay for this later, guaranteed.

Joe walked over to his bookcase and chose his favourite picture book. Sure, he could read chapter books now, but he hadn't grown out of the words, sentences and rhymes that he'd been brought up listening to. Linda read it with him three times, cover to cover, but it didn't tire him out. Far from it. His eyes still looked at her, hungry for more. She looked at the clock on his night light and, as her eyes squinted, the footballers who adorned the wallpaper surrounding them seemed to come to life. Her mind was playing tricks with her, and it was getting silly now.

'Right then, mister, it's definitely time for sleep. You've got to be up in a few hours' time to go to Maria's,' she said. Joe recognised the voice. It was the one Mummy used when she was at work, the one she told naughty patients off with. It was the one that meant business. The one that he didn't argue with. 'Come and lie down and let's snuggle.'

She lay down and he cuddled into her, his back against her stomach. Linda shut her eyes. The middle-of-the-night wake up she hated. These cuddles though… They were everything.

Linda stroked her son's side, and he tensed up. She'd forgotten about the graze. Her sigh was deep and the shake of her head almost imperceptible, but she couldn't say anything, could she? She asked so much of Andrew and Sophie, after all.

After about half an hour he was asleep, announced by the noise he made. It was uniquely his – not quite a snore, but with a little squeak as a kicker when he exhaled. She fully intended to go back to her own bed, to try to at least get a few hours of something approaching meaningful kip, but Joe had wedged himself into her armpit and to move him would risk waking him. She reasoned that a couple of hours of uncomfortable sleep was better than none and, as she closed her eyes and tried to time her breathing with the melody from Joe's sleeping lips, drifted off.

Joe's door always creaked if it was opened slowly. Linda knew it, and so did Chris. That's why, in the middle of the night, she had pushed it shut quickly. Now, as she was awoken in a daze by the shrieking percussion of those hinges squeaking and threatening to wake Joe, she froze. The look that she shot at Chris could have turned boiling water to ice. He held his hands up in apology, hoping against hope that Joe's stirring would revert back to the deep sleep that he

23

had been in, and stood rooted to the spot. Linda looked at the clock. She could've had another hour of sleep. Furious, but too tired for an argument, she lay there until Chris had finished in the bathroom. When she heard him going downstairs, she extricated herself from Joe's grip.

She dragged herself out of his bedroom and went to the bathroom where she splashed water over her face, grabbing a towel by instinct and drying the drips that had hit the mirror.

As she looked into it, a broken woman stared back at her.

She went downstairs. The kettle was on, teabags in mugs. Chris made conciliatory noises about helping out more at night, but she was too tired, too drained, to go there. She went into the lounge and curled up on the sofa, her eyes just feeling too heavy to keep open.

'Mummy?'

Linda pulled herself out from the deepest of sleeps. Was she dreaming?

'Mummy?'

She opened her eyes. Where was she? The lounge, of course. Her tea sat on a coaster on the table, but the steam had long since died away. In front of her, Joe. Staring at her.

'What are you doing down here, Mummy?'

A burst of adrenaline jolted her upright, and she looked at the clock.

'Shit,' she muttered.

It was 6.40 a.m. and she had just twenty minutes to get Joe to Andrew and Sophie's house if she wanted to be at work on time.

'Quick, upstairs,' she said to Joe. She scooped her boy up into her arms and rushed up the stairs. They only had time for the bare necessities. Teeth brushed and, in her case, a quick roll of deodorant under the arms. No time to wash.

Iron her uniform? Forget about it. She threw it on; the creases would fall out anyway, then grabbed some of Joe's clothes and chucked them into a bag. His pyjamas would have to do for the drive to Andrew and Sophie's house.

They were out of the house by 6:55 a.m. and arrived at the Wicks' just after 7 a.m. For once, Linda had no time to feel the slightest pang of jealousy at just how bloody lovely their house was, how not a brick seemed to be out of place, how all the tiles on the roof matched and the cars on the driveway were lined up in perfect symmetry. She knocked on the door and, as Sophie answered it, Joe ran inside. She didn't have time to resent her best friend's silky smooth, naturally blonde hair, and how she always carried herself with panache.

'I'm so sorry,' Linda said, flustered. 'I overslept. He's got some clothes here but he hasn't had breakfast yet. Are you alright to give him some?'

Sophie's smile was one of pity, and Linda knew it. The contrast between the two of them couldn't have been more marked. Linda's skin wasn't glowing. Every day may have been a good hair day for Sophie, but she hadn't had one since... She couldn't even remember.

'Are you alright, Lin?' Sophie asked. 'You look done in.'

'Joe was up in the night,' Linda replied, running a hand through her hair, almost able to feel the grey roots that were growing by the day and fighting against the winds that had sent it wild. She looked at her watch, before shaking her head. 'Sorry but I've got to dash. I'm running late, love. I'll see you about six, all being well. Thank you again.'

'You don't need to thank us,' Sophie replied. Her voice was small, and Linda barely heard her as she turned and ran back to her car, battling a headwind that was trying to keep her from getting in. In the distance, she heard a bin topple. The seagulls cawed their approval as they dived in for the scraps. She slammed her door shut, keeping the winds at bay, just as Joe ran to the front door. She saw him. He saw her. And his face was tinged with a sadness that wounded her.

'Mummy!' he shouted.

Linda waved.

'Mummy!'

'For fuck's sake,' Linda muttered to herself, instantly regretting her words. She was tired. She was in a rush. But she knew she had no right to take it out on her little boy.

She jumped from her car and ran back up the pathway where she scooped her little boy off his feet. This was typical of how it had been for the weeks, months and years gone by. A whirlwind, of snatched cuddles, misty eyes and all too frequent goodbyes.

'Mummy loves you,' she said, nuzzling their noses together. 'More than chocolate.'

He laughed. The smile was back.

'Love you, Mummy. I wish you were coming with us,' he replied.

Chapter 3

DS SUE WILLMOTT

Three Hours Before

In another part of town, another mum was awake and getting ready to creep out of the house.

'Thanks for having her, Mum,' DS Sue Willmott said, as she walked into the lounge.

'Never a problem,' her mum replied with a smile.

'What time did you get here?' DS Willmott asked, picking up the mug of tea that was sitting on the table, ready and waiting for her.

'Didn't you hear?' her mum replied.

DS Willmott looked at her, blankly. She'd been dead to the world right up until her alarm had blared in her ear just twenty minutes before.

'That wind came whistling through when I opened the door,' her mum continued. 'Banged it right against the wall.'

'Didn't hear a thing,' DS Willmott replied, taking a long swig on her tea. It was like nectar as it hit her lips and, from the temperature of the liquid, she knew that her mum had been there for a while.

'What time are you home, love?' her mum asked.

'Four, all being well,' DS Willmott replied. 'Is that alright?'

Her mum smiled and nodded. There was no place in the world she'd rather be than with her granddaughter, and DS Willmott knew it. It went some way to soothing the sting of leaving her little Lottie in bed.

'What have you got planned?' DS Willmott asked, picking up the coat that she'd thrown over the side of the sofa the day before and slipping her arms inside. She caught sight of herself in the lounge mirror. A thousand investigations or more were painted across her face, reaching inside every frown line, and touching every blemish. Her hair was short. Practical. Her round-rimmed glasses were not for fashion, but for function. She'd lived, breathed and bled to be the copper she was now, and it showed. She'd earned her stripes alright.

Her mum looked out of the window. Morning may have broken, but it was still dark with heavy clouds overhead. The silence inside was punctuated by a tiny whistle of wind that was sneaking through a hairline crack in the beading of the window frame.

'I think we'll stay here, do some baking or something,' her mum said.

'Good plan,' DS Willmott replied.

It was 6.30 a.m. The clock in her car told her that she had time to spare as she drove to work. She pulled down the sun visor in her car, not to protect her from the sun that was hidden behind angry clouds overhead, but to look at the photo of the little girl she had left at home, sleeping like an angel. It was a couple of years out of date, way back when Lottie had been just six years old, but the smile she wore had lent itself to being one of 'those' photos that every parent had. In a world where camera phones were everywhere, only a few photos would stand out and make the cut. This was one of them.

Beachbrook Police Station occupied a prime location in town, with views out over the sea that property developers would have given their collective right arms for. About a mile from the main sands, it had a personality and charm all of its own, one that was the preserve of the older police station that was becoming a thing of the past up and down the country. It had character. The hallways and offices could tell stories of times gone by, of different ages of policing. Hell, DS Willmott could herself write a book about her own twenty-five years of policing within those very walls. She was as much a part of the fabric as anything else in there.

She made her way into the CID office that had been her working home for twenty years, first as a Detective Constable (DC) and, for the past ten years, as a Detective Sergeant (DS). She was the first in, but it didn't surprise her. She always was. She knew the others would soon follow – no one would dare fall foul of her 'ten minutes early is better than ten seconds late' rule, but for now, she just took in the silence and shuffled into her office.

Lottie's face smiled up at her from a picture frame on her desk, and she smiled back at it. In an ideal world, of course she'd still be at home with her, but she was a pragmatist. She was a realist. And she loved her job to boot.

She heard movement, and watched through the slats in the blind from her office as the detectives in her charge filed in. She looked at her watch, and smiled.

'Morning, team,' she said, as she walked amongst the open-plan desks where the daily grind occurred. A collectively murmured response was all she elicited.

'Let me check prisoners in the bin,' she said, 'then I'll

dish them out. Anyone want to put their hat in the ring for the first one?'

She was doing it for sport. For amusement. It was amazing how, in an office filled with detectives who were trained on body language and how to read a suspect, that none of them were willing to make eye contact with her. She grinned, and went back into her office where she woke her dormant computer from its nightly slumber and flicked onto the night duty DS' report. A couple of burglaries. A case of taking without owner's consent (TWOC) that turned out to be an insurance scam. A bin arson that had melted a couple of the council waste receptacles, and would likely have local councillors demanding a robust policing response that would never follow, and the usual couple of assaults that were par for the course on a Saturday night in town. All very normal, and all very Beachbrook.

She created a new email, addressed to the DI, and typed in the subject box.

SUNDAY EARLY TURN DS REPORT

Better to get ahead of the game, she thought, as she wrote the surnames of the prisoners and which unlucky members of her team were being allocated to them. As she got up to go and break the news to the DCs who were waiting to hear their assignments, she hid the email in the background.

She could add to it as the day progressed, she thought.

Chapter 4

ANDREW

Two Hours Before

Andrew struggled to open his eyes; they felt glued shut. A couple of beers had turned into a few more after the Jamiesons had gone home, and the resulting elbows in the ribs from a sober, pregnant wife during the night had certainly stopped his snoring, but they hadn't helped him get the full eight hours that he needed.

His weren't the only snores that drifted across the room that morning. Sophie was up, but Maria lay in her space facing her dad, mouth open and throat rattling gently. Andrew lay still, listening. How was it that the purrs of sleep could sound so melodic, so harmonious? Snoring was an affliction, something to be annoyed by, but not now. Love may have been blind but, here and now, it was also deaf. Hard-of-hearing though he may have been when it came to his daughter's snores, he was far more attuned to the noise coming from beyond the safe sanctuary of his duvet and the bedroom. The wind outside was whipping up, and it wasn't kissing the windows. It was pounding against them.

He looked at his bedside clock. It was far too early on any

31

day, let alone a Sunday, but the doorbell had given him fair notice that it was time to get up. Time to face another day.

'Hmmmm,' Andrew mumbled, sitting up and rubbing the sleep from his eyes. Maria didn't stir. She was too busy catching flies.

'Oi, you, how did you get in here?' he said softly while gently tickling her in the ribs. She screwed her face up with stifled laughter but kept her eyes shut. Like her dad, she wasn't a morning person.

'We'd better get up, poppet,' Andrew whispered.

Andrew stretched, then got out of bed. He scooped Maria up in his arms and, with her grunts of disapproval ringing in his ears, carried her downstairs.

'Morning, bud,' Andrew said, bashing fists with Joe, who was sitting in the kitchen eating some toast and still wearing his pyjamas.

'Morning, Ange, morning, Maria,' Joe said with crumbs spilling from his mouth.

Andrew bumped into the kitchen island as he walked away from Joe, wincing as he rubbed his hip. The pain melted away as he felt the recently boiled kettle. Getting up second had its benefits. He made a mug of coffee as a yawn drifted from his lips, and looked out of the kitchen window. High up in the sky, thick and moody clouds were overhead.

'So, what's the plan today then?' Sophie asked.

'Beach!' Maria said.

'No chance,' Andrew said, chuckling.

Maria's face turned stone cold.

'We're not going to the beach,' Andrew said. His face was resolute.

'But you said we could,' Maria said, as she turned to her mum.

'I said we'd see,' Sophie replied.

Maria looked across to Joe for support. His eyes widened. Stuck between a rock and a hard place, he really didn't want to get in the middle.

'You want to go as well, don't you, Joe?' Maria said.

He didn't reply, and she nudged him under the table.

'Don't you, Joe?' she repeated.

'Whatever Maria wants to do,' Joe replied, looking down to the floor.

Andrew sighed. It was the weekend, it was early, it took a conscious effort to keep his eyes open and he really, really didn't need this. He looked to Sophie for support, but she looked down at the floor. She wasn't giggling yet, but it was a scene that had played out a thousand times before. The resolution rarely went in her husband's favour.

'Cinema?' Andrew said.

'Beach,' Maria replied.

'Have you seen the wind?' Andrew muttered.

Maria, it seemed, had an answer ready for this.

'Yeah, well I've got that new kite,' she shot back in an instant. 'You said we needed wind to fly it.'

'We could just drive past, to have a look?' Sophie said.

Andrew looked out of the window as leaves blew across the front garden like confetti at a wedding. He'd lost, and he knew it. He walked out of the kitchen without saying another word. His stomping feet on the stairs said it for him.

Maria looked at Joe and giggled, as a grin spread across her cheeks. He mirrored it, though the intensity of his emotion didn't match hers. Without saying a word they both ran up the stairs and into Maria's bedroom, slamming the door closed behind them.

Andrew sat on the end of his bed and watched as the

outside world painted a picture for him from beyond the windows. Nature was wielding her teeth, and his worrying mind actually, for a moment, wondered if it was possible for a kite to carry grown children away. He heard excited squeals coming from Maria's room, and shook such thoughts from his head.

'Stupid,' he whispered to himself, as Sophie's soft feet trod a path across the bedroom floor until she sat with him.

'We won't be long down there, will we, love?' Andrew asked.

'You know what they're like,' she replied. 'If we get down there soon, we'll be home early enough to do something else.'

Andrew leaned in and gave Sophie a hug, then gently stroked her tummy. He tried to give her a kiss but she pulled away.

'Your breath stinks,' she said with a giggle.

'Who said romance was dead?' Andrew replied, trudging to the bathroom.

Washed and teeth brushed, he put his ear to Maria's bedroom door and heard her and Joe playing. He couldn't work out what they were saying but it was clear who was in charge of whatever game they were playing.

'We're leaving in half an hour,' Andrew shouted through the door.

'YESSSSSS!' Maria shouted back, pulling the door open and stopping dead in her tracks. 'What is THAT?' she asked, pointing at his upper torso.

'Just a shirt,' Andrew replied, looking down at the top he was wearing; it screamed lairy with almost psychedelically floral patterns. He hustled towards the stairs so that his daughter and Joe didn't see his cheeks turning a deep shade of red. Shamed by a six-year-old, he made his way down to the kitchen and put on a jumper that didn't scream tourist, then put on a shell jacket, just to make sure.

'Christ,' Andrew muttered to himself as he opened the front door and the outside world introduced itself to him with a short, sharp slap on the cheeks. Maria and Joe jostled past him, his daughter clutching her new kite, still sealed in its wrapping, firmly in her grip. They raced to the car and clambered in as Andrew, open-mouthed, shook his head. 'They're mental,' he grumbled.

Sophie heard, and smiled before stopping in her tracks.

'Yeah, I guess they are,' she replied, slipping her hand into his as they walked to the car. Andrew's fingers were cold. It was the height of summer, but it felt like one of those autumnal days where everything was on the turn.

'Alright back there, kids?' Andrew asked, looking in his rear-view mirror as he pulled off the driveway. Maria was fiddling with the wrapping that housed the kite.

'Waves will be ginormous,' Maria whispered, her voice trembling with excitement.

'REALLY ginormous,' Joe whispered back, though without Maria's level of enthusiasm.

'Really really *really* ginormous,' Maria said. She had to have the last word.

Maria popped both thumbs up in the air and flashed a grin that was far brighter than the weather closing in all around them.

'Joe?' Andrew asked.

'All good, Ange,' Joe replied. 'Your car's cool. Can you talk to it again?'

'Sure, mate,' Andrew replied, pressing a button on the steering wheel. 'Play Coldplay,' he said.

Blasts of 'Paradise' sang from the speakers.

'We can't do that in my daddy's car,' Joe said.

Andrew looked at the pair of them in the mirror. Maria, his life, his world. Joe, different team, but the same league. He loved them both.

He pulled up on a deserted Beach Road just as the first drops of rain began to bounce against the windscreen. He looked at the sky and, for as far as the eye could see, it was just a river of grey, a depressingly bleak canvas. If the day before had been postcard perfect, then this was a vista from the opposite end of the spectrum.

'Well, we said we'd have a look,' Andrew said.

'Looks good to me,' Maria replied.

Andrew had scarcely had time to put the handbrake on before Maria had thrown her door open and was running down to the beach, holding her kite under her arm, the tail of which had found its way out of the packaging and was floating on the wind. She had learned how to turn off the child lock in the car about a year prior and it was a running battle between her and Andrew about it being on or off.

Joe sat in his booster seat, unsure if he should follow Maria or not. Andrew forced a smile and nodded at him. He climbed out of the open door and ran after Maria, but to try to catch up with her was to chase his tail into the fog. She was always too quick.

Andrew and Sophie slogged down the slope towards the beach, and watched as Joe tried in vain to tag Maria who, in turn, was trying to wrestle her kite from its case. Their hair whipped around their faces as the wind bit, but they seemed oblivious to it. In the distance, and through eyes wet from sea spray and the drop, drop, dropping of rain, Andrew could just about make out a dog walker in the distance.

'We're not the only crazy ones.'

'What's that, love?' Sophie asked.

'Nothing,' Andrew replied, shaking his head, before turning towards his old nemesis. From horizon to shore, she was raging.

'I'll unlock, you get water?' Sophie said.

Andrew nodded, his eyes looking out to sea. Water, from the public tap. Water for a cuppa. Not *that* expanse of water. Not that beast. He shook himself back into the present, listening as Maria and Joe's joyful shrieks juxtaposed with the grim panorama that stretched all the way as far as the eye could see.

'Do you need help with that kite?' he shouted, his words being swallowed by the weather as they made their way through the air.

Maria stopped dead in her tracks and looked at him, shaking her head as she fumbled with greater intensity at the Sellotape that was keeping the kite caged in its wrapping. Behind her, Joe gained ground until, finally, he got her.

'TAG!' he shouted.

Maria glowered at her dad, as he walked from the hut to the water tap with a jug.

As he walked back, he heard protestations coming from the beach hut. Maria and Joe were both standing on the promenade, tugging furiously at their clothes. Maria's *Frozen* top had already been discarded and was lying on the ground in front of her, while Joe struggled with an Arsenal top that was just a tiny bit too big for him. In front of them, lying pristine and flat, were their matching orange wetsuits, still damp and with grains of sand clinging to them from the day before.

'Don't even think about it,' Andrew said. This time, his voice was firm. This time, he meant it.

'I've already tried,' Sophie said. 'I told them that you would say no too, but they didn't listen to me. Come on, kids, don't be silly.'

Maria scowled at Sophie, then turned to Andrew. 'Daddy...'

'No,' Andrew replied. They were his guns, and he was sticking to them.

'Come in with us, then,' she said, her voice quivering as tears began to fill her eyes. 'Come on, Daddy, you never do.'

She had pulled out two big guns of her own. Daddy, not Dad. And the sea. The churning, raging sea. It unnerved him, just like she knew it would. Andrew's eyes flickered upwards, beyond Maria's tiny frame and at the rolling waves. Like hell was he going in there. His eyes lowered, and fixed on his daughter's. She was begging him without saying a word and he needed an out that didn't involve him getting wet.

'Shall I get the kite out?' Andrew asked, reaching for the now abandoned toy that lay on the floor.

'After,' Maria replied.

Andrew looked at her. He looked at Joe. And he looked at Sophie. Was that a touch of concern that he could see in his wife's eyes, he wondered?

'I'll tell you what,' he said. 'You can go in the little sea. Just at the edge. That's what's called a compromise.'

Maria looked to the clouds. 'I know what a compromise is, Dad,' she said, with sarcasm dripping from her lips.

'You don't have to go if you don't want to, mate,' Andrew said quietly to Joe, bending down and out of earshot of Maria. He could see a slight look of apprehension on Joe's face. 'It's horrible out there, we can get the football out if you like?'

Joe looked at Andrew and forced a smiled. 'Maria wants to play so I'll go with her to make sure she's okay,' he said.

'Well, as soon as you've had enough, come back and we'll go home. Deal?' Andrew said.

'Deal,' Joe agreed.

'Shake on it?' Andrew asked.

Maria stood close by as her dad and best friend went through their ritual. Joe counted it out, just like he always did, before he wrestled his wetsuit on. That it was damp made it adhere to his skin as he climbed into it, and he winced as the neoprene material rubbed against the graze on his side.

Andrew grimaced. He'd been a little boy once, and he knew just how much those injuries could hurt. He pulled Joe's stuck arms through the sleeves, and looked at his watch.

'Right, you've got fifteen minutes, then we're getting out of here,' he said.

In spite of the weather, the kids jumped from the promenade and floated across the sand until they were at the edge of the little sea. Andrew set his chair up, facing directly at them, the raindrops that had greeted their arrival having turned into a soaking wet blanket of drizzle that swarmed his face and clung to his skin.

'Should I go down and keep an eye on them?' Andrew said, as much to himself as to Sophie.

'We can see them from here,' Sophie replied, peering around from inside the beach hut. Andrew sensed just the merest trace of anxiety in her voice, but her face masked it well. Was it a mother's lot, he wondered, to cover up her worries? Or was that the exclusive reserve of a father?

Andrew looked down at Maria and Joe as they jumped around in the little sea. Safe. Disconnected from the big sea.

No tide, no current. Behind them, though, in the distance, a violent orgy of waves, being whipped up by the wind. Frenzied. Out of control.

'Tea's up,' Sophie said as she came out with two mugs. Andrew wrapped his fingers around his cup to get some warmth into them and took a sip. Beach tea always tasted different to house tea. Whether it was something in the water or the salty air infusing itself into the mix, Andrew had never been sure. Now, though, he barely noticed. He was focussing on one thing only. Watching the kids. The brew in his hand was simply fuel to keep him alert.

'Thanks, love,' Andrew said. He was shivering, but didn't take his eyes off Maria and Joe. 'Are you watching?' he asked.

Sophie nodded, and Andrew stood up. He backed into the beach hut and looked around. Sophie had taken great pride in the décor with signs and bunting and pictures. A large mosaic of photos hung on the wooden wall. The six of them, on sunny beach days. Chris, Linda and Joe. Andrew, Sophie and Maria. It had been something that Chris had given them, a present at the start of the season. In all the pictures, it seemed that everyone wore a smile while messing around on the sands. Everyone, except Andrew. In the middle of all the photos, there stood a sign in big, bold words. *Home From Home*. Andrew shook his head. It wasn't a home from home. It was a shed.

He dug into the box of clothes at the back of the beach hut that they kept for emergencies, and pulled out a brand new, cheap but thick black coat that he'd brought down for bad weather days. He pulled it from the plastic wrapping, and slipped it on.

Four layers. Surely it was enough to keep the rain at bay. He sat back in his chair, sliding his phone, keys and wallet into the pockets of the coat and zipping them closed. The drizzle was like death by a thousand cuts and he could taste salt as the mist of sea spray descended upon them. She was a spitting cobra, her venom, everywhere.

'Christ, you must be cold,' Sophie said. 'I forgot you even had that coat down here.'

'Same,' Andrew replied.

After Andrew and Sophie had finished their cups of tea, Andrew shouted down 'Ten minutes!' his voice fighting its way through the elements on its way to the kids. Even from a distance, through the misty haze that was the barrier between them, Andrew could see Maria scowl. 'I'll go down and keep an eye on them,' he said.

'We can see them from up here,' she replied. It wasn't just Andrew with eyes fixed on the kids. Hers were wide and focussed like lasers. 'They'll only moan that you're spoiling their fun... Then we'll have to stay even bloody longer.'

The drizzle lifted, as heavy, bulbous beads of rain began to beat down all around them. They thudded onto the promenade, each drop bouncing before finally settling.

Andrew looked at his watch again. Time was crawling past.

'Five minutes!' he bellowed.

'Alright, five minutes,' Maria shouted back, clearly not impressed.

It was a rumble of thunder piercing through the howling winds around them that brought Andrew to his feet. The groaning sky seemed to heighten the roar of the waves that raced towards the shore, and he'd seen enough. Those five minutes could be put in the bank for next time. He got to his feet, bracing himself for an argument that, this time, he was going to win. He jumped down from the promenade

41

onto the sand, this time oblivious to any pain that his knees might have grumbled about, and began trudging through the thick, wet sand towards the kids. He was still thirty metres away from them. They'd seen him coming, and had inched away from the little sea. As he opened his mouth, it wasn't his words that reverberated around him, though.

'Lex, heel!'

He turned his head, trying to find the voice.

'Lex, here NOW!'

Andrew scanned, tracking towards the voice. There was panic laced within it. Something was amiss.

'Lex, NO!'

A black mastiff was running along the promenade, in the direction of Sophie.

'LEX, GET BACK HERE.'

It picked up pace, galloping, as candlesticks of spittle hung from its jaws.

'LEX!'

Andrew turned away from the kids.

'FUCK'S SAKE, LEX!'

Andrew had seen enough. His trudge lightened as he breezed back across the sands and clambered up the steps of the ladder, fuelled by a raging adrenaline that coursed his veins. As he stepped up onto the promenade, the dog reached Sophie, who was sitting in her chair, and jumped straight up at her, landing squarely on her pregnant belly. Andrew grabbed the mastiff by the scruff of the neck.

'Lex!' the dog walker shouted as he jogged along the promenade.

'Come and sort this fucking dog out!' Andrew yelled. Lex tried to resist, but he was no match for a seething father-to-be. 'Will you hurry the fuck up?' Andrew shouted.

'I'm really sorry,' panted the dog owner, as he finally arrived. 'He's just a baby.'

'And that's my baby in there,' Andrew spat back, pointing at Sophie's tummy. Wet, sandy pawprints were etched all over her clothes.

The dog walker mumbled something unintelligible before taking control of Lex and slipping a lead onto him. The Andrew of ten years before might have dealt with it in a markedly different way, and it took every ounce of control that he possessed to keep a lid on his simmering rage.

'You okay, love?' he asked, his breathing ragged with ire as the dog walker and Lex melted away.

'I think so,' Sophie replied. Her hands shook slightly as she brushed Lex's sandy imprints off her dungarees.

Andrew helped her to her feet, holding her hands gently and stroking her trembling fingers.

'Let's go home,' Sophie whispered.

Home. Andrew looked at his watch. Time was well and truly up. He turned to shout for Maria and Joe.

The empty little sea. The thundering big sea.

And nothing in between.

'Sophie, where are they?' Andrew said with panic in his voice. He didn't wait for an answer. He turned away from her, leaping from the promenade onto the beach and ran down to the water's edge, his trainers churning the wet sand in his wake.

'MARIA? JOE?'

There was no reply, his words dissolving in the crashing waves. A breathless Sophie was only a few paces behind, maternal fear having driven her legs to sprint in her husband's footsteps.

'Andrew, there,' Sophie cried, pointing towards the

breakwater. Andrew looked and, just beyond the cresting waves, there was something. Orange. A wetsuit. One of the kids. It was barely visible as the waves obscured it from view before it re-emerged once, twice, three times. Amidst the swirling seas, it was being tossed around like a ragdoll in a washing machine. As a child, the sea had failed to claim him. Now, it seemed she was trying to settle the score.

'Get help,' Andrew cried. Then he was in the water. Back in her grip, for the first time in thirty-five years. The waves clung to him as he took steps that were too big, making him fall as she tipped him from his feet. The taste of salt brought it all back, but didn't stop him. Nothing could, for a father's love trumped everything.

Deeper, he strode. Blinkers on, and with tunnel vision his guiding instinct, he fought the waves that broke over him. Knee high. Then waist. Chest, then face. It was without warning that he was picked up by a rip current that pulled him in the exact direction of the wetsuit.

'FUCK'S SAKE,' he shouted. He didn't just remember what had happened all those years before – the trauma of it was ingrained into his body. Adrenaline shot through his veins as the air was squeezed from his lungs, and his heart raced to keep up with his every sense screaming at him.

'MARIA!' he screamed. Salt water filled his mouth. 'JOE!'

He looked around, but the beach was getting lost through the haze that was being kicked up by the waves. How many metres away from solid ground, he couldn't even begin to guess. What he knew, though, was that with every kick of his legs, with every swing of his arms, the rip was dragging him further away from the safety of shore. He was being held captive, a prisoner in the clutches of the sea. The waves smacked him in the cheeks, and dragged him under.

He forced his head above the surface, treading with futile fervour against the rip beneath, as his eyes darted all around him. Where was she? Where was he? Where were they?

And then he heard her.

'DADDY!'

Her words quivered with absolute, naked fear, barely a whisper above the swirling water that surrounded them. The ten metres that separated them seemed like an ocean all of its own but, inch by inch, foot by foot, metre by metre, he fought to get to her. The fibres of his thick coat grew heavy as they became bogged down in water but he was driven by paternal brawn. Nothing was going to stop him getting to her.

Nothing.

PART TWO

During the Storm

Chapter 5

SOPHIE

During the Storm

'Maria! Joe!'

Sophie's words bounced back at her, making no progress through the storm as she screamed again and again while, in her ears, Andrew's words rang.

Get help!

'Andrew!' she screamed, but the foaming, rolling waves were dragging him further from her. His thick, black coat was swelling as it became saturated from the battering it was receiving from the surf. As each second passed, it became more and more distant. He was being dragged beyond the breakwater and into the unknown.

'Kids!' she bawled, unable to differentiate her tears from the salty sea mist that was stinging her face.

Get help!

Her ankles were wet as she walked towards the waves and the scummy bubbles that sat atop its surface clung to her calves.

She took another step forward, unsure whether to go in after them all, but Andrew's parting words echoed in her ears.

Get help!

In that moment, they gave her purpose.

Turning on her heels, she sprinted back over the sodden, clumping sand. The thirty-metre sprint felt like a marathon and, as she clambered up the ladder onto the promenade and grabbed her mobile phone from her bag in the beach hut, she shook with fear.

'Come on,' she shouted, as her wet fingers struggled to unlock the phone. Maria's picture stared back at Sophie as the front camera somehow recognised her contorted, anguished face.

'Emergency, which service?' a voice at the other end of the line asked.

'Um, police? I don't know! The kids, my husband... The sea's swept them out, they need help!' Sophie screamed.

'Connecting you now,' the operator said.

Sophie paced the promenade, staring and squinting through the mizzle but it was no use. She couldn't see a thing beyond the shoreline.

'Fucking come on,' she muttered, her teeth chattering and her legs feeling weak. The seconds that passed felt purgatorial.

'Police emergency,' a voice finally said, 'what's your location?'

'The beach,' Sophie replied in an instant.

'What beach?' the operator asked.

'Beachbrook,' Sophie replied. 'Main sands.'

She could hear the furious tapping of a keyboard in the background, but couldn't wait for more questions. She had to fill the quiet void as the operator typed.

'The kids... the sea,' she continued without pausing for breath, trying to string together coherent sentences. 'They've been washed out.'

Again, more tapping of keys clicked across the phone line.

'Come on,' Sophie said, 'please.'

'Just updating the log and sending across to Coastguard,' the operator said.

It was taking mere seconds, but time had become malleable. It wasn't progressing linearly for Sophie. Those seconds felt like minutes. Hours.

'What children are in the sea?' the operator asked.

'Maria and Joe,' Sophie replied.

'Ages?' the operator asked.

'They're both six,' Sophie wailed, as she stared out to sea and the enormity of what was happening ran roughshod through her every sinew. 'They're just babies.'

'Can you see them now?' the operator asked.

Sophie strained her eyes, willing them to penetrate the gloom that was a fixed and seemingly immoveable barrier, but it was no good.

'No,' she whispered.

'I've sent it up the line,' the operator said, as they tapped the information on their keyboard with even greater intensity. 'Your name, please?'

'Sophie,' she replied, 'Sophie Wicks.'

The rest of the call passed by in a haze and, as she hung the phone up, she clung onto it for dear life. It was her lifeline. *Their* lifeline.

Without a wasted second, she made her way back down the ladder and onto the sand. Her cheeks were raw and the wind beat into them but she didn't notice. Nothing mattered. Nothing, except for those kids.

The lethargy of pregnancy was overridden as she near-sprinted across the sand, spurred on by maternal instinct. She reached the shoreline and waded to her knees as lightning filled the air in front of her, bringing a momentary fork of brightness to the gloom. The sea was alive. She could see that much. It was angry. And it was as if those bolts from the heavens were a cattle prod, urging it on, making it rage.

'MARIA!' she screamed, her voice growing hoarse. 'JOE! ANDREW!'

So warped was her perception of time that it could have been two minutes or twenty before she heard the first siren wailing softly, fighting with the waves for audible supremacy. Then, another. Soon, a crescendo of noise filled the air around her and, as she turned around, a sea of blue was filling the clifftops.

'SOPHIE,' Andrew called.

She spun back around in an instant. There, he was. Dragging himself from the surf, fighting against the waves that were trying to pull him back in. Slumped on his shoulder, Sophie saw one of the kids, their head behind him and hidden from view.

'ANDREW,' she screamed, wading further into the water until she reached waist high. Andrew was being dragged about, his thick coat anchoring him to one spot before a wave swept him to the next. At certain moments he seemed to be just a passenger, but he was making progress. He was getting closer to her. To shore. To safety.

Five metres away.

Four.

Three.

Two.

Then, one.

Andrew almost collapsed into her arms, but it wasn't him that she wanted.

'Maria,' she whispered, as she lifted her daughter from his shoulder.

Maria's face was blank. Vacant. Her chest was moving, though. Her eyes were open. Whatever shock she was in, it was almost irrelevant. She was alive.

'Joe?' Sophie asked.

Andrew shook his head softly and, in an instant, turned around and strode back into the sea. His coat sagged, weighing him down as its padded fibres soaked up every drop of seawater it came into contact with. Still, he reached the breakwater. Then, beyond.

'Is anyone still out there?' a voice shouted from behind Sophie.

She turned around, and saw several police officers racing across the sand towards her while, in the air, yet more sirens wailed. The cascade of flashing blue lights that filled the clifftop had grown intense. The balloon had well and truly been sent up.

'Miss, is anyone still out there?' the police officer asked, his voice dripping with urgency.

'Yeah,' she said, 'Joe. Joe's still out there.'

The police officer relayed the message into his radio as yet more police officers poured onto the dark, wet sands and spread out in formation, each maintaining a watching brief as the rolling waves crashed to shore, yet Sophie didn't notice. She was too consumed by Maria, too wrapped up in trying to bring some warmth to her daughter's cold skin. She rubbed furiously, trying to radiate heat into Maria's back, her cheeks, her hands, her everything, but none of it worked.

'My daughter,' she said, weakly. 'She needs help.'

The police officer looked at her, then at Maria who lay

limp in her arms. His mouth was agape. It just wasn't a drill that the police rehearsed for.

'Give her here,' he said, scooping Maria from Sophie's clutches and running as fast as his heavy work boots would allow him.

'Wait,' Sophie shouted, as she struggled to keep pace, desperate not to be separated from her baby girl for even a moment. She hadn't noticed just how wet she was, and how heavy the rain had set in until, as her head swung from side to side, her hair matted together as one, solidly sodden entity.

Beach Road, located at the top, was alive with activity. Police cars filled the street, and yet more were arriving by the second. A fire engine. The coastguard. And, in tandem, two ambulances.

'There,' the police officer panted breathlessly, pointing at them. On solid ground, his footing was a bit steadier but the sand and the slope had taken it out of him. Regardless, he hot-footed it to the front ambulance as it screeched to a skidding halt, with Sophie matching him pace for pace, stride for stride. She was so close that she could hear his radio.

'Control to all patrols,' the operator said. 'Coastguard helicopter in the area and en route. ETA one minute.'

She could hear it already. It was a light fluttering sound that, within seconds, was thundering overhead, its spotlight shining down and lighting up the gloom like a finger from the gods. It took her breath away, but she didn't have time for any of that.

She was a parent, and her every maternal sinew screamed at her. Maria needed her, now more than ever.

Chapter 6

DS SUE WILLMOTT

During the Storm

'Sarge…' A voice trailed from the main office.

'I'm on it,' DS Sue Willmott replied. She looked up from her computer, her eyes flicking from the computer-aided dispatch (CAD) log that was being updated in real time to the window of her office that looked out over the sea. Rain pelted the glass like bullets from the sky.

'What the fuck were kids doing out there?' she whispered to herself. She reached for her police radio, not even sure if the battery was charged so seldom did she need to use it as a detective, and hoped for the best. It crackled into life, and was a mishmash of garbled, panicked messages from the officers on the ground and the helicopter in the sky.

'One child out of the water.'

'One still missing.'

'Adult also unaccounted for.'

'RVP is Beach Road, above the beach.'

'Weather hindering progress.'

'IC11 to control, we're now on scene and overhead.'

'Lifeboat en route.'

'Lifeguards making way.'

'Considering declaring major incident.'

She watched her computer monitor as, somehow, the person in the control room did their best to steady a swaying ship. Line by line, the updates from the scene were inputted and managed in some form of coherence. Gently shaking her head as the transmissions from the scene continued, she looked at the photo of Lottie that adorned her desk and felt the tiniest of lumps develop in her throat. She was a mum. She had to do something.

'Alright, Skip?' someone asked as she strode with purpose through the main office.

'I'm going down there,' she replied, reaching for one of the communal umbrellas that had somehow grown into a large collection, stacked by the coat stand.

'Have they asked for CID?' someone else asked.

'No,' she replied, bluntly. 'It's about to be called, though. Won't be long before the phone goes.'

The team knew better than to ask any more questions. Major incidents weren't two a penny in a sleepy town like Beachbrook, and if it was about to be declared as such then the duty DS would have to go anyway, to investigate what had happened. Force policy dictated so. Besides, DS Willmott had a look on her face that she wore only occasionally. Rarely, even. It was the 'don't get in my fucking way' mask, and it was nothing to do with being a copper. Instead, it was borne of something that only a parent – no, a mother – could appreciate.

'Give us a shout if you need anything,' someone said, but she was halfway out of the door before their words arrived.

It was only a mile around the coast, but traffic was at a standstill as soon as she turned left out of the police station.

In an unmarked car, without the assistance of blue lights and sirens, she was just one of the masses in a queue who had somewhere to be. In the distance, she could almost see her destination and, for a few fleeting seconds, she considered turning around, parking back up at the police station and making her way on foot, despite the weather. Instead, her saviour appeared from the police station behind her. More resources were being called in to comb the coastline, and a marked police car beat a path through the gridlocked road. All she had to do was follow, and ignore the silent glares of those she was overtaking.

As she snaked and weaved between the cars on the road, the updates on the radio kept coming.

'Lifeboat on scene.'

'Still one child unaccounted for.'

'From IC11, we have visual on an adult male in the water.'

'Adult now coming ashore.'

'More resources needed.'

'Put in request for Havington District to send over patrols.'

'Major incident.'

'Repeat, major incident.'

'Request DS to attend.'

She was glad she'd pre-empted her attendance. The earlier she got her finger on the pulse of what was happening at the scene, the better the quality of any subsequent investigation would be. Sure, she could've maintained a watching brief from the nick, listening to the radio updates and seeing the CAD be updated, but that wasn't for her. It never had been. She'd found being there, in amongst it, served her better. Besides, something deep inside told her she needed to be there. It was that mother's instinct, once again.

She picked up her radio, and pressed the transmit button.

'Control from DS Willmott,' she said, 'already aware and en route.'

She squeezed her accelerator just a touch more as the patrol car in front gained a bit of ground over her. It wasn't quite top speed, but she knew the ramifications if she was to have a fender bender while breaking the highway code in an unmarked vehicle. Finally, as she navigated her way past the last of the stationary vehicles that formed the queue to get to Beach Road, she pulled to a stop at the rear of a procession of marked police vehicles. Many of them still had their blue lights flashing in the gloom, their occupants having abandoned them knowing that every second counted.

She climbed from her car, and into the elements.

'Jesus,' she muttered. She tried to open her umbrella, but the wind immediately pulled it inside out. Instead of trying to right it, she tossed it back in the car and hurried along the road to what was a hastily arranged rendezvous point (RVP) at the top of the slope that led down to the beach.

It was a hive of activity. Emergency personnel from all the different services were running around, carrying out varying tasks. Drone operators were setting up. Thermal imaging teams were ferrying equipment around. And still, the sirens rang in the air. It wasn't so much a balloon that had gone up, more an airship.

'Where is she?' someone asked loudly.

A man, drenched from head to toe emerged from the top of the slope. He was shouting almost deliriously and wobbling from side to side.

'Maria,' he shouted, 'where is she!?'

DS Willmott watched, as police officers converged on the male to provide assistance. She'd learned long before that, in situations like this, an observing brief was best for the anonymous lady from CID. Let the uniforms do their bit at the start, then pick up when it was her turn. In the meantime, her analytically driven brain worked overtime, taking everything in.

'Andrew!' a female voice shouted.

DS Willmott turned to one of the ambulances, from where the shout had come. A woman clung to the rear door. Her face was a picture of terror, and her voice had sounded just as anguished as that of the male's.

DS Willmott's eyes tracked the man as he ran over to the ambulance and, in an instant, clambered up the steps and into the woman's embrace. Mere seconds later, the door closed behind them.

'Boss,' DS Willmott said, recognising the duty inspector who was trying to co-ordinate his troops and scribe his actions in the face of the storm that had set in overhead.

'Sue,' he replied, nodding at her as raindrops pelted off the two pips that he wore on the shoulders of his reflective tabard.

'What's happening?' she asked.

'Shit show,' he muttered. 'That's the dad of the one who got out of the sea,' he said, pointing to the ambulance with the now closed door. 'There's one kid still out there.'

'Want me to get an account from the dad?' she asked, as the inspector juggled his sodden day book with a radio that was barking at him for more orders, more instructions, more updates.

'Please,' he replied, patting her back as he marched past her and down the slope. She watched him as he stomped a path in front of him, his shoulders sagging under the weight of pressure that bore down on them. Every decision he made, she knew, had ramifications. Every time he spoke into the radio, the result could be life or death. Where to deploy his officers, where to focus his attention, what needed to take priority.

'Poor sod,' she said to herself, as she walked towards the ambulance.

Standing outside it, she steeled herself, rolling her shoulders once and clenching her fists before allowing her fingers to relax. She tapped her knuckles on the door, and it was opened by one of the paramedics.

'Can I help you?' he asked.

'DS Willmott,' she replied. Her voice was different. Just like a teacher in a classroom, when a professional entered the field of play, the first thing to change was their tone, their pitch, their presentation of words. 'May I have a chat with…' She scanned her brain, but came up empty. She didn't know his name. '…the gentleman who just came out of the sea, please.'

She peered inside, where she saw a young girl sitting on a stretcher. From neck to toe, she was covered in blankets. Above that, an oxygen mask was fixed over her face.

'Is she alright?' DS Willmott asked.

'We need to get her to hospital,' the paramedic said. 'She'll be fine, we just need to get her checked over. She's not hypothermic so don't worry about that. We think she swallowed a bit of water. It's just a precaution in case of aspiration.'

DS Willmott nodded, and looked squarely at the man who was standing next to the girl on the stretcher.

'I'm Detective Sergeant Sue Willmott,' she said, 'from Beachbrook Police Station. Can I have a word outside?' The question may have been framed politely, but her tone informed everyone that it wasn't a request.

'Yeah, of course,' the man tremored. 'I'll just be outside. Okay, darling?' he said to the little girl as he climbed out of the ambulance. She just stared straight ahead, without responding.

'Over here,' DS Willmott said.

The man followed, as she led him to the middle of the road where a hastily erected multi-agency major incident gazebo swayed in the wind. The gusts may still have chilled them, but at least it afforded some degree of respite from the rain.

DS Willmott wrestled with her day book and pen as she made some notes. She wrote about the weather, about the squalls, the rain, the wind. The occasional, errant raindrop painted a picture of its own on the pages, smearing her ink and providing documentary evidence of the appalling conditions that surrounded them. It was all context, a means of her being able to recall the conditions at the scene, should she need to in the coming days, weeks or months.

'What's your name?' she asked, gently.

'Andrew,' he replied. 'Andrew Wicks.'

They stood in silence for a moment. Though it was daytime, the weather made it seem like dusk. Beyond the cliff top, the helicopter still hovered over the sea, its search light burning through the murk and shining on the sea. Distant sirens still cut through the air.

A small crowd was beginning to gather, despite the weather. 'Press will be here soon as well,' DS Willmott said, quietly.

'Joe?' Andrew whispered. 'Anything? Have they found him?'

'What happened?' she asked, gently.

'I don't... I'm not... I can't...' he mumbled. He was

shaking, from his core to his extremities and, as DS Willmott peered over the top of her glasses, she saw it with her own eyes.

'Wait there,' she said, as she walked over to the ambulance, and knocked on the door.

'Can we get a blanket out here, please?' she asked.

One of the paramedics passed her a thick, freshly folded sheet. She marched back over to Andrew and gave it to him as he peeled his outer layer off, lairy shirt and all.

'So…?' DS Willmott said. She had her day book and pen in her hand, poised and waiting. No matter the emotion of the moment. There was a child missing, and it needed investigating.

Andrew looked all around. Up, and down. Left, and right. Anywhere, it seemed, to avoid making eye contact with DS Willmott. She let the silence develop until it was entirely uncomfortable and, eventually, he had to meet her gaze.

'I don't know,' he said, his voice breaking with emotion and hoarse from salt. 'I just couldn't get them both in.'

DS Willmott's pen worked double time.

'What were you doing here?' she asked. It was a fair question.

'The kids wanted to come, I think,' he replied. 'I'm sorry, it's just all a bit, you know, my head's all over the place.'

DS Willmott had always been able to read people. Enough years of doing the job had only served to refine those skills and, as she looked at the man standing before her, with his shoulders slumping to the floor and his chin nearly touching the top of his chest, he was every inch a defeated human being.

The ambulance door opened and the paramedic poked his head out, looking all around until his eyes fixed on Andrew.

'We're going now, are you coming with us?' the paramedic called.

Andrew looked at DS Willmott, who snapped her day book shut and pointed her eyes in the direction of the ambulance.

'We'll need to go through this in a lot more detail,' she said, as he shuffled away from her. 'You know that, right?'

Andrew nodded.

'Is there any update on Joe?' he asked. 'Anything at all?'

DS Willmott shook her head softly and, as their eyes met, the streaks of salt that ran down Andrew's face were now from the tears that had begun to flow. He sobbed. Oh, how he sobbed.

'His parents?' Andrew asked quietly, between the tears.

DS Willmott looked at him.

'His dad… He's a copper, in Havington.'

Chapter 7

ANDREW

During the Storm

'Are we ready?' the paramedic asked.

Andrew looked around. The crowd of onlookers was swelling by the second. It was now formed of rows of people rather than just the odd bystander. He caught DS Willmott's eye and they nodded mutually. Andrew closed the door and sat in one of the fold-down seats next to Sophie, the blanket across his shoulders and draped over his lap. He reached for Maria's hand and, when their palms nestled together, he felt Sophie take hold of his other arm. The three of them, as one, were soaking wet and frozen cold from the weather, from the sea, from everything that had gone before. There were so many things swimming through his mind, so many questions that needed resolving.

Why did they go to the beach?
Why did they let the kids go in the little sea?
How the fuck did they end up in the big sea?
And… And… No, that was a question, for another day.
And Joe? Oh, Joe.

'Daddy?' Maria said. She was looking at him, her voice muffled by the oxygen mask.

'Princess,' he croaked. He coughed, and tried again. 'Alright, princess?' It was no good. The frog was staying resident in his throat.

'Daddy,' Maria said again. Her voice was spiked with a panic that Andrew had never before heard as tears began to fall from her eyes. She pulled the oxygen mask away, freeing her face but not easing her angst.

Andrew stood up and shot the paramedic a look that told him not to say anything about seatbelts or health and safety. He gathered Maria in his arms while she lay there, and held her as tightly as he possibly could. Her wails drowned out his own blubs. They'd been through it together. They'd both been witness to what had happened and they'd share the scars forevermore.

The ambulance eventually stopped, but Andrew still held his daughter, not wanting to let the outside world in. In the confines of the ambulance, they were safe. In each other's arms, in that cocoon of love, they were secure. To breach it would be to face up to what was going on outside it. He just wasn't sure that he was strong enough.

'We're here,' the paramedic said.

Andrew looked up. He knew he'd have to let go and, begrudgingly, stepped back. Sophie's hand slotted into his, but it didn't help to fend off the smothering fog of despair that cloaked him.

'Daddy, are you coming?' Maria asked as her neck contorted so that she could see him.

'Of course I am, princess,' Andrew replied.

Maria was wheeled into the accident and emergency department. People looked. Of course they did. It was something far removed from the norm, after all. A child on a stretcher. An adult, wearing a blanket who left a trail of water behind him as he walked. A mother, pregnant and cheeks red raw. Something had gone on and it wasn't just a kid falling out of a tree or something.

'What have we got?' a doctor asked.

'Six-year-old girl,' the paramedic said. 'Pulled from the sea. Query aspiration. Not hypothermic. SATs and BP all okay.'

It was all too much for Sophie to bear and, as she held Maria's little hand, knocking the oxygen saturation (SATs) monitor from her finger, a nurse unapologetically moved her to one side so she could reattach it.

Eavesdroppers lurked, everywhere. The staff were attuned to it and, accordingly, found Maria a private bay.

'How are you, sweetheart?' a nurse asked, as he took the ambulance mask from her face and gently placed a new one over her nose and mouth.

Maria looked at Andrew, wide-eyed.

'It's alright, love,' the nurse said, stroking her forehead, 'you're in good hands here.'

Maria's eyes didn't divert once. They remained fixed on Andrew throughout, as doctors and nurses went about their work.

'Just a few stickers, poppet,' the nurse said, sticking electrodes to her chest, ankles and wrists. 'No talking now,' he added, as he completed the echocardiogram, though there was no danger of that. The constant beeping of the machinery was the only noise, occasionally punctuated by some reassuring words from Andrew and Sophie.

'You're doing great, sweetheart,' Andrew said. He took hold of her hand. It was warm, now, though she recoiled as

66

his skin touched hers. He'd yet to generate any heat of his own.

'You're cold, Daddy,' she said.

'There's going to be a little squeeze on your arm,' the nurse said as he attached a cuff to Maria's lower bicep. 'Jeez, mate,' he said, as his hand brushed against Andrew's. His voice was different. For Maria, it had been his best paediatric tone. Soothing. Reassuring. For Andrew, it was an octave lower. 'You're freezing.'

Andrew had barely been noticed yet, as the nurse looked him up and down, from the blanket over his naked upper half to the puddle of sea water that he had brought to the emergency room from his saturated trousers, his teeth once again began to chatter and his hands trembled without control. Shock? Cold? A combination of both? Either way, the nurse now took notice.

'Trousers off,' he instructed, reaching for a fresh blanket, and passing it to Andrew before leaving the room momentarily.

As he opened the door, the outside world came pouring in. Beeping, from all those other monitors in the A&E department. Voices, some raised, some drunk, some laced with grief. It was a brief snapshot of any emergency room anywhere in the country. The door closed, and shut it all out once again. Andrew took off his trousers and stood in his underwear, unsure how far the instruction to remove his lower clothing went.

'Here,' the nurse said, as he walked back into the room, wrapping Andrew in a foil blanket and putting a cheap, cellophane-wrapped grey tracksuit down on the chair next to him. 'It's on us,' he said, winking at the near-naked man in front of him, who was swallowed up by the foil. 'Kecks off as well,' the nurse said, now that Andrew had some degree of modesty. There was no argument, and Andrew slumped into his chair. Instructions he could take. Directions were fine. What he couldn't do, though, was think of anything other than Joe.

If he'd been thinking straight, he'd have noticed that Maria didn't complain once. Contrary to her normal, feisty self, she acquiesced to every request.

As for him? Questions. So many questions, so few answers. Why had they been there? Why? Why? Why?

The minutes strung together until they were a sizeable, solid chunk of time. A yawning silence developed as Andrew and Sophie, now also dressed in one of those unflattering, hospital tracksuits, took turns to sit right beside Maria and stroke her hand, just how she'd always liked it.

'Where's Joe?' Maria asked, rousing Andrew from the depths of despair and shaking him to the core.

A question so blunt, yet so innocent. What did she remember, he wondered? And what could he say? Before he could even begin to formulate a response, he heard two distinct male voices in the corridor outside.

'I just need to talk to him,' one of them said, and the door swung open. Andrew knew the voice. He'd known it for many years. He'd heard it, through the good times and the bad. Now, it sounded like he'd never heard it before.

It was Chris.

Chapter 8

LINDA

Two Hours Before

'Come on,' Linda whispered to herself as she looked time and again at the clock on her car. 7.14 a.m. She couldn't be late again.

The roads were empty and her right foot heavy as she made her way through the squally streets of Beachbrook, heading towards the coastal road away from town. She thought about what the day would bring. Her years spent in the green uniform gave her enough knowledge to know that it would be mostly weather-related calls. Car crashes, slips and falls, maybe the odd dementia patient who would decide to go walkabout. She snaked her way along the winding road, and flicked on the windscreen wipers. It wasn't raining, but the sea was throwing up a mist as it erupted next to her.

She pulled down her sun visor. There was no dazzle to reflect, no burning sun to bat away from her eyes. Instead, like other parents the world over, she was looking at a photo. The edges may have been frayed, chewed up by the time that had passed since it had been taken years before, but it captured the very essence of her boy. A cheeky grin. Flowing blond locks.

Dimples beside his mouth. Holding a football in goalkeeping gloves that were several sizes too big.

She sighed as tears filled her eyes. She didn't want for much, and she'd already sacrificed enough.

'Get a grip,' she mumbled, admonishing herself. Family wasn't a burden but, still, life was hard. Being a working mum was harder. Missing her boy on a grim Sunday morning when they should still be snuggled up in bed was the hardest.

As she swung a hard left into Havington Ambulance Station car park, she looked at the clock in her car. 7.29 a.m. She'd made it in time. The melancholy that had been her passenger for the journey would have to take off its seatbelt and depart. She had work to do.

'Morning, Linda,' Sam called. He was sitting at a table in the staff office, drinking a cup of coffee. 'You alright?' he asked, looking at her with concern. The dark rings around her eyes had developed into saucers.

'Just about,' Linda replied breathlessly. 'Thought I might've been late this morning. Bad night with Joe.'

'Go and get sorted,' Sam replied. 'I'll make you a drink and sort out the handover.' Early shifts had been like this for a while now. The sleepless nights were taking their toll on her and Sam was really beginning to notice it.

'Thanks, love,' Linda said to Sam, flashing a weary smile. He'd been a godsend, and she knew it. He was in his early twenties and wise beyond his years. He'd only been doing the job for a few months but had taken to it like a duck to water, and Linda knew that he'd go far. One day she'd have to let him spread his wings and fly but, for now, he was in her charge.

She walked into the locker room and relaxed, before looking

at herself in a mirror. The bags under her eyes still bulged. After kitting up she went and found Sam who was sitting at the same table and, even better, had a cup of coffee waiting for her. Black, strong and no sugar.

'You look like you need it,' Sam said.

'I do,' Linda replied. 'All okay with the handover?'

'Yep, fine,' Sam said. 'No issues.'

They drank their coffee and then went out to their ambulance.

'I'll drive if you like,' Sam said. Linda wasn't going to argue. 'We're call sign AM 21.'

Sam drove out of the ambulance station and parked up in Havington High Street. This was a central spot in the district and meant that they were in a good position to be able to respond to calls within the set response times. Linda checked her phone to find there was a message from Chris waiting for her.

Morning, sweetheart, hope you're okay? Joe alright? Bad night? Xxx

She paused before replying. No shit, Sherlock.

Didn't you hear him!? He was shouting. That bloody window, the wind was howling through it. Please, please can you sort it? Tired mummy = grumpy wife. X

She threw her phone into her lap so hard that it stung her thigh. Pissed off. She was royally, totally pissed off. The speed of Chris' reply suggested he knew that as well.

Sorry, sweetheart. I'll get on it as soon as I get back later. Love you xxx

She shook her head and forced a smile. If she didn't, she'd

cry. Anyway, despite her tiredness, and notwithstanding her husband's ability to snore his way through her sleepless nights, the flames of love still burned brightly.

Love you too, numbnuts xx

She flicked her phone onto silent. Outside, it was a ghost town. Shops were still shuttered, and curtains were still drawn. Not many people would have been out and about at that time on a Sunday anyway, but the stormy winds buffeting the ambulance from one side to the other would have put off even the most hardened of early morning walkers.

While they waited for their first call they heard a few other crews being sent to elderly, housebound patients who had fallen overnight. Carers would find them while doing their rounds and call for assistance. They were the usual early morning calls. Absolutely nothing out of the ordinary there.

'So what happened last night then?' Sam asked.

'Oh, the same,' Linda replied. 'Joe's been playing up recently with his sleep and I was up with him for a couple of hours again.'

'Can't someone have him for you one night just so you can get a good night's sleep?' Sam asked.

'Afraid not,' Linda said, sighing. 'My mum and dad are long gone, and Chris doesn't get on with his dad. I'll just have to kick Chris out of bed to do him one night.'

Sam laughed.

'How's Joe doing, anyway?'

'Apart from not sleeping? Yeah, he's good,' Linda replied. 'Bloody horrible graze up his side from the beach yesterday, though.'

'What's that?' Sam asked.

Linda bit her lip. How could she even begin to suggest that she was unhappy that her boy had been given back to her with an injury? To say it wouldn't have happened on her watch would have been churlish. Ungrateful, even.

'Doesn't matter,' she replied.

She reached for her phone and touched the screen, bringing it to life. Joe looked back at her, all big eyes and mischievousness. He was holding an ice lolly; one bought for him by Andrew and Sophie. It had been *their* day out, that photo sent to her by Sophie months before. It was all she had of yet another day in the past that had been his best ever, ever. All of his best ever ever days seemed to have been spent with Andrew and Sophie.

It was the guilt that got her. Until she'd become a mum she only felt guilt over irrelevant, immaterial stuff. Snogging her best mate's boyfriend when she was sixteen. Snapping at her mum when she was only trying to help. Now she had Joe, everything made her feel guilty. Being impatient to leave, yet missing him desperately the next moment. She didn't know anyone else who had to spend so much time apart from their child, just to make sure that the bills were paid. What she'd give to be able to find something different, to be able to spend her every Sunday morning under the duvet with Joe. To stay at home with her kid, just like Sophie did. She didn't want for much in life, but in the blink of an eye her baby was now a boy.

She looked out of the passenger window, hoping that Sam wouldn't have noticed her eyes threatening to leak. He had. He reached his hand across and patted her knee.

They sat on the High Street, watching as Havington slowly woke up. Curtains were drawn. Shop shutters began to rise, creaking as the winds tried to keep them down. A few cars passed here and there, but still there was no one silly enough to wander the streets. Linda looked at the clock on the radio. An hour had passed by. Much as with Joe growing up, time marched on relentlessly. She was about to message Sophie to see what they were up to when they got their first call of the day. It had taken a while but, eventually, it was their turn.

'Control to AM21, please attend Hollingwood Tunnel, northbound. Reports of a two-vehicle injury RTC. Police on scene. No update on injuries yet.'

'Received and en route,' Linda replied to the operator. 'We'll be out of comms while we are in there.'

Hollingwood Tunnel was notorious for two reasons. It was an accident hotspot, and their radios didn't work while inside.

Sam flicked on the blue lights, activated the siren and pressed the accelerator to the floor. Hollingwood Tunnel was a strategic road linking Havington with towns north of it. After twenty minutes of navigating deserted local roads, with the winds rocking the ambulance from side to side, they found the approach to the tunnel was backed up for at least half a mile by the time they arrived. Sam forged a path down the centre of the two lanes of the dual carriageway, and as they made their way into the tunnel the lights and sirens became amplified. Aggressive shades of blue bounced off the enclosed walls and the wailing noise echoed along the length of the structure.

Sam parked the ambulance next to the police car that was already at the scene. One of the vehicles had substantial damage to the front end. The other was facing in the wrong direction with damage to the rear. Sam went to the vehicle facing in the wrong direction while Linda ran over to the vehicle with damage at the front. She spoke with one of the police officers who was talking to the driver, who was still in the vehicle.

'Hi, Linda,' the police officer said. She was on Chris' team and they knew each other.

'Alright, Tash,' Linda replied. 'What have we got?'

'This is Drew,' Tasha said. 'He's forty-five, and has got some pain in his neck and back. We haven't tried to move him yet, but he's starting to feel light-headed. He's got his seatbelt on still. We've got a fire crew on their way to help get him out if needed.'

She stood up and moved back while Linda manoeuvred herself into a position where she could speak to Drew. The driver's door was crumpled beyond repair.

'Hi, Drew,' Linda said. 'I understand you've got some pain?'

'Yeah,' Drew moaned. 'My back and neck are killing.' His eyes were shut and he sounded in genuine distress.

'We don't want to move you at the moment then,' Linda said. She could hear the distant sound of sirens as a fire engine fought its way through the ever-growing backlog of traffic. As she spoke with Drew, she noticed Sam by her side.

'All okay over there?' Sam asked. 'Can I help?' He may have been wise beyond his tender years, but he had yet to deal with the extrication of a patient from a vehicle. Linda took him just out of earshot of Drew.

'This is a good one for you,' she whispered. 'Fire will need to cut him out. Fancy taking the lead on it?'

'Yeah, great,' Sam replied.

Linda stayed in the background while Sam dealt with Drew, close enough to him to provide reassurance but far enough away to allow him the space to work. She watched, smiling with almost maternal pride as he liaised with the fire fighters and police officers while they set about extracting their patient. Drew moaned as the boys in yellow sliced and diced his car all around him, popping the top off as though simply removing the lid from a tin can. Drew's pain was genuine. Linda could tell, even from a distance, that he wasn't chasing whip-cash. Sam supported his head as he had been taught to do and guided Drew through the process, keeping him involved and informed.

'Top job,' Linda said to herself as, finally, the screeching sound of sliced metal came to a halt and Drew was lifted onto their waiting stretcher. She nodded her approval to Sam, whose smile told a story of its own. Another tick in a box, another job well done.

Then, more sirens. Quiet at first, but louder as the cavalry entered the tunnel at the far end. *Strange*, Linda thought. They had all the emergency service personnel they could possibly need down there. As the dimly blue lights grew brighter, and the sirens reached almost unbearable volume, it seemed stranger still. Another police car, followed by another ambulance. They may have been out of radio contact, but there was certainly no need for reinforcements.

As she and Sam wheeled the stretcher with a stricken Drew lying on it back towards their ambulance, her eyes remained firmly fixed on the arriving crews.

The ambulance parked next to Tasha, who spoke to the paramedic on board. Linda didn't recognise them – it was a crew from a different district. She could see from their faces that something was very wrong.

'Are you alright a second, Sam? I'm just going to check something out,' she said.

'Yeah, all good,' he replied.

Linda walked over to Tasha and the paramedic. Tasha's eyes were wide, her cheeks flushed with panic.

'Linda, you need to get to Beachbrook Beach right now,' Tasha said. 'Jump in my car and I'll drive you. That other ambulance crew will take over here.'

Linda's heart skipped a beat. Then it pounded.

'What's happened?' she asked, quietly at first. Tasha failed to find the words, so Linda repeated the question. This time she raised her voice; it echoed around the tunnel and brought everything to a standstill. Her naked terror stopped everything dead in its tracks.

'Something's happened with Joe,' Tasha replied. 'He's been in the sea and they can't find him. Chris is there but he can't get hold of you on your phone. Get in and I'll take you.' Tasha only knew as much as the paramedic had told her.

The echoes of Linda's screaming voice had barely subsided before they were replaced by something much more guttural. Her boy. Where the fuck was he? What the fuck was happening? Her knees trembled as her body lost all sense of coordination. Her balance shifted and Tasha caught her just as she was about to fall down.

Sam ran over and took hold of her arm. He looked into her eyes and saw the horrors that lay beyond them.

'I'll get you there as quickly as I can,' Tasha promised, as she and Sam guided Linda to the front passenger seat of the police car.

Linda sat down, and the door was closed. Outside, she heard a muffled conversation between Tasha and Sam. Hushed voices. Swear words. She didn't process any of it. She just needed to get there.

Beachbrook was about twenty-five minutes from Hollingwood Tunnel. As Tasha emerged from under the artificial lights, the roads were quiet and the weather atrocious. A wall of rain battered the windscreen. Tasha made good progress, yet Linda willed her to go faster. Quicker. With more urgency. She had to be there, near her boy, with him.

The police radio was alive with ongoing commentary. Tasha didn't know what to do. Keep it on, or turn it off? She settled for turning it down. As soon as she did, Linda turned it back up.

'All beaches covered.'

'Helicopter launched and at scene.'

'Weather atrocious.'

'Lifeboat on scene.'

'Rain teeming down.'

'Is media officer aware?'

'Major incident, notify the CI.'

It was a garbled, incoherent mishmash of information that was being broadcast in real time by first responders who were each trying to fit their own piece of the jigsaw. Individually, it was hard to pull it all together to paint a picture.

'Do you want me to try to get an update before we get there?' Tasha asked gently. Linda nodded.

'Control from Hotel Victor 25,' Tasha said.

'Two-five, go ahead,' came the reply.

'Hotel Victor 25, I'm conveying PC Jamieson's wife to Beachbrook. I'm not state twelve, but please can we have an update, over,' Tasha said.

The radio went silent for about five seconds, then came the reply, the operator's voice cracking as she spoke. 'Control to two-five, last update from DS Willmott at scene. Female child out of sea, male child still not accounted for. Major search operation is ongoing. No further information, over.'

Linda shut her eyes as the message was relayed. This

was a scenario not even played out in the deepest, darkest recesses of her imagination. She slipped into a state of semi-consciousness, internally cocooning herself from reality. Time passed without her realising, before Tasha's soft voice brought her back to the present, as if waking from a dream. She looked around, trying to orientate herself. Abandoned police cars. Crowds of onlookers. A helicopter in the distance, hovering like an ant set against a grim, grey canopy. And the sea. A beast of nature, spitting waves towards shore with tempestuous fury. It was no dream. It was a living nightmare.

'Linda, we're here,' Tasha said softly.

Linda bolted upright and sprang out of the car. This was familiar territory, but it felt totally alien. She ran towards the slope. Towards the beach. Towards the sea.

'Where is he?' she screamed, oblivious to the many eyes that were on her.

As the fine mizzle began to cling to her clothes, an arm halted her progress. The comforting hand at the end of it held her shoulder gently.

'It's Linda, isn't it?' a police officer said. He was wearing stripes. A sergeant. 'My name's Mike, I work with Chris. I brought him here. He's on the beach.'

Linda had heard enough. She ran into the wind, into the rain, into the storm, screaming Chris' name.

She found him standing on the beach and staring out to sea.

Chapter 9

CHRIS

During the Storm

Chris' alarm had gone off at 5 a.m. that morning. He hit it straight away, not wanting to wake Linda. It wouldn't have mattered. As he sat up and looked across, she wasn't there anyway. He slipped quietly out of bed and sat on the end of it, rubbing his eyes. He loved being a police officer, but the early mornings... Not so much.

He opened his bedroom door as quietly as he could and crept across the landing towards the bathroom. Joe's door was ajar and, inside, he could hear the two very distinct sounds of sleep from the two people he loved the most. His mind wasn't in gear. As soon as he gently pushed the door open, the hinges creaked their disapproval.

Chris froze. Shit. He'd been saying for days that he'd WD40 them. Joe stirred and Linda's eyes opened. Her stare cut through him. What could he do? He just held his hands up and waited, praying for Joe to stay asleep. As he walked away and into the bathroom with the softest steps he could muster, he closed the door and sat on the toilet. Great start to the day.

He liked to be organised. He always had a shower the night before an early shift so that he could just have a quick brew, brush his teeth and be out the door. Those extra twenty minutes in bed each morning were precious. He had laid his uniform out the night before as well. More seconds saved.

He went downstairs to the kitchen and looked out of the window, whistling quietly to himself at the sight of Joe's toys laying upturned and in a line against the side fence. Footballs of all sizes bounded from pillar to post as the winds played their own game with them.

Alone, and sitting stubbornly on the floor, was a solitary egg-shaped ball. Chris was trying to get his boy into rugby, but it was a losing battle. If only Joe knew the joy that fifteen-a-side could bring, how it had tempered a young Chris and gave him purpose. Discipline. A different path from the one he'd trodden as a young man.

He held his hand up to the window frame and felt a small draught blowing through. Another job to add to the list. One day, he'd get them all done.

He heard footsteps upstairs. Linda hadn't gone back to sleep, obviously. She stumbled downstairs just as the kettle boiled.

'Bad night?' Chris asked.

'Shit night,' she replied. 'Didn't you hear him?'

'Nah, I was out like a light,' Chris said, knowing that it was the wrong thing to say as soon as the words passed his lips. 'I'll do tonight, I promise,' he said.

Linda didn't reply. Her eyes were closed and her head bowed.

'Go and sit down, love,' Chris said gently. 'I'll bring you a brew in.'

Linda turned and walked out of the kitchen. Chris watched,

those pangs of guilt growing more and more pronounced. She was the best wife. The best mum. She deserved more. He needed to step up.

He made her drink in a mug, and his in a travel cup to drink on his twenty-minute drive to work. He walked into the lounge wearing his best smile, but gentle snores told him that his wife had fallen asleep. What to do, he wondered? Wake her? Leave her? Set an alarm for her? Whatever he did would probably be wrong. She looked so peaceful, so serene. So different, in fact, from the shattered woman who had stood before him just minutes prior. He quietly set her mug down on the table and left her to sleep. She'd probably set her phone alarm, anyway. She normally did.

He liked the drive to work. It was a good time to turn off from his personal life and switch into police mode. It was especially good on weekend early shifts as the roads were so quiet, but the journey that morning was hideous. There were some exposed roads on the way there and the wind was potent. More than once, he felt his car being sideswiped by a sudden, invisible gust and it took every ounce of his advanced driving skills to stay centred on the road. Dawn was breaking and thick clouds lurked, waiting to unleash a deluge. He'd been a copper long enough to know that it was going to be car crashes and fallen trees all day long.

He arrived at the station at 5.40 a.m. and went to the locker room to get kitted up before the 5.45 a.m. briefing. Most of the team were there.

'Morning, all,' Chris said. Sleepy greetings were exchanged all around. No matter how long anyone had worked shifts, earlies were still a killer.

'Good morning, team,' Sergeant Mike Adams said as they

all sat at the briefing table. There were ten constables along with Sergeant Adams. A big, steaming pot of tea sat proudly in the centre. Chris picked it up and began pouring.

'Aren't you getting a bit old for this, Chris?' Jim Croft, one of the younger police constables (PCs) joked. Chris smiled and raised his eyebrows. Jim had a point, though. At forty-one, Chris was the oldest on the team by over ten years. He was the only one with a child. Hell, he was old enough that some of those sitting around the parade table could BE his child. Generally speaking, most officers had moved on to specialist roles by the time they passed into their forties, but Chris still enjoyed the challenges of being out on the streets.

Not only that, but Chris was the elder statesman on the team. He was the longest serving by a distance and they all looked up to him. Sergeant Adams appreciated having someone like him around. On more than one occasion, Chris had been an effective conduit between him and the troops and, since they were the closest in age, a healthy respect had grown between Chris and his skipper.

The briefing only lasted a few minutes. Nothing had changed since the day before. Briefings were rarely updated at weekends – the nine-to-five brigade were still tucked up in their beds. Instead, Sergeant Adams flicked onto a weather forecast. Warnings of wind and rain filled the projected image on the wall.

'Weather's shit out there today,' Sergeant Adams said. 'It's going to be a busy one so be safe and back each other up where you need to, alright?'

The team murmured their assent as Sergeant Adams read out the crewings for the day and allocated various tasks and enquiries to different officers. Chris' pen twitched in anticipation, but he hadn't been given a callsign.

'Have you forgotten me, Sarge?' he asked at the end of the briefing.

'No, mate, you're riding with me today,' Sergeant Adams replied. 'I need to talk to you about a few things.'

'Anything to worry about?' Chris asked with a nervous grin.

'Not unless you've got anything to worry about?' Sergeant Adams replied, pokerfaced, before bursting into laughter. 'No, mate, nothing to worry about,' he said.

Chris smiled wearily. He was tired and the day had barely begun. Jim had been right. He was getting too old for this.

He assembled his kit, then went to get the sergeant's car ready. A quick once-over, a check of the mileage book and he was ready to go. He'd never crewed up with Sergeant Adams before and didn't have a clue what he wanted to speak to him about.

'I'll drive, mate, you look knackered,' Sergeant Adams said.

'Whatever you like, Sarge,' Chris said. Being chauffeured around by the sergeant was a bit of a luxury.

Sergeant Adams got into the driver's seat and set his driving position. He had only been with the team for about six months, having moved there on promotion from the firearms unit. Chris didn't know him well, but he already had a lot of time for him.

'Makes a bit of a difference to running around with guns, doesn't it?' Chris asked.

'That's a bit of you, isn't it?' Sergeant Adams asked.

'Not me,' Chris replied, 'I'm happy enough doing what I'm doing.'

Chris had seen it all before. Once someone had got onto a specialist team, one of the Gucci roles like firearms, then promotion to a patrol team was just a blip on the radar. Sergeant Adams was serving his dues. Before long, he'd be back on that unit as a firearms skipper.

'So what did you want to talk to me about, Sarge?' Chris asked as they drove out of the police station gates.

'It's Mike in here, mate,' Sergeant Adams replied.

'Okay, Mike,' Chris said. They sat in silence for a few seconds. It was strange for a sergeant to allow a constable to address them by their first name, but Chris wasn't going to argue.

'I want to talk to you about where you're going with your career,' Mike said. 'I've been here about six months now and, I've got to say, you're wasted here. The team all respect you. So come on, have you ever thought about doing the exams?'

Chris sat, quietly thinking for a few seconds. A lot of what Mike had said had struck a chord. Chris knew that he was a decent copper, and it was true that he'd been the one to go to when others on the team had a problem. Promotion wasn't something that he had ever really thought about but he knew that, eventually, it was a logical progression.

'It's just that we need someone to act up on the team when I'm not here,' Mike continued. 'You know how much they keep moving me about to cover custody and public order stuff at the moment. The chief inspector wants someone from our team to step up rather than having to shuffle all the other skippers about. Would you be up for it?'

Chris sucked a lungful of air down. Talk about being put on the spot.

'I've never really thought about it, to be honest, Mike,' he said, eating up the seconds while his mind whirred.

Was he ready? Of course he was.

Did he want to do it? Maybe. Actually, more than maybe. Yeah, he did.

'I suppose I could give it a go.' He smiled. It had been a shit start to the day, but things were looking up.

'That's great, mate,' Mike replied. 'I'll get all that sorted out tomorrow then. You can do some shadowing with me. That's why I crewed us together.'

It made sense to Chris now. In the six months that Mike had been with the team, the skipper hadn't ever crewed up with anyone to go out for a shift. Chris knew that the rest of the team would be gossiping at the moment and wondering if he was in trouble for something. He grinned at the thought of those very conversations being about as wrong as could be.

'Weather's grim, isn't it?' Mike said. It was raining sheets and the outside world was littered with the remnants of a Saturday night of excess blowing all around them.

'Yeah, what a difference a day makes,' Chris replied. He idly flicked his phone onto the main screen. Joe stared back at him. Golden locks, cherubic smile. His boy.

'It's just the one you've got, isn't it?' Mike said, noticing Chris looking down at his phone.

'Yeah, Joe... One and done!' Chris said, laughing. 'You've not got any, have you?'

'Nah, not me, mate,' Mike said, also laughing. 'None that I know of anyway. Your wife is on the buses, isn't she?'

'Yeah, she's on now actually,' Chris replied. 'Can pop in the ambulance station for a brew later if you like?'

'That's a plan,' Mike replied. 'Who's got your little man today, then?'

'Friends of ours,' Chris replied.

They drove around Havington for a while, lifting a few

fallen bins out of the road and removing some small branches from the carriageway.

'You live over this way, don't you?' Chris asked the sergeant.

'Sure do, just in town,' Mike replied. 'You're in Beachbrook, aren't you?'

'Yeah, born and bred,' Chris replied.

'Family still there?' Mike asked. It was one of those throwaway questions, a conversation filler rather than one that actually required a deep answer.

Even so, Chris went silent for a couple of seconds. A straightforward question, but not a simple answer.

'My dad lives just out of town but I don't see him,' Chris replied, praying for a change of conversation.

'All good?' Mike asked.

'You know what it's like,' Chris replied. 'Families, eh?'

Mike got the hint, and they patrolled in silence for a few minutes. Chris looked at the clock on the central console of the car. It was 7.15 a.m. Linda would've dropped Joe off by now, he thought. He sent her a text message to check that everything was okay, but she'd be on the road now.

'Any patrol available for a three-car injury RTC, London Road, Havington?' the radio operator barked. There wasn't anything going on anywhere else, so the whole team made themselves available.

'Fancy it?' Mike asked Chris.

Chris smiled and flicked on the blue lights.

They made their way to the incident at speed, but what was reported as a three-car injury RTC was actually a two-car accident with no injuries. Still, the road needed closing, and both Mike and Chris were wise heads when it came to volunteering to do exactly that. Sitting in a car, blocking a road, was certainly preferable to standing outside in THAT weather and doing the necessary paperwork.

'That ain't gonna be the only one today,' Chris said, as they watched their colleagues take a drenching on the roadside with smug grins on their faces. The rain was pummelling the windscreen and the wind was howling outside. It wasn't the weather to be going out for a Sunday drive, nor was it the weather to be dealing with a car accident. Chris thought that he could get used to the privileges of being a sergeant after all.

'Fancy a cuppa?' Mike said to Chris, as a recovery vehicle finally arrived and the operator set about their work. 'I've got a few bits of admin to tidy up at the nick. You can listen out and fill in for me while I'm doing that if you want?'

Chris nodded. 'Sounds great,' he said.

Chris made the tea while Mike sat at his desk, typing up some reports. It was the less glamorous side of supervising, that was for sure. Chris listened as his radio burst into life with another call.

'Any patrol available for a two-car injury RTC, Hollingwood Tunnel?' Hollingwood Tunnel was on the outskirts of Havington and had recently been opened as a relief tunnel for access to the motorway leading to London.

'Hotel Victor 25, show us attending,' said Tasha. 'Please let the sergeant know that we will be out of comms while we're dealing with it.'

'Received that,' Mike said over the radio. 'PC Jamieson is taking the reins for a while. Any problems, please go through him.' Chris swelled with pride. Apart from the two car crashes and the odd tree down, though, nothing else was happening. It was a quiet morning, though Chris would never dare to say the word. Mention it, even just the first letter, and all hell would break loose. It was one of those unwritten rules of policing. Never, ever, say 'quiet', 'Q', or anything related.

Chris sat back in one of the chairs in the sergeant's office. As he felt the cushioned lumbar support and the soft arm rests, he knew where the furniture budget had gone that financial year. He busied himself with some reports of his own and kept a beady eye on the CAD system as calls came in and were resolved. Proper sergeant work, that. He looked at his watch, then his phone. Joe. Little, happy Joe. He unlocked the keypad and sent a message to Andrew.

Alright, mate? How's it going? How's my little man? Weather is shite here, reckon it'll be on top of you now. What you up to? Xx

As he pressed send he locked his phone and Joe's sweet little face turned to black.

And so the morning continued. Chris and Mike tapping away at their computers while, outside, Mother Nature unleashed her fury on the world. After a while, the radio flickered into life. This time, though, the operator's voice was different. It was more urgent, more panicked.

'Control from Sergeant, are you receiving?'

Chris' ears pricked.

'Control from A/PS Jamieson. I'm acting for a couple of hours. How can I help?' Chris replied.

'Control to A/PS Jamieson, have you got some patrols we can send over to Beachbrook? We've got a potential major incident over there,' the operator said. Her words were rushed, her tone almost pleading. Whatever it was, it was serious.

'Of course, Control,' Chris replied. 'Take who you need.'

'Control to A/PS Jamieson, thank you,' the operator replied. 'Control to Hotel Victor 26 and 27, please make your way on immediate status to Beachbrook Beach. Change radio channels to Beachbrook frequency for further details.'

Chris' vision blurred. Beachbrook Beach. 'What's going on over there, Control?' he asked.

'Control to A/PS Jamieson, something has happened on the beach. Details are sketchy at the moment, but it looks like some kids have been washed out to sea,' came the reply.

Chris' blood turned cold.

'Who's the informant?' Chris asked, as his panic rose.

'Standby...' came the reply.

The wait was hell.

'Control to A/PS Jamieson, informant is a Sophie Wicks.'

Chapter 10

CHRIS

During the Storm

'Mike!' Chris shouted, jumping to his feet.

'You okay, mate?' Mike asked.

'Joe's in the sea, he's been washed out. We need to go!' Chris yelled. His heart was pounding out of his chest.

'Hold on, mate,' Mike said, closing down the CAD system for Havington and pulling up the Beachbrook calls.

There it was, in black and white.

'Informant, Sophie Wicks. A garbled 999 call. Two kids, swept out to sea. Her husband has gone in after them. Coastguard lifting and lifeboat deploying. Fire and Ambulance en route. Nothing further.'

Chris' face was deathly white. With a million thoughts racing through his mind, the blood had drained away from his cheeks.

Mike took hold of his radio and transmitted. 'Control, show me and A/PS Jamieson attending,' he said quietly. 'Please inform the duty inspector that one of the children involved is the son of A/PS Jamieson.'

Everyone heard Mike's broadcast, and a deafening silence followed across the airwaves.

Chris bolted from the sergeant's office, closely followed by Mike. His mind was racing. What the hell were they doing at the beach? He wouldn't have taken a dog there, let alone kids? What the fuck were they thinking?

They got into their police car and Mike illuminated the blue lights and activated the siren. They made their way out of the police station gates at a speed Mike hadn't before attempted. The high-and-low-pitched wails of the siren cut through the gloom all around them. The deluge was getting heavier and was irradiated in the blue lights, as shining shards of rain were driven through at breakneck pace. It didn't matter that the driving conditions were appalling. Mike pushed that police car to the very limit of its potential, and far beyond.

All Chris could do was sit there, stuck in some kind of hellish nightmare as Mike thrashed through corners and gave way to no one. Every part of him was willing them to get there quicker. He took out his telephone and tried to call Andrew. The phone line wouldn't connect. He tried to call Sophie but it rang straight through to answerphone. And Linda. What would he say to Linda? Maybe she already knew and was at the scene? He tried to call her.

'Hi, you're through to Lind—'

'Fucking answerphones,' Chris whispered, as he hung up.

'We'll go straight to the beach when we get there,' Mike said to Chris. He was driving with a surgeon's precision and poise, dissecting the junctions and stitching together a clean route ahead.

They were making good progress but, for Chris, it was too slow. Too leisurely. It was a dawdle when it needed to be a sprint.

'Come on,' he growled. Mike heard him and pressed the accelerator just a little bit harder.

Time, that irreversible constant, was being warped. Seconds felt like minutes. Minutes, like hours.

Chris looked out of the passenger window as the connecting road between Havington and Beachbrook wound around the coast. The sea spat with fury, and it made him feel sick. Not nauseous. Sick. In the pit of his stomach, and all around. Sick.

'Control from A/PS Jamieson, is there any update in Beachbrook?' Chris barked into his radio, his voice sizzling with the torment of a parent apart from their child.

'Control to A/PS Jamieson,' came the reply. 'Have you got your phone with you? I'll give you a call.' He pulled his work phone from his pocket.

'Go,' Chris said. Within seconds it began to ring.

'Hi, Chris,' the operator said. She knew him. She'd met him enough times, and her voice was loaded with sympathy. 'Patrols are at the scene now and the coastguard helicopter is overhead. Updates are coming in all the time, but it looks like one of the kids is out of the sea. One of them is still in there. We haven't been updated with any other details at the moment.'

The inner turmoil that had been eating away at Chris boiled over. 'Who's still out there?' he shouted down the phone.

'It doesn't say on the log,' came the reply. 'I'm so sorry, Chris.'

Chris hung up. He needed answers, not pity. Not sympathy. Just answers. He tried to call Linda again.

'Hi, you're through to—'

Mike retuned the car radio set to the Beachbrook frequency as Chris threw his phone into his lap and buried his head in his hands. It was all too much to bear. On the operational channel, it was a hive of chaotic and confused messaging. Someone needed to cut through the muddled broadcasts, and provide the control room with a clarified update.

DS Willmott was that person. 'Control from DS Willmott, an update for you. Can confirm that the female child is out, repeat, out of the sea. Male child is unaccounted for. Rendezvous point for further patrols is Beach Road. Will give further information when available. Over.'

Mike momentarily turned to Chris. His face was ashen. They were about five minutes away now and Mike pressed the accelerator a little harder still. He could make it in four, flat out.

'Come on,' Mike whispered, as the rev limiter kicked in along a lengthy, straight stretch of road.

Chris could feel his ire rising, cheeks flushing and fingers trembling. Close. They were close.

'Daddy's nearly there,' he mouthed, silently.

As they arrived in Beach Road and screeched to a halt, vapours of steam rose in their wake, the engine screaming after being pushed beyond anything it'd experienced before.

Chris threw his door open and jumped out of the car, sprinting through puddles on the road as he ran towards the slope down to the beach. Mike jumped out and followed him, but he just couldn't keep up. He was no match for a tormented father.

'Wait up, mate,' Mike shouted. Chris didn't look back at him. He raced along the clifftop and down the concrete slope. The sand was a dark shade of brown where it was so wet and, as he ran onto it, his eyes surveyed a vista alive with the flurry of activity. The Coastguard helicopter was over the sea with a powerful searchlight looking down onto the rolling waves. Lifeguards were out on surfboards fighting against the pull of the currents and the onslaught of the breakwater as they searched through the spray for signs of life. For Joe.

Police officers were fanned out on the beach at regular intervals for as far as Chris could see. He saw that everything that could be done was being done, but still it wasn't enough.

'What's going on?' Chris shouted as he ran towards the nearest police officer. He knew some of the local officers in Beachbrook, but didn't recognise this one.

'Calm down, mate,' came the reply, as the police officer backed away. The first thing he saw was a uniform. A colleague. Someone there in a professional capacity. One and one didn't make two, in the police officer's mind, and he hadn't twigged just who Chris was. 'The dad got the girl out, but we don't know where the boy is. Probably too late by now if you ask me. Parents must be going mental.'

All of the building tension in Chris was unleashed. The storm, the rage, the not knowing and the cheaply callous words from the officer all combined to expose the part of Chris that he'd kept a lid on for all those years.

Fists clenched, knuckles white, Chris swung at the officer and caught him flush in the face. Rationality had gone out of the window and, as the officer dropped to the floor clutching his left cheek, Chris stood over him, wild and ready for more. Mike may have fallen behind, but he arrived just in time to save Chris from himself.

'Chris, move away,' Mike shouted as the officer scrabbled to his feet. His cheek was red and swelling already.

'What the fuck was that?' the officer yelled, flexing his own fists. Chris was agitating to get at the officer but Mike was holding him back.

'It's his son out there!' Mike shouted. 'Show some fucking respect!'

Other officers who were standing sentry along the beach looked over and saw the commotion. In a matter of moments, various uniforms were swarming around them.

'Get back to your posts!' Chris screamed. The sea wasn't being watched. Joe needed them to be looking for him.

'He's right,' Mike shouted. 'Back to your posts, please. I'll deal with this.' The officers all saw Mike's sergeant stripes and melted back to their watching brief.

'Right then, mate,' Mike continued, addressing the officer who Chris had struck. 'This was either an accident where you fell over and banged your head on a rock, or we can investigate it... starting with anything inappropriate that you might have said. What's it going to be?' He stared at the officer, daring him to argue back.

The officer looked at Chris, still being restrained by Mike. 'Slippery as shit around here, Sarge,' he said. 'Really sorry, mate,' he said to Chris.

No reply came but, as Mike released Chris, he didn't lunge for the officer. A sideshow wasn't required. He just needed to get to Joe. He barged past the police officer, spinning him a full one hundred and eighty degrees, and ran down to the shoreline. Closer to Joe. Closer to finding him. Mike followed behind, and grabbed hold of Chris just as his feet were swallowed up to the ankles by the frothing breakers.

'You can't go in, mate,' Mike said, holding his hands up as Chris wrestled himself free and pushed his boss away. 'They've got professionals out there doing their thing. If you go in then it's going to be you who needs rescuing.'

Mike was right, of course. Chris knew it. Yet, still, it took every ounce of self-control he could muster to stop himself from diving in. Joe was out there. To do nothing seemed perverse.

'Gotta do something,' he mumbled repeatedly, while pacing in and out of shore.

His feet were soaked inside his heavy-duty work boots, but he didn't feel a thing. He looked out at the sea, at the savage rolling swells, and his broken heart sank into the pit of his gut. The lifeguards were struggling in the waves and the helicopter was pitching back and forth as if in the very eye of the storm. Watching, it seemed, was all he could do. Joe was out there somewhere, all alone. Scared. Maybe calling for his mummy, his daddy. And they weren't there for him. The very thought of it broke him.

Mike stood beside Chris, his feet also soaking. He placed his arm around the shattered man next to him, but didn't say anything. Words wouldn't help.

'I've got to get hold of Linda,' Chris whispered, choking on his emotions. He didn't know if she was aware of what was happening or where she was. He looked at his phone. No signal. She needed to know.

'Mike, can you try to get hold of Linda, somehow?' he said.

Mike looked at Chris. 'If you promise you won't try to go in,' he said.

Chris nodded, but didn't take his eyes from the sea. Mike took his phone and strode away as quickly as the wet sand underfoot would allow. Chris was right. She needed to know.

Alone, and with just the sea for company, Chris stared long into the distance. He watched the waves breaking. He watched the layer of foam that always sat atop the breakwater on a windy day be churned underneath as the surf crested and broke, releasing so much power, so much energy. When the cycle was complete, and the next wave was just beginning to form, he could see all the way to the horizon. He couldn't tell where the sea ended and the sky began. It was endless. Limitless. And Joe was somewhere in between.

'Chris, I've just spoken to Ambulance Control,' Mike said, running up behind him. 'She's at the RTC in the tunnel and hasn't got any signal. I've told them what's happening and another ambulance is on the way to take over from her. She'll be on her way here as soon as possible.'

And when she arrived, what was Chris to do, he wondered? What was he to say? What could he say? He had no answers, only questions.

'Chris?' came a voice from behind them. Both he and Mike turned around. DS Sue Willmott was walking towards them, trying to balance the day book that she held in her hand with the wind that was threatening to lift her from her feet.

'Sue,' Mike said. 'Is there any update?'

'I'm not sure what you know at the moment,' DS Willmott replied. 'Maria has gone off to hospital but she will be fine. Andrew brought her in. I'm really sorry, Chris, but there's no news on Joe yet. We're doing everything we can.'

Chris didn't answer. Whatever they were doing, it wasn't enough. Nothing ever would be, not until Joe was found.

'Did you know they were coming to the beach today?' DS Willmott asked him.

'I never thought they'd actually come,' Chris whispered, casting his mind back to the night before when the kids had been so insistent upon it. No, when Maria had been so insistent upon it. It was one of the questions that he desperately needed an answer to. Why the fuck had they been at the beach?

'Where's Andrew?' Chris asked.

'Gone with Maria. Have you spoken to him?' DS Willmott asked.

'What do you mean, gone?' Chris asked. 'Joe's still out there and he's fucked off because his kid's safe. Are you fucking kidding me?' He had been so preoccupied with his concern for Joe that he hadn't given a moment's thought to Sophie and Andrew. His cheeks burned in anger as his emotions threatened to boil over once again. He flexed his fists and his knuckles, red and grazed already, whitened.

'We don't know what's actually gone on here yet, really,' DS Willmott said, trying to pour water onto the fire that was beginning to rage within Chris.

'I dunno, I think I've got a pretty good idea,' Chris said, turning his back on her.

Mike put an arm around Chris and, just as DS Willmott was about to speak, raised a finger. No words. It was Chris' moment, Chris' time for release.

'What the fuck were they thinking?' Chris said, staring at the sky and letting the mizzle blend with the tears that were leaking from his eyes.

The spray of the sea, the rain in the air, the tears on his cheeks, it was all just too much. The floods of water in his hair, on his face, and dampening the fibres of his uniform all combined. He felt like he was drowning. He turned and walked away. To where, he didn't know. He trudged around and around, circling the same stretch of sand until his boots were heavy with sand, both inside and out, and his tracks were one solid trench rather than a series of footprints. He stood alone, staring at the sea, as the minutes crept past with unremitting dependability.

'Where are you, mate?' he whispered, begging for an answer to come his way.

'Chris!' He turned around and Linda was running towards him. His heavy boots made hard work of the ground beneath him, but her voice had cut him to the core. His pain was hers, and vice versa. It resided in every sinew of them both. He needed her as she needed him and, as their bodies collided in an embrace of parental heartache, their individual nightmares became one terrifying entity.

Neither had the words. Instead, the noise came from a clamour at the shoreline.

'There's something there,' shouted one of the officers who was standing sentry.

Chris and Linda could barely make out his words over the crashing of the waves and the thudding of the helicopter rotors, but instinct and intuition told them to run towards the voice, quickly.

They could see what he was pointing at. What he had seen.

There was a dark object in the sea, about twenty metres from the water's edge. Underwater. No signs of life. It had been spat clear of the breakwater by the waves. One of the lifeguards out at sea had noticed something going on and, as she paddled towards them, the waves pummelled her. They were trying to keep her away from their prize.

'Please, no,' Linda whispered, as they watched the lifeguard arrive at the object and survey it, poke at it with her oar and, eventually, and with great difficulty, haul it onto her board. Its weight nearly sunk her, more than once.

Whatever it was, it clearly wasn't Joe. Chris breathed ragged breaths. What if it had been him? What if... He couldn't even bring himself to think it.

The lifeguard struggled to stay afloat as she manoeuvred herself, her board and the object from the sea into shore. Despite her tender years, she was professional at navigating perilous waters. She caught the crest of a wave and rode on it as it brought her to solid land. The object was a big, thick coat, fully saturated and as heavy as a pallet of bricks. The manufacturer's price tags still hadn't been cut out of it. They were soaked, but they still clung on, affixed to a piece of string that was looped around the inside label.

'Lay it there, search it and get CSI down here now,' DS Willmott instructed the officer. He gently lay the coat down on the sand, safely away from the shore. He put a pair of gloves on and searched the pockets. He pulled out a set of keys, a mobile phone and a wallet with the driving licence of Andrew Wicks inside.

Chris looked at it, then turned and paced the beach.

What the fuck had they been doing there?

So wrapped up was he in his own world, Chris didn't notice the flurry of activity out at sea. Away from DS Willmott and Mike, who were watching from a distance but not approaching out of respect for his and Linda's private turmoil, he didn't hear the sombre tones on the radio. Walking around and around on the thick, clay-like sand, physically together but mentally miles apart, neither parent saw the lifeboat scrambling with pace towards the now stationary searchlight of the helicopter, beating down on one, fixed point, way out to sea.

What snapped them back to reality was the look on DS Willmott's face as she approached them. Mike followed, wearing the same, grim expression. Chris and Linda both recognised it. They'd worn it themselves, many times.

It was the look of death.

Words weren't needed. Not there, and not then. They knew. They both knew.

Linda fell into Chris' arms and not even the sea could consume her wails of anguish.

Chapter 11

MIKE

During the Storm

'In here, love,' Mike said.

He guided an almost catatonic Linda into the front seat of his police car and nodded to DS Willmott, who stood guard outside the vehicle, shielding Linda from the crowd of onlookers who had seen the broken woman slump into the passenger seat. It was obvious who she was, and what had happened. Grief had descended upon Beachbrook, and it touched everyone. Anyone dying at sea was a tragedy but, when it was a child, the wounds ran deeper.

Mike ran back along the pavement and down the slope, finding Chris exactly where he had left him, resolutely refusing to be parted from the sands, from where he could see exactly what was going on out at sea.

Mike stood next to him, with his arm placed delicately around Chris' shoulder. There were no words. Just two men watching as a lifeboat chugged through choppy waters to port, carrying a cargo that they had been desperate to avoid finding. Slowly, almost reverentially, it rode the waves that had taken Joe. Chris watched through broken and glazed eyes as the boat charted a course due west, eventually rolling out of sight. He craned his neck, but it had gone beyond the cliffs to the right, around the coast and heading for Beachbrook Port. He looked at Mike. He had to be there when it landed. Mike nodded. He knew.

They walked up the beach, Mike's arm not once leaving Chris' shoulder, and trudged up the slope to Beach Road.

'I'm so sorry, mate,' Mike whispered, as they approached the police vehicle. He'd said it on the beach, but Chris hadn't processed it.

Mike climbed into the driver's seat while Chris and Sue sat in the rear. Linda hadn't moved a muscle and, as they drove away, the only noise – other than nature's percussion beating down on the windscreen – was the sound of the seatbelt warning system informing Mike that Linda wasn't plugged in. It beeped quietly at first, louder as he drove away and then loudest as he pulled to the side of the road. He reached across Linda, took hold of the belt, and pulled it across her. She didn't even flinch. Chris stared out of his window at a world that was no longer pure. It had been polluted by Joe's passing, permanently stained by his being gone. The drab, moody skies seemed apt. Nothing would ever be the same. Everything had changed. It was irrevocably different.

Mike navigated a cautious path to the port, his funereal pace entirely appropriate. He knew what awaited them, what was to follow. He looked at Chris in his rear-view mirror. His colleague. His charge. His crewmate. What hell was he going through? His eyes met Sue's as he scanned the roads to the rear. The following minutes, hours, days would be the hardest of their respective careers, bar none, and they nodded faintly at each other. Respect the anguish, recognise the pain, and be present in those deepest, darkest moments. It's all they could do.

They arrived at the port well before the lifeboat. Mike drove through no-entry signs, ignoring the stares of officials and onlookers. On a day like that, with bereaved parents in his vehicle, no one was going to stop him, least of all some jobsworth with a clipboard. He rolled to a gentle stop next to the slipway.

He looked once more at Chris in his rear-view mirror, whose eyes were fixed and staring out to the point where the clouds met the sea on the horizon. Mike looked too, knowing what Chris was searching for. There was no lifeboat in sight yet, though. It was just a rolling mass of grey, a solidly bleak vista where it was nigh on impossible to differentiate sky from ocean.

Mike climbed quietly from the vehicle and opened the rear passenger door. He took hold of Chris' hand as the broken man clutched at anything in reach that would aid even the most basic of motor skills. The driver's headrest. The edge of the car door. Mike's grip was tight as he helped Chris find his way.

'My boy,' Chris mouthed.

The lump that had begun to form in Mike's throat grew large as, behind them, a black, nondescript but very shiny van approached. It parked a respectful distance away, but Mike knew who they were. So did Chris. The police dealt with undertakers all the time, death being part and parcel of the job. Sue approached and spoke with the driver and the passenger, both in mourning suits, while Mike's arm never left Chris' shoulder as they looked out to sea.

They waited. And waited. Eventually, through the sea haze, the lifeboat came into view. It was a speck on the ocean to start with but, as it got closer and closer, Chris could see bowed heads on all those aboard. They'd gone to rescue a child. Instead, they'd recovered a body.

Chris tensed up, then walked away from Mike.

'Chris…' Mike said, following him.

'I need to get to him,' Chris whispered, as the lifeboat approached its mooring.

'Let them bring him up, mate,' Mike said quietly. 'We'll see him when he's here.'

That reassuring arm once again held Chris' shoulder as, heads bowed, the two men watched as an oversized body bag was lifted ashore.

Mike could feel Chris' heart breaking. Shattering. He felt the little twitches, he heard the involuntary whimpers. The shaking, the murmurs, the racing heart. It radiated from Chris and took Mike's breath away. A child's body, barely filling a quarter of the bag in which it lay. It was just so wrong. So manifestly unfair.

'I'm so, so sorry, mate,' Mike mumbled, feeling he needed to say something but knowing that, whatever words he said, they were just so utterly meaningless.

Chris wept and stumbled forward, his knees buckling under the weight of the shroud of grief that sat squarely on his shoulders, yet Mike didn't loosen his grip.

The lifeboat crew carried Joe with such dignity, such poise, as they traversed the slippery ramps up to solid ground. A trolley was waiting, the two undertakers standing by it and looking on. They dealt with death every day, but this wasn't their usual, run-of-the-mill job. Far from it. Children weren't meant to die. Parents weren't meant to outlive their kids. It just wasn't how things were meant to be.

The lifeboat crew set him down on the trolley and took a

few paces back. Their work was done, and they bowed their heads collectively, instinctively.

'They'll be taking Joe to the hospital,' Mike said softly, as he and Chris inched closer to the trolley until they were standing beside it.

It started as an involuntary humming noise, being emitted from the side of Chris' mouth. Then it grew louder. Deeper. Harsher. His eyes rolled and his entire body shook as the yawning chasm in his life that Joe's demise had exposed was laid bare.

Chris wept on his knees, free of Mike's grip. He yowled. He wanted his boy. He needed him.

'We'll follow them to the hospital if you like,' Mike said, holding Chris' hand as he and Sue gently helped him to his feet.

Chris nodded and stroked the shape of his boy's head through the closed body bag that was wrapped around Joe, the smooth material feeling like sandpaper as he rubbed his fingers over it. So close, and yet so very, very far apart. Worlds away from each other. Separated by spirit and reality. By life, and death.

As Chris slumped once more into the rear of the police car, Mike gently closed the door behind him. He looked through the front window. Linda hadn't moved a muscle.

Mike looked towards Sue, and beckoned her to one side, where they were out of earshot.

'It's fucked,' Mike whispered.

'Awful,' Sue concurred.

The brake lights on the private ambulance lit up, punctuating the mizzle with a glow of red. They were ready to go.

'Is this your job?' Mike asked.

'Kid dies, CID take it on,' Sue replied.

'What do you reckon?' Mike asked.

Sue sighed. 'You know how it goes,' she replied. 'Start big, follow the evidence.'

'What the hell were they doing at the beach?' Mike asked.

Again, Sue sighed, and shook her head.

'Needs answering, doesn't it?' Mike said.

'Damn right it does,' Sue replied, firmly.

They climbed back into the car and Mike remained silent, listening as DS Willmott began to fill Chris and Linda in on the formalities of what was to follow. Their paths hadn't crossed too many times before, but Mike knew just how professional she was. Just how diligent. He knew just how much she cared.

Mike looked at Chris, and Sue's words mostly seemed to bounce off him. Some sentences penetrated his barriers, but only sporadically.

'The coroner will have to release Joe.'

'Post-mortem.'

'We have to make sure there's no crime.'

'No crime?' Chris spat back. That one speared him.

'I'll investigate it like Joe is my own,' Sue said. 'I promise.'

Mike winced. Promises. A police officer should never make one.

Mike swung slowly into the rear of the hospital, to the unmarked and un-signposted anonymous building that housed the mortuary. It was one of those buildings that police officers and ambulance staff knew well, but the general public were oblivious to. Mike climbed from the car and stood by Chris' side as the trolley carrying Joe was lowered from the private ambulance and wheeled in through the doors. This was where their escort ended, but

Mike didn't need to say it. Chris knew. Right now, Joe was a crime scene.

If it pained Mike to think of him like that, then he could only imagine how it made Chris feel. It was the kind of thing that Mike had said so many times to others, his words calming and gentle as he explained to bereaved families that the body of their loved one may have evidence that could assist the police in investigating the circumstances of their death. It was always as if he was reading from a script, that his words were part of a scene from something theatrical where he was just a member of the supporting cast. Now, he was doing his best to assist one of the lead characters. Now, as he thought about Joe, the crime scene, the post-mortem, what was to come, it was a horror story too macabre to even imagine. In the blink of an eye, the trolley had been wheeled into the mortuary and out of sight. Joe was gone.

'Where's Andrew?' Chris asked. His quiet voice couldn't mask the venom laced within.

'I wanna know as well,' Linda said. She'd emerged with stealth from the front seat of the car, and Sue stood behind her.

'I'm not sure now's the time...' Mike began to say.

'Now's exactly the time,' Chris replied, walking off and through a side door.

Linda ran after him, and Mike stared at Sue, wide-eyed with mouth agape. He reacted first, though Sue was only a heartbeat behind.

'Look, guys, it's really not the place to do this,' Mike pleaded, as he caught up with them.

His words fell on deaf ears. Instead, it only prompted a collective lengthening in the bereaved parents' stride.

'I can arrange a meeting,' Sue added, struggling to keep up.

Again, nothing. Again, a hastening in their march.

'Guys, stop,' Mike said, barging his way past Chris and Linda and standing in front of them, temporarily halting their charge. They were in an empty corridor, one of those that only people in the know were aware of. 'Come on, there's a way to do it and this ain't it.'

'Mike, I know you're here to help,' Chris murmured, 'but get the fuck out of my way.'

Mike looked at Sue, both of them stuck in a situation that no amount of training could prepare them for. What were they to do? Arrest two grieving parents to prevent a breach of the peace? Not a chance in hell.

'I'll take you to them,' Mike said calmly, trying to ramp down the tension. 'But only if you promise it's not gonna go off. We're in a hospital.'

Chris' blank face did little to assuage Mike's trepidation. The nod that followed didn't, either.

Mike escorted them through the labyrinth of hallways that led to the A&E department. It was jam-packed full of people, but Linda knew exactly where to look. Mike's eyes followed hers as she surveyed the whiteboard in the triage area. Maria Wicks. Room eighteen. Just down the corridor.

'Guys...' Mike said, but Chris and Linda were two steps ahead of him. Their pace quickened.

'Chris, Linda, remember we're in a hospital and there's going to be a scared little girl in there,' Mike said. Suddenly this seemed like the worst of ideas.

'I just need to talk to him,' Chris said as he opened the door.

Chapter 12

ANDREW

During the Storm

When the door to room eighteen opened, the smell of salt hung heavy in the air. A beeping monitor from next to Maria's trolley provided a steady, constant soundtrack but aside from that, there wasn't a sound. Not a word was spoken.

Chris and Linda stood motionless in the doorway, while another police officer wearing stripes stood close behind them. Andrew looked up, and the mask of composure that he had been wearing to pacify his little girl slipped from his face. He felt Sophie's hand grasping for his, her palm wet with sweat.

They all stared at each other, waiting for someone else to make a move, to take a leap. The ice that fell across the room was spiked with the pain that had befallen them all.

'Hi, Chris, hi, Linda,' Maria said. Seeing them was normal. Familiar. Andrew looked at her, and watched as the smile on her face melted away under the glare of Joe's mummy and daddy.

'Where's Joe?' she whispered.

Andrew shot her a look, as if by instinct. What was she

thinking? What was her mind telling her? What memories were trying to escape?

His eyes shifted once more in the direction of the door. There, he saw pain in its purest form. It was etched all over Chris and Linda's faces, the kind of pain that could only manifest itself in one way. Anger. Andrew recognised it and, as he finally stood, his words cut through the tension like a hacksaw through bone.

'Let's go outside if you want to talk,' Andrew said firmly.

'I think that's a good idea,' the police officer with stripes said in agreement.

Chris and Linda turned around without saying anything and strode back along the corridor.

'Daddy will be back in a minute, okay, poppet?' Andrew said to Maria, pressing his dry lips against her forehead. 'I've just got to go and talk to Chris and Linda about something. Won't be long. Mummy will stay with you.'

Andrew walked out into the corridor and saw that Chris and Linda had already disappeared from view. 'I'm Sergeant Mike Adams,' Mike said, keeping his hands firmly by his side and not offering a handshake. 'I'm Chris' supervisor. He's on edge as you'd expect, so that's why I'm here with him.'

'Thanks,' Andrew replied. 'It all just happened so quickly...' His words trailed off. 'Is there any update on Joe?'

Mike stood rooted to the spot. Andrew saw it in his eyes, long before words parted his lips.

'I'm afraid Joe died,' Mike said. There was no sugar-coating it, no way of glossing the news. It was the textbook way of passing on a death message. Straight to the point and no ambiguity.

Andrew held his hand to his mouth.

'No...' he whispered. The boy he loved as if he was his own

112

had been snuffed out, his life ended, his game played. Joe's curtain had crashed down, and there was to be no encore. 'No, Joe, boy,' Andrew whispered again, as the hand covering his mouth rose up his face to shield his eyes from Mike's steely gaze. 'I just, what I'd give to—'

'Stop,' Mike said, holding his hand up. 'They need to hear it, not me.' The flick of his hand towards the length of corridor that Chris and Linda had walked wasn't quite dismissive, but it wasn't exactly friendly.

Andrew slowly turned and walked in the direction of the exit. The floor may have been smooth and shiny, as in any hospital up and down the land, but he might as well have been walking over boulders. He stumbled. He tripped. He overbalanced. His legs couldn't string together two solid steps, such were the shockwaves that were spreading across him.

Chris and Linda had made their way outside and gone to the garden area that was adjacent to the A&E entrance. The sheeting rain had chased away anyone who had been hoping for a crafty cigarette, and they sat on a bench as those bulbous drops slapped down upon them. Chris held his head in his hands while Linda sat next to him, staring up into the sky, at whatever may be up there beyond the clouds. Andrew's footsteps slapped through the puddles as he approached them. He didn't know what he was going to say. He owed them something but, what that something was, he had no clue.

Chris looked up at him. 'Well?' he asked. One word, but uttered with toxicity.

Andrew didn't reply immediately.

'What the fuck happened?' Linda shouted.

Again, words evaded Andrew. He knew there was nothing he could say. What dialogue could he string together to explain why they had gone to the beach? Why he had been too weak to resist? Why he had allowed them to play in the little sea? In the cold light of day, everything was inexplicable.

'I don't know how they got in the sea,' he said weakly. 'They were just playing in the little sea, you know, like they do. A dog ran and jumped up at Sophie and because she's pregnant I tried to get it away from her. When I looked back, they weren't there.'

'So you went straight in after them?' Chris asked. His eyes burned scorch marks in Andrew's mind.

'Of course I did,' Andrew replied. 'But I'd put a coat on after they'd gone to play. It just weighed me down.'

'And?' Linda asked. 'What happened?' Tears were falling, but the drops of rain that clung to her cheeks masked them.

Andrew saw their pain. Their sheer heartache. Their anger. Chris' nostrils flared, and Andrew understood. He got it. Roles reversed, he would've been in a police cell by now, with Chris in a hospital bed. From their perspective, he knew that it was impossible to be rational when dealing with actions that were demonstrably irrational. Why hadn't he just taken that fucking coat off? Would it have turned out differently, if he had? Again, a stream of endlessly unanswerable questions flooded his mind.

He looked at Chris and Linda. Grief poured from them, and was manifest in their every movement, their every breath. It was ingrained in their very being. Andrew knew just how easily it could have been Maria who had suffered Joe's fate. It could have been him and Sophie mourning the loss of their child, their baby.

'Well?' Linda said. 'What happened?'

'I only saw Maria,' he said quietly. 'I didn't see Joe at all. He was already gone.'

Linda recoiled sideways, slumping into Chris' shoulder. Chris held her head tightly against his own as shards of water slapped their faces, little razor blades in a fog of grief. Mike stepped forward and placed his coat over Linda. As he did so, Andrew noticed that something on Mike's utility vest was flashing red. It was the 'record' function on his body-worn camera. Mike had activated it to record their conversation.

Andrew shuddered, as the colour drained from his face. His words were now committed to the record.

DS Willmott had been lurking in the background, barely able to pick up any of the conversation over the torrent of rain that was falling. Now, though, the conversation had finished and she walked over to Mike and helped him lift Linda to her feet.

Chris had heard enough and stormed off, shooting Andrew a look beneath contempt as he went. It was far from over, but it was more than he could stomach. As DS Willmott and Mike escorted Linda away, DS Willmott turned to look at Andrew.

'I'll be in touch,' she said. 'We need to talk, don't we?'

Andrew nodded. He knew it and, as he watched them disappear back into the hospital, his own gnawing grief was compounded by a sense of foreboding. As he sat on the bench, and the rain washed over him, he lost all sense of time. For the second time that day, he sat in saturated clothes, but his mind was playing the events of the morning on repeat to the exclusion of everything else around him.

Why had they gone to the beach?

Why had the kids ended up in the sea?

Why had he not just taken that fucking coat off earlier?

Why hadn't he just told the tru... No. He could never do that.

'Andrew, what's going on?' Sophie asked. 'Maria wants you.'

He looked up at her. Grief wasn't yet a part of her features. She was still in the dark about what had happened to Joe, and he had to tell her.

'Joe's dead,' Andrew whispered. She instinctively squeezed his hand, then pulled hers away, her eyes widening before filling with tears.

'No… he can't be,' she said, fumbling for the words to express herself. 'He… No. No, Andrew.'

Andrew pulled her close to him in an embrace. 'We need to get back to Maria,' he said. 'She's on her own.'

He wondered what was going through her poor, innocent mind. What would she remember? Would her six-year-old brain deem it too damaging and repress it all?

Andrew took hold of Sophie's trembling hand. He led her out of the garden and back towards the A&E entrance. She walked slowly, her mind completely at odds with her stumbling feet. As they were about to enter, her phone started to ring. She took it out of her pocket and looked at the screen. It was an unknown number.

'You answer it,' she said as big tears snaked down her already raw cheeks, handing Andrew the phone.

'Hello?' Andrew said, his voice still hoarse.

'Hi, Andrew,' DS Willmott replied. 'I left before we could speak properly.'

Andrew remained silent. He'd said enough, he thought.

'You'll appreciate that I need to get to the bottom of what happened,' she continued. 'I'll need to speak to you and Sophie about it, and Maria as well when she's up to it. We'll do you first, though. Are you free today? Beachbrook Police Station, ASAP?'

Andrew swallowed hard. The immediacy of the request shook him, but a refusal might make it look like he had something to hide.

'Yeah, of course,' he replied. 'I just need to check on Maria then I'll make my way there.'

They ended the phone call and Andrew took a deep breath.

'Was that the policewoman?' Sophie asked.

'Yeah, I've got to go there in a bit to speak to them about it all,' Andrew replied. 'She said they'll need to speak to you at some point.' He paused. 'Maria, as well.'

Andrew and Sophie made their way back to Maria's room where they found her asleep and a nurse sitting by her bedside.

'She's just gone off so I thought I'd sit with her until you got back,' the nurse said. 'She shouldn't really be left on her own after such a trauma.' Sophie's eyes, only just dry from the news of Joe, began to fill up with tears again.

'I'll get this police thing out of the way,' Andrew said. 'I'll be back as soon as I can.' He looked at Sophie, then at Maria. His wife's eyes told him that she didn't want him to go, but he knew he must.

It had to be done, and he had to do it.

He had a daughter to shield. He had a family to look after.

And, now, he had a lie to protect.

Chapter 13

DS SUE WILLMOTT

During the Storm

She always kept a couple of changes of clothes in her office for days just like the one she was experiencing. She pulled the blinds and prised the wet two-piece from her skin, knocking her glasses upwards as her shirt came over her head. She put them back over her eyes, and gazed at the photo of Lottie on her desk. Golden curls. A cheeky smile. Eyes that could churn cream into butter. Dimples on her cheeks. Every inch an angel. Her angel. Just like Joe had been, to Chris and Linda. Stood semi-naked, with just her underwear protecting her modesty, she felt vulnerable. She felt exposed. Not physically. Not at all. Emotionally, though. Spiritually, even. Something about Joe's story resonated with her and, as her glazed eyes sucked in the image of her own baby girl, her heart ached.

'I'll find out what happened,' she whispered, to herself as much as anyone, as her phone rang. It was from the front counter.

She let it ring out as she climbed into a dark suit that befitted the events of the day, and ran a brush through her hair, squeezing the last drops of rain out as it glided through the strands. Suitably attired, and well and truly back in the game, she let out a deep breath and picked up the phone.

'DS Willmott here. You just tried to call me,' she said.

'Got an Andrew Wicks down here for you,' came the reply. She looked at her watch. He'd got there quick.

'It's going to be a little while,' she said. 'I've got a few things to do before I speak to him.'

'I'll let him know,' the front counter officer said.

DS Willmott wasn't lying. She was waiting for Mike to download his body camera footage for her to review prior to getting Andrew's account. He had told her that there wasn't anything on there that he thought was of evidential value, but she was a meticulous detective who liked to have everything in order before proceeding. Mike had been privy to the conversation between Andrew, Chris and Linda, but she had only managed to catch the odd word here and there, keeping a distance in the rain that she deemed respectful while still being in a position to assist if it kicked off. She'd seen enough mistakes be made by people not checking the small details in the past. Besides, if there was anything – *anything* – that needed to be scrutinised, then she wasn't going to leave it to chance.

Assume nothing. Believe no one. Check everything. Until she had evidence that no crime had occurred, then her role was to investigate. A little boy had died and, in death, he depended on her to do just that. It mattered more than anything and, at the moment, all she had was a colleague's kid in the morgue and not a lot else to go on.

She looked at her watch. Mike had dropped her at the station on his way to taking Chris and Linda home, and had been gone a fair while. That was understandable, though. He had enough to deal with from a supervisory perspective, let alone on a human level.

She went over Andrew's incredibly brief first account that she had scribed on sodden paper in her day book outside the ambulance. She committed it to memory as, eventually, her door opened and Mike walked in.

'I've got the download here, Sue,' he said to DS Willmott. 'Do you want a look?'

DS Willmott looked at her watch. Andrew had been waiting forty-five minutes. She viewed the footage and made a couple of notes.

'How were they both?'

'Not good, if I'm honest,' said Mike. 'What do you reckon?'

She shook her head slowly. She knew better than to guess about things.

'Child neglect?' Mike asked.

She sighed. It was a stretch, but one she was willing to make if necessary.

'Enough to ask him some questions,' she replied, standing up and holding her day book close to her chest.

She made her way to the front counter area, and took a deep breath before entering the public arena. Steeling herself, she opened the door and looked around. Amongst a veritable assortment of grifters, chancers and bail signers, Andrew stood out. He didn't belong there. This just wasn't his field of play.

'Do you want to come through,' she said.

Andrew climbed to his feet, and she watched as the thick-set man with arms like boulders walked meekly towards her. There was something about a police station, she'd found, that reduced those who'd never stepped foot inside one to cowed, almost submissive, entities.

'Alright?' she asked, as Andrew walked behind her through the door.

She stopped in the hallway, and turned to face him. He looked like a deer, caught in the headlights of an oncoming juggernaut.

'Had to borrow a tenner off a nurse to get here,' he mumbled. 'I'll pay her back, though.'

She nodded.

'So we're going to sit in an interview room,' she said, her voice professional yet forgiving, 'and I'm going to ask you a few questions about what happened.'

Andrew nodded, but didn't reply.

'It's just a first account of what happened,' she continued, 'just so we can get it down on the record.'

Again, Andrew nodded at her, but didn't add to what was a one-way conversation.

'You'll appreciate just how serious this is,' she said, 'I know you were close to Joe. I won't make this any harder than it has to be but... Well... I've got to get to the bottom of it all, for Joe's sake.'

She eyed Andrew from over the top of her glasses. Just the mention of Joe had made him twitch.

'And for Chris and Linda's, obviously,' she added.

'What do you mean "the bottom of it"?' Andrew whispered.

She smiled kindly. This must have been hell on earth for Andrew.

'No stone unturned,' she replied. 'You'll appreciate that, I'm sure.'

She led him into a room and watched as he took it all

in. Metal, soundproofed walls with little holes punctured in them. Dim, moody lights. A desk and chairs, all bolted to the floor to prevent them being used as weapons. Recording equipment on said desk. Nothing else.

They sat in silence while DS Willmott loaded a DVD disc into the recording equipment and completed a few pieces of paperwork prior to the interview commencing. There was no small talk, now. She was in the zone. This was where she plied her trade, and she was at the top of her game.

A short time later, the interview commenced.

DS WILLMOTT: Thanks for coming in, Mr Wicks. You're here because a child has died and I'm investigating the circumstances of that death. This interview is just to get an initial account from you, but I do need to advise you that you are being investigated on suspicion of child neglect. Therefore, I need to caution you. You do not have to say anything, but it may harm your defence if you do not mention when questioned something you later rely on in court. Anything you do say may be given in evidence. You are not under arrest and you are free to leave, and as you're here at a police station you may have a solicitor advise you free of charge. Would you like a solicitor?

It was quite an opening salvo and, as she reeled it off with the gusto of someone who'd done it all a million times before, she looked closely at the man sitting in front of her. His head sank as mists of doubt rolled in all around him. She'd seen it before, oh so many times.

ANDREW: That's thrown me, to be honest. Do I need a solicitor?

A question that every police officer expects from a first-time interviewee. She was ready for it.

DS WILLMOTT: I can't advise you on that, I'm afraid. What I can say is that it is an ongoing right and that if you decide you don't want one now, you can always change your mind later.

His lips parted, but no words came out.

DS WILLMOTT: How does that sound... Okay?
ANDREW: Okay.

She looked into his eyes and gave him a little nod and the hint of a smile. Sometimes, people just needed a bit of encouragement to open up. Tense interviewees seldom gave good interviews.

DS WILLMOTT: Mr Wicks, tell me what happened today.

Some coppers tended to go for elaborate, verbose openings to an interview. Not her, though. She'd always found that clarity was found in simplicity.

ANDREW: Well, we were at the beach. That's me and Sophie with Maria and Joe. We had Joe with us because his mum and dad were at work. The kids were adamant that they wanted to go to the beach but the weather was awful. I keep wondering why I didn't just put my foot down and tell them that we were staying at home.

She looked at him, but his head was tilted down. The cowed man that had presented himself to her at the scene earlier in the day was still bogged down in the trenches.

DS WILLMOTT: What happened at the beach, Andrew?

Her voice was softer still. It was classic policing. Textbook. Be human. Develop a relationship. Gain their trust. Be their friend.

ANDREW: They were playing in a bit of water away from the main sea, Maria and Joe. We call it the little sea. The weather… It just came out of nowhere. Well, not nowhere, I guess, but you know, it'd been just a spit and blow at home. At the beach, it just got worse and worse, so bad that I had to go and put on my coat that I keep in the beach hut. Really, really bad. Anyway, a dog came and jumped at Sophie. She's pregnant, you know. So I was trying to get the dog away and then I looked around and they weren't playing there anymore. They'd… gone.

DS Willmott watched as tears fell down his cheek, and she couldn't help but feel some pangs of sympathy for his plight. He'd have to live with what happened, forever.

DS WILLMOTT: Gone where, Andrew?

ANDREW: I don't know. I ran to where they had been and it's all a bit of a blur really.

He shifted in his seat from side to side as his hands reached for his eyes and rubbed the tears away. DS Willmott let the silence develop, just a bit longer than she knew was comfortable.

DS WILLMOTT: I've reviewed some footage given to me by Sergeant Adams. He was with you when you had a conversation with Joe's parents earlier. Maybe if I introduce the content of that, it might help you to recall what happened?

Andrew's eyes fluttered, and DS Willmott's pen twitched in her fingers.

ANDREW: It's okay, I can remember what I said to them. I saw something out there, one of them. They were both wearing matching wetsuits, you see, so I couldn't tell who it was. It was about twenty or thirty metres out, I guess, where the waves were up and down, and I dived straight in and went right over, but I was panicking, you know. I hadn't taken off my coat or anything and it was pulling me down. So heavy. I don't know why I didn't just take it off to start with, I really don't. Anyway, I got out there and it was Maria and I just about managed to get her in. Then I went straight back out to try to find Joe.

It didn't matter that it was being recorded. DS Willmott still made notes, as much to plan her next question as anything else. With every word that Andrew said, she could feel the tension in the room rising. Why that was, though, she couldn't quite put her finger on.

DS WILLMOTT: But you took your coat off at some point, didn't you?

The speed of his response surprised her.

ANDREW: I did, but it's a blur. I just can't remember when.
DS WILLMOTT: Why didn't you take it off to start with?
ANDREW: You don't think I've asked myself that? It was brand new, I wasn't used to wearing it I guess. That's the best I can come up with. I'd only put it on in the beach hut right before, the weather was just foul.

Her pen scratched the paper in her day book, deliberately and without pace. She was looking at him as she wrote, a skill she'd perfected through years of asking the questions and getting the answers.

DS WILLMOTT: So did you see Joe at all when he was in the sea?

Her voice was so soft that it could barely be heard over the whirring of the DVD disc. Again, she'd only just finished the question before the answer jumped from his lips. He was loud, and authoritative.

ANDREW: No, I didn't see Joe.

It was enough, she reasoned. She had his account. She went into the finer points of detail on what he had told her, but the fundamentals had been established in those early exchanges. She wrapped up the interview when she was satisfied that she had all of the information that Andrew could provide.

'Thanks, Andrew,' she said after she turned the tapes off. Another unreturned smile radiated from her face to his. 'I'm going to need to speak to Sophie and Maria as well in due course,' she continued. 'I'll be in touch to arrange it. In the meantime, we found your coat and I've got your wallet, phone and keys here. The phone probably won't work, but the wallet and keys should dry out okay.'

'Thanks,' Andrew said, grabbing his things and putting them in his pockets. If she didn't know better – and she did, of course – then she'd have said that he was keen to get out of there as soon as possible.

She watched as he double-stepped outside from the front counter area and into the rain that had followed them around the coast, and shook her head. Andrew looked one way, then the other, before staring to the heavens. Then, he was gone.

DS Willmott returned to the CID office. Mike was still there, talking to a couple of DCs. Chris may have worked in the next district, but he was still a boy in blue. One of the family. One of them. The events of the day had hit everyone hard.

'Need anything, Skip?' DC Amy Flanagan asked. Some cases hurt. DS Willmott's face told Amy that this was one of them.

'Coffee, cheers,' DS Willmott replied.

'I'm on it,' DC Tom Harris said, scooting past DC Flanagan and heading towards the kitchen.

'How did it go?' Mike asked.

'I'm not really sure,' replied DS Willmott. Wasn't that the truth. 'You know what they're like when they get interviewed for the first time, clamming up and all that. He just seemed a bit… I don't know… Odd.'

'Understandable?' Mike asked.

'Guess so,' DS Willmott replied, quietly.

She turned to DC Flanagan.

'Amy, can you get that coat from the beach down to CSI?' she asked.

'Course,' Amy replied. 'What are they looking for?'

DS Willmott shrugged her shoulders.

'Haven't a clue,' she replied.

Something was niggling her, though, and she couldn't quite put her finger on it.

PART THREE

After the Storm

Chapter 14

LINDA

Seven Hours After

Linda's cup of tea from earlier in the morning sat on the coffee table. The words emblazoned on it cut her to the core.

Best Mummy EVER!

It had been hours since Chris had placed it in front of her. Now it was just a cold, undrunk reminder of what had gone before. How she yearned to have those hours back, but time had marched on relentlessly and without remorse. 'Before' was now a lifetime ago. She wanted it back. She needed it back. Those moments had gone, moments when Joe had been sleeping upstairs, safe in his dreams and snug in his bed, protected by the same footballers on his duvet who kicked balls on the wallpaper. She craved his smell, that unique, dried odour of mud that oozes from every six-year-old boy who flings themselves around the garden with a ball at their feet. She was desperate to hear his voice, to feel his head nestled into her chest. The space that he had occupied had been replaced with a numbness, a dawning of a grief so vast and profound that she didn't want to contemplate it. How could she continue? How could she navigate life without her child? Did she even want to?

Instead of the warmth of family, a cold, reverberating void had settled upon them. Upon her. No noise from upstairs. No football slamming against the wall outside. No sudden giggles when the ball hit the patio window by mistake. No constant requests for juice, for a snack, for a story. Just an overwhelmingly sad silence that hung heavy in every room, in every corner.

She looked to her left, to her husband. Physically close, but so many miles away. Wedged between them was death's sceptre, a hulking presence in the company of two bereaved parents.

Her mind drifted, lost in a sea of hopelessness. Beyond her tea, photos adorned shelves and mantelpieces. On the wall, canvases hung proudly. All of them with her boy front and centre. His blond locks drew her in, just as they always did. His cheeks, full and rosy. That grin. Her lips tremored. THAT smile. Here. There. Everywhere.

That smile. And always, always with a ball in hand.

Love you, Mummy.

It cut through her, sending shockwaves to the tips of her fingers.

Love you, Mummy. I wish you were coming with us.

His last words to her echoed, bouncing off the four walls that were closing in all around her, but only she could hear it. Those words, said as she'd hurried away from him to a job she didn't want to be at, in a life she'd created but would have given anything to have changed. All she wanted was to be his mother, to share his life. To make moments, to create memories.

The day drifted by, but it didn't matter. Nothing mattered. And what came next? She didn't know. Of course she didn't. She barely knew what came now, let alone at some juncture in a future without her boy.

The shrill tone of Chris' mobile phone rang in her ears, but it barely registered.

'Yeah?' Chris asked, his voice hoarse.

Linda didn't look up. Her eyes were closed, a barrier preventing the real world from getting in.

'An update?' Chris asked.

Linda scrunched her eyes tighter.

'So what, you nicked him?' Chris asked. 'How can someone let a child go in the sea in a raging storm and it be a tragic accident?' he shouted. 'I'm not putting up with this shit!' he yelled and hung up, throwing the phone onto the sofa with such force that it bounced into the air and then down onto the floor.

He threw himself back down.

'What's happened?' Linda croaked.

'They're saying it could be an accident,' Chris replied, his voice muffled as it travelled through the fingers that were propping his head up.

The floodgates opened once more.

'It wasn't an accident though, was it, Chris?' Linda asked, between sobs. 'I mean, they knew that he wasn't a strong swimmer. He should never have been there, should he?' She wept, barely noticing Chris storming out of the room.

Her grief devoured her, and time passed without rhyme or reason. She reached into her bag and picked up her phone. It was instinct and her fingers worked from muscle memory as she clicked on her WhatsApp icon. Sophie.

The last photo on the message stream, a picture of Joe at the beach. Smiling. Those cheeks. His blond locks. And a ball in his hand. Always, a ball in his hand. Sunny. Yesterday. Before it happened.

The phone tumbled from Linda's hand into her lap as she raised her fingers to her mouth. An involuntary whelp passed her lips as her mind caught on fire.

Sophie, her confidante. Sophie, the one she would always turn to for help, a chat, to put the world to rights. Sophie, her friend across the baby years. The chalk, to her cheese. The liberal to her conservative.

Now, Sophie, the one who had taken her baby to the beach and hadn't brought him home.

'No,' she whispered again. 'No, no, no.' Louder, she spoke. More agitated, she became. 'No. No. NO!'

She clicked through the photos and video clips.

I wish you were coming with us.

His words blasted in her ears, both tormenting and consoling her in equal measure.

She ran upstairs. A bit of mud here. She'd told Joe about wearing his trainers on the carpet. A forbidden Ribena stain there. She'd told him about carrying drinks upstairs. A pair of goalkeeping gloves on the landing. She'd told him about putting things away. She threw his bedroom door open, far too quickly for the hinges to murmur their creaking dissent, then fell onto his bed, breathing him in as she held the pillow to her face.

Time, once again, drifted by. Without reason, without purpose, she didn't feel it passing her by. It could have been seconds, minutes or hours until she felt Chris sitting next to her, holding her hand. She let it lay limply in his palm and, as dusk became night, neither of them moved. Neither of them spoke. The room was near black when Chris stood up and gently pulled the duvet over her. She didn't flinch. The hinges squeaked as he closed the door, but she didn't react. She didn't murmur. She just lay there, as inanimate as the boy she'd left behind in the morgue.

Chapter 15

CHRIS

Twelve Hours After

He sat in the lounge, staring at nothing. The curtains were open, and darkness was beginning to creep in. On the floor, his phone chirped at him. He leaned forward, feeling grief's weighty mass crush him as he moved, and picked it up.

Mike.

A message.

Sue said she spoke to you, mate. I'm not sure what I can say, other than I'm here for you. And Linda, of course. Anytime, at all. Just know that we will all be doing whatever we can to put the pieces together for you. Sending so much love your way.

He tossed the phone on the sofa next to him without replying, watching Joe's flawless face on the screen darken as the backlight faded, then disappear as the phone locked itself. His heart thudded against his ribs, the rhythm quicker than normal. He let it pound away. How often did someone think of their heart, he wondered? A vital organ, working to keep us alive every second of every day. Not Joe's, though.

Joe's little heart didn't beat anymore, and it drove a dagger through his own.

He stumbled into the garden. He wanted the rain again. He wanted a thunderstorm, a monsoon, a deluge. He wanted it to beat down on him. Anything to distract him from the pain inside. Instead, a thin layer of cloud hung overhead, a haze that barely masked the moon behind it.

He sat on a garden chair and felt the rainwater that had saturated its fabric dampen his trousers all the way through to the skin. What did it matter, though? What did anything matter anymore? He ached. Oh, how he ached. Every part of his essence was being deconstructed stitch by stitch, inch by inch.

How often had he told bereaved families that time was a healer? How many times had he dished out advice to others, that grief is a process? Words that he had been taught to say, but that didn't sit right with him at all. Not now that he'd experienced it. Not now that he'd suffered that loss. As he sat there, staring into the void behind his closed eyes where darkness resided, he felt a feeling beyond failure.

The caw caw cawing of seagulls roused him occasionally, but he didn't open his eyes. Instead, he spent the hours venturing deeply into his racing mind. It wasn't sleep, just a journey into his subconscious. Besides, he wouldn't sleep, even if he wanted to. Waking would have just brought the revelation all over again that his baby boy was gone. For a couple of seconds there might have been a fleeting sense of normality before reality crushed him. That, he didn't need. That, he couldn't face.

Instead, he had thought of the holidays they had shared. Holiday camps mostly. God, how Joe had loved them. Halcyon days, where the sun had shone and they wouldn't have chosen to be anywhere else in the world but there. He thought of the short life that Joe had experienced, of the future that he would never get to live. He wondered what kind of man Joe would've become. Would he have loved, and been loved in return? Would he have been a good dad? Would he have lived long, lived happy, lived true?

Chris thought of his own childhood. When he was Joe's age – long before things got difficult with his dad – he'd been a happy boy. A single child, like Joe. He'd loved his sport, like Joe. The parallels ended now, though. Chris had grown into a teenager, a man. Joe was forever stuck in time, the concluding part of his story written before he'd had chance to finish the introduction. He'd always be a victim. People would think of him not as the little boy who he'd been, but as the little boy who'd gone.

'Oh mate,' Chris murmured, wanting to say something but failing to find the words.

How many other fathers had stumbled along this particular track, he wondered? Which other daddies had ventured into the darkness and stared into the abyss that he was falling into? What other parents did he know, really? He was the only one with kids at work. Outside of that, it was only Andrew. Just thinking of him made the hairs on the back of his hands rise, in the worst way possible.

Aside from that, there was his own father. The seagulls went silent as he sat, thinking of a time long before, when he had been the child and his father had been the doting one. Hatchets were made to be buried, but that was one for another time.

Being a dad had been Chris' dream, and he had lived it. Now, though? To call it a nightmare would be too cliched, too simple. It was hell. Pure and utter torment. He bit down on his lip as he opened his eyes.

He'd been robbed. Joe's life had been stolen, and everything that came with it snatched away. Happiness. Contentment. Purpose.

Mother's Day and Father's Day would forever be dates for condolence, not celebration. Exam results days would bring pain, not satisfaction. Birthdays and Christmases? Pointless. The only anniversary that would have meaning was this one, their own personal D-Day.

To lose your child was to lose your reason.

Chapter 16

ANDREW

Five Hours After

Andrew had returned to the hospital from the police station, but he couldn't yet face his wife and daughter. The interview had left a stain in his mind that simply couldn't be cleaned. Instead, he sat on the very same bench on the hospital grounds that was still damp from a few hours before. He closed his eyes, lest they begin to leak once more.

Those waves from earlier in the day crashed over him in his mind with such vividness that he could feel them flooding his mouth, the taste of salt so sharp that it dried his tongue.

His eyes flew open, and he jumped to his feet. As he marched away from the gardens and towards the A&E entrance, he shook his head with such vigour that it cricked his neck.

He found Maria sitting on Sophie's lap on the bedside chair. She was dressed in clothes that he didn't recognise, but she was up. Her cheeks had colour in them. The small smile on her face that greeted him melted his heart and, just for a few, fleeting seconds, it skipped a beat as relief washed over him, momentarily numbing the angst within.

'Daddy!' she shouted. She jumped off Sophie's lap and ran to him, wrapping her arms around his legs and clinging to him. Still Daddy. Not Dad. 'You're not going again, are you, Daddy?' she asked.

'No, princess, I'm not going anywhere now,' he replied, returning her smile with one of his own.

'Apart from home,' said Sophie. 'The doctor has just been round, he's writing up the discharge papers.'

Their eyes met. Andrew saw a pain residing in her that he'd never before seen, and straight away he knew that he'd got his priorities wrong. What the hell had he been thinking, leaving his wife and baby to go to the police station? They should have come first. Never again would that happen. Never.

'How are you doing?' he asked Sophie, stroking her cheeks and trying to soothe the wounds that ran deep within.

'I'm alright,' she replied. A lie, for sure, but he understood. Appearances were everything, especially with Maria watching on.

Maria sat on Andrew's lap on the way home, silently sucking her thumb and staring out of the rain-spotted window. He held her, much tighter than usual. She stroked the skin on his elbow with her spare hand, just like she had as a toddler.

'We're home, poppet,' Andrew whispered as the taxi rolled to a gentle stop.

Maria wrapped her arms around his neck as he lifted her from the vehicle and carried her indoors. He closed his eyes, expecting the blissful clinch of his daughter to bring peace.

Instead, it brought it all back.

The sea confronted him. Maria's hands had been wrapped around him then, as now. The waves crashed all around him. Over him.

Once more, he forced his eyes open and felt his neck go tense. A bead of cold sweat ran down his forehead, dribbling onto his nose and dripping onto the floor. There were demons swarming and, by God, he knew they were coming for him.

He carried Maria into the house and laid her on the sofa in the lounge.

'Do you want anything, princess?' he asked.

'Juice please, Daddy,' she replied, cuddling into the pillows that surrounded her. It was safe. A cocoon in which she could bask. She was home.

Andrew walked into the kitchen, but stopped as soon as he felt the cold, smooth tiles underfoot. His eyes fixed on the kitchen table and he shuddered, biting his bottom lip so hard that he could taste blood flowing. Joe's pyjamas were folded up neatly and lying on the table. Little footballers, crudely stitched and their bodies stretched where they had been worn so many times, running amok on the fabric.

He picked them up and pressed them against his face, breathing in. Joe's scent rushed up his nose, that sweet, innocent and unique smell of a child. Tears the size of raindrops slowly trickled down his cheeks as he felt someone pulling gently at his arm. Sophie took hold of his hand and let her tears fall as well, a private moment that they had not yet been able to have together. They muffled their sobs in their fingers so as to avoid Maria coming to investigate their source and, more than once, Andrew again held Joe's pyjamas to his face before finally passing them to Sophie. She folded them back up, handling them as if the most delicate item in the world.

'We'll get through this,' he whispered to her.

She nodded as she turned her face away.

'What happened?' she asked, barely audibly.

141

'Later,' Andrew whispered back, pointing towards the front room. It was a conversation that needed to be had away from prying, vulnerable ears. Not one for there. Not one for then.

As sure as night follows day, though, later came. Andrew and Sophie sat either side of Maria's bed until long after she had fallen asleep, watching her tiny mind drift away into a slumber that they hoped would last the night. Her night light displayed a dim moon floating on a backdrop of tranquil blue and, though it was still light outside, the blind trapped most of it at source. Andrew looked around, finding shadows everywhere. Lullabies played in the background, each a composition that contrasted so radically with the events of the day. Still, it was all that they could do, to try to radiate some kind of serenity into the air all around their little girl.

The cracks at the edges of the blind eventually grew dark. Andrew looked at Sophie, and she nodded towards the door. She walked out, pausing to look at her little girl. He followed in his wife's footsteps as she led him downstairs and into the kitchen.

Andrew stared out of the kitchen window as the light of a nearly full moon shone back in at him. The sky was clear, the night still. In every sense, it was the calm after the storm. Sophie was behind him, and he knew she had questions. He knew that she wanted to talk about what happened, that she *needed* to, but he just couldn't bring himself to make the first move. Instead, he bathed in the moonlight, closing his eyes and hoping against all odds that he could open them and find it had all been just the worst kind of nightmare.

His mind was a canvas of black just for a moment. Earlier in the day, when he'd closed his eyes, the images of the sea that had plagued him had been instant and vivid.

Now, though, it was the sound that came to him first. A low, humming noise, from both sides of his head, growing louder by the second. The hum became a drone. The drone, a roar. Then, images in the clearest of resolution. The rip, dragging him. The waves, pummelling him.

His eyes flew open, and he looked up to the moon, and the man on it frowned back at him. It was a spotlight under which he couldn't crack. Sophie's hand slipped into his, and he slowly turned around to face her.

'It doesn't seem real, does it?' she said.

'Why did we go there?' Andrew asked, shaking his head.

Her breath was ragged, but it was a conversation she was determined to have. In all the years they'd been together, Andrew knew when she was battling against the torrents that raged within her.

'It just all happened so fast, didn't it?' she said. 'The dog and all that, I swear we didn't take our eyes off them for more than a second, did we? What were they doing?'

'I don't know,' he whispered.

'Maria will,' Sophie said, quietly.

Andrew took a short, sharp breath. Hers wasn't the only ragged voice in the room, now.

'Maybe,' he replied. 'Can't force that, though.'

'Obviously,' Sophie said. 'Police will know what to do, though, they'll have specialists or whatever, won't they, to speak to her?'

Another sharp breath in. Another pause.

'Maybe,' Andrew said. The hairs on the back of his hands stood to attention once more, as silence filled the air.

'I want to speak to Linda,' Sophie whispered. Her voice was so small, so frail, and the tears that she had been steeling herself against finally began to fall.

'We've got to give it time,' Andrew mumbled.

'I know,' she said, 'God I know, but I just want to see her, to speak to her, to say… Sorry. Sorry, Lin. I'm so sorry, darling.'

'I know,' Andrew replied, pulling his sobbing wife in and holding his clammy hand around the back of her neck, 'and me too, love, me too.'

Sophie pulled her head back from Andrew's. She needed to know what had happened, why it had happened, how it had happened.

'Did you not see Joe in there at—'

'MUMMY, DADDY!' Maria screamed.

They looked at each other, wide-eyed, for barely a millisecond before they ran for the stairs. It was thirteen steps, bottom to top, but it felt like running through wet sand as Andrew made his way to the top. They ran into her bedroom, where they found her sitting bolt upright against the headboard of her bed, crying hysterically and her body rigid. Her eyes rolled as the screams continued. Andrew picked her up and held her tightly. Maria was kicking and thrashing about as her parents tried desperately to calm her down.

'Maria, sweetheart, Mummy and Daddy are here,' he soothed.

Her screams lessened in strength and intensity until they were sobs.

'What happened, darling?' Andrew asked, gently rocking his daughter in his arms.

'I don't know, Daddy,' Maria replied, still sobbing. 'I had a bad dream.'

Sophie took Maria from Andrew's arms. He'd always been in awe of how strongly her maternal flames burned but, right there and then, what he'd have given to be the one comforting his little girl.

'Alright, sweetheart,' she said, rocking her daughter from side to side.

Maria's hand was drawn to her mouth, and she sucked her thumb. She hadn't done that for years.

Andrew walked out of the room, barely able to stomach it. He knew what her dream had been about. He stood on the landing, pacing up and down, until Sophie poked her head through the bedroom door.

'I'm going to take Maria in with me,' Sophie whispered. 'Are you alright to sleep in here tonight?'

'Course,' Andrew replied. He walked back into Maria's room, and forced a smile onto his face. She tried to smile back, but behind her eyes was a sadness that told him everything. Andrew scooped her up into his arms, and carried her away from the night light and the lullabies and into his and Sophie's marital bed. Softly laying her down, she closed her eyes as soon as her little head hit the pillow.

'I'm going to make a tea,' Andrew whispered to Sophie. 'Want one?'

Sophie shook her head, and, with her eyes firmly on her little girl, climbed into the bed next to her and held her from behind.

Andrew walked downstairs and turned the kettle on. Though he made the tea, he left it untouched.

Only one thought occupied his mind. After seeing Maria react like she had, there was no way in hell that DS Willmott or any copper were going to get their hands on his little girl to ask her questions about what had happened. She'd seen enough. She'd been through enough.

Over his dead body were they going to make it worse.

Chapter 17

CHRIS

One Day After

The slowly rising sun brought the light of a new day. The storms that had battered Beachbrook gave way to something more serene, more tranquil. Chris had seen the early breaking of dawn still in the garden, having given up on the idea of sleep. He sat on the same chair, still wearing the uniform of the day before, still damp from nature's soaking. What came next, he wondered? For him? For Linda? For them? How to arrange a funeral for a child, for example?

Everything was wrong. Life was all about order, and a parent burying a child wasn't how it was meant to be. It wasn't fair, and it wasn't right. Children put their parents to rest when their time came, then lived on. That was the way things went. Life's script had been messed with, though. Scenes had been moved about. Joe's ending had come before the end of his first act, and the encore had been deleted long before the curtain fell.

Joe's funeral. They were two words that he'd never, ever imagined he would utter.

And then what was to follow? He couldn't see a minute in front of him, so what was yet to come? How would the hours, the days, the weeks, and the years afford him anything other than the frozen, barren landscape that filled his vision?

And what of his wife? How the hell were they going to navigate this journey, together?

He'd seen grief before. He'd worked with it, helped people through it and he knew how invasive to life and living it was. It consumed everything, and spared nothing. Not dealt with properly, it could be an insidious force. Pervasive, too. How would the community react? Was he at fault? Should he have been with his boy, to prevent any of this from happening?

The next night, sleep came. The following night, the same. Chris had worked shifts long enough to know that it was taken when needed. When he slept, it was to allow function. It wasn't for rest and it certainly wasn't for the pleasure that some people find in their dreams. It was simply a means of allowing waking hours to follow, to operate, even at a sedentary level. It was instinctive. Animals need sleep. The body will do it eventually, with or without its occupier's consent. He knew that resisting it was futile, so he allowed his eyes to close. The nightmares followed, as he suspected they would. When he woke, it was light. Groundhog Day.

Reminders of his boy were everywhere. Football figures on the floor. Joe had been bought Subbuteo for Christmas, only two seasons before. Whenever he'd broken one of the little players, he'd gone to Chris to use the glue gun to fix it. Now, the red and white Arsenal team seemed to follow Chris around the house, turning up wherever he walked. There were pictures on the fridge. Photos, all around. The three of them on holiday, all smiling, all carefree. School pictures. Class photos. Now, just memories.

At some point, would those reminders be removed? Bit by bit, would they be cast aside? Would the carpet stains be cleaned, the books taken down, the pictures filed elsewhere, the photos replaced? What would become of Joe's room? Would it forever be a shrine to their boy, or at some point would it be taken apart and dismantled?

He looked across to Linda's side of the bed, at the empty space next to him. Today, they'd speak. Today, their burdens would come together as one. He needed it and, he was sure, so did she. He climbed from his bed, but he didn't need to draw the curtains to know the sun was shining once more. It filled the room through the cracks, bringing light to the darkest recesses of the room.

Going onto the landing, he picked up Joe's goalkeeping gloves. They'd lain there for days, and now he held them to his nose. Through the latex and rubber, the smell of Joe was there. He breathed it in, sucking down the essence of his boy as, in the background, he heard the faintest of purrs coming from Joe's room. Linda was still in there, and she was resting at last.

Chris went downstairs and crumpled onto the sofa. His phone sat next to him, unmoved from days before. The battery had long since run out. With a deep breath, he brought it back to life, and two answerphone messages flashed up on the screen straight away. Grimacing, he dialled through to the voicemail.

'Hi Chris, it's Sue again. I completely get your anger. Really, I understand. I just want you to know that I will be doing everything I can to work out exactly what happened and why. I know how important this is to you, believe me I do. I just want you to know that it is very important to me as well.'

She paused, before continuing. Chris could hear her voice cracking.

'I'm a parent too. I get it. I just... I can't comprehend what you're going through. I promise if there is something to be found out, then I will find it. If you need anything then please call me.'

She could wait.

'Hi Chris, it's Mike. Just checking in before briefing. Sorry it's so early but I have been thinking about you guys all night. Anyway, I'm here if you need anything, mate.'

Chris pressed the call return button which dialled Mike's number. It was answered before the second ring.

'Chris,' Mike said, his voice hurried and almost paternal. 'How are you doing, mate?'

The silence was uncomfortable.

'Sorry,' Mike said. 'Stupid, shit question.'

'Bearing up,' Chris replied, eventually.

'And Linda?' Mike asked.

Again, a pause. Longer, this time. How to respond when you don't know the answer?

'Oh I dunno, Mike,' Chris replied. 'It's just... so hard, you know. I'll speak to her in a bit, properly.'

'Do you need anything?' asked Mike. 'Anything at all.'

'We're okay,' Chris replied. 'Just gonna take time.'

'Of course,' Mike said. 'Time, we've got. You've got as much as you need, you know that.'

Chris didn't say anything. He looked around the lounge. The walls felt closer, breathing on him with the putrid stench of grief.

'You there, mate?' Mike asked.

'Mike, this is breaking me in half,' Chris said, quietly. 'I know you said to take some time out but I just... you know.'

'Know what, mate?' Mike asked.

'Dunno, walls are closing in at home,' Chris said.

'Whatever you need, mate, I'm here,' Mike replied.

'Just a change of scenery,' Chris whispered. 'I dunno, a cuppa with the team, something, anything... It's just... It's broken here, you know?'

Chris heard Linda's footsteps on the stairs.

'I've gotta go, Mike,' he said. 'Lin's coming downstairs.'

He hung up, as his wife walked into the lounge. He stared at her. She was a shell. What was once vibrant, was now gaunt. What was once radiant, now distinctly dulled. Her blue eyes looked grey, their luminosity deadened by the dark rings that circled them. Hers was a jigsaw with pieces now missing.

'I'll get you a cup of tea,' Chris said.

Linda nodded and went into the lounge. Her mug from days before was still sat there, the layer of scum now fully formed and floating on the top. She dropped onto the sofa, resisting its velvety, warm embrace as she sat on the edge. Faux comfort wasn't needed.

Chris handed her a cup with steam rising from it, and she looked at him. He looked at her. His wife. Joe's mother. A woman, shattered to the core.

'How are you doing, love?' Chris asked softly.

She shook her head as a million thoughts crossed her mind.

'You know what the last thing he said to me was?' she said, her voice breaking as Chris sat next to her.

He took hold of her hand. Cold. Clammy. Frosty, from the winter in her mind.

'Love you, Mummy. I wish you were coming with us,' she whispered.

'He loved you so much, sweetheart. There's nothing you could've done. You couldn't have known,' Chris said, stroking her hand and trying to link his fingers with hers but getting nothing in return.

'I heard you talking about getting out of the house,' she said.

Chris fixed his gaze on her. To see her in such pain only exaggerated his own.

'I've just got to do something,' he said quietly. 'I'm struggling as well. I feel everything. I'm angry. So, so angry. All the time I'm sitting here I'm just watching the walls and thinking about it. I need to just do something, anything. Does that make sense?'

Nothing made sense, yet she nodded. An argument over how to deal with their individual grief was a bridge too far for either of them.

The front doorbell rang, but neither Chris nor Linda made a move to stand up. Again, it rang. Then, once more. She looked at him, and he at her as, simultaneously, they got to their feet and, together, they shuffled out of the lounge into the hallway. On the floor by the front door, a pile of mail had accumulated. They may have been mourning, but life outside had gone on. A gentle knock replaced the ringing bell. Whoever it was, they weren't going away.

It was now Linda who was clinging to Chris' hand. He'd already made contact with the outside world. He'd already spoken to someone, even if it was on the phone. Now, he was leading her, helping her to take the first, tentative steps into the unknown. A world apart from what it had been before.

A world where nothing really mattered. A world without her little boy. Sure, it was probably a delivery driver or the postman, but it was still a step forward.

No one else ever came to their door, after all.

Chapter 18

SOPHIE

One Day After

Sophie walked up behind her husband, the early morning sun shining in her eyes and forcing them shut. Not a breath of wind was in the air. Instead, the only sound that daybreak had brought was the gentle humming of birds, speaking to each other from their perches way up high. Aside from that, there was nothing. No leaves fluttering, no branches swaying, no floating debris from the battering Beachbrook had taken just twenty-four hours before. Just peace. Just silence. It was mournful.

'How did she sleep?' Andrew asked.

'Yeah, she's still up there,' Sophie replied, rubbing Andrew's shoulders as he sat, facing away from her with his eyes also closed. 'Did you get any?'

Andrew's shoulders slumped. It answered her question at least.

'You?' he asked.

'A bit,' she lied.

She stood over him as reality began to bite. It was Monday morning. Outside of their little bubble, life was going on.

153

Andrew was meant to be at work. Maria was meant to be at school. Monday was the day she did the big shop. The fridge and cupboards needed filling. And yet, her grief was so resounding, so intense, that none of it seemed to really matter.

'You need to tell them you won't be in today,' Sophie said quietly.

'I know,' Andrew replied. His eyes stayed firmly shut.

'Will you get behind?' she asked.

'I don't think that really matters,' he said, before walking indoors through the bifolds.

Sophie didn't say anything. Ever since Maria had been a little seed in her womb, Andrew had shared with her a vision for their future. He would provide, and she would always be there. It wasn't, he'd explained, a masculinity vs femininity thing, like those archaic marriages of yesteryear. Far from it, he'd said. He had just wanted Maria to have a constant in her life, a presence who would always be there. The sacrifice wasn't only his. Sophie had turned her back on her own career, selling her salon and hanging up her scissors. Maria had been worth it, though. More than worth it, in fact.

She followed Andrew as he walked into the kitchen. He stopped dead in his tracks, and she knew why.

'I'll move them,' she said, picking up Joe's pyjamas that still lay neatly folded over a chair and holding them tightly in her bosom. As Andrew walked over to the sideboard and retrieved his work diary, she looked down at the pyjama top. A milk stain. A dried dribble of chocolate. Reminders of the little boy who had only recently filled the fabric. She licked her finger and rubbed them without thought. A parent's instinct. Yet, as the chocolate disintegrated to dust and fell to the floor, ice gripped her veins. It felt like sacrilege, a desecration of the memory of Joe.

'Hello,' Andrew said.

Sophie looked up. He was holding his work phone to his ear.

'Weekend? Yeah, not bad,' he continued. 'Listen, I won't be in today,' he said. 'My apologies, but something's come up.'

Something's come up. Sophie winced.

'Tomorrow?' he said. 'No, away tomorrow as well,' he continued. 'I'll be there Wednesday.'

Sophie could only hear one side of the conversation, but she saw the blood drain from Andrew's face. She saw the tremor in his fingers, as the phone bounced away from his ear. She knew where the conversation had diverted to. It was a cul-de-sac, where torment resided.

'Saw it on the news last night,' Andrew whispered.

Sophie froze, that ice in her veins rooting her to the spot. There was nothing in her stomach to throw up, but she felt sick regardless.

'You're right,' Andrew continued, his eyes closed and head tilted towards the floor. 'Just tragic. Awful.'

He hung up and turned the phone off. Sophie's feet remained glued to the floor.

'She…' Andrew began.

'I know,' Sophie replied.

'She said…' Andrew continued.

'I know, love,' Sophie interrupted.

'She said "What were they doing at the beach?"' Andrew said, persevering to the end.

Sophie's stomach tightened and her lungs deflated, squeezing every last breath of air from them. Just hearing someone else speak of it, hearing them pass even mild judgement, nearly floored her.

She summoned the strength from somewhere deep within to lift her feet, one at a time, and walk over to her husband. His hands gripped the top of a chair, his knuckles white as he clung on for dear life. She took hold of his fingers, prising them away, but they were rigid. Inflexible. As stiff as a dead body.

'I'll get onto the school,' she said, taking her phone from the table and walking into the lounge.

She unlocked it, and opened the phone app. In the call log, a stark reminder of what had befallen them over that fateful, tragic weekend confronted her. A call to 999. Calls from withheld numbers, the police's calling card. She scrolled backwards. The school was on there, somewhere. Scrolling. Scrolling. Scrolling. Past phone calls, to and from Linda, too plentiful to count. Occasionally, Chris too. Then, the school.

'Welcome to Beachbrook Primary School,' the automated voice said. 'Please press one for the absence line, or two to be connected to the school office.'

Option one... It simply wouldn't cut it, would it? Leaving a message wouldn't explain the magnitude of what had happened. And what would she say? Her mind ran away on a tangent of its own design. Would it go something like this, she wondered?

Maria isn't in because her best friend died and all because we were looking after him and took him to the beach and... and... and... and I'm hanging up now because I'm too weak to speak to a real life human and tell them what has happened, so I'll hide behind this sickness line voicemail. Thanks and I'm not sure when she'll be in again but it's alright, because I can just call this fucking sickness line and do it again and again and again and again and...

'Hello, Beachbrook Primary,' a stressed-sounding receptionist said. Sophie had pressed two without even realising.

'Oh hello,' she said, guided by autopilot but flustered all the same, 'Maria won't be there today.'

There was silence. She'd not said who she was, or what class Maria was in. The receptionist had nothing to go on but, it appeared, she knew exactly who was calling.

'Mrs Wicks?' she said.

'Yeah,' Sophie squeaked.

The receptionist breathed, heavily.

'How's… How's Maria doing?' she asked.

'You've heard what happened?' Sophie asked, softly.

Again, silence. Again, Sophie filled the blanks in her mind. She knew she was being judged.

'She's asleep,' she continued. 'Don't want to wake her.'

'I think you need to speak to the headmis—' the receptionist said.

'No need at the moment,' Sophie interrupted. 'I'll be in touch.'

She hung up without waiting for a reply, as a stark realisation struck her. Had Linda needed to make the same phone call, that very morning? Had she been confronted by an automated voice, asking for the absence line, to say that Joe wouldn't be at school that day, or for the rest of all time? What would she have said? Sophie felt sick thinking about it.

Linda. Her friend across the years, who would at that exact second be wrestling with a pain that Sophie could only imagine in the deepest, darkest corners of her mind.

Andrew sidled up next to her, but she pushed his hand away.

'I just want to see Lin,' Sophie wailed, 'I want to give her a hug, to talk to her, to be with her, you know?'

She didn't receive an answer, but she didn't need one. She knew just how burned that particular bridge was.

'Mummy?' Maria said, standing in the doorway.

'You're up?' Andrew replied, as Sophie rubbed furiously at her eyes, willing the tears away.

It was normally the stomps of an elephant that announced her descent down the stairs. That morning, she'd been quieter than a mouse.

'Morning, sweetheart,' Sophie said, jumping to her feet and rushing over to her little girl. She scooped her off her feet and, as Maria's hair flirted close to her lips, she could taste the salt that still clung to it. 'Bath time,' she said.

It was normally a bone of contention, a point of resistance for Maria, but not now. Instead, she just nodded, acquiescing to Sophie's instruction.

'Why are you crying, Mummy?' Maria asked. 'Is it about what happened?'

Sophie's panicked eyes shot towards Andrew.

'What do you mean, "about what happened"?' Sophie asked.

'The beach,' Maria said. 'The sea.'

Sophie tried so hard not to, but she just couldn't help it. With her hands entirely occupied holding her little girl in her arms, she couldn't rub the tears from her eyes before they began to fall once more. Andrew put his arms around them both, pulling them close.

'Let's talk about that bath then,' he said quickly.

'Good idea,' Sophie said, welcoming a change of subject.

'Is Joe at home?' Maria asked.

Andrew walked over and took Maria from Sophie's grasp.

'Joe...' Andrew began, before words failed him.

Sophie wiped her tears on her sleeve, before turning to face her husband and daughter. This was 'mum' time, when she had to compartmentalise. To put Maria first. To do what she always did, and be the rock, the foundation.

How to do it, though, she wondered? How to tell a child that their best friend had died? And what was death to a child, anyway? Something unfathomable, incomprehensible. Something totally abstract. She thought back to the conversation she'd had with Maria a year ago, when she'd first explained the concept.

'Remember when Grandma became a star?' she said, her words quivering as her voice struggled to deliver her explanation. 'And we look up to the sky and we see her sparkling every night? Joe's with her now, he's a star as well.'

'Joe's a star?' Maria asked.

'The brightest one,' Sophie whispered into her ear.

She stared at her little girl, who had a look on her face of someone who wasn't going to let it go that easily. Her six-year-old mind was a muddled pool of confusion, and Sophie knew it. The problem was that she just didn't have the answers.

She took hold of her and carried her upstairs to the bathroom. A star had been the best that she could come up with on the hoof, but was that the right thing to do? Weren't you supposed to treat kids like adults when it came to all things death? She didn't know. At least it got Maria through the day without asking any more questions about it.

No more queries about Joe passed her lips, all the way to bedtime and beyond.

'NO!!!! MUMMY!!!! DADDY!!!!'

Sophie raced to her daughter's bedside, but her soothing words seemed to have no effect. Andrew tried too, but it was one of those night terrors that needed to resolve itself, it seemed. That it only lasted a minute was of little comfort to either of them. Sophie felt helpless. Hopeless.

Once again, Sophie shared the marital bed with Maria. Andrew offered to stay with them but, under that duvet, they both knew that two was company and three was a crowd. Maria was a wriggler. She always had been, ever since they could remember. She held her daughter in a loose clinch, and settled in to a night where the kicks from her little girl just bounced off her. They didn't matter.

Sophie woke from a sleep that she didn't know she'd fallen into. She looked at the clock. 6 a.m. Maria was still. Silent. Peaceful. Sophie extricated herself from the bed with the deft touch of a parent who had done it before and found Andrew sat upright on the sofa, a snore coming from his mouth.

'Andrew, love,' she said, gently touching his shoulder.

'What's that?' he barked, opening his eyes wide and shifting his head sharply from side to side.

'Only me,' Sophie whispered, 'I'm going to get some bits from the shop. Need milk and stuff for Maria's brekkie. Can you go lay with her?'

Andrew grunted and made his way upstairs, as Sophie slipped out of the front door. Again, if it was just the two of them, they'd make do on whatever scraps they could muster. Not with Maria, though. She needed food. She needed drink. She needed continuity, reassurance, normality. Sophie was a mother, and this was maternal compartmentalising at its very best.

It was Tuesday morning, well before the day had got going

for most people. It was safe, she reasoned. A good time to escape the crowds. The sun was peeking through the thin clouds overhead, bringing with it the warmth of summer that a beach town basked in. Sophie, for her part, was dressed for winter. Maternity jeans and a hoodie. She caught a glimpse of herself in the rear-view mirror as she drove. Dark saucers ringed her bloodshot eyes. Her cheeks, normally glowing, were dull and ashen. She even had a spot on her chin. She hadn't had one of them since she'd been a teenager.

She parked in the car park and put her sunglasses on as she climbed from the car and walked the short distance to the entrance of the supermarket. She only needed to get a few bits. A basket would do. It wasn't a full trolley shop, just some essentials. Enough to keep them going, for now.

She didn't mean to look at the newspaper racks but, then, why wouldn't she? She probably did it on a subconscious level every time she passed them, but the news didn't normally impact upon her life so headlines would never have stuck out to her in the past. This time, they didn't just stick out. Instead, they screamed at her. Early editions, only just placed on the shelves.

DEATH IN A STORM, raged one of the local rags.

BEACH TRAGEDY, LOCAL BOY KILLED AT SEA, shouted another.

And, though there were only a few other shoppers milling about, she was sure they were looking at her as she stood, frozen to the spot, in the eye of the tabloid storm. An old boy. Not looking. A businesswoman. Not looking. A mother with a child. A familiar face, from the school gates. She was looking. Boy, was she looking. Gawping. Staring.

'Fuck,' she whispered to herself. It would have gone all around the school like wildfire.

Parent communities are a law unto themselves and she was a member of a lot of group chats. Now, she realised, there had been radio silence. Not a single message referring to the events of the weekend. People knew, and they knew she was at the epicentre of it. She bowed her head and turned away, making a beeline for the exit before it turned into something where she had to acknowledge the other woman or, God forbid, have a conversation.

Back in the car, her heart thumped so hard that it felt like her ribs were being bruised from the inside. She still needed to get some bits, but not there. It was too public, too open. Instead, a corner shop would do, and she knew just the one. Out of town. Out of the way. A drive, sure, but worth it to avoid anything like that happening again.

She made sure to look straight ahead as she passed the newspaper racks and, as she made her way up and down the tight aisles, where space was a commodity and squeezing two people past each other was nigh on impossible, she felt herself breathe for the first time since the supermarket. It was better. Much better. She paid on the self-checkout, not once having to interact with another person, before finally heading towards the exit.

Big, blooming red roses reeled her in as she walked past them and it was almost an involuntary act as she leaned forward to sniff them. That aroma provoked memories in her of the one lady who loved red roses more than any other. Linda.

Sophie sighed, and stared at the roses. She sniffed them again, closing her eyes this time, their floral notes throwing vivid images into her mind. Linda always had a bunch of roses on the go somewhere. Always. Sophie had to get them. She just had to. What she was going to do with them was another issue entirely, but she had to have them.

She drove on autopilot with the windows closed as the perfume flowed from the flowers and filled her car with the scent of happier times. Beachbrook came into sight, and she navigated a path towards where the flowers would fit in best. She wasn't even thinking about her end destination as her nose guided her. That she rolled to a stop outside Chris and Linda's home was just as much a surprise to her as it would have been to anyone else.

'What the...' she whispered to herself. She had no right to be there. None at all... But her heart ached for her friend. She longed to hug her, to tell her that they'd get through it together. Her brain would have told her something else entirely but, in a battle between heart and mind, there was only one winner.

She climbed from the car, still working from the same auto-pilot that had got her that far, and shuffled forward, roses in hand. She'd walked that path countless times before. She still had a key for the front door on the keyring she held in the other hand, yet everything seemed so different, so changed. What was once bright seemed dull. Shadows reigned. Death had paid a visit, and left his mark.

She stumbled towards the front door and set the flowers down, before turning away.

But then, she reasoned, it wasn't fair for Linda to find a random bunch of flowers on her doorstep. No, if she was going to give them to her, then she wanted to hand them over. It was only right. It was the decent thing to do, and she was a decent person.

Her finger hovered over the front doorbell for at least a minute before she summoned the courage to press it. As soon as she heard the chimes inside, the pit of her stomach churned. She was committed now. She had to go through with it and, in any case, it's what she had wanted to do from the outset. To see her friend. To comfort her.

She rung the bell again, before gently tapping on the door.

Footsteps. Two sets of footsteps. Then, the door opened and Chris and Linda stood, hand in hand, their faces haunted from chin to hair by death's passing visit.

'Lin, love,' Sophie began to say. Her head tilted forward but her eyes looked up, entirely fixed on the broken lady who stood, shoulders slumped in the doorway.

The look Chris shot across the threshold almost wilted the roses that Sophie held in her hand, and stopped her mid speech. The confidence she'd built up to knock on the door evaporated in an instant. The three of them stood and stared at each other, the silence punctuated only by the cawing of a seagull above their heads.

'Lin, Chris,' Sophie whispered, looking to the floor as the seagull flew into the distance, taking with it any ambient noise. Now, it was just them. 'I, just…'

She touched her tummy by mistake, not knowing what to do with her hands, and Linda noticed. Boy, did Linda notice. It wasn't a scream that came from her lips but, as she turned and ran back into the lounge, it was more a guttural sob that rung loud in the air.

'Get the fuck outta here.'

'I just—' Sophie replied, but Chris was having none of it.

Before she could say another word, the door slammed in her face.

Chapter 19

CHRIS

Four Days After

It was a job that no parent should even have to contemplate, let alone carry out. Chris had been resisting and resisting, putting it off and ignoring the phone calls, but eventually something had to give. He had to do it, for his boy. For his wife. For himself.

He walked to the sideboard where he opened a drawer and removed a bundle of papers from underneath some rather more mundane banking paperwork. He'd hidden them, hoping they would deal with themselves, but knowing they wouldn't.

He looked upstairs, straining his ears to listen, but there was no creaking hinge, no squeaking floorboards. Instead, there was a silence that informed him that Linda was sleeping. He held the bundle close to his chest, and walked to the dining room table where he sat down and thumbed through the contents. He'd avoided looking at them but the funeral director needed to know what their wishes were.

A sigh escaped his lips as he read the first line of the front page. The documents had been printed directly from the website page.

'If you need to arrange a funeral for a child, we will carry out our services for free.'

It was so kind, so benevolent yet so... He couldn't think of the word... Clinical? 'Child' and 'funeral' should never be words in the same sentence and, just to see them there in black and white reignited the smouldering embers within. Doing his level best to douse the cinders with the cooling reflections of how he was best going to fulfil one last paternal duty, he dragged a pen across the pages in front of him, scratching his words as he committed them to paper. Joe's name. Date of birth. All of his other details. Those questions were easy, and he treated it just as if he was filling out a passport application,

The next ones, though... They were hard.

What should he be dressed in?

What coffin was preferred?

By Christ, it was too much. They were questions that he wouldn't wish on his worst enemy.

He did his best, but the pages became soaked with tears. His prose became smudged. Still, every page completed was one less left to fill in. The stack steadily reduced in size until eventually, and by the light of the moon that bathed him as he sat, he'd done it. He'd go through it all with Linda, of course, but only when she was up to it. The steps she'd already taken were small.

This was far too big a leap to ask of her right now. What he needed, what he craved, was someone to share with. It was his load to bear, his weight to carry, but he was being smothered by the mass of anguish that rode with him wherever he went. He walked back to the sideboard, and reached for the phone book. The physical one, that every home used to have. This number was from a time well before smart phones.

And yet... He couldn't bring himself to do it. He didn't even need the phone book. He knew the number. Once upon a time, they'd been his digits too. In a fit of rage, well in the past, he'd scrawled out the name *Dad* and replaced it with *Trevor*. Was he too proud to call, he wondered? As he flipped the phone book shut and put it back in its place, he knew the answer. Trevor had never met Joe. It felt wrong that the first place he'd encounter his grandson was at his funeral.

He looked around, at the dining room walls. He'd never been claustrophobic, but his chest tightened as, inch by inch, the walls grew closer still. Soon, he felt, they'd be squeezing the life out of him.

A tap on the front door pushed those walls back a bit. He ignored it, but it grew persistent. Louder. Whoever it was, they weren't going away and the last thing he wanted was for the front doorbell to ring and disturb his wife upstairs. He fumbled for his phone, and looked at the camera screen for the front door video that Andrew had installed only weeks before. He'd not got around to using it properly but, after Sophie's intrusion, he'd fired it up. It wasn't Sophie this time, but it was still a red rag to a bull.

The front door flew open, and Chris' suspicions were confirmed. He'd seen enough members of the press at crime scenes over the years to know what they looked like. The lanyard around the reporter's neck told Chris they were from the *Beachbrook Herald*. Local. Still, the nationals would follow. They would find them. They always did.

'Mr Jamieson,' the reporter said, 'I'm so sorry for—'

'Don't ever come here again,' Chris barked, slamming the door in his face.

His heart pumped furiously as his ire rose. He wasn't so naïve as to think that this wouldn't have hit the news. Still, though, to encroach on his family home? To intrude on his private grief? It was a disgrace.

He crept upstairs. Joe's bedroom door was open, and Linda was lying on his bed, still cuddling the same book that she'd read to him all those nights before. The edges were fraying as the days passed, but the words those tattering pages contained could never be lost. Chris stood and looked at her.

'Lin?' he whispered, but there was no response. She needed to eat, but he wasn't going to force it just yet. Her tipping point might be coming, but he had to give her time. He had to give her space.

He pulled the door to – quickly enough to avoid the creaks in the hinges, for once – and tip-toed back downstairs. Another day had passed, and it had been yet more of the same.

Grief. Tears. Pain.

In the lounge, he reached for his phone. He wasn't one for social media. He was an analogue man, he'd once chuckled, in a digital world. There'd been messages aplenty, but he'd deleted them all without reading them. It was far too much, much too soon. He didn't need to read about it on the news, to see what every man and his dog was saying about it all. Instead, he settled on the message thread between him and Mike. The team were on lates. He knew that much. Their five-week shift pattern was ingrained in his mind, for so long had his life been dictated by it.

What he'd give just to have a moment's respite from being a prisoner in his own mind, to get out of the four walls where he'd been captive for days and days and have a brew with the boys and girls in blue. He wasn't the quickest at typing, unlike his wife who could knock out an essay in mere seconds. Instead, he was more of a voice note man. Easier, he'd always argued, and you can make a point with your voice far better than you can with your fingers.

'Hi, Sarge. I know you're on lates so I hope this catches you on a quiet moment. Shit. Sorry. Said the Q word. My bad. Anyway, just wondering if I can get in for a brew or something sometime. Just need a bit of time out, a bit of air, a cuppa or something, with the team, you know. What you reckon?'

Two blue ticks told him that Mike had listened to it straight away, and the reply was almost instant.

'Of course, mate. Of course you can. Anytime you like. When's good? Want a lift or anything? Let me know and we'll sort out whatever you want.'

Chris puffed his cheeks, before recording once more.

'Brilliant, thank you. How about next week when you're on nights, can I come in for briefing on the first of the set? I'll be fine getting there, cheers. One more thing, Sarge, I've had the press here. I got rid of them, but is there anything you can do?'

'You're kidding? I'll get on to Sue right now, that's not on at all. Parasites. I'll see you for a brew next week, and I'll let you know as soon as Sue gets back to me. Keep well, mate.'

It was a weight lifted, a step of his own in the right direction. He knew that Linda couldn't yet face the world and, of course, he'd be there for her when she needed him, but he just needed a bit of something else other than the house, where memories lurked in every corner.

Chapter 20

LINDA

One Week After

Whenever Linda considered going outside for a walk, all she could think about was how she'd felt when Sophie turned up at her door with flowers. She'd realised that the outside world wasn't for her. Not now. Not ever. No one in the world beyond her four walls could understand what she was going through.

Just seeing Sophie, just hearing her voice, just the vision of a bunch of flowers, it all reminded her of a time gone by. That was then. This was now. They were two different periods, the before and the after. Merging them would have been a stain on the memory of her baby boy.

Not only that, though. There'd been phone calls. There'd been other knocks on the door. A couple of camera crews had plotted up outside. Pleas for privacy went ignored until, eventually, they'd given up. She wasn't going to give them what they wanted, to add fuel to the fire. She wanted quiet. She wanted peace. She wanted Joe.

Each night, she'd slept in his bed. The sheets still retained his scent but, as the hours passed and became yet more days gone by, the strength of his aroma weakened. It wouldn't be long before it was gone forever. Something else lost. Another part of him, extinguished. She thumbed his books, remembering with clarity how they read together, how she pointed to the words and how they both knew the stories off by heart. He wasn't the best of readers but, by God, when he put his mind to it, it was magic that passed his lips. She remembered how his voice mirrored hers as they spoke in harmony, the words of the page singing as they came to life through their collective narration. But his voice was just a memory, and it was already beginning to fade. Hers remained loud, and real. As she read alone, the words no longer made sense. They were just letters on a page. It took Joe to bring them to life. Without him, they were just empty sentences.

Chris was beginning to sit up and take notice, she realised. It had been day number... she didn't know... since Joe had gone, and she was lying in her usual position atop his bed, cuddling his duvet, when her husband finally took the plunge.

'We've got to get you some help,' Chris had said to her.

'Okay,' she'd replied. An argument wasn't what she'd needed, nor wanted.

The doctor had visited, but she'd told him exactly what he needed to know. She knew how to game the system, after all. His answer had just been to prescribe something to help her sleep, and that worked for her. At least Joe visited her in her dreams, she thought, but it wasn't enough. Being awake, being without him, made the dreams that much harder to cope with.

While Chris had talked of his desire to get out of the house, to be amongst his peers, nothing had been further from Linda's mind. The prospect of having to speak to people made her feel nauseous. Her colleague Sam had tried to call her a few times, but she had diverted it to answerphone. His text messages had been deleted before they had even been read. The last time she had seen him had been before it had happened. Now, she was living in the after, and she didn't want company.

Chris had a plan, and it was to immerse himself in routine. Linda's strategy was to just be. Not to live. Just to be. Time passed and, as the seconds rolled into minutes, into hours, into days, it was more than she could cope with. The load was too much to bear.

She didn't want Chris to worry. Joe aside, she loved Chris more than anything.

It was the *Joe aside* part of it all that got to her the most, though. She couldn't put it aside. It wasn't a book that could be put down, mid-chapter, and picked up again later. It wasn't a TV show that could be paused and resumed at a later date. It was all-consuming, all-encompassing, devouring her every fibre.

What to do, she wondered? How to deal with it? The days and nights finally took care of themselves as, in her mind, a plan slowly fell into place. It was out of the fire and into the furnace as, with something entirely different motivating her, she finally broke out of her slump wearing a mask of acceptance.

Though a shell of her former self, she still maintained function and awareness. If Chris knew what she really wanted to do, he'd have her sectioned, after all. She knew that. She put her brave face on, and said the things he needed to hear. She needed him out of the house and, if she needed to paint a counterfeit picture of a woman slowly coming to terms with her bereavement, then so be it.

'Alright, love?' Chris asked, as Linda put the vacuum cleaner away.

She forced a smile.

'We'll get there,' she said, allowing his hands to slip into hers. He raised them to his nose, tracing the scent of bleach that rose from her fingers.

'Been cleaning?' he asked.

'Bathroom needed doing,' she replied.

She saw the edges of his lips curled up, for the first time in what felt like forever, and knew that she had him on the hook. Cleaning was a part of her DNA. Always had been. Andrew and Sophie might have had the bigger house, she'd always joked to Chris, but theirs was the cleaner. Her steps may have been small, but they were moving in the direction they needed to. Grief was a process. She'd preached that to enough people in her working life, and now it was time to put those words into action. In many respects, she was a thespian playing her greatest role.

'Kitchen next,' she said, forcing one foot in front of the other. She was no actor, though, and it was exhausting her.

As she lay in Joe's bed that night, in the protection of a duvet that was just a little bit too small for her, on a mattress that was just a little bit too narrow, and a little bit too short, she took hold of her phone. She'd never been a part of any of the mum WhatsApp groups. Sophie had always done that, for the both of them.

Sophie.

They hadn't discussed Andrew, Sophie or Maria, or anything about what had happened. It wasn't so much an elephant in every room, more a herd, but neither Chris nor Linda could bring themselves to confront it, let alone discuss it.

Sophie.

Linda thumbed through her phone, to her contacts. Through the alphabet, and settling on the letter 'S'.

Soph. A little heart emoji next to her name.

Soph ♥

At any other time, she'd be the one to talk to. She'd be the one to go to. She'd be the one to drink coffee with, to drink wine with, to share the goss. Not now, though. Not again. When she'd seen her at the front door, roses in hand, she'd lost control of her emotions. Seeing Sophie had only served to make her realise how ill-equipped she was to continue on in a life without her boy. Her Joe.

She hesitated, before dropping the guillotine. She took a deep breath as, with two swipes of the finger, Soph ♥ was consigned to the phone book bin. Like Joe, gone in the blink of an eye.

Chapter 21

CHRIS

Twelve Days After

The night shift started at 9 p.m., but the team were there early. It was the same briefing room, with the same personnel sitting at the same seats. Their faces, though, wore different emotions to any he had seen before.

Chris stood in the doorway, dressed in jeans and a t-shirt, and the looks he received from his colleagues, his friends, bordered on awkward. While they were used to dealing with loss and bereavement as part of their daily duties, this was different. Death had paid a visit to one of their own and stolen something from them, and not in a peaceful way. It wasn't as if the scythe had fallen while an elderly relative had slept. Joe's passing was about as upsetting as things got.

Only Mike was missing and, as Chris surveyed the faces of his colleagues, they sat in silence just staring at him. Seconds passed and no words were spoken. Was it a mistake, Chris wondered? Coming back so soon? The truth was, that none of the team had kids. Hell, most of them were just kids themselves. They couldn't relate to the utter joy of parenthood, in the same way that they couldn't empathise with the harrowing loss that Chris had experienced. Sure, out on the street they could find the words to comfort someone, but this close to home? To Chris? None of them knew what to say or do.

Tasha made the first move. Unable to stand the silence anymore, she jumped from her chair and ran to Chris. Though almost half his size, her arms blanketed him as she held him close. The team breathed and the tension in the air disappeared as quickly as it had risen.

'Chris,' Mike said as he walked through the door, 'so good to see you, mate.'

'Thanks, Sarge,' Chris said. He looked around, as everyone took a breath of relief. The ice had been broken. 'Do you mind if I say a few words to the team before briefing?'

'Of course not,' Mike replied. 'It's all yours.'

'Thank you,' Chris said. He'd spent a good chunk of the previous few days rehearsing what he was going to say. He just hoped the words would flow exactly as he planned.

'You all know what happened the other week. Truth is, it's knocked me massively. I know there's an investigation going on, but that's all over in Beachbrook. Linda is still really struggling and I almost didn't come tonight but she told me to. I just needed a brew, to get out. Gets claustrophobic, just sitting there and thinking about it all the time. All the fucking time. Sorry. Just… you know. All I wanted was to see you all, to have a drink with you and chew the fat for a bit. And please, just treat me like normal. That's all I ask. Fair enough?'

Chris sat down at his chair around the briefing table, hoping that they had listened to him and taken on board what he had said.

'In that case, you can make the teas then, you egg-chaser,' Jim said.

Chris smiled.

'On it,' he replied, walking out to the kitchen to make a pot. The small talk returned to the briefing room as he left and he let out a sigh of relief.

It was exactly what he needed. Briefing table banter. Gossip. It was as it should be. As the team filtered out, to tackle the criminals who stalked the shadows of the night, Chris and Mike sat alone.

'Occy health have been on to me,' Mike said. 'They told me to put you in touch with them when you're ready. Do us a favour and give them a bell in the morning, will you?'

'Yeah, course,' Chris replied.

'How are you, mate, really?' Mike asked. 'And Linda?'

What could he say?

'Linda's still working through it, mate,' Chris said. 'It kills me, just absolutely kills me. I can't say anything else about it, you know? I'm doing my best, but I can't seem to get through to her. Nothing I say feels enough.'

So many times, he'd found the words for other people. For strangers. For bereaved parents. Now, though? He found it impossible. What use were words, after all, when their meaning had been removed?

Chapter 22

LINDA

Twelve Days After

While Chris had gone to see his colleagues at the nick, Linda was sat on the floor at home in the lounge, surrounded by photos. Memories.

There were pictures of her breastfeeding, of Joe covered in some kind of mucky puree, spread across his face from cheek to cheek while he grinned. That eternally beautiful smile. And, yet more photos. More memories. Joe, riding his first bike. Joe, winning the egg and spoon race, that triumphant grin etched from ear to ear again. The obligatory first day at school outside the school gates, of course. She wanted to reach into the album, to be a part of the photos again. She looked at a picture where Joe was asleep on her shoulder. She could feel him there, the way he used to breathe heavily on her as he slept, the way he used to pinch her skin gently to comfort himself. It wasn't stuck in a picture, consigned to history. She could feel it.

Linda put everything away, just as it should be, not wanting to leave a mess. That wouldn't be fair on Chris. Upstairs, she made sure the bed was made and clothes put away. Once a clean freak, always a clean freak, she thought.

Love you, Mummy. I wish you were coming with us.

She looked around for him, needing his touch, longing for his arms to be around her. No sooner had she felt his embrace when looking at those photos downstairs, it had gone. Disappeared. Never again would it be a physical reality. She knew that. She'd accepted it for what it was, and what was coming wasn't a cry for help. It wasn't a plea for attention. It was a rational, thought-out decision.

She slowly tidied his books away, and folded his duvet over in the inviting way that only a mother can, as his voice screamed in her ears through the silence.

Love you, Mummy. I wish you were coming with us.

'Love you too, Joe,' she whispered.

She left the night light on and gently closed the door as she walked out. The hinge groaned, and she smiled.

Linda walked downstairs, guided by muscle memory. Every creak of the stair provoked a memory, every breath through her nose aroused a scent from the past. It was both comforting and torturous.

She walked into the kitchen and flicked the light on. She'd charged her phone especially for this. She knew all about GPS and live cell tracing. It wouldn't be fair on Chris to leave him not knowing where she was.

She looked around, to where Joe had stained the carpet when he'd been sick on it, to where he had taken his first step, to where he'd fallen off the counter and cut his head, needing stitches. Those memories felt hollow, trapped in a place and time when life had simply been better, a world where aching pain was something she managed in others, not herself.

She closed the front door quietly as she left the house. She was carrying Joe's favourite book with her, frayed edges and all. She hadn't put it down for nearly two weeks.

Linda climbed in her car. She knew where she wanted to go. She just needed to get there.

Chapter 23

CHRIS

Twelve Days After

'I spoke to Sue Willmott earlier,' Mike said. 'She said she's tried to call you a couple of times but hasn't been able to get through to you.'

'Yeah I'll speak to her this week,' Chris replied, as her 'tragic accident' message from weeks before reverberated around in his head.

'Well she told me to pass on to you that she's still working on it. She told me that you got upset with her on the phone, and I completely understand why. I've got to tell you that she's been trying to get Maria in for a video statement but Andrew is refusing to allow it at the moment.'

The tips of Chris' ears turned a dark shade of red, but his face remained neutral. He had to keep a lid on it. There would be a time of reckoning, for sure, but the investigation had to run its course. Regardless of Chris' poker face, Mike saw right through it.

'They're just trying to do what's right for Maria at the moment, mate,' he said. 'I'm sure they'll come around once the shock has gone. I know it's really hard to hear but she's only Joe's age and it's going to be really hard on her as well. I know

181

you're going to be angry, but all I'd ask is that you bring that anger to me rather than taking it elsewhere, if that makes sense?'

There were so many things that Chris wanted to say. How dare they? How fucking dare they?

'Yeah, thanks, Mike,' Chris said calmly.

'That's okay, mate,' Mike replied. 'Right, another brew?'

Chris nodded. His knuckles were white as he handed his mug over.

The radio was alive with the usual incidents that a night shift brings – fights, domestics, drink drivers. Nothing out of the ordinary was happening.

'Same shit, eh?' Chris said, as yet another flash call came across the airwaves.

'Never changes,' Mike replied.

Chris caught sight of the clock.

'Shit,' he said.

'Time flies, eh?' Mike said.

'Does indeed,' Chris said, reaching for his phone. It wasn't the time for a voice note, just in case Linda was asleep. Instead, his fingers tapped slowly as he typed.

Just checking in, love, hope you're asleep and this doesn't wake you if you are. Leaving soon. Good to see the team. Love you xxx

'Thanks, Skip,' Chris said, shaking hands with Mike in the rear car park of the police station.

His phone vibrated in his pocket. He smiled at his boss as he took it out and, as he unlocked it, the harsh glare of the screen in contrast to the moody darkness of his surroundings made him squint.

Slowly, surely, his focus adjusted. The blurry lines became letters, and he read the reply from his wife.

Chapter 24

LINDA

Twelve Days After

For the first time since her boy had passed, she had purpose. It wasn't the road to nowhere that she was driving along. Instead, she had clarity. She had lucidity. She had reason. And, as she rolled down her window and let the night air in, her aching muscles relaxed. Grief had ravaged her. Now, it was time to tame the beast.

As she rolled to a gentle stop, the calmness she felt almost overwhelmed her. For the first time in forever, her breaths felt almost natural, not forced. The moon soaked her in light as she climbed from her car and she stood, just for a moment, looking out to sea. The waves barely rippled as they lapped into shore. She looked at the top of the slope that led down to the beach, and wandered over.

Bunches of flowers, some dead but many still living.

A few teddy bears.

Cards.

A makeshift memorial, dedicated entirely to her little boy.

She bent down, and picked one of them up.

'We didn't know you, brave little man, but we'll remember you.'

She placed it back down and a whimper passed her lips. What humanity. What compassion. What benevolence. She reached for another.

'This should never have happened, such a tragic, tragic thing.'

'Damn right it shouldn't,' she whispered.

Her phone vibrated in her hand. Chris. Oh, Chris. She read his message once, twice and three times. Sleep was coming, soon.

She had messages of her own to send, but Chris would be the last to get his. He deserved that much, to know that he was the last one she thought of. It would give him crumbs of comfort, she hoped. For the others she needed to message, grief had concentrated her concealed anger until it had become toxic. She wanted to hurt them. She had plenty of pain to spread around, and they needed to have their share.

First, Andrew.

You are responsible for this. For all of this.

Then Sophie, her phone number now just a series of random digits at the top of their message thread.

You took him there and didn't bring him home. Fuck you.

Linda followed the cliff path for about fifty metres as it wound upwards, before stopping abruptly. She'd rarely seen out over the bay from up there, but she knew this was it. This was the place. This felt right. If she looked in a straight line out to sea, it was about there that Joe had been found.

She sat down and took it all in. It was so calm, the weather peaceful. There wasn't a breath of wind in the air and the moon lit the sky like a beacon. Perfect, she thought.

She looked at her phone, at the message from Chris, and remembered the good times. Their wedding. Their life. But every memory was tainted by the loss of Joe, by their boy who simply no longer was. There was no coming back from it. Her grief had flooded her with insidious intent, and she just needed to be with her boy.

She looked over the cliff edge. Rocks. The gentle tide didn't rise high enough to cover them. At least it would be quick.

She agonised over what she should say to Chris. She composed several messages, trying to explain her feelings, her thoughts, her grief, but words didn't do it justice. In the end, she settled for something simple. An apology. A declaration of love. A farewell. It wasn't perfect, but it would do.

Her finger hovered over the send button, until a burst of adrenaline hammered it down.

She looked up, and the man on the moon smiled down at her. Once more, she looked out to the sea. She'd never seen it glowing by moonlight before. While the sun normally threw diamond shards everywhere, the jewels bouncing from the moon on the calm surf were much more subtle. It was glorious. It was... dare she think it... perfect.

Now she was committed.

Now there was no going back.

I wish you were coming with us.

'I'm coming, Joe,' she whispered.

Chapter 25

MIKE

Twelve Days After

Chris dropped the phone on the floor.

'What's up, mate?' Mike asked, as he bent down to pick up Chris' phone. The screen had cracked, but the message got through loud and clear.

Sorry, Chris. I love you. Goodbye.

A suicide risk. That much was obvious, and Mike kicked into action.

'Control from Sergeant,' he called into his radio.

'Go ahead,' came the reply.

'We've got an active suicide risk over in Beachbrook,' Mike said, his voice tight as his mind ran at a million miles an hour. 'I need a unit deployed to PC Jamieson's home address on immediate status. Entry to be forced if no answer. Subject at risk is Linda Jamieson, I repeat, Linda Jamieson.'

'Received,' came the reply.

'Can you create a CAD and bump it up to the duty governor for live cell site authorisation, phone number to follow.'

'Doing it now,' came the reply.

'And deploy whatever you've got to the area, vehicle details to follow in case she's not home,' Mike said, barking instructions on the hoof.

'Received and will do,' came the reply.

'Get an ambulance en route as well,' Mike said, his authority tinged by panic, as he checked his phone book and relayed Linda's phone number for the trace to be activated. 'Come on, Chris, we're going, mate,' he said as he began to run to the police car.

Chris remained rooted to the spot.

'I can't face it, Mike,' he said quietly. 'I can't do it again.'

The message ran through Mike's head over and over.

Sorry, Chris.

An apology? What was she sorry for?

I love you.

Declarations of affection tended to precede something either very good, or entirely bad.

Goodbye.

A farewell that spoke for itself. The inference was obvious.

'Chris, you've got to come, mate,' Mike said louder, the alarm in his voice obvious. 'You know you've got to. We don't know what's happened and we might be able to get there in time if she's done something, but we've got to go now.'

Mike was right. Chris forced one leg in front of the other and ran to the police car. Mike was speeding off before Chris had even had chance to close his door.

It was a cruel journey, following the same route, and in the same car, that Mike and Chris had navigated all those days before. Tragedy had been at the end of that road. This time? Mike dreaded to think.

'Try calling her,' Mike instructed, as the tyres in his command squealed with displeasure.

Chris thudded his phone screen with fingers that seemed too clumsy to function, but eventually he made it work.

Hi, you're through to Linda...'

'Voicemail,' he muttered.

Mike wanted to look across to Chris, to put that big, comforting arm around his shoulder, to be something paternal to a man who was a few years his elder, but he couldn't. The tarmac was being eaten up underneath them, and it needed his total concentration. It was like déjà vu. They'd been in that sinking ship together only a matter of weeks before.

'Control to Sergeant,' the radio operator said.

'Go,' came the reply from Mike. He had no time for pleasantries, his concentration being on getting to Beachbrook as quickly and as safely as possible.

'No signs of life at the property,' the radio operator said. 'Entry being forced.'

'Is her car there?' Chris shouted into the radio.

'Standby,' came the reply. Then twenty seconds later, 'Negative. No car at scene.'

'She's gone,' Chris said to Mike.

'How are we doing on that live cell trace?' Mike asked the operator, as he squeezed the accelerator until it hit the floor.

'Just waiting for authorisation,' came the reply.

'Fucking get it done,' Mike growled into the radio. In normal circumstances, that would've invoked the wrath of some desk dwelling inspector, but not now. Now, it was all hands to the pump.

'Try her again,' Mike said.

Chris tried calling Linda once again, but each time it went straight to her answerphone.

'Linda, love, I got your text,' he said, as Mike flicked off the sirens to let his words flow without intrusion. 'I know you're struggling at the moment. I should've been home with you. I'm so sorry. Please, please don't do anything. I'm coming to find you and we'll work this out together. I love you.'

'We'll go to your house first,' Mike said. 'You'll know if anything is out of the ordinary.' He'd preached to the team often enough that, when it came to suicide risks, minutes mattered. Seconds counted.

'Control, any update the area search?' Mike asked the operator. 'On the cell site analysis? On the house? Anything?'

'Negative at the moment,' the operator replied. 'Are you able to go over to the Beachbrook frequency, they're running the incident on that channel.'

Chris frantically retuned the car radio set, and the Beachbrook radio frequency was alive with updates from all directions.

'Control from Havington sergeant,' Mike called up. 'I'm on my way to the home address. I have PC Jamieson with me. He is the husband of the Misper. Is the on-call DS aware? We're going to need POLSA there too.'

Chris' teeth clenched together as his jaw locked. Linda was a Misper. A missing person. Because of the nature of her text message, she had been instantly assessed as high risk which meant that the balloon had gone up over Beachbrook once more. On-call personnel. Police Search Advisors. The whole mob were being called in.

'Control from DS Willmott, I'm the night duty DS. Please advise Sergeant Adams and PC Jamieson that I will meet them at the home address.'

Mike looked at Chris, but he was staring straight ahead

as the car devoured the road, spitting it out behind them with violence. It wasn't quick enough, though.

'We'll meet Sue there and work out a plan,' Mike said.

'Where are you?' Chris whispered.

'Where could she be?' Mike asked.

Chris' breaths were sharp.

'She'd have gone to Sophie's… Before,' he spat out, barely able to mention her name. 'Talk to me, Linda, where are you?'

'Chris, we're here. Come on, mate,' Mike shouted, putting the police car out of its misery as he screeched to a stop.

Mike jumped from the driver's seat, and looked at Chris' house. The front door was hanging off its hinges and there were blue lights bouncing up and down the entire length of the road. Curtains twitched as neighbours snuck a look, trying not to be seen but unable to resist the urge to gawp.

'Steady, chaps,' a police officer said, holding up a hand as both men made to barge through the front door. 'Crime scene. Got to sign you in.'

'Sergeant Adams, PC Jamieson,' Mike yelled, slapping the officer's hand down. 'It's his house.' They marched past the officer standing guard on the door, and stood in the hallway.

'Carefully,' Mike said, 'I need you to tell me if anything's out of the ordinary.'

They walked from room-to-room downstairs.

'It's all normal,' Chris mumbled.

They crept upstairs.

'Joe's room's been tidied,' Chris whispered.

Mike peered in, and straight away felt like an intruder. It may have been a potential crime scene, but it was Joe's home. It was Chris'. It was Linda's. It wasn't for outside, prying eyes. He heard footsteps walking up the stairs behind them, and turned around.

'Chris, I can't even begin to imagine what you're going through,' DS Willmott said, joining them on the upstairs landing. She was holding a hand-held radio, that was tuned to the Beachbrook frequency. The personal radio that Mike held was still tuned to the Havington frequency. DS Willmott's hissed into life.

'Control to DS Willmott, we've had a ping on the cell site analysis. Mobile phone was last active on the mast adjacent to Beachbrook Beach. Phone no longer switched on.'

Mike looked at Chris, who began to shake, his arms and legs trembling at the realisation of where Linda was.

'She's gone to Joe,' he whispered.

The three of them ran downstairs.

'Sign us out,' DS Willmott shouted at the officer with the scene log as they sprinted from the house.

'Sue, jump in here,' Mike called to her. She had come to Chris' house in an unmarked police car, ill-equipped for running red lights and being thrashed to death.

Blue lights and sirens saturated the night skies as every available resource raced to Beach Road.

'I want the area flooded with patrols,' Mike barked into the radio, 'and I want the chopper up now.'

'That'll need authorisa—'

'JUST FUCKING DO IT!' he shouted. It wasn't a request. 'Wake Coastguard and Trumpton up, get whatever dog handlers are on area there and get Search and Rescue. I want every resource, right now.'

The ABS didn't kick in as Mike skidded to a stop on Beach Road. The last time they had been there... No, he thought. Don't go there. Job to do. Head on, and focus.

'Chris, is that Linda's car?' Mike asked.

Chris looked to where Mike's finger was pointing. It was. Parked neatly on the road. Anonymous. Just any other car. The front door was open, though, and there was no one inside.

'Chris, stay here,' Mike shouted, as his angst-ridden colleague ran towards the car. 'Sue, get on the radio and get a dog unit here now. They'll be able to track her.'

Overhead, the soft, humming of a helicopter announced its imminent arrival. Soon, that hum was a din. Then it was deafening as the blades from the low-flying bird threw dust and sand up all around them. As it climbed into the moonlit sky, it showered them in blinding, artificial light. As it swooped around the clifftop, and refocussed its area of search to the bottom of the cliff, it was a scene that Mike had seen play out so many times before. The stretch of land up top was notorious for it.

'Dog handler en route,' Sue said breathlessly.

The police helicopter hovered close by, moving slowly as it scanned the rocky terrain below, its operators expert at this particular part of the job.

Sirens rang out from all corners, as radio traffic intensified.

'No trace length of Beach Road,' one copper shouted.

'No trace Beach slope,' another called.

'Searching cliff top,' another screamed, fighting the noise of the chopper that was so close to them they could feel their teeth thudding.

Then, the helicopter stopped, dead in the air. Its spotlight remained fixed on a single set of rocks down below.

The radio chatter went silent.

And a sombre voice came on the airwaves.

'Control from India Charlie One. Visual confirmation. Body on the rocks.'

Chapter 26

MIKE

Twelve Days After

'Control from India Charlie One. Visual confirmation. Body on the rocks.'

It was the radio message that changed everything.

It wasn't so much the words, more the instant reaction they had provoked in Chris. He'd been stalking the same stretch of tarmac, pacing over his own footsteps on repeat as Mike had been co-ordinating search parameters with local resources and partner agencies. It was the police helicopter operators who had seen her first and, as they hovered above her broken body, their blades made her hair flow in the artificial wind that filled the air beneath. Mike watched, as Chris' feet remained rooted to the spot, his body paralysed by fear.

'India Charlie One, no signs of life.'

Mike looked at Chris. He was still frozen, fear carved into his features.

'India Charlie One, injuries appear incompatible with life.'

And that was that. Mike knew that a tipping point had been reached.

The scene was one of chaos and noise but, as Mike walked

Chris back to the police car, a protective arm draped around his shoulder, their colleagues stood still and silent. They bowed. Collective tears fell as battle-hardened police officers felt the aching chasm that had been inflicted upon one of their own. His son gone, his wife dead, what else did he have to live for? How was there any coming back from this?

Mike turned all the radios off in the car. Linda was dead. What need was there for a running commentary on the extent of her injuries, the recovery of her body or the initial investigation into the circumstances surrounding it all? They drove slowly and in silence, as Mike bought some time. Time, for him to work out what he was going to do with Chris from there. Time, for thinking. For reflection. For wondering what the hell came next.

Mike's mind was running at a million miles per hour. He'd dealt with bereaved colleagues before, but those deaths had been expected. An elderly parent or a partner with cancer. Never a kid. Never a wife committing suicide. Never both, and so brutally. There was no manual for something like this, no terms of reference or operational order for dealing with it. Chris would be drowning in grief, and it was up to Mike to provide some level of buoyancy. How he did that, he hadn't the first clue. How do you pluck a man from those depths? Around and around in circles, Mike's mind ran. As he eventually turned into Chris' road, he knew he had to say something.

'I'm going to be here for you all the way, mate,' he said as he rolled to a gentle stop. 'You've got my word on that.' An empty promise, it was not.

Mike followed footstep for footstep as they walked into the house that Linda had left behind not even hours before. Chris sat on the edge of the sofa in the living room, staring into oblivion, not moving a muscle.

'Chris, can you talk to me?' Mike asked.

There was no response, just silence.

'I can't even begin to imagine what you're thinking or feeling, mate,' Mike said, once again putting a defensive mitt around Chris' shoulder, 'but I've got to be honest, I'm worried about you. Shall we get you checked over?'

Death hung heavily in the air and held Chris in its dark, morbid grip. He wasn't for moving, nor speaking, and it troubled Mike. He stroked his chin, anxiously. Was Chris broken beyond repair? Or a volcano, lying dormant before an eruption? What to do? How to move forward? He walked out of the front room and into the kitchen where he quietly turned on his radio and tuned back in to the Havington frequency.

'Sergeant to Control,' he said.

'Go ahead,' came the reply.

'Please can you ask Hotel Victor 25 to attend PC Jamieson's H/A?' Mike asked.

Over twenty miles away, back at Havington nick, the same shroud of sorrow that plagued the skies over Beachbrook had descended. Normal policing had gone out of the window, as Chris' team gathered in the briefing room. It may have been busy out on the streets, but the radio was silent. The operators understood. They got it. Resources were being mined in from other areas, other districts. For that team, in that moment, all that mattered was Chris. His chair remained empty, and none of them knew if he'd ever be there to sit in it again.

'Hotel Victor 25, received that and on my way,' Tasha replied almost immediately, jumping to her feet and running from the briefing room. The tears may have dripped from her chin as her face bounced in time with her feet, but there was no way she wouldn't be there for him.

'Sergeant to Control, received and thanks,' Mike said quietly. 'Please could you also arrange for the out of hours doctor to attend as well? I want PC Jamieson assessed here please.'

Mike slipped back into the front room. Chris was still sitting in the same position, still staring into the abyss, and still without expression on his face. Mike held Chris' shoulder.

'I've got Tasha coming over,' he said. 'She'll sit with you while I sort a few bits out. I've also got the doctor coming, just to have a chat.' His voice was soft and calming, and his words finally elicited a response from Chris.

'I don't need a doctor,' he replied. He spoke without agitation or hostility but, aside from his lips opening and closing, not a single muscle twitched.

'What do you need then, mate?' Mike asked.

The tension in Chris' shoulders seemed to intensify. He took a deep breath in, released it slowly and whispered, 'Can you get my dad please?'

'Of course,' Mike said, as relief washed over him. His dad. Of course, his dad. He racked his mind, thinking back to their conversation from all those days before. 'It's just your dad, isn't it? I think you said your mum passed away a while ago? I just don't want to get anything wrong when I get there?'

'Yes, just Dad,' Chris said. 'You'll have to tell him what's happened. I haven't seen him for years.' His eyes filled with tears. 'He never met Linda or Joe.' The tears stayed put, glazing his eyes but not staining his cheeks.

Mike felt some brewing in his own eyes, but he forced them away. This was about Chris, not him.

'Okay, as soon as Tasha is here I'll go and pick him up,' Mike said. 'You'll have to give me his address.'

'Hopefully he's still where he was ten years ago,' Chris replied. 'Can you cancel the doctor? It's not for me.'

Mike got it. Doctors did the job for some people, but not everyone. He nodded, and squeezed Chris' shoulder.

'Sergeant to Control,' he said into the radio. 'Please can you cancel the on-call doctor. Full update to follow.' He turned his radio to silent.

'Dad lives at The Glades on Hillside Approach, just out of town,' Chris said.

It only took about fifteen minutes for Tasha to arrive, the twenty minutes it should have taken being a moot point when it came to being there for her friend when he needed her the most.

'Thanks, Tash,' Mike said, opening the front door to her gentle tapping. 'You know what's happened. It's fucking shit, no other way of describing it. I couldn't get anything out of him for a while but he's talking now. He's asked me to go and get his dad so are you alright to sit with him while I do that and then we can work out what's going to happen from there?'

'Yeah, of course I will,' she replied. 'Go on, we'll be good.'

She walked into the house and shut the door, leaving Mike outside and alone for the first time since the events had unfolded, finally able to collect his thoughts. He sighed and, as he breathed out, the lungful of air that emerged was ragged. He walked to his car. He got into the driver's seat and pulled away at a snail's pace. It took thirty minutes to drive the empty streets to Chris' dad's house, and on his way he struggled to come up with his opening gambit.

'Hi, the daughter-in-law and grandson you never met are both dead.' How was he going to deliver that? However he dressed it up, it was a shitty situation. It was like no death message he had ever passed on before, that was for certain.

197

It was a big house. Detached, and set in acres of land, but everything about it was shabby and unloved. From the outside, it looked tired. Under the light of the moon, the weeds in the front garden fought with wild flowers for space. It was a battle they were clearly winning.

Mike took a deep breath and rapped on the door firmly with his knuckles, before a thought crossed his mind. Chris' dad's name. He hadn't thought to ask that.

A soft shuffle from inside at least told him that someone was home and, as the door opened, Mike knew immediately that he had the right place. Putting aside the aesthetics of the gaunt, haggard and unshaven slip of a man who stood before him, the eyes gave it away. Though he'd clearly just been roused from his sleep, he was Chris' dad, alright.

'Hello, are you Mr Jamieson?' Mike asked, offering a sympathetic smile of the kind that only a police officer of experience can deliver.

'I am. Trevor, please. Is everything okay?' His voice croaked. It seemed painful for him to speak.

'I'm sorry to have woken you, Trevor,' Mike said. 'Do you mind if I come in?'

'Of course,' Trevor replied, gesturing for Mike to come in. 'Please excuse the state of the place, I don't really have visitors.'

Mike walked through the front door and into the front room. A solitary, threadbare armchair sat in the shadows in the corner of the room. The moon may have afforded light through the curtainless window, but it was the gloom that stood out. There was no other furniture. Paint was peeling from the walls and there was mould and damp covering vast swathes of the ceiling. It was a scene familiar to Mike. He had been to many houses such as this where an ageing person lived alone and, in many cases, died without anyone noticing. Photos sat on a shelf but they were steeped in sepia; Father Time had taken away their soul. They were faded, washed-out memories of a forgotten time, long since passed.

'How can I help?' Trevor asked.

'There's no easy way to say this,' Mike replied gently. 'Chris asked me to come here. His wife and son have both died and he wanted you to be with him. I know you haven't seen each other for a while, but I'll take you to him now if you want me to.'

Trevor stood still for a moment, and then staggered over to the armchair where he slumped into its frayed, balding fabric, and held his head in his hands.

'I don't know what to say,' he croaked.

'I'm sorry, it's a massive shock,' Mike said. 'If you want to go and get dressed, Chris is waiting at his house to see you.'

Trevor stood up unsteadily. His arms and legs were skeletal, almost to the point of atrophy. He made his way upstairs, the faint echo of his footsteps magnified by the bare wooden floors.

'Can I make you a tea or something?' Mike called up the stairs.

'Kettle's knackered,' Trevor called back.

Minutes later, he reappeared downstairs. He was dressed, but how could he ever be ready for what was to come? He nodded at Mike, and the two men walked through the front door onto the porch. The lock creaked as Trevor twisted the key, its mechanisms groaning with resistance as they were put to work for the first time in God knows how long.

'Is there anything I should know before we go to see Chris?' Mike asked. 'He's suffering at the moment as you'd expect, and I just want to make sure that we can manage any issues that might arise.'

There was silence for a moment. Both of them knew what Mike was really asking.

'Cancer,' Trevor said. 'Riddled with it. Not sure how long I've got. Now please, take me to Chris.' Words were effort, and he got by on the bare minimum if he could help it.

The journey back to Chris' house was silent. Each man was deep in thought, their minds separately occupied by the situation that faced them. Mike's expression was blank, but he was deeply concerned about what kind of impact Trevor's reintroduction into Chris' life would have. Already, like the great snooker players of the world, he was thinking several shots ahead. Frankly, Trevor was a lot closer to the end than he was the beginning. Months? Weeks? By his appearance, days might not have been out of the question. How much death could one man deal with?

Mike rolled to a stop outside Chris' house, and both men walked up the pathway, side by side, Mike gently guiding Trevor as they made slow progress. The driveway next to them was empty, Linda and Chris' cars having taken two very different journeys earlier in the evening. Mike rang the doorbell and Tasha opened the door.

'Wait here, Tash,' Mike said as Trevor walked in ahead of them, 'let's give them a minute.'

Chapter 27

CHRIS

Twelve Days After

'Son?'

Chris looked up. It was a voice from a lifetime before and, though he was the one who had sent for his dad, just hearing it again in real life brought everything back to him.

'Dad,' he replied, climbing to his feet from the sofa in which he had slumped into hours before. He tried to meet his dad's eyes, but the older man was looking around. Chris followed his gaze, looking at the family photos and canvas' that had made the house a home.

'Oh, son,' Trevor said.

'Yeah, Dad,' Chris whispered. The flames of grief were burning him, from head to toe. His every nerve was raw. He itched his skin, trying to scratch away the pain that was plaguing him inside and out, but nothing was helping. Nothing at all.

'The policeman told me what happened,' Trevor said, shaking his head as he planted his eyes directly on Chris. 'I'm so sorry, son. So, so sorry.'

Chris wanted to walk over to his dad, but he was all

out of sync with his senses. Commands issued by his brain simply weren't being carried out by his body. He met his father's gaze, and he felt helpless. In an instant, Trevor was by his side. Chris knew only too well just how deep paternal bonds ran and, as his dad stood within hand's reach, it was obviously something that was never lost. The wasted years of estrangement melted away as, arms wide open, the two men embraced.

No words were spoken as the seconds in each other's arms turned into minutes. Chris' trembles quivered in time with Trevor's shivers. So lost was Chris in the colossal cloak of sorrow that enveloped him, that Mike's words bidding them farewell just bounced off him.

'I'll be back in the morning,' Mike said.

'Thank you,' Trevor replied, neither loosening his grip on his son nor taking his eyes away from the little boy who he'd held in that very clinch on so many occasions in the distant past.

'Tell me about them,' Trevor said, his words bringing their embrace to an end.

They sat next to each other on the sofa and Chris took his time as he composed his words carefully.

'What to say?' he whispered. 'Joe... You'd have loved him. Like, properly loved him. He loved his football, but you'd have probably forgiven him that.'

'What position did he play?' Trevor asked, looking at a photo of Joe in his little Arsenal kit that sat proudly on the mantelpiece.

'In goal,' Chris replied.

'As close to rugby as it could be, then,' Trevor said. His voice was hoarse, creaking under the strain of a conversation about a dead grandson that he had never met.

'He was brilliant, Dad,' Chris said, oh so quietly. 'Like… brilliant. Just… brilliant.'

'I can only imagine,' Trevor said.

'And Lin,' Chris said, his own gaze shifting to a canvas of his wife and son that hung proudly on the wall opposite, 'she was the best. Just the best. She… I don't know, I just can't tell it how it is, you know? She was just the best wife. The best mum. Just the best.'

He held his head in his hands. It was all just too much, speaking of them both in the past tense. It went against everything that he knew to be right in the world.

Neither father nor son slept. Despite the heartache that had brought him to his knees, just talking about his Linda, his Joe, gave him some small crumbs of comfort. Sharing brought them back, if only in his heart, in his mind. His dad mopped up the tears as they tracked their way down his face in a way that only a parent could. A lifetime ago, he'd done it whenever Chris had grazed a knee or trapped a finger. Here, now, the injury that caused them was on a truly different scale.

Trevor's presence when he had walked through the door had blinded his son to the obvious. All Chris had seen was the man his dad had once been, the man trapped in time, a figure from the past but, as they sat, spoke and the years caught up with them, it was clear that time waited for no man.

'Are you ill, Dad?' Chris asked.

Trevor nodded, smiling sadly as the conversation turned from two tragic deaths to an impending, more natural one.

'Yeah,' he said. 'I am, son. Cancer. They've tried treating it, but there's nothing they can do for me now.'

'Why didn't you come to me, Dad?' Chris whispered.

'Honestly don't know,' Trevor replied. 'The amount of

times I wish I'd tried to find you. I didn't even know if you still lived in the area, to be honest. I've been on my own for so long that you just kind of get used to your own company.'

'I always guessed we'd bump into each other one day,' Chris said.

'I don't really go out,' Trevor replied. 'Just to the hospital for my appointments, that's it. Since you went… Well, it's been a struggle.'

Both men looked away from each other, contemplating what could have been. What should have been.

'But we're here now,' Trevor said quietly. 'That's what matters.' He placed his hand on Chris' shoulder.

'I don't know what I'm going to do, Dad,' Chris said. His voice was weak. Though he'd cried rivers, there were still lakes to flow. 'How am I going to get through this?'

'I don't know, son,' Trevor replied. ' All I can say is that, whatever it takes, I'll be here with you. I wish I'd known them,' he rasped. He'd barely held a conversation for years, and a whole night of talking was playing havoc with his vocal chords.

'Me too,' Chris replied. He couldn't mask the regret laced in his voice.

'I saw something on the news last week about it,' Trevor said. 'When something happens locally you notice it, don't you? I had no idea… What happened, son?'

Chris took a sharp breath in, and his eyes narrowed. His fists clenched, and the veins on his temples bulged.

'I trusted someone with him,' he muttered.

Chapter 28

DS SUE WILLMOTT

Thirteen Days After

Sue had stolen a few moments with her little girl at home while grabbing a change of clothes and a shower, but even the tenderest of hugs that morning couldn't lift the dark clouds that followed her.

'You alright, love?' Sue's mum asked, packing Lottie's schoolbag for the day ahead.

'Not really,' DS Willmott replied. 'Work stuff.'

'That case?' her mum asked, as Lottie ran in and attached herself to Sue's shoulders.

'Last night,' she said. 'It got a whole lot worse.'

'You work too hard,' her mum said, standing up and prising Lottie away from her.

'Got to do it,' Sue replied, standing up and draining the last dregs of the coffee that she hoped would sustain her through the day. 'Now, you, give me a kiss, pickle.'

Lottie's sweet, innocent chirps as she struggled to stop her mum tickling her only served to drive home the angst that awaited her at work.

Those dark clouds that followed her had spread through

every inch of Beachbrook nick. Grown men and women had shed midnight tears at Chris' plight. He may not have been a Beachbrook copper, but he was still one of their own, part of their extended family.

As she sat at her desk, everything felt heavy. Her limbs, the atmosphere, the world. And it was all sitting squarely upon her shoulders.

'Alright, Sarge?' DC Flanagan asked gently, poking her head around the door.

'Gonna need a few on this, Amy,' DS Willmott replied. 'Can you and Tom put off whatever you had on today, please?'

DC Flanagan nodded. She shuffled out of the door and made her way back to the workstation she shared with DC Harris.

'Is the skipper alright?' Tom asked.

'Her eyes,' Amy replied. 'She's knackered.'

Knackered, she was. Not only was she now charged with investigating Joe's death, but now she was the lead detective on Linda's suicide as well. She'd investigated plenty of suicides before. It was always a DS who had to get up at a coroner's court and present the facts, and the job never got any easier. But, this time, it felt different. Cliff jumpers were a sad fact of life, or death, in a coastal community. This one, though? The inevitable public interest? The reasons why? It was an entirely different animal.

She leaned back in her chair and nodded as Tom set another coffee down in front of her. One swig was followed by another. It was caffeine that was going to get her through the day, to help her get her the answers that she needed. That Chris needed, even more. She had been with him when Linda had been found, when that fateful message had been relayed across the airwaves. He hadn't shouted, he hadn't sworn, he hadn't screamed or cried, he had just closed the world out. He had been a man completely crushed by loss.

In death, though, Linda was with Joe. Their bodies lay side-by-side in the mortuary fridge. That had been DS Willmott's first instruction as soon as Linda's wrecked body had been recovered from the rocks.

DS Willmott had snatched a couple of broken hours' sleep at home before making her way to the mortuary before work. Linda hadn't made pretty viewing, though DS Willmott had seen enough pieces of the broken jigsaw to be able to sign the identification forms. Joe had been a sleeping angel, pure and innocent, taken by the sea but not a blemish left on his skin. Linda's demise had been a hell of a lot more violent.

Her phone rang, a welcome distraction.

'DS Willmott, it's the comms office here,' the voice on the other end said. 'We've had a lot of enquiries from the local and national press about the jumper last night, possible links with the boy who died in the sea.'

DS Willmott sighed. That hadn't taken long.

'Can you give us something?' the comms officer asked.

'Later,' DS Willmott replied, hanging up.

'Amy, Tom,' she called, summoning the two young detectives into her office.

'Sarge?' Tom said, as they both walked through the door.

'Need one of you on the post-mortem today, please,' DS Willmott said. 'And one of you on house to house.'

Tom and Amy looked at each other, and her eyes narrowed ever so slightly. Tom sighed. There was no point arguing.

'I'll do the PM,' he said.

'Good lad,' DS Willmott replied. On any other day, she'd have had a laugh about the power dynamic between them, but it just wasn't that kind of day. 'Amy, you crack on with house to house please, Beach Road and Linda's road, and I'll get the ball rolling on the coroner's report.'

'Nothing sus about this one?' Amy asked.

'Define sus,' DS Willmott replied. 'All I know is that we've got a dead boy, and a dead mum. Think of the what-ifs. What if someone was with her last night. What if she was pushed. What if, what if, what if? Until I'm satisfied that all those what-ifs have been answered, then we treat it as suspicious.'

Until she had definitively proven that no crime had taken place, her starting point from an investigation perspective was one of suspicion. Assume nothing. Believe no one. Check everything. She had gone to the nth degree in dishing out actions overnight. CSI had spent hours combing the clifftop, searching for any evidence of foul play. Linda's car had been recovered and was awaiting examination to establish whether Linda had been alone on her journey from home. She owed Chris that much.

As Amy and Tom melted back to their desks, suitably told, DS Willmott reached for a sealed evidence bag. She took some scissors from her drawer, and sliced it open, donning a glove before she took out Linda's phone, and held it in the sunlight. It bore only superficial wounds from her descent to death, her body taking the full brunt of the impact and the phone, stowed in her pocket, wearing only a couple of scratches on the casing. DS Willmott twirled it in her fingers as the screen caught the sunlight and bounced it off the office walls around her. Not usually one for melancholy, a thought crossed her mind. Not twelve hours before, a desperate mother had held it in her hands, typed into it a message indicating her intent to die, and jumped from a cliff with it in her pocket. Now, it was here. For evidential purposes it would require a full download, but just so she could determine if there was anything on there of preliminary interest, she unlocked it. Joe's birth year, Chris had mumbled the night before when asked if he knew the password. It made sense. Even if he hadn't told her, it would've been DS Willmott's first guess.

Joe's little face stared up at her as the screen came to life, and she looked at him for a few seconds.

'But for the grace of God…' she whispered to herself.

She scrolled through the recent call list. There was nothing of interest there. DS Willmott closed the call register and opened WhatsApp. The last message sent was the one to Chris.

Sorry, Chris. I love you. Goodbye.

It was chilling, and DS Willmott felt the ice creep down her spine. She scrolled to the next message. It was to Sophie.

You took him there and didn't bring him home. Fuck you

Then, to the next. It was to Andrew.

You are responsible for this. For all of this.

She read them, and then read them again.

'Jesus,' she whispered.

Those messages weren't just going to stoke the fire that already raged within Chris. They were going to be incendiary, fuelling the flames and fanning them until something blew up.

There was no way she could keep it from him. That wasn't in her power, nor was it her right. He'd find out about it eventually, either during the investigation or at inquest. It was evidence of Linda's state of mind, demonstrable proof of the motive for her suicide.

DS Willmott closed her eyes. The caffeine from Tom's brew had barely kicked in, and her head ached.

As she was formulating her investigation plan, her mobile phone started ringing. She didn't recognise the number.

'Hello?'

'DS Willmott? It's Andrew Wicks,' came the reply. 'I'm a bit worried about a couple of messages we got in the middle of the night from Linda. I was hoping I could tell you and you could see if everything is alright.'

DS Willmott froze. Of course Andrew didn't know yet. His voice was small, his concern obvious. Now, having received those messages from Linda, he was a witness who the coroner would probably have a very keen interest in hearing from. DS Willmott's headache was getting worse.

'I know about the messages she sent you,' she said, her voice quiet and sombre. 'I've got her phone here in front of me. Look, Andrew, it's not easy to do this over the phone but I'm sorry to say that Linda died last night. I know how this will make you feel bearing in mind what was said in those messages.'

The line went silent for a few seconds.

'You still there, Andrew?' DS Willmott asked. She could hear heavy breathing on the other end of the line before the phone line went dead. 'Shit,' she said, dropping her phone onto the table.

Her day had just got a lot more complicated. That emerging headache was developing into a throbbing one that pounded against her skull from all angles.

Her investigation into Joe's death had gone as suspected. Sophie had given an account where she wasn't able to offer anything other than what Andrew had already told her, and there was no way that she was going to put a young, traumatised Maria through the wringer to get an account from her. Even if she wanted to, it'd never get the thumbs-up from her bosses further up the chain. Now, with Linda thrown into the melting pot, it was an investigator's nightmare.

She tried several times to call Andrew back but his phone rang straight through to answerphone. She sighed and rubbed the back of her head, scribbling in her day book as she tried to see through the fog and work out a strategy moving forward.

The ringtone on her phone stabbed her through the ears, and she picked it up quickly to make the noise go away. This time, it was a withheld number.

'Hello?' she said.

'Sue? It's Mark in the CSI office here,' came the reply. 'I've got the results on the forensics for the coat from the sea that you asked for the other week. Shall I email them to you?'

'Brilliant, thanks, Mark,' DS Willmott replied, her eyes squinting as the sunlight intensified the throbbing that lurked beyond them.

Her inbox pinged, and there it was. An email from Mark. Subject: Forensic Analysis of Item MJT/01 – Coat recovered from Beachbrook Beach – Report.

She double-clicked on it and set about reading the results. A lot of it was the usual scientific jargon, but not the conclusions. There, in layman's terms, was the answer that DS Willmott had been looking for. Confirmation of the hunch that she'd had when she decided to submit the coat. All of a sudden, she was wide-eyed.

Everything had changed.

The headache that had been prowling in the foreground dissipated.

'No shitting way,' she whispered to herself. She jumped from her chair and, light of foot, sprang from her office, floating across the floor until she stopped at Amy and Tom's desks.

'House to house can wait,' DS Willmott said, 'PM isn't until later, I need you both with me now.'

DC Harris sat in the back of the car as DS Willmott briefed him and DC Flanagan. Their mouths dropped open at what she was saying.

'Always follow your nose,' DS Willmott said as they arrived at Andrew's house. 'And remember your ABCs.'

'Assume nothing, believe no one, check everything,' DC Harris said.

DS Willmott walked up the driveway with coils in her shoes springing her forward, and rapped the door loudly. She was a detective on a mission. Andrew answered the door. He was staring at the floor but, as he looked up, his eyes were red and glazed. He looked surprised to see DS Willmott at the door. They'd not long got off the phone with each other.

'I'm sorry I hung up on you,' he said. 'It was a lot to take in. Do you want to come in?'

'I do,' DS Willmott replied. She walked in to the front room where Sophie and Maria were sitting and playing a board game. Sophie's eyes were raw, but she kept up appearances.

'Can we speak in private please, Andrew?' DS Willmott asked. He pointed her down the hallway to the kitchen.

'What's going on?' Andrew asked as he closed the door quietly, once more staring at the floor. 'I was going to call you back, I just needed a moment,' he said.

'It's not a social call, I'm afraid,' DS Willmott replied. 'Andrew Wicks, I have received further information relating to your possible involvement in child neglect. Therefore, I am arresting you on suspicion of that offence.'

Chapter 29

ANDREW

Thirteen Days After

'You do not have to say anything but it may harm your defence if you do not mention when questioned something you later rely on in court. Anything you do say may be given in evidence.'

The blood drained from Andrew's face.

'I... I... I don't understand,' he stuttered. 'I told you everything I could the other day.'

'Don't say anything now please, Andrew,' DS Willmott replied. 'Save it for when you're on tape. Would you like to go and tell Sophie what's happening or do you want me to go and speak to her?'

'No, no, I'll do it,' Andrew said quickly, marching into the lounge.

'I'm just going with DS Willmott, love,' he said to Sophie. 'Got to help them out with a couple of bits. I'll be back as soon as I can.' The blood still hadn't returned to his face. He was deathly pale, and he was acutely aware that DS Willmott would be making a mental note of it all.

'Are you alright?' Sophie asked. 'Can't it wait? We've been

through enough, haven't we?' She may have been looking at Andrew, but her question was clearly aimed at DS Willmott.

Andrew gave her a kiss. 'It'll all be fine, love. Maria, look after your mum for me until I'm home, will you?'

'Don't go, Daddy,' Maria said. She ran up to him and wrapped her little arms around his thighs, clinging on tightly.

Andrew looked at DS Willmott, but her face was granite. 'I'll be back soon, princess,' he said. 'I promise.'

Sophie lifted a crying Maria from her embrace with Andrew, and he saw DS Willmott nod to his wife. All he'd received from her was a raised eyebrow and his rights being read.

He trudged behind DS Willmott as she led him away from the house, wondering if they were going to slap some handcuffs on his wrists. He didn't know what the procedure was. These just weren't the circles that he ran in. He sat in the back of the car, and looked at the male detective who was sitting next to him. He didn't know his name, and so he fixed his eyes on DS Willmott as she drove away.

'What's changed?' Andrew asked, quietly.

'Better for you that we don't speak until you're on tape,' DS Willmott said, staring at him in the rear-view mirror. Her eyes were smouldering, and Andrew looked away.

The rest of the journey passed in silence. Andrew looked out of the window as they navigated roads that he knew well. From the inside of the police car, though, they looked dirty. Tainted. His heart was pounding so much that he had to force himself to breathe, to concentrate on inhaling, exhaling, inhaling, exhaling, until it was muscle memory once more. He was petrified and then so much more.

'I know you haven't been arrested before, so we'll take it

one step at a time?' DS Willmott said as they got out of the car at the police station.

Andrew nodded, but remained silent. As they walked into the custody suite, the first thing he noticed was the smell. Mouldy, festering socks. Then the noise. Someone was banging on a cell door and someone else was screaming blue murder. It was about as far removed from Andrew's world as was possible and his face indicated as such.

'You get used to it,' the male detective said, as he searched Andrew and logged his belongings. 'Good to go, Sarge.'

The custody sergeant towered over Andrew like a composer on his podium as DS Willmott outlined the circumstances of the arrest. It was a whirlwind of information for Andrew to comprehend and he struggled to understand exactly what was happening.

'Do you want a solicitor?' the custody sergeant asked.

'I don't think so,' Andrew replied. 'I didn't need one last time. Do I need one now?'

'Up to you,' the custody sergeant said. 'I'll put no. Let me know if you change your mind. Want to read the *Codes of Practice*?'

'The what?' Andrew asked.

'Book that tells us how to look after you while you're here,' the custody sergeant replied.

'I dunno. I guess so. Why not?' Andrew replied.

The custody sergeant peered over his glasses.

'Not been here before, have you?'

'No,' Andrew said quietly.

'Been doing this four years and you're the first to say yes to reading the *Code of Practice*,' he laughed. 'I'll see if we can dig one out for you.'

'Come this way, Andrew,' DS Willmott said, leading

215

him down a long corridor to a cell. 'You'll need to take your shoes and belt off,' she said. Andrew guessed that after the shitshow of the past few weeks, she was taking no chances. 'I'm just going to get a few things ready, then I'll be back to get you for interview.'

She shut the thick, heavy metal door and, as the bolts secured themselves, Andrew winced. He'd never thought himself claustrophobic but, already, beads of sweat were beginning to form on his brow. Moments later, they were dripping down his face. As the minutes passed, his top became damp. It wasn't particularly warm in his cell but, by God, he was feeling the heat.

He paced up and down, listening to the goings on in the corridors beyond his four walls, painting pictures in his mind with only his ears as a guide. As the minutes passed into an hour gone by, the knot in his stomach grew into a bird's nest that it seemed would never be unravelled. Finally, the door opened once more, and DS Willmott stood at the threshold.

'Let's crack on then, shall we,' she said.

She led him back down the corridor, past the custody sergeant and into an interview room. There, it was silent. No screaming, no banging, just her, and him.

She sat in the interviewer's chair and arranged her paperwork. Everything she did seemed meticulous, from the way she shuffled them into order, to the way she pulled open the plastic wrapping on the DVD discs. Andrew could see that she was in total control, in complete command of her brief, and it unnerved him.

'Right then,' she said. 'It'll be the same process as before. Are you ready to go?'

Andrew nodded as he mopped sweat from his forehead with the sleeve of his top.

DS Willmott loaded the discs into the digital interview recorder and pressed 'record'.

She looked Andrew up and down, and he looked away again. For her, it may have been showtime but, for him, he wondered if it was the endgame.

It was a solid beep that lasted for about fifteen seconds. Other than that, there was silence. Andrew looked at DS Willmott, but her eyes remained fixed on the paperwork in front of her. The friendly, perhaps understanding detective was long gone, Andrew realised. He was on his own.

DS WILLMOTT: Mr Wicks, you have been arrested on suspicion of child neglect after further evidence has come to light relating to the investigation. For the avoidance of doubt, this is in relation to the investigation into the death of Joseph Jamieson. Before we begin is there anything that you would like to tell me that might differ from the account you have already provided to me?

Even her voice was different. Officious. Vicious.

ANDREW: I don't think so, no. I'm confused about why I'm here to be honest. I told you everything last time.

It wasn't just the pressure of the situation that was weighing down on him. There was remorse, too. Survivor's guilt, maybe. What did DS Willmott have that he hadn't accounted for? It must be a witness. Someone must have seen him. What else could there be?

DS WILLMOTT: I'd just like to clarify some of the details from the first interview, if I may?

Andrew opened his mouth, but she didn't wait for an answer.

DS WILLMOTT: You went to the beach on the day in question. The weather was awful but the children were adamant that they wanted to go. Is that right so far?
ANDREW: That's right.

What have you got? he wondered.

DS WILLMOTT: Joe and Maria were playing away from you. You then went and put on your coat from the beach hut because the weather was so bad. A dog jumped up at you and you took your eyes off the children, then…
ANDREW: No, the dog jumped up at Sophie. I was protecting her because she was pregnant, you see.

The trap she was weaving was one he didn't even realise he was walking into.

DS WILLMOTT: My apologies. You're right, the dog jumped up at Sophie and you tried to get the dog away. You then looked around and the children weren't playing any more. They had gone. You ran down to the sea and saw one of them in the water. You went into the sea and saw it was Maria. You managed to get to her, but you were weighed down by your coat. At some point you took the coat off and at no point did you see Joe. Is that about right?
ANDREW: Yeah, that's about right.

His eyes filled.

DS WILLMOTT: Are you okay to continue?

Andrew heard her tone. It was hard. Granite. It might've been a question that sounded caring, but it was delivered with indifference.

ANDREW: Yes, I'm okay, thank you.

He wiped his eyes and took a deep breath.

DS WILLMOTT: There are just a few things that I need to go over in a bit more detail. When you got to the beach, where did Maria and Joe get changed?
ANDREW: Outside the beach hut. I helped Joe with his wetsuit and Sophie helped Maria with hers. They were still wet from the day before, see, they were harder to put on.

His answer was slow and deliberate. He was looking for traps. Searching for holes. Listening for anything that she could use to trip him up.

DS WILLMOTT: Did either of them go into the beach hut at all?
ANDREW: No, they got changed and then went onto the sand.

He couldn't see where this line of questioning was going, but it seemed innocuous enough to him.

DS WILLMOTT: When was the last time that Joe had been in your beach hut?

ANDREW: I don't know. We'd been down there the day before, but the kids don't go in the beach hut. They're not allowed. Kettle, and gas, and all that. They're always on the beach.

DS WILLMOTT: I see. Moving on then, tell me about the coat that you were wearing when you went in the sea.

ANDREW: Oh that, not a lot to say really.

He didn't notice DS Willmott's eyes flicker.

ANDREW: It was brand new. Weather was bloody awful, like hideous, and it was cold as well. It was just one of those cheap coats you buy, just doesn't matter if it gets dirty or damaged, you know?

DS WILLMOTT: So where do you keep it? On a chair, hanging up? I'm just trying to paint a picture in my head.

Andrew just couldn't see where it was going. Still, it was pretty inane stuff.

ANDREW: No, I mean it was in a box that we keep our extra clothes in, you know, for rubbish weather. It was brand new, in a bag.

DS WILLMOTT: Oh sorry, I see, like a cellophane bag type thing?

DS WILLMOTT: Kids ever play with it?

ANDREW: No.

Weird question, he thought.

DS WILLMOTT: And you had your keys, phone and wallet in the pocket of it when you went in to the sea?

ANDREW: Yeah, you gave them back to me last time you interviewed me.

It was all mundane stuff, nothing they hadn't already covered. He wasn't relaxing, not by any stretch of the imagination, but she hadn't landed a killer blow just yet.

DS WILLMOTT: That's right. Now I just want to go over what happened when you were in the sea in finer detail. When interviewed last time, you said that it was all a blur. Now that a bit of time has passed, have you had a chance to think of anything else that might help me with the investigation?

He took his time before he answered. This was trickier territory, and he needed to be careful.

ANDREW: Well, like I said, I saw Maria and went in to get her. My coat was weighing me down but I managed to get her in. Then I went back out to try to find Joe, but I couldn't see him anywhere.

DS WILLMOTT: So you had your coat on when you got Maria in, then?

ANDREW: I believe so, yes. I think I took it off when I went back out to look for Joe.

DS WILLMOTT: And at no point did you see Joe in the sea?

ANDREW: No.

There was silence as Willmott met Andrew's gaze. He held it, determined not to break it first.

DS WILLMOTT: I have a couple of issues with what you have told me.

What now?

DS WILLMOTT: When you were in the ambulance on the day of the incident, I asked you what had happened. I made a note of your answer to that question. You said 'I couldn't get them both in.' What did you mean by that? Why say that you couldn't get them both in if Maria was the only one that you saw?
ANDREW: I... Errrr... Well, I guess I was in shock and wasn't thinking properly. That's the only way I can explain it.

Was that it? he wondered. That was explainable. Defensible. It didn't prove anything.

DS WILLMOTT: So you only had the option of saving Maria? You didn't see Joe at any point in the water?
ANDREW: That's right.
DS WILLMOTT: So why is his DNA all over the shoulder of your coat, then?

And there it was.

DS WILLMOTT: Andrew? Any answer to that question?
ANDREW: Well... I... Errrr... What do you mean?

He closed his eyes.

DS WILLMOTT: It's a wonderful thing, DNA, especially now. Did you know that clothes can go through the washing machine a lot of times and still retain DNA that had been on them before they went in? It's the same deal with your coat. It doesn't matter that the sea soaked it wet through. Joe's DNA was absorbed by the cotton. Pretty clever, don't you think?

ANDREW: I don't know, maybe, do you think, it might have been from earlier in the day maybe?

His sentences lacked structure. They were just fragments, providing a fractured defence. DS Willmott had him by the throat, and she tightened her grip.

DS WILLMOTT: But it can't have been, can it? Joe didn't go into the beach hut. Not allowed. Kettle. They got changed outside, remember?

ANDREW: I don't know, maybe he brushed up against me at some point then.

He was despairing in his attempts to provide a defence.

DS WILLMOTT: But the coat was brand new. Fresh out of the packet.

Again, she let the silence fill the room until it was screaming so loudly at Andrew that he had to break it.

ANDREW: I just don't know.

DS WILLMOTT: Would you like to clarify what you meant when you told me that you 'couldn't get them both in' in the ambulance?

Fuck. Andrew thought of Sophie and Maria, at home alone. He wasn't getting back to them anytime soon.

ANDREW: I think I'd like to speak to a solicitor now.

Chapter 30

DS SUE WILLMOTT

Thirteen Days After

She couldn't have scripted it any better. Outwardly, her composure remained steady. Inside, she was euphoric. Her set-up questions had left him absolutely no wriggle room.

DS WILLMOTT: That is entirely your right. I'll stop the recording now so that we can arrange for a solicitor to attend.

She stopped the recording and sat in stony silence as she ejected and sealed the DVD discs. She looked at Andrew. He was looking at the ground and his head was slightly rocking back to front.

'I'll need to put you back into your cell until your solicitor gets here,' she said. 'Do you have any preference or do you want the duty solicitor?'

'I don't know,' he replied. He lifted his head, and his eyes darted to every corner of the room. 'I guess whoever will do.'

DS Willmott led him back to his cell and shut the door. She softly put her ear up to it and heard very heavy breathing from the other side of it, followed by the sounds of a man trying to suppress tears.

For the first time in the course of those tragic two weeks, she felt a modicum of professional pride. It was so rare to have something to work with, where webs could be spun and traps laid. She'd grown so used to having her interviewees answer every question with 'no comment'. Now, through a bit of good, old-fashioned coppering, she was one step closer to figuring out what happened in the water that day. She felt a new-found determination as she walked down the corridor and arranged for the duty solicitor to attend.

The duty solicitor arrived about thirty minutes later. DS Willmott knew her well, having locked horns with her many times before, both in interviews and at court.

'Hi, Jill,' DS Willmott said as she walked into the custody suite. 'Quite an interesting one for you today.' While they may have been adversaries on a professional level, they got on well enough with each other personally. 'Come through and I'll give you disclosure.'

DS Willmott and Jill went into a side room where DS Willmott laid out the evidence against Andrew. Jill rolled her eyes.

'Well that's going to bring the newspapers back, isn't it,' she said.

DS Willmott nodded. She stood up and left the room, fetching Andrew from his cell for his consultation with Jill. His eyes were bloodshot, his cheeks red and blotchy. She was impatient to get him back into the interview room and back on the record. The consultation lasted a lot longer than she thought it would, however. She thought that it would have been a very quick bit of advice – to tell the truth, and to take it on the chin. The clock kept ticking though. Eventually, after about an hour, Andrew and Jill emerged. He looked pained, like a wounded animal going back into battle for its life.

The interview recommenced shortly after.

DS WILLMOTT: This is a continuation of the interview with Andrew Wicks. Mr Wicks, please can you confirm that you have received the legal advice that you asked for during your previous interview and that you are happy to now proceed?

JILL: Having consulted with Mr Wicks, he is offering the following prepared statement: 'I, Andrew Wicks, refer to and stick with my previous statements made in relation to the tragic death of Joe Jamieson. I do not know how his DNA got onto my coat but suggest there are other, logical reasons why it may have been there. A play fight, maybe. It may have happened in the sea if he came across it after I had taken it off. For the avoidance of doubt, I did not come into contact with Joe in the sea. I will not be answering any further questions in relation to this matter.'

DS WILLMOTT: Andrew, are you really saying that Joe's DNA got onto your coat after you had discarded it in the sea?

ANDREW: No comment.

He spoke quietly.

DS WILLMOTT: And your statement about not being able to get them both in?

ANDREW: No comment.

DS WILLMOTT: Tell me the truth, Andrew. They

were both there, weren't they? You could've rescued them both, couldn't you?

ANDREW: No comment.

DS WILLMOTT: This is going to eat away at you if you don't tell me what happened, Andrew. We know that he came into contact with your coat. Your explanation... Well... You know it doesn't add up, don't you? Are you sure you don't want to tell me? Come on, Andrew, what happened out there? Don't you owe it to Chris?

Andrew screwed his face up, and DS Willmott let her words linger. They had raked over a raw nerve.

JILL: My client is asserting his right to silence at this time. He won't be answering any further questions, DS Willmott.

DS WILLMOTT: If that's the case, Andrew, then I'll end the interview. Is there anything else you want to say before I do?

ANDREW: No comment.

She had him, and she knew it.

DS Willmott turned off the recording equipment. The interview had gone as well as it could have from her perspective. She had got everything that she needed from it, and the only defence that Andrew had eventually provided seemed preposterous.

'You're going to be bailed so I can speak to the CPS about all of this,' DS Willmott said coldly. She was sure that she had sufficient evidence to charge him already, but she wanted to put an appeal out to locate the dog walker before she sought charging advice from the local prosecutor. He might have further evidence to strengthen the case against Andrew, she thought.

Andrew didn't answer, and she wasn't particularly bothered about hearing anything else from him anyway. He'd have to answer for Joe's DNA, one way or the other.

She bailed him, and watched from the front office window as he left the police station. He looked to the heavens, before disappearing out of sight.

For her, the investigation had come roaring back to life.

Chapter 31

SOPHIE

Thirteen Days After

Call it the hormones of pregnancy, call it the overwhelming grief that came with the death of a child on her watch, or call it the punch in the guts that completely knocked the wind out of her following the news of Linda's suicide. It was only the fact that she had to keep her focus on Maria that kept Sophie from shutting down completely.

She couldn't turn to social media, knowing just what toxic content would be spreading across the web. She couldn't turn on the television, through fear of an unwanted headline coming her way. She couldn't even bear to look at her phone, so numbingly silent had the usually busy mums WhatsApp groups become. Instead, she only had Maria to focus on, and that's what she did.

'When's Daddy coming home?' her little girl asked, clinging to her leg for the third time in ten minutes.

'Soon, sweetheart, soon,' Sophie said, running her fingers through Maria's hair, trying to lighten the tension in her voice.

The clock told her it had been mere hours that had passed. It had felt like days. Whatever the case, it was dark when he finally arrived home. Maria was already asleep. As she went, she had wept for her absent father.

'Where the fuck have you been?' Sophie hissed.

Andrew's interrogation from DS Willmott may have been over, but his wife's had only just begun. Her face raged from a day spent assuaging a scared child and struggling to deal with her own trauma. He owed her something.

'Well?' she asked, her face showing little sign of softening.

'Sit down, sweetheart,' Andrew whispered, 'I don't want you stressing.'

'Don't want me stressing?' she shouted, before her voice lowered. 'Your daughter has been going spare, and so have I.'

'I'm sorry,' Andrew replied, looking down at his shoes as he ushered Sophie into the lounge, closing the door behind them.

A table lamp provided the dimmest of glows, and Andrew grasped for the edge of the sofa as Sophie sat down on it.

'Well?' she asked, again.

Andrew took a deep breath.

'I've got something to tell you,' he whispered.

Sophie's eyes met his. She'd never before seen pain in them quite like now. It was something so bare, so raw, and it thawed her icy stare in an instant.

'Go on then,' she said, softly.

Andrew remained standing, looking at the window but staring far beyond the glass.

'Look at me,' she said.

'Don't deserve to,' he replied.

'What is it?' Sophie asked, needing to know what it was, pleading for him to tell her.

'They found Joe's DNA on that coat I wore in the sea,' he mumbled.

He could feel Sophie's eyes boring a hole in his skull from behind, as a silence so deafening that it pounded Andrew from all corners descended upon them.

'So?' Sophie asked.

If Andrew had turned around, he would've seen confusion on her features.

'So... So...' Andrew stuttered. 'S-s-so, I haven't told you the truth.'

Sophie gripped the slack of her trousers until her fingernails made indentations on her palms, but she didn't make a sound.

'The truth,' Andrew continued, quietly, 'is that when I went into the sea, the kids were both there.'

He opened his eyes and shuffled towards the window, looking for a moon and stars that were hidden by clouds.

'And I tried, love, I tried so hard to get them both in. I promise, I tried, but I just couldn't do it. It was too much, and I was going under as well. Then they drifted apart from each other, and I could only swim to one. I had to choose, Soph, I had to let one of them go.'

Sophie clenched her trousers tighter still, and felt her heart pound inside her. No tears came, though. She was all cried out.

'You what?' she whispered.

'I couldn't save him,' Andrew replied, as the clouds momentarily parted and the moon glowed. 'And then I panicked, and lied.'

'What the f...' she began to say, before her voice trailed away to nothing, her head spinning.

Never in their years together had Sophie seen or heard him so exposed, so helpless, so vulnerable.

Yet, something had changed. Something fundamental. Something that went to the very roots of their marriage.

Trust.

Their vows had mentioned respect, all those years before, and in those intervening years the truth had been their bedrock. Now, though? He'd let her believe that Joe had gone without a trace, had been taken by the sea without even the slightest chance of saving him. That hadn't been the truth, and if he could withhold something like THAT from her, then what else was he capable of hiding?

She looked up. Andrew was facing her, but she saw him through different eyes.

'I'm sorry, Soph,' he said, crying.

Her heart was thrashing to a beat she'd never before experienced. Before that fateful Sunday on the beach she'd always been so rational, so well-equipped to deal with whatever it was that life threw at them. Since, though? She'd been quietly getting on with getting on just for the sake of her family.

In the depths of her gut, she could feel her stomach turning. No, she realised. It wasn't her stomach. It wasn't that at all.

'I'm gonna be sick,' she blurted out, running from the lounge and shutting herself in the downstairs bathroom, bolting the door shut behind her.

Inside her womb, their baby kicked, disturbed by the stress that coursed through Sophie's body. As she gagged and vomited into the toilet, she heard a knocking at the door.

'Soph, love,' Andrew said.

'Give me a minute,' she croaked, heaving until there was nothing left to come up.

She didn't hear footsteps walking away, though.

'Andrew, please, give me a minute,' she repeated. Her voice was resolute. Iron. Not to be messed with.

The creaking of floorboards faded away as Andrew retreated to the lounge. As she flushed the toilet, and mopped the cold sweat away from her face and the back of her neck, her stomach growled. She felt empty, but not only physically. She may have been sitting silently on the bathroom floor, but her husband had just lobbed a proverbial grenade into the family home.

She stared at herself in the mirror.

Who are you?

The weeks of grief had taken their toll on her. She dragged her fingers through her hair, but they got lost in a maze of knots and tangles.

What's going to come of this?

Her lips trembled, their shakes rooted in the feeling that only comes from familial distress.

Joe. Oh, little Joe.

She thought she had no more tears to shed, but they flowed once more at the thought of that poor, sweet, innocent little boy, fighting for his life and being left on his own, his fate determined by Andrew's choice. What would he have thought in those last moments? How would he have felt? Abandoned. Alone. Scared.

Can we get through this?

'Alright, love?' Andrew asked, climbing to his feet as she finally emerged from the bathroom and into the lounge.

She looked at him, and he at her. She wasn't the acquiescing type. That's what Andrew had always said he loved about her. She said what she thought and wore her heart on her sleeve. Yet, here? Now? What was there to say?

'Guess so,' she replied.

Baby Wicks nudged her.

'I'm so sorry, Soph,' Andrew said. 'The guilt has been

eating me alive, every single day. The guilt of leaving Joe out there, and the guilt of lying to everyone about it.' He paused for a moment. 'The guilt of lying to *you* about it.'

He held her hands, and she let him. They felt like she knew they would. A bit calloused from all those years on the tools, his skin hard and his palms dry. But... She just couldn't explain it properly, in her own mind... They felt different. Not like the hands she knew. Not the hands she had always felt so safe in. Were these the same hands that had let Joe go?

'Family comes first,' she said, the words spilling from her lips instinctively.

'Totally,' Andrew replied, nodding. 'I mean, I had to choose Maria... Right?' he asked, desperation in his eyes.

'I didn't mean it like that,' Sophie said, quietly. She let her hands drop to her side. 'I meant that Maria and bump are what we should be thinking about. Now. Always.'

Andrew nodded again. Sophie's head was facing the floor once more, and she knew he was trying to make eye contact with her.

'Soph,' he said.

She looked up, and Andrew's eyes stared deep into hers.

'Yeah?' she asked.

His pain diffused in the air all around him. Sophie could feel it, alright. She could almost taste it. It reeked of that dead little boy who'd filled their house with joy on so many occasions.

'What would you have done?' he whispered.

It was a question she just couldn't bear to think about the answer to.

Sleep didn't come that night. Instead, she lay on her side, facing the wall. Andrew's lack of snores told her that he, too,

235

was locked in his own ruminations, but neither of them spoke. When morning came, and the sun rose, she was first up.

The rustling of the post coming through the letter box told her it was 7 a.m. without the need to look at her phone clock. They'd always joked that they could set the time by their postman.

She left Andrew in the bedroom alone, and walked downstairs. She picked up four letters that lay on the floor by the front door, and eyed them with suspicion. Each was housed in a brown envelope, all addressed to Andrew and each with 'private and confidential' written on the front. She may not have dealt with the family finances, but she was by no means naïve to the fact that Andrew hadn't been working, nor that there were bills that needed paying. Their life may have been on pause for a while, now, but outside of their cocoon, it was playing at normal pace.

Family comes first.

She pursed her lips, and walked through to the kitchen, dropping the envelopes on the table, and filling the kettle. Behind her, footsteps.

'Morning, love,' Andrew said.

'Morning,' she replied, feeling his hands wrap around her from behind. She didn't flinch.

Family comes first.

Andrew's hands lingered, sitting on her hips. Eventually, he removed them and walked away to the table. She heard him grunt as he ripped open the envelopes.

'All alright?' she asked.

Andrew was leafing through the contents of the envelopes. Sophie watched, looking at the papers that he held in his hands. The writing on them was in bold, but it wasn't in red ink. Not yet.

'Just a bit behind,' he said.

'Anything I can do?' she asked.

'All good,' he replied. 'You just keep growing that baby for us.'

Family comes first.

'Will do,' she said, nodding and ignoring the elephant that was running rings around her. 'I reckon it's time we sorted things out properly with baby girl as well.'

'Maria?' Andrew asked.

'She's got to go back sometime,' Sophie said.

Andrew nodded.

'Tomorrow?' he said.

'I'll get onto the school,' Sophie replied.

'And I'll get on the phone to see what work is about,' Andrew said.

After the nightmares of those first few nights without Joe, Maria had seemed settled, even if she had regressed a bit in terms of her maturity. That much, they had noted. They were still Mummy and Daddy, after all, not Mum and Dad, and she'd lost the edge that she'd been developing before... it... had happened. It was almost as if the stubborn independence that she'd built up over the past year had disappeared, and her confidence in arguing the toss about everything had diminished. But they still had her and, whatever life threw at her from that point, they'd be there to guide and shape her.

Family comes first.

Sophie hoped that she had simply pushed the trauma out of her mind, that she had been too young to process it so she had simply erased it from her memory. Children were fickle creatures, after all. Yet, still, she had remained at home. Was it parental cowardice, Sophie had wondered, that had prevented her from returning? Was the fear of being under the magnifying glass at the school gate preventing them doing what was best for their little girl? Would the spotlight have burned too brightly upon them at drop off and pick up? The supermarket visit from before was still seared on her mind, when the headlines had screamed at her, when the other parents had gawped. It would be that, times a hundred. Times a thousand. Yet, still it was a bridge that needed to be crossed.

'Can you come with me?' she asked.

'Course,' Andrew replied. 'What's up?'

'We need to talk to her,' Sophie replied. 'Without the kid gloves, without hiding behind it all. We've got to do it.'

She'd spent countless hours on websites of every variety, searching for ways and means of addressing a child's grief while attempting to navigate her own. Every day, she had put it off until tomorrow. Just let the little girl have some space, she had told herself. Now, it appeared, that tomorrow had finally arrived.

'Maria,' Sophie said, gently cushioning her words so as not to wake her baby girl with a start.

Andrew stood behind Sophie, as she stroked Maria's forehead. In her sleep, her thumb lay in her mouth while soft lullabies hummed in the background.

'Sweetheart,' Sophie said, as Andrew moved in closer.

Maria opened her eyes, and screwed them up before opening them fully once more. She was never good at waking up, but both her parents were there. It was different to normal.

That and the outermost cracks of her blind let in enough light for her to know it was morning.

'Morning,' she said, rubbing her eyes and sitting up, before lying straight back down.

'Morning, love,' Sophie said, still stroking her forehead. 'Mummy and Daddy need to talk to you.'

Her voice told Maria it was something important, and she sat up again.

'You know you've not spoken about Joe since the other week,' Sophie said, holding Maria's hand as it began to tremble. 'So we wanted to let you know that it's okay to talk about him,' Sophie continued.

'He's a star, you said,' Maria replied.

'That's right,' Andrew replied, 'the brightest one up there.'

Maria nodded. They'd already told her this.

'Thing is,' Sophie said, 'that Joe's mummy went to be with him as well.'

'Linda?' Maria asked.

'Linda,' Sophie said, nodding.

'She's a star as well?' Maria asked.

'She is,' Sophie replied, desperately forcing back the emotion that surged inside from her forehead to her toes.

Maria sat still for a moment, with her eyes darting from Sophie to Andrew.

'Is Chris a star, too?'

'No,' Sophie replied, 'Chris isn't a star.'

'Can we see them later,' Maria asked, 'Joe and Linda?'

'When the moon's up, of course we can,' Andrew said.

Maria nodded. She understood about as much as she needed to. And, when night came, she pointed them out to her parents. Sophie hid under the dark blanket that the canopy above them afforded her as a few tears escaped. It was at once cathartic to see Maria processing everything, and heartbreaking at the same time.

The next morning came in a flash. It was a car journey that

Sophie had taken so many times before, but in many ways it was brand new. For a start, there was an empty seat in the back, one that was filled only by memories of the boy who had once sat there on so many school runs. Sophie couldn't help but look with misty eyes in her rear-view mirror at the silhouette of crumbs and dirt that had collected at the edge of where Joe's booster seat had been.

'Joe was the brightest, wasn't he, Mummy?' Maria asked.

'Sure was, baby girl,' Sophie replied quietly.

'It's nice, isn't it, that they're next to each other,' Maria said. 'Will they always be there together?'

'Yeah,' Sophie replied. It was all her faltering voice could manage.

It was cleansing, in a way, to see and hear her daughter speak about it without the barriers of maturity blocking her path and, as she parked on a road parallel to the school, she steeled herself. It was time to run the gauntlet. She kept her eyes straight and her head down, but the whispers followed her all the way to the school gate.

Family comes first.

It was all she could do just to keep the bubble around her intact. If someone strayed into her eyeline, then she looked down. If someone walked in her path, her sidestep was deft. The chatter all around was of Linda, of Joe, but she shut it out. Communities grieve as an entity in their own right, and the school one was close. Sophie knew that. She got it. And she knew that things would never be the same again for her, for Andrew, for them. It didn't matter. What did matter was Maria, and that was her focus.

Family comes first.

As she walked through the front door, the load certainly felt lighter. She found Andrew sitting at the kitchen table, his phone idling in his hand and his wall planner spread in front of him. As far as she could see, it was a sea of blank spaces.

'Alright?'

'It's fucked,' he replied, his voice dripping with alarm.

'What do you mean?' she asked.

'Called everyone, the sites, the subbies, everyone,' he replied. 'It was a massive no, everywhere. Wasn't so much the no, though, more the way they said it.'

'Like what?'

'Like, you know when you know if someone is bullshitting you,' he replied. 'Well they were all bullshitting me. Couldn't get off the phone quick enough, most of them.'

'Why?' Sophie said, as much to herself as to Andrew.

'People know, Soph,' he replied. 'We're on the outside, and there's no way in.'

Chapter 32

CHRIS

Twenty-two Days After

Soft choir music played in the background and the air was scented with the perfume of arranged flowers. Antique wooden panels lined the four walls, and candles flickered on the shelves around the room. It was perfect. Utter serenity. Chris was by no means a religious man but, in that moment, he felt what he only imagined those with faith experienced when in their place of worship, in the presence of their God.

There had been no precedent for what he had been through. No pamphlet, no guide book. There was no one who could talk him through the process or empathise as he navigated his way through the depths of his own, personal hell. All he could do was follow his instincts and look for the angels who floated on his shoulder. They'd guide him. They'd be there.

He'd met the funeral director a few times in the run up to his visit. Lucy. Nice lady. Professional. Now, as she spoke, her words drifted past him, only a few of them finding their way into his ears.

'Linda's coffin is closed.'

'Died instantly.'

'Didn't suffer.'

He nodded.

'They're down there waiting for you,' Lucy said. 'And, honestly, please take as long as you need. When you're finished, you don't need to come and find me. You know where the door is, just let yourself out if you need to.' She leaned towards Chris and squeezed his arm with an affection borne of years of experience. Chris nodded and smiled weakly at her, then cautiously walked down the steps. The door shut quietly behind him. He was alone, and the air was cold.

Then he saw them. Two coffins, side by side. One open, one closed. One full length, the other half the size.

His family.

Choosing those coffins, mulling over what was to be his wife and baby boy's eternal place of rest, had broken him.

His feet felt cemented to the spot in which he stood but, by God, he was going to get to them. The tiny steps that he took were progress enough and, as he finally stood in the narrow gap that separated mother and child, they were united. The three of them, back together once more.

He looked at Joe. His boy. Entirely peaceful, eternally at rest. His face, so pale that his skin seemed to shine. His hair, washed and brushed, and fashioned in a side parting just how Linda had always liked it. There was no evidence of the trauma of the post-mortem, and the sea hadn't left a mark on him. He just looked like he was sleeping, dressed in his school uniform. He had always loved school and Linda had always been such a stickler for taking a photo of him every September before the first day of term that it had only

243

seemed right that he be laid to rest in it. He was every inch the boy who Chris had been so proud of in life.

His hands had been placed on his stomach, his left hand covering his right, which in turn had a single white rose underneath it. Chris gently took hold of his left hand. It was icy cold, and instinct caused him to flinch momentarily. Still, he held on tightly to his baby boy's small, delicate fingers. Warm or cold, in life or death, Joe was still his son, and he was right there with him. Rigor mortis had long since passed and Joe's hand fell softly into Chris'. It still fitted like a glove.

'Hi, mate,' Chris said quietly. 'Daddy's here.' He interlocked his fingers with Joe's, just how Joe had always done to him. He felt his eyes filling with tears, but he was resolute in his determination to get through this without breaking down. He owed them that much.

'I'm so sorry, mate. I'm sorry that you had to go through that on your own. Remember we talked about heaven a few times? I hope Mummy has found you and that you're together somewhere now and that you're happy. You look after her for me, won't you, mate?' He felt tears falling. He couldn't stop them, but they didn't matter. He just had to get his words out, to pass on what he wanted to say. His voice quivered as he continued. 'I've brought your favourite book with me. I know that Mummy reads it best, but do you mind if I have a go?'

He gently placed Joe's hand back on his stomach, and took the book from his bag. It had been precious treasure, recovered from Linda's car on the night she'd gone to be with Joe. He opened it to the first page and began reading. The words flowed, just as they had from Linda's lips on so many occasions before. He didn't want it to end but, as the sentences turned into pages gone by, he knew it had to.

'Time to sleep now,' Chris whispered softly. He bent over

him and kissed him on his forehead. 'Night, son. Daddy loves you. Always, Joe. Always.' He stroked his forehead, moving a single, loose strand of hair back in place, before kissing him gently. Tenderly. With the love of a parent who would be forever lost without him.

He turned to the closed coffin. A bunch of red roses lay on top, next to a photo of Linda. It was from their wedding and she had a glass of fizz in her hand, a huge smile plastered over her face. Exactly how Chris would remember her, he thought. The shell that lay inside the coffin wasn't her. It was just the organic material of a woman who had long since lost her soul.

'Hi, love,' he said. 'You remember what you told me, about Joe's last words to you? "Love you, Mummy. I wish you were able to come with us." Well, now you are with him. And please, just know that I love you too, my beautiful wife. Always did. Always have. Always will do.'

He stroked the smooth, shiny pine wood that entombed her. That beautiful, mournful music in the background carried on playing as he spoke.

'What do I do, Lin? How do I do this without you? Without my wife, my boy? Am I supposed to go back to how everything was, on my own?'

No answers came his way. Instead, candles just twinkled all around him, radiating just a modicum of warmth into the otherwise chilled air.

'I'll always remember...' he began, his words petering out as his chain of thought was lost.

'I know why you did what you did and I don't blame you,' he said, his voice suddenly stronger. 'Look after our boy for me, won't you? I know you will.'

He stared at the photo. Their wedding day had been full

of love and laughter. Happy times, from halcyon days in the past.

'The police are looking into what happened,' he said. 'I promise you, love, I promise you that they won't get away with it.'

He turned and marched out of the chapel. He had said what he needed to say and done what he needed to do. He didn't say goodbye to Lucy, instead he walked straight to his car and sat in the driver's seat, his heart racing and his mind whirring. He closed his eyes and pictured Joe lying there, so calm. So restful.

And so dead.

His life had been stolen from him.

Chris breathed deeply, trying to quell his rising anger. Eventually, he felt calm enough to drive.

The rest of the day passed him by as he lay on his bed, contemplating the funeral the next day. It would be full of people. The thought of being in the public gaze, all eyes on him as he dealt with the most profound sorrow, filled him with dread. The news hounds were back in town, more so since Linda had gone. They'd come for him, but he'd hidden away. Mike had taken care of one or two who had pushed the envelope a bit further than they should have. The funeral would be his first step into whatever it was that came next for him.

Sleep hadn't come. He hadn't tried particularly hard to force it, either. But he did force himself to stay in bed. It was 6.30 a.m. when he walked to the bathroom and stood with his eyes shut under a hot shower until his skin began to wrinkle. He shaved again. Twice in two days, he thought. Progress? Maybe. He dressed in a beige suit, with a pink tie. No black today. Dark days would surely follow, but not now. And then, he just sat on his... their... bed, waiting. Waiting until it was time. Waiting to see his family one last time. Waiting for what was to come.

'Good morning, son,' Trevor said.

Chris looked at the clock on the wall. It was 8 a.m. Time was inching forward.

'Morning, Dad. You're up early,' he replied. He had asked for the funeral to be early in the day to avoid clockwatching. He was glad he had. Looking at his watch, the time was almost upon them.

'We'll get through this,' Trevor said. 'Together.'

Chris nodded.

Trevor hadn't known either Linda or Joe but the stories and memories that Chris had shared had brought a bit of life to what he knew was his last rodeo in the sun. Today wasn't about him, though. His job was to be there in a supporting capacity for Chris. He couldn't make up for the years that had been lost in the past, but in the here, the now, and the future, he could make his mark.

'I'm proud of you, son,' he said.

'Thanks, Dad,' Chris replied.

'Wish I'd known them,' Trevor mused. 'Wish they'd known me. All those years...'

'In the past,' Chris replied.

Like two peas in a pod they both nodded, their collective assent at exorcising the ghosts of their past.

'I'm sorry,' Trevor said.

'Me too,' Chris replied.

'I shouldn't have hit you,' Trevor whispered.

'And I shouldn't have pushed your buttons,' Chris replied.

'You were my boy,' Trevor said, sadly.

247

'Still am,' Chris replied.

'So stupid. So fucking stupid,' Trevor said.

Again, Chris nodded. Years and years of estrangement, and all because of an argument that got out of hand.

The front doorbell went. Chris took a deep breath in and walked out of the house with Trevor following closely behind.

Three vehicles were waiting for them outside the house. The hearse at the front was escorting Linda, the middle hearse carried Joe, and the vehicle at the back was for Chris and Trevor. Chris took a second to look at Linda and Joe. Today was a day of lasts. The last time that they would be at the house. The last time the three of them would ride together. The last time that he would have with them without the intrusion of a crowd of mourners.

The ten-minute journey to the crematorium passed in silence. Nothing needed to be said. Chris kept his eyes firmly fixed on the procession ahead of them, Joe's coffin visible through the rear window of the hearse in front of them. As the cortège moved forward, life around it stood still. People watched. Many wept.

The driveway leading to the crematorium was long and winding, with towering oaks lining the way. As the three vehicles pulled up, rows of people stood silently at the side of the driveway awaiting them. Strangers. Well-wishers. The occasional camera flash, but Chris blocked them out. The tragedies had resonated with so many and they wanted to pay their respects. It was to them whom he was most attuned, most focussed. Most grateful.

Chris climbed out slowly, followed by his dad. The older man placed a protective arm around the younger as they watched the coffins being unloaded from the hearses.

'Lin... Joe...' Chris whispered, his weeps being absorbed by the sea of tears that were flowing all around him. He buried his face into Trevor's shoulder, the fabric of his dad's suit muffling his sobs.

Trevor led him inside the chapel, guiding him to his seat at the front of the room. Chris sat and bowed his head. The funeral march began and the congregation rose as one. The piercing chords of Chopin's masterpiece – *Marche funèbre, Piano Sonata No.2, Third Movement* – tore through Chris, so much that he grasped for Trevor's arm. His dad was right there next to him, his hand warm, ready and waiting.

The coffins were carried down the middle aisle of the chapel, Joe first, then Linda. Chris looked to his left as they drew level with him, and then kept them in his sight as they were placed next to each other to the left of the lectern where the celebrant was to speak from. Six white roses on Joe's white coffin, Linda's adorned with red. Innocence, and vibrancy. Chris shut his eyes again, and let the last few bars of music wash over him. After their journey to the crematorium, Linda and Joe were now together again, side by side, never to be parted.

The service may have been short, but it was beautiful. Chris didn't look around once, but the stifled cries of those behind him rang in his ears. That Linda and Joe had touched so many people brought him crumbs of solace. The words of the celebrant passed him by. They were just an assortment of words; he knew the truth about his wife. His son. They were everything, and more. There was one thing that resonated with him, however. One turn of phrase that made his hairs stand on end, and his every muscle go tense.

'A candle that burns twice as bright, burns half as long.'

For Linda, maybe. Not so much for Joe. Half a life would

have been a blessing for him. Those smouldering embers inside his soul were stoked once more.

The funeral ended and the congregation was asked to stand. Though a smell of flora permeated throughout, it was death that hung heavy in the air. Chris was the last to get to his feet, but he couldn't raise his head. He knew what was coming next, and he wanted to eke out the seconds before the end came. With a fractured heart, he lifted his head. It was happening. It had to. It was all part of the process. Through eyes that had leaked a thousand heavy tears, he sobbed as a purple velvet curtain was slowly pulled across the entire width of the chapel, shielding the coffins from view as their encore began. This wasn't one for an audience, though. It was to be just them, and the furnace. Chris couldn't bear to watch, but he refused to shift his gaze until it was done.

'Goodbye,' he whispered, so softly that even Trevor didn't hear him.

Chris bowed his head and turned and walked out of the chapel, past rows of mourners who were staring at him through glazed eyes of their own. Tissues in hand, dabbing at faces. Adults, and even a few children. Kids. No older than Joe. He recognised some of them.

A gentle wind blew, and the leaves of the trees sung their own song to him, whispering in the breeze as only ancient oaks can. It was one tune that he'd always listen to, especially in a setting so tranquil, so peaceful.

Then, Chris saw him.

Andrew.

He was keeping his distance, trying to find camouflage amongst the oaks, but it was definitely him. Hidden beneath a hat and sunglasses, and wearing black, not the lairy shirts that were his trademark.

Chris' blood ran cold. Was his mind playing tricks on him? He looked again. Not a fucking chance. It was him, clear as day.

He'd gotten to within five metres of Andrew when Mike appeared and grabbed hold of Chris, forming a human barrier between him and Andrew. He'd been watching. Waiting. Anticipating.

'What the fuck are you doing here?' Chris screamed. His body shook with rage as he fought to free himself from Mike's grasp.

Andrew didn't say anything. He held his hands up to placate Chris, but there was no appeasing a man who had lost everything. It was the rage of his youth, long since buried, coming to the surface once more.

'Get out of here, now!' Mike shouted at Andrew.

'I'm sorry,' Andrew said softly. His eyes were bloodshot and his cheeks were red.

'GO!' Mike shouted. Andrew turned and bowed his head, before making a sharp exit.

'You did this, you wanker, you murdered my family!' Chris screamed as Andrew retreated. 'You wait, you fucking wait, you fucking murderer!'

PART FOUR

Those Left Behind

Chapter 33

DS SUE WILLMOTT

Thirty-six Days After

CPS Charging Decision:
Case of: Andrew Wicks
Investigating Officer: DS Willmott
Deciding Prosecutor: Jenny Atherton

I have reviewed the case file in relation to the death of Joseph Jamieson and the associated paperwork relating to the arrest and interview of Andrew Wicks. I have given full consideration to the circumstances surrounding the death, and at present do not feel that there is sufficient evidence to charge the suspect. There is no evidence of wilful neglect when referring to the Code for Public Prosecutors. It is the opinion of this office that this was a tragic accident. The DNA evidence, while showing that the suspect and the deceased came into contact, does not in any way provide evidence of child abuse or neglect. It may show that his account is not true but it doesn't come close to meeting the threshold for charging with the offence for which he was arrested and interviewed.

Final Decision: No further action.

DS Willmott sat at her computer and read the email several times as she processed the words. She stared at the picture of her own little girl that sat on her desk. She was a parent. She understood Chris' pain, though she could never begin to know what it felt like. She looked up at Amy and Tom, who stood in front of her desk.

'NFA,' she muttered.

'You're kidding?' Amy replied.

'Why?' Tom asked.

'Saying it was an accident,' DS Willmott replied. 'No evidence of abuse or neglect.'

The two junior detectives each walked around the desk and read the email on DS Willmott's computer.

'Pretty blunt,' Amy said.

'Rude,' Tom added.

DS Willmott sighed. Beachbrook was a small community. A tight one. Would it be accepted that this was, as the CPS had said, just an accident? And Chris? How the hell would he take the news?

'Let's map it out and break the offence down,' Amy said. 'A person who has attained the age of sixteen.'

'Fits,' Tom said.

'Who has responsibility for any child or young person under that age,' Amy continued.

'Keep going,' Tom said.

'Wilfully, intentionally or recklessly,' Amy continued.

'Still fits,' Tom said.

'Assaults, ill-treats, neglects, abandons or exposes him in a manner—'

'Likely to cause him unnecessary suffering or injury to health,' she said, finishing the legislative wording of the offence of Child Cruelty, Neglect and Violence. 'We all know it fits,' she concluded.

Dead ends had been down every road she had travelled. She'd spent several fruitless shifts on the beach trying to locate the owner of the dog that had jumped up at Sophie, questioning plenty of dog walkers but finding no witnesses.

'Can we get the kid in for an ABE interview?' Tom asked.

'You know how that one goes,' DS Willmott replied. 'A six-year-old kid, who's lost her best friend? It's a can of worms opened.'

'Worth a shot, though?' Amy said.

'CPS aren't gonna run it, either way,' DS Willmott replied.

The issues surrounding interviewing Maria were complex. She was a child who had experienced a traumatic event. DS Willmott could compel her to provide evidence, but it was to be used as a tactic of last resort, given the potential for inflicting psychological trauma on her. She had decided to seek CPS guidance prior to deciding whether or not to do so, but the email she had just received had resolved the issue for her.

Andrew Wicks was to face no formal sanction for his involvement in the death of Joe Jamieson.

DS Willmott pulled the case file onto her desk and flipped it open. She had affixed a photo of Joe to the underside of the file to remind her of the life that had been lost every time she opened it. His smiling little face sent bolts of electric guilt racing through her body. She hadn't got to the bottom of what had happened. Not by a long shot. She looked from him, to the photo of Lottie, then back again. But for the grace of God went she.

And what came next? DS Willmott had been at the funeral, hiding at the back. As the investigating officer into both deaths she had been duty-bound to attend. Mike may have been the one to jump between Chris and Andrew first, but she'd been close behind. She'd witnessed at close quarters the reserves of anger that Chris held. If Mike hadn't intercepted him so quickly, God only knew what might have happened.

There were two things that she needed to do. One of them, on the phone, and the second, in person.

She took out her mobile phone and dialled Andrew's number. He answered almost immediately.

'Hello, Andrew, it's DS Willmott,' she said, her voice emotionless and reserved.

'Hiya,' he replied. She could hear his nerves jangling through his voice.

'I'll keep this short, Andrew,' she said. 'The CPS have advised that you are to face no charges in relation to Joe's death. You don't need to come back to the police station and I will be cancelling your bail notice.'

Andrew didn't say anything.

'There will be an inquest, Andrew,' she continued. 'I'll be presenting all of the evidence that I have gathered there.'

She closed her eyes and pictured Joe, scared and alone, as the sea raged around him. Her voice lowered as she opened her eyes and fixed them on the photo of Joe that sat in front of her at the front of the case file. 'I know you didn't tell me the truth, Andrew. I know something else happened out there. You've got to live with that. Just a word of warning though...'

She paused to choose her words carefully. 'The truth always comes out.'

She hung up without waiting for a response.

That was the easy job done, she thought. The next was going to be much more difficult. As she dialled Mike's number, she felt numb.

'It's bad news,' she said. 'CPS have NFA'd Joe's death. Can you come with me to tell Chris?'

'I'll be with you in half an hour,' he said.

He was in DS Willmott's office twenty-five minutes later and, as they drove from the police station, one thing occupied both of their minds.

'What are we going to tell him then?' Mike asked.

'What do you reckon?' she replied.

'God knows,' Mike said.

'He deserves to know,' DS Willmott said.

'Yeah, of course he does, but...' Mike replied. They both knew what that specific 'but' related to.

'It's all going to come out at inquest anyway,' DS Willmott said. She was staring out of the window as Mike drove along the coastal road that ran adjacent to the cliffs. Linda's cliffs. She looked out to sea. Joe's sea. It was all a mess, both on paper and in her mind. The only thing she had any clarity on was that, in Chris' shoes, she'd want to know what the CPS had said and why.

'You saw him at the funeral, Sue,' Mike said. 'How the fuck is he gonna process this, now?'

'Wouldn't you want to know?' she asked. 'I would.'

'We're not him, though,' Mike replied. 'The shit he's been through, the shit he's got coming, I mean, it'll tip him over the edge.'

'It's gonna come out at inquest,' she said.

'Fair point,' Mike replied.

'So what's better,' she asked, 'him having a pop at everyone at coroner's court, getting in the shit there, or us doing it now, controlled?'

Mike sighed, but didn't argue the toss. DS Willmott was right.

Mike knocked on the door. There was shuffling inside, before Trevor's face greeted him. They hadn't seen him since the funeral two weeks before.

'Hi, Trevor, is Chris about?' Mike asked, eyeing the older man with concern.

Trevor looked like he had taken a turn for the worse. The weight that he had gained since moving in with Chris had fallen from him, leaving him with features even more gaunt than when he had first reunited with his son.

'He's still in bed,' Trevor croaked. 'Hang on, I'll go and get him for you. Let yourselves in.'

Trevor turned around and slowly made his way upstairs, his heavy, laboured breathing indicating that each step was harder than the last. Mike and DS Willmott went into the front room and sat down on the sofa. A stale aroma greeted them, the type that normally follows a night on the tiles, and it certainly hadn't come from the older man.

Clumping footsteps on the floorboards above suggested movement, and, within a few minutes, Chris stumbled into the room. Every copper up and down the land was able to maintain a look of indifference in the face of alarm, but both DS Willmott was knocked for six at the man standing before her. Spiky, ungroomed stubble spread from Chris' neck to his cheeks, above which his eyes were bloodshot and with bags hanging heavily around them. His hair was wild and greasy and the grim smell of musty booze seeped from his pores. Trevor stood in the doorway, leaning uneasily against the doorframe.

'Hi, mate,' Mike said with a cheery tone, trying to rouse the Chris of old.

'You're here to tell me something, I guess?' Chris replied. Even from a distance, his breath smelt rancid.

'We are,' DS Willmott said, her voice was business-like but her features gentle. 'And it's not good news, I'm afraid, Chris. The CPS have decided to take no further action against Andrew. We tried. I tried. But they have said that it is just a tragic accident.'

Chris was breathing deeply.

'One, two, three,' he mouthed. He didn't get to ten. 'How the fuck did they decide that?' he shouted. 'They took my boy there in a fucking storm and he didn't come back. So what, they're going to get away with it? They're just going to plod along, life all normal, and that's it? What kind of shit case file did you send them, for fuck's sake?'

Conflict raged in DS Willmott's mind as she struggled to maintain a placid demeanour. Chris deserved the truth. She'd resolved in her head that he was going to get it, as well. But now? With him acting like this? Still, surely now was better than at inquest? Or was it? He was a copper. One of them. Like her. Like Mike. One of the family, a brother in blue. She had to make a decision, and quick. In front of her, a man was bending and, in a few seconds time, he was going to snap.

'There was good evidence, Chris,' she said softly. 'I thought it was, anyway. This may come as a shock to you, and I really do want you to remain calm when I tell you this. Promise me, Chris?'

Chris sat down on the sofa next to Mike. He held his head in his hands, his fingers locked together.

'Tell me,' he snarled.

DS Willmott looked at Mike before continuing. A slight nod of his head was all the endorsement she needed to continue.

Fuck it, she thought.

'Joe's DNA was found on the jacket Andrew wore into the sea,' she said, so gently that it was a voice she herself didn't recognise. 'The basic explanation from our perspective is that Andrew came into contact with Joe in the sea. Andrew has denied it throughout. When I challenged him on it, he went no comment. As I've said, this will all come out at the inquest, it's just courtesy to you as a dad, a husband and a copper that we're telling you now.'

Chris pulled his hands slowly down his face, stretching his eyes open as he did, revealing rivers of red on a canvas that should've been pure white.

'And Sophie? Maria? What did they say?' he barked.

'Sophie's account was nothing different to Andrew's,' DS Willmott said. 'Maria... Well, we haven't got a statement from her. Andrew and Sophie wouldn't allow access and now that CPS have said it was an accident I'm not going to be looking to do it, I'm afraid. I know you don't want to hear that but I want to be honest with you.'

Chris looked at DS Willmott, staring into her eyes. They burned with injustice. With outrage. Wrath was his only outlet.

'I think you've said all you need to say,' he said coldly.

He got up from the sofa and marched out of the room. They heard him stomping up the stairs and a door slam. Trevor shuffled into the front room and sat in the seat just vacated by Chris.

'He's been drinking, you know,' Trevor said. His voice was weak.

'Thought so,' said Mike. 'Could smell it. How have things been?'

'Up and down,' Trevor replied. 'No. That's a lie. There's been no up. Just all down.'

You probably heard everything that we said to him,' DS Willmott said. 'It'll be a massive shock to him, obviously. What we don't need, for his sake, is for him to create any problems with Andrew or Sophie. The process isn't over yet. We've still got the inquest where the coroner will make a ruling and we don't want to jeopardise any of that.'

'What happens at an inquest?' Trevor croaked.

'The coroner investigates deaths that are unnatural or where the circumstances are unknown,' DS Willmott replied. 'It works like a court.'

'So what can they do about it?' Trevor asked.

'I present the evidence, and they make a ruling,' DS Willmott said. 'Loads of variables, but they give a conclusion. You would've seen some of them when they make the news, the verdicts, if you like. Things like a narrative conclusion, natural causes, accidental death, unlawful killing…'

Trevor looked up as those last two words dripped from her lips. He looked hopeful, but she knew there was no chance of that.

'Just need you to keep a good eye on Chris,' Mike said.

'Please,' DS Willmott added.

'I will,' Trevor replied.

'Any problems, you just call 999. Okay?' Mike said, as he stood up from the sofa.

They walked into the hallway where, from upstairs, they heard sobbing. They let themselves out of the front door and got back into the car.

'What do you reckon?' DS Willmott asked.

'I reckon he's on the edge,' Mike replied. 'The old man hasn't got long left either. It's a mess.'

'Any ideas?' DS Willmott asked.

'I'll get Andrew's address tagged for any calls to be treated as urgent,' Mike said. 'There's not much else we can do, to be honest.'

'Do you think he'll try anything?' DS Willmott asked, her voice quieter than before.

'Honestly?' Mike replied softly. 'He's lost everything. Nothing would surprise me.'

Chapter 34

CHRIS

Thirty-six Days After

Breathe in. One. Two. Three. Four. Five. Breathe out. One.
Two. Three. Four. Five.

Ten minutes of that still wasn't enough to stop the veins
in Chris' temples from throbbing. His blood flowed so fast
that if he didn't do something about it, they might explode.

DS Willmott's words reverberated in his ears.

No further action.

I tried.

Tragic accident.

He thought of Andrew, and his heart thumped even
harder.

'You fucking coward,' he muttered. 'You total, fucking
coward.'

He'd tried to hide in plain sight behind a 'no comment'
interview, with Joe's DNA on his coat unaccounted for.

And he was going to get away with it.

Something had happened in the sea. Something had
gone on.

A tragic accident.

'Like FUCK,' he shouted, his words echoing on his bedroom walls and slapping him right back in his own ears.

In his gut he knew that DS Willmott would have led Andrew on a merry dance through his interview, tying him in knots and tripping him up with his lies. And yet...

The fucker was going to get away with it.

Around and around his mind whirred. Something had happened. Something. Some. Thing. Why go 'no comment' if there was nothing to hide? Why shield Maria from the investigation? Why not let a grieving dad, a tortured husband, have answers?

He stomped the length of his room, the floorboards beneath the carpet groaning as he pounded down on them, turning to face the photo that lay on his bed. The one that he cuddled every night as he went to sleep, and kissed every morning when he woke. His boy. His beautiful, handsome little man. And his wife. Joe's radiant, amazing mother. Both of them were now just a pile of ash, waiting to be scattered.

He'd promised them both that he'd get to the bottom of it all. He'd made a vow. A solemn, binding agreement with them. If no one else was going to get it done then he would do it himself, and his tormented mind knew just how.

He peeled off the clothes that he had been wearing for days and beat a track to the bathroom. The man in the mirror wasn't someone he recognised, but it mattered not. He had work to do. First, he had to be presentable.

He turned on the shower and the scalding water cleansed him of the grime that had accumulated since he had last washed. It was like acid rain, burning him from the outside in but, as his skin reddened in the boiling spray, it was nothing compared to the fire raging inside. Anyway, pain was good. It showed that some of his senses were still working.

A tragic accident.

He turned off the shower and, with steam rising from his body, he stood back in front of the mirror.

'Better,' he whispered to himself as he dragged a razor across his cheeks, ridding his face of the untidy bristles that looked so out of place. Now, there was a semblance of recognition when he looked up. Now, he looked a bit more like himself. A bit more human. By no means good, but better.

He retraced his footsteps back to his bedroom where he climbed into some clothes. Dark chinos and a short-sleeved shirt, and a pair of sunglasses in his pocket. Nondescript. His chinos had grown so loose that he needed to punch another hole in his belt to hold them up. He pulled out a winter coat from his wardrobe and put it in a rucksack. He'd need something thick when he got there, but it was warm out. If he wore it now, he'd draw attention to himself and that was the last thing he needed.

With soft steps, he crept onto the landing, and waited, looking at his watch. Time was on his side, but he needed his dad in the kitchen, away from the lounge. He didn't want anyone in his way, least of all his father.

'Can you chuck the kettle on, Dad,' he called down the stairs. It was a conscious effort to sound so normal, so controlled, so ordinary. In the face of what had come before, he marvelled at himself.

A tragic accident.

He heard his dad, coughing as the lounge door opened.

'Course, son,' Trevor replied. 'Tea?'

'Please,' he replied. He heard footsteps shuffling across the downstairs hallway, and the sound of the kettle being filled in the kitchen.

Bingo.

Like a coiled spring, lubricated and ready for action, Chris double-stepped down the stairs, past the lounge, across the hallway, and burst through the front door, not stopping or looking back as he bounded over the front garden, across the pavement and disappeared from sight before his dad had even had a chance to react.

As he stalked the streets, hugging tight lines against fences and hiding in the shadows like the criminals he'd chased in his previous life, a feeling of calm washed over him. He was going to find out what had happened to his boy.

Where DS Willmott had failed, he was going to succeed.

The distant wailing of sirens encouraged him to quicken his pace. His dad would have called the police, he knew that much, but he also knew where the cavalry would be heading. He didn't allow himself a smile. That'd be too much. Instead, he just continued his march under the canopy of the tree-lined streets as the sirens remained far away. They weren't getting louder. They weren't getting closer.

He pulled his sunglasses out and put them on as his destination drew closer and closer. Having seen himself in the mirror earlier, he wondered if anyone would recognise him. With each step he took, DS Willmott's words still rang loud and true in his ears.

A tragic accident.

He shook his head.

I tried.

Not hard enough.

No further action.

'Oh there will be,' he whispered.

Chapter 35

ANDREW

Thirty-six Days After

'So, that's it?' Andrew asked, holding his phone tightly to his ear.

The line had already gone dead.

'What is it?' Sophie asked.

Andrew turned to face her. She was standing at the kitchen sink, as he dropped his phone on the kitchen table where some more of those brown enveloped letters with bold writing had been scattered.

'They've decided not to prosecute me,' Andrew whispered. It was all that he had processed. DS Willmott's warning about the truth always coming out had barely registered as a range of contrasting and powerful emotions surged through him.

How could it be, he wondered, that he felt elated at the case against him being closed? In truth, he wasn't. Guilt soon overcame him, first as a trickle, then in waves. His joy at being free from further investigation was utterly overwhelmed by self-reproach. In many ways, he was escaping the punishment that he privately felt was necessary. A victory, it may have been, but a pyrrhic one at best.

Sophie nodded at him, but there wasn't a smile attached to her lips.

'Alright, love?' Andrew asked.

Again, she nodded.

'Sure?' he asked, doing his best to ignore the pain in her eyes.

'Family comes first, right?' she said.

It was Andrew's turn to nod with a hint of reservation. For several nights, he'd heard his wife creep down the stairs in the witching hour. He'd heard her muffled sobs in the lounge. He'd followed, and found her alone, her phone pressed to her ear, with Linda's voicemail on the other end. He may have been fighting demons of his own, he'd realised, but his wife was battling hers as well.

'You wanna talk about it?' Andrew asked.

'About what?' Sophie replied.

'About...' Andrew said, clutching for words. 'I dunno... Linda? Joe?'

He watched, as that pain in her eyes intensified.

'Not really,' she said.

Andrew got the hint. He'd seen her cry the tears of a lifetime over her friend. It was like that particular avenue of grief was a cul-de-sac that she wanted to visit alone, without him.

'Are we good, Soph?' he asked.

'Yeah,' she replied, turning her back on him and reaching into the sink for the dishes.

Andrew watched, as she scrubbed them until scratches began to form on their surface. Her shoulders were twitching and, as he walked over to her, she could stifle her sobs no longer.

'Soph,' he whispered, as he sidled up beside her.

'It's alright,' she said, 'I'm alright.'

He took hold of her hand, but she shook it free, wiping the bubbles from her palm on the ever-growing bump. Her fingers lingered over Baby Wicks.

'Got to dry up,' she said.

'Okay, love,' Andrew replied, walking away with his shoulders sagging.

He walked out of the house and into the garden. The outside world had been somewhere he'd avoided since the scene at the funeral. Out the back, he was safe. Out the front? No chance.

In a world where social media is king, Chris' words had spread like wildfire around Beachbrook, fanned by the wind of public opinion. All of a sudden, everyone knew where Joe's father and Linda's husband was laying the blame. To say that Andrew felt like the world was heavily against him would do an injustice to weights.

He'd avoided doing the school run. Sophie had run that particular gauntlet each day, morning and afternoon, taking shade and ignoring the whispers that, if anything, had only intensified.

Family came first. That's what they'd agreed. As he fell into a chair, and felt the gentlest of warm breezes on his cheeks, he knew that she was doing her bit. It was him who needed to step up to the plate. Each morning, he'd dreaded the postman arriving. The ink was getting bolder. Sometimes it was red. The font was getting larger. The reminders had started to bear phrases like 'final notice'. Something had to give, but his phone calls for work weren't being answered. Messages went ignored. In a community grieving the loss of two of their own, his card had been well and truly marked.

Andrew closed his eyes, remembering how he'd scurried

through the front door on the day of the funeral just a few weeks before, Chris' words replaying over and over in his head and his face screaming murder as he struggled like a wild animal to get past Mike and at him.

Fucking murderer. What else needed to be said?

ANGE!

Joe's scream echoed through Andrew's head.

ANGE, PLEASE!

He could see the waves, crashing. He could hear them. Feel them. Taste them.

ANGE, PLEASE! MARIA!

Somewhere in the house, his work phone rang. It dragged him back from the torment of his subconscious, and Joe's words disappeared into the ether. His legs trembled as he tracked the sound of his ringtone.

By the time he'd found it, previously slung aside behind the kitchen table after he'd tried in vain to find something, anything, that would cover the bills, an answerphone message had popped up on the screen.

'Message for Mr Wicks. It's Sergeant Adams. This is a courtesy call to tell you we have been to see Mr Jamieson and have told him that you aren't to face any further action in relation to the death of his son. We have no indication that anything untoward is going to happen but, after the incident at the funeral, I am advising you to call 999 if he turns up at your house or if you feel threatened in any way.' That was it. No farewell, or best wishes.

He listened to the message several times. There was no indication as to what they had said to Chris, only that he had been informed that there would be no further action taken against him.

Stumbling through the bifolds back into the garden and

272

sitting heavily on the rattan sofa, he looked around. It was always so peaceful in their garden. That gentle breeze had gone and, without a breath of wind to interrupt them, the birds sang. Andrew sat and listened to them, trying to work out what his place in the world was. Soon, though, the tweeting birds were interrupted by a soft wailing in the air. A siren. It grew louder. Somewhere, someone was in need.

It grew louder still. Closer and closer, the sirens screamed until they were deafening.

The noise suddenly stopped, but was replaced by the noise of tyres squealing as a car skidded to a halt outside the front of Andrew's house. He couldn't see it, but he knew that it was a police car, and he knew why they were there. He just wondered how they had got there before Chris.

Jumping to his feet, guided by a primal instinct that told him he needed to protect his wife, his unborn child, he ran back into the house just as the front door began to be pummelled from the other side. He opened it, and was met by two police officers.

'Is he here?' one of them asked.

'Who? Chris?' Andrew replied. He looked at Sophie and saw his own worries reflected in her face.

In the background, an unmarked vehicle screeched to a halt. Andrew watched, mouth agape as DS Willmott and Mike jumped out and ran up the pathway towards him.

'Have you heard anything at all from Chris?' Mike asked, his voice strained with urgency.

'Nothing,' Andrew replied. 'Why would I?'

Chapter 36

CHRIS

Thirty-six Days After

Those distant sirens became totally mute as Chris reached his destination. A busy, one-way street. Rows of parked cars on either side of the road. Yellow zig-zags, forbidding any stopping between 8 a.m. and 4 p.m. A hazard sign, warning that a lollipop lady operated there. Chris knew the layout well. Very, very well. He'd done the drop off and pick up enough times, after all.

It was break-time. He'd timed it to perfection. The sound of children playing, though, drove daggers through his already shattered heart. Joe used to be one of them. Hordes of kids were kicking balls of all colours and sizes. Joe would've been fending them off, saving shots from every direction, his goalposts made up of school jumpers on the concrete playground floor. Now his boy was just a memory, a footnote in the school's history.

A tragic accident.

Chris stood and watched, scanning the playground, looking for his mark. Where was she?

There she was. His eyes stopped scanning and fixed on the

little girl he'd known since birth, standing on her own, at the furthest point from him and close to the school building. In a sea of children, where innocence sprang from every single corner and sang in the words of every child who played on the playground before him, she looked lost. Alone. In a world entirely of her own. He'd not seen her since… Since.

He took the thick coat from his rucksack. School security had been beefed up nationwide following a number of high-profile incidents, and Beachbrook Primary School had been no different. In addition to automated gates controlling access to vehicular traffic, tall fences with anti-intruder spikes had been erected around the perimeter of the school. Chris knew how to breach them, though. He'd been to enough burglaries in his time to know the tricks of the trade. He pulled the heavy coat from his bag and threw it over the top of the fence, watching with smug satisfaction as it nestled in between the spikes above. He pulled himself onto that thick, snugly protective barrier that prevented his hands and legs from being sliced wide open.

He slipped over the fence with the stealth of a man on a mission, and prowled across the playground. He knew that time was of the essence. No matter how much he tried to blend in, a scene was likely to follow. It was written in the stars.

He was yards away from her. Feet away from her. Then, inches away.

Maria looked up at Chris, brown eyes wide. It wasn't the familiar face that she had known since before she could remember. But, somewhere, somehow, a flame must have been ignited inside her. Happy thoughts. Good memories. And she smiled.

She knew him, but he wasn't happy. No. He was angry. His

face spewed malice, and the rage oozing from his every sinew stripped her smile from her face in an instant.

'Hello Maria,' he hissed.

She didn't reply.

'What happened to Joe, Maria?' Chris asked.

He saw confusion in her eyes, as she tried to connect the dots.

'He's a star,' she replied quietly.

'What happened?' Chris barked.

'EXCUSE ME!' an adult voice shouted.

Chris looked around. The teacher on playground duty was running towards them, the teaching assistant ushering the other children back to the classroom.

'Tell me, Maria,' he growled. It was now or never. 'Answer me!' Chris demanded. That was it. His time was up.

'It was just an accident,' Maria whispered.

'What was!?' Chris shouted. 'What do you mean?'

His face was twitching with rage as he watched tears stain her cheeks. It was too much for her little mind to cope with. Maria screamed and lost control of her bladder. Urine began to seep down her legs.

He could hear the commotion around him, and the adult voices were getting louder.

'I'm calling the police. Get away from her!' a teacher screamed, arms outstretched across some other children.

Chris' time was up.

'Shit,' he muttered.

His chance had gone. He turned away and marched back across the tarmac, head bowed. Teachers had emerged from all corners to form a protective blanket around the children being ushered out of harm's way.

'Stop!' a teacher hollered.

'Mr… Mr Jamieson?' another asked.

'It IS!'

A collective realisation dawned on the teaching staff, as Chris broke into a gentle jog across the playground. Those strides became a sprint as, in the distance, he heard the tiniest of wailing sounds.

Twenty metres from the fence. He heard footsteps banging on the concrete behind him. An arm grabbed at him, but he shrugged it off.

Ten metres.

'STOP!'

Five metres.

A *tragic accident*.

He leapt at the fence.

No further action.

His scream was guttural. An animal, mortally wounded. He reached for his coat, still astride the top of the fence as, in his periphery, he saw teachers, male and female, big and small, old and young, converging on him.

He clung to the heavy fabric, his coat protecting his hands from getting savaged but also stopping him from finding the traction he needed to hoist himself over. He scrambled to pull himself up as those wailing sirens grew just a little bit louder.

'Will you STOP!'

A set of hands grabbed him, around the waist. Another pair locked onto his left foot, then his right.

'Mr JAMIESON! What are you doing!?'

Three teachers. Four, then five. They tugged at every part of him, yanking him down.

'Alright, alright,' he said. It was a fight he was never going to win and, anyway, that siren was beginning to cut through the air around him.

'What are you doing?' a teacher asked.

With knees digging into his back, and his arms held tightly to his sides, he forced his head up. He didn't answer. A mouthful of dirt didn't allow him to. His eyes shifted and, amongst the children being herded inside the building, he saw Maria exactly where he'd left her. A teacher stood sentry over her, while another wrapped her in a blanket.

She stared at Chris, though, and he stared right back at her.

It was just an accident.

She knew something.

A tragic accident.

'Like fuck,' he whispered to himself.

Chapter 37

ANDREW

Thirty-six Days After

'Sarge, you've got to hear this,' a police officer shouted from out in the street. DS Willmott and Mike both turned around, as the chaos turned to silence. Radios were turned up. The operator was diverting patrols to another incident.

'Control to all patrols, please respond immediately to Beachbrook Primary School. Subject has been seen at that location and is trespassing on site. No further information.'

Everyone in the house heard the call being broadcast, Andrew and Sophie included.

'MARIA!' he screamed. He ran from the house, grabbing his car keys from the shelf by the front door and joined at the back of the procession of police cars that were making their way on blue lights to the school. He didn't have emergency lights or a siren, but he kept up with them, jumping red traffic lights and speeding. He had to get to Maria and, for once, Sophie didn't protest as he pushed the car to keep pace with those ahead. Instead, she just gripped the handle above the passenger window, squeezing until the tips of her fingers were numb. It was a fear that wasn't borne of Andrew's driving.

A river of blue lights greeted Andrew and Sophie on their arrival at the school. They jumped from the car and ran towards DS Willmott who was just leaping out of one of the convoy of marked police vehicles ahead of them.

'Andrew, Sophie, over here,' she called to them. She was standing at the main entrance to the school building, not far from where Chris had confronted Maria.

'Where is she?' Andrew shouted. Tears were streaming down his cheeks and he didn't even know if Maria was safe. All he knew was that Chris had been at the school.

'She's in there,' DS Willmott said, pointing into the building.

Neither parent waited for any further explanation. They ran past DS Willmott and through the open door into the school, where they found their daughter in a side room being tended to by a range of people. Andrew elbowed his way in front of them, with Sophie gripping his arm from behind. All they cared about was Maria, and she was now in front of them, sitting on a chair.

Andrew stepped towards her and then faltered. Something had happened to her. She had a blanket wrapped around her legs. She wore an expression of abject fear that Andrew had not seen before.

'Hiya, princess,' Andrew whispered. 'Daddy's here now.'

She reached out her arms to him, and Andrew scooped her up into a tight embrace, squeezing her close. He could feel her little heart thud, thud, thudding against his chest, every beat more powerful than the last.

'Andrew, can I borrow you for a minute?' DS Willmott said, squeezing into the room behind them. Her voice, softer now, more measured so as not to alarm Maria.

'You'll have to wait,' Andrew replied gruffly. He didn't

turn to look at DS Willmott, his attention utterly focussed on the needs of his daughter.

'Meet me outside when you're ready,' DS Willmott said. 'Take your time.' She got it. If it was her girl, she'd be exactly the same.

And take his time, he did. He continued to hold his daughter until her breathing had calmed and the tension had dissipated from her tiny muscles.

'Let me take her,' Sophie whispered.

Maria looked around, Sophie's voice like a harmony in her ears and stretched her arms out to her mother.

Andrew saw the smile that Sophie was wearing, and forced one across his own face. Whatever was eating away at Sophie's guts, whatever ailed him, none of it mattered.

Family comes first.

Sophie had nailed it, and they needed to front it out for the protection of their little girl. Satisfied that Maria was safe in his wife's arms, Andrew quietly slipped out of the room to speak with DS Willmott in the corridor.

'Where is he?' Andrew asked, his voice shaking with anger.

'Chris has been arrested to prevent a breach of peace. It doesn't look like he's actually committed any criminal offences,' she replied, bracing herself for Andrew's response.

She was right.

'Nothing criminal?' he shouted. 'Have you seen my daughter?'

'Trespassing on a school site is a civil offence, Andrew,' DS Willmott said. 'He was seen talking to Maria. We don't know what about, but she wet herself.'

Andrew's breathing was laboured as the gravity of what had happened finally caught up with him.

Fucking murderer.

Chris' words reverberated in his mind.

'Steps will be taken to make sure that something like this doesn't happen again,' DS Willmott said.

Andrew was still standing close to her, chewing his lips as his senses went into overdrive, swamping his mind with a litany of emotions. Anger. Guilt. Fury. Shame. Contrition. She leaned in even closer.

'I guess he's trying to find the truth,' she said. 'Like I told you, it will come out eventually.' She spoke so quietly that Andrew barely heard her, but her words tore through him.

He stepped away. What depths would Chris sink to in order to get to the truth? If even Maria wasn't off limits, then how far would he go? He turned and walked away from DS Willmott. Her whispered words had told him all he needed to know. Unless Chris did something catastrophic, he was on his own.

'If you get any more problems, you know where we are,' she called after him. Her voice sounded reassuring, but Andrew knew that her words were hollow.

This was something that he would have to sort out himself.

Chapter 38

CHRIS

Thirty-six Days After

The ground was dry and the dust from the dirt filled his mouth. Face down on his back, pinned to the floor by teachers who were fuelled with adrenaline, he knew what was coming, and it was going to hurt.

'Over here,' one of the teachers shouted.

Chris tried to lift his head, but it was held firmly into the ground by hands that felt clammy on the back of his neck. Whoever was doing it, he almost felt sorry for. They were shaking, their fingers trembling as they applied pressure to him. He could've fought back. He could've probably forced his head up and away from them, but he didn't. This wasn't about the teachers. They were just doing their job, protecting their students. He knew that.

That he wasn't resisting didn't matter a jot. Chris put himself in the shoes of the coppers he could hear running towards him. He'd been on that side of the fence so many times before, and he knew how they were feeling. A school? An intruder? Their adrenaline would be pumping. For all they knew, it was someone trying to touch the kids.

Sure enough, the police officers took hold of an arm each and bent them behind his back. Chris lay prone, letting his body go limp so as to let them know that he wasn't going to give them any problems, but it made no odds. For all they knew, he was a nonce with a weapon, and they weren't willing to give him the benefit of the doubt.

'It's Joe Jamieson's dad,' one of the teachers said.

Chris winced as the rigid handcuffs were cracked onto his wrists, the metal cutting ribbons into his skin where they were fixed in place two notches too tightly. From his position on the floor, he forced his chin up and looked towards where Maria had been. A crowd were watching him. Teachers. Children. No Maria, though. Some of them stared at the mad man with suspicion. Others looked on with sympathy. Some knew who he was, and some were none the wiser.

'On your feet,' one of the police officers growled.

'Easy with him,' another teacher said.

Chris didn't have the chance to try to manoeuvre himself into a position where he could stand without the use of his arms. Instead, he was pulled from the ground so roughly that his shoulders nearly separated. He could feel the balls being wrenched from the sockets and scrambled to gain a footing on the turf before any lasting damage was done, breathing a sigh of relief as the police officers' grip finally moved from his biceps to the handcuffs that sat in the small of his back.

'You're nicked,' the copper said.

Chris didn't reply. He knew the score.

Beachbrook wasn't his district. It wasn't his nick. He'd worked there a few times, though. Coppers always got around, one way or another, and he knew a lot of the officers and staff who worked there. Not the arresting officer or his crewmate, though. Still, it was probably better that way. They

284

manhandled him away as other patrol cars began to arrive and, before an account had even been taken from anyone at the school, he was in the back of the police car and on his way to Beachbrook nick.

As he stood in front of the custody sergeant though, in the cell block at the police station, it was a whole other matter.

'Name?' the sergeant asked, staring at his computer. It was just another prisoner, just another cell to be filled, and he was busy enough as it was.

'Christian Jamieson,' came the reply.

The sergeant peered over his glasses.

'Chris, is that you?' he asked, squinting at him.

'Yeah, Sarge,' Chris replied.

'Shitting hell, mate,' the sergeant said. 'Barely recognised you.'

Chris looked at the sergeant. Conflict was written all over his face, but Chris nodded and winked an eye.

'It's alright, Skip,' Chris said. Again, he got it. He'd put the skipper in a position, and he didn't want to make it awkward for him.

'Circumstances of the arrest, please,' the sergeant said to the arresting officer.

'We were called to Beachbrook Primary School following reports of a trespasser on site,' the officer began. 'Upon arrival, the male here had been detained by staff at the school. Tensions were running high and he has been arrested to prevent a breach of the peace.'

The sergeant looked at Chris. 'I don't know why you were there, Chris, but you know that I've got to authorise your detention here so that we can get to the bottom of what has happened and to work out what happens next. You know all of your rights and entitlements so I won't bore you with those. How are you feeling?'

'Been better,' Chris replied, breathing deeply as the handcuffs were finally removed from his wrists, taking a fine layer of skin with them. 'I just wanted to know if she knew anything—'

'You know the score, Chris,' the sergeant said, cutting him off. 'We can't talk to you about it now. If they need anything from you then they'll interview you but you've only been arrested to prevent a breach of the peace. I'll have a chat with someone and work out what the plan is, okay?'

Chris nodded. Of course he knew. He'd said it himself often enough.

'You fancy a brew?' the sergeant asked.

'Cheers,' Chris replied, nodding once more.

He was led to a cell and, even though he'd heard the sound of the heavy, metal door slam so many times before, it sounded so much harsher from where he now stood. It was a taste of policing from the other side of the game. Waiting for him was a plastic cup, far too small to moisten his dry mouth, with steam rising from it. He took a sip, regardless, and recoiled. He'd tasted custody coffee before, but it had always been when having a chat with a colleague or on those stolen visits on nights when a movie was on the TV. Now that he was locked up, it tasted so much more bitter.

He looked around the four walls. The paint had been gouged from them as previous occupants had carved their own décor into the coop they'd found themselves locked up in. A basic metal toilet was in the corner, no toilet seat though. Nothing that could be wrenched free, that could be used as a weapon.

He could do nothing but sit and wait. Discussions were

being had about him at a senior level and behind closed doors, he reasoned. He hadn't crossed the line in committing a criminal offence. All he had done was enter a school site as a trespasser and speak with a child he knew. He'd possessed no weapons, nor had he committed any public order offences by being threatening or abusive. There had been no damage to the fence and he had not assaulted anyone. He was giving them nothing to charge him with, as had been his intention from the outset.

Time passed as he waited, but he had no point of reference to determine just how long. Time hadn't mattered since his family had gone, and he'd long since stopped wearing a watch. He tried to lie down and shut his eyes but there was no way that sleep would come. The adrenaline that had been pumping through his veins still left him with twitchy limbs and a racing heart. Besides that, his wrists were throbbing. The cuffs had drawn blood, and the dents in his skin would leave bruises that would last for days. He bore no grudges, though. They'd just been doing their job, much like he would've done if he'd been in their boots.

The echoes of a busy custody suite seeped through the cracks in the door until, finally, Chris heard some footsteps booming down the corridor before coming to a stop outside his cell door. The lock to his door clunked as metal slammed against metal. It swung open, and he saw DS Willmott standing in the doorway, accompanied by a uniformed superintendent.

'Chris, meet Superintendent Murphy,' DS Willmott said. 'She needs to speak to you about a couple of things. Boss, this is Chris.'

'Hello, ma'am,' Chris said, raising his head, eying the crowns on her shoulder and meeting her gaze.

'PC Jamieson,' Superintendent Murphy said. 'I'm from the Professional Standards Department, and I need to give you formal notice that you are suspended from duty, effective immediately. You'll understand that your behaviour today wasn't acceptable and we need to look into it fully.'

Chris nodded. That much was to be expected.

Superintendent Murphy took an age to fill out the many forms that she needed to, all of which needed to be witnessed by Chris. It didn't bother him. He didn't have anywhere else to be.

'DS Willmott has filled me in on everything that has been happening, Chris,' Superintendent Murphy said. Formalities completed, her voice softened so much it almost sounded human. 'Firstly, I'm so sorry for your loss. If you have any welfare needs, you'll still have full access to anything required. I understand that Sergeant Adams has been dealing with that. If you need anything, anything at all, then please do get in touch with him.'

'Thank you, ma'am,' Chris said. 'Would you mind if I speak to DS Willmott alone?'

'Of course,' Superintendent Murphy replied, nodding at him with a flicker of compassion, before turning around and walking out of the cell.

DS Willmott listened as the boss' footsteps echoed into the distance, before pushing the door so that only an inch of the outside world was allowed in.

'What the fuck were you thinking, Chris?' she hissed at him. 'Do you know the shitstorm you've created?'

'Well you weren't going to speak to Maria so I did,' Chris replied. 'She knows something, Sue. She's covering up for her dad.'

'She's six years old, Chris!' DS Willmott said, raising her

288

voice. 'Covering for her dad? That's fucking ridiculous. Now listen to me, and listen good. Andrew and his family are off limits for you. That means no contacting them, no accidentally bumping into them in the street, nothing. I promise you that if something like this happens again then I'll put the papers in to the court myself to get you charged with something. You scared that poor girl half to death today.'

That last sentence was a red rag to a bull.

'Half to death?' Chris shouted. 'HALF TO DEATH!? My boy is completely fucking dead and you've got the gall to spout that shit to me? How about you investigate what happened? You know, how about finding out why my boy died?'

'I'm sorry for saying that, Chris,' she said, holding her hands up. 'I really am. You need to understand that the investigation is over, though. The CPS said there isn't an offence there. It wouldn't matter what Maria said and I wouldn't be able to justify forcing her to give a statement, especially after the way she reacted to you today. It's tough to hear, but you've got to let go.'

She turned and walked out of the cell without waiting for a response, pulling the door shut with enough force for it to bounce twice before the lock engaged.

Chris held his ear to the metal grate as DS Willmott retreated towards the custody desk. He was straining to hear if anything was said as she retreated past the uniformed sergeant, but he knew that any conversations would be had behind closed doors. In his mind, he knew how it would go. There'd be the usual chat about if the breach of the peace had ended, or if it was likely to continue if he was released. There'd be a discussion about how long to hold him until they were sure there was going to be no further breach. It was usually a couple of hours, in his experience. Long enough to let things settle down, not too long that the police would worry about being sued for unlawful detention. Of course, they could present him at court the next day, to bind him over to keep the peace. That was always an option, but he knew how the optics would be. A grieving father? Sent to court for trying to find the truth? There was no way the police would go for that.

Besides, court wasn't a part of his plan, and he knew all the right things to say and do to avoid it. Even so, those couple of hours took an age to pass by, so much so that he began to wonder if they'd made that decision. Eventually, his door opened. The custody sergeant was standing in the doorway.

'Hi, Chris,' he said. 'How are you feeling?'

'Hiya,' Chris replied, staring at the floor and putting on the most contrite voice he could muster. 'Better now, thank you. I don't know what came over me earlier. Just trying to work out in my head what happened, I suppose. I really hope the girl is okay, I never meant to upset her.' Excellent words, he thought. That should work.

'I need to be sure that there are going to be no further issues, Chris,' the custody sergeant said. 'I'm trusting you on this.'

'My word is my bond,' Chris said.

The custody sergeant had heard enough and showed Chris out of the custody suite. As he did, he looked him in the eyes and shook his hand. The two men nodded at the other, the custody sergeant in sympathy and solidarity, and Chris in appreciation and respect. He was offered a lift home, but he said he'd walk. He wanted to be alone with his thoughts, to breathe some fresh air.

To contemplate what came next.

Chapter 39

ANDREW

Thirty-six Days After

Andrew stood in the doorway to Maria's bedroom, watching as his wife lay with his little girl. He dare not breathe as, finally, she went limp in Sophie's arms. The clock next to her read 8.30 p.m. It had taken ninety-four minutes of gentle parenting for Maria to drift away from the horrors that had befallen her earlier in the day to the serenading sounds of a lullaby playlist.

The lightest of purrs drifted from her lips. Andrew took a step forward, but a floorboard creaked under him. Sophie looked up, and held a finger to her lips as those snores intensified. He froze on the spot, one foot in front of the other, watching as Sophie extricated herself from Maria's grasp with maternal expertise and settled her head onto the pillow. It moulded around her, and she fell further into the slumber that had threatened never to come.

Andrew took hold of Sophie's hand as she tiptoed across the room towards him, but her fingers didn't squeeze his as he did so. He looked at her, and she beckoned him out of the room. They both stood in the doorway, looking at their little girl, listening to her humming snores. Andrew closed the door gently, waiting for a few seconds with his ear to the wood, checking that she didn't wake. She didn't.

Finally, she slept. Finally, her little mind was resting. Finally, Andrew and Sophie could talk about what had happened, free from her innocent ears.

He followed Sophie as they crept down the stairs. He'd kept a check on his emotions all day, his anger simmering under the surface while he'd kept up appearances for Maria's sake but, now that it was just the two of them, it all came spilling out.

'The fuck did he do?' he vented, shutting the lounge door behind them as Sophie paced the floor in front of him.

'I don't know,' she whispered.

Andrew's mind was whirring. What Chris had done had crossed a line in the sand.

'And they've just let him go?' Sophie asked.

Andrew nodded slowly, and he closed his eyes.

ANGE! Joe's voice hit him again, as the waves from THAT day crashed across his mind.

'Do you trust me?' he asked, opening his eyes and looking at Sophie.

'What do you mean?' she replied.

'I'm going out for a while,' Andrew said, his voice cracking with emotion but his demeanour calm and measured.

'Where to?' she asked.

Andrew looked at her, and she at him. It was obvious, he thought. She must be able to see it, just from looking at him. There was a fire raging within his body, and it was exploding out of his eyes.

'To Chris?' she said. 'You can't.'

'Like fuck I can't,' Andrew replied, pivoting his head from

side to side, trying but failing to release some of the tension that was consuming him.

'Stay here,' Sophie whispered.

'Can't, love,' he replied, lifting his head up high and then dropping it down so his chin touched his chest. 'I've got to do it.'

'Andrew,' she called, as he turned and walked from the lounge.

Standing in the doorway, he held a finger to his lips while pointing at the stairs. Sophie stood before him, wide-mouthed. In any other time, in any other situation, he'd never have dreamed of leaving her like that. Not now, though. Not after what had happened.

Family comes first.

He turned and walked out of the house, closing the door gently behind him. He hadn't a clue what he was going to do. He just knew that he had to do something.

It was a route that he'd navigated so many times before that he could do it with his eyes closed. As he arrived in Chris' road he was still unsure what he was actually going to do, yet he was surer than at any point on his drive there that it needed to be done.

As he closed his car door a fair distance from Chris' house, the air around him was so still, so silent, that the clanging of the metal catch reverberated all around him. With only the faint glow seeping from behind the curtains and blinds of the houses he passed to guide him, he relied on his wits and his senses to navigate a path along the pavement. The moon was safely tucked in for the night, hidden behind a thick layer of cloud overhead. It was one of those nights where rain was due but the air was thick with summer's throes.

Stuffy.

Humid.

Tense.

Andrew sucked in a breath, but it felt suffocating. It was the kind of weather that could fray the very best of temperaments, even without provocation. Andrew felt sick yet, still, on he marched. He was there for Maria, and he'd defend her to the death.

He stopped short of Chris' house. Downstairs, darkness. Upstairs, lights on and curtains pulled. Both Chris and Linda's cars were on the driveway. He waited for a minute, trying to work out what his opening gambit would be. In his head, nothing sounded right, but it'd come. The right words would find their way out.

He stumbled up the pathway, and came across his first dilemma: knock, or ring the bell? The doorbell struck him as being too cheery. A knock on the door sounded better, he thought. A good, loud rap of the knuckles on wood. Confident. Authoritative. He knocked four times, each strike louder than the one that came before. No response, and no sounds of movement inside. He knocked again, and heard it echo inside. No one could've missed that. Sure enough, from inside there was the sound of shuffling down the stairs, and Andrew's every hair prickled with anticipation.

The front door opened slowly, its hinges creaking in the still of the night as Andrew braced himself for what was to come. Staring at the figure standing in the doorway, he opened his mouth to speak, but no words came. It was Chris, but it wasn't. The face was like a badly aged caricature of him, the body wasting away and the voice hoarse and rough. Andrew remembered him, alright. It was the man who'd stood at Chris' side at the funeral.

'What are you doing here?' Trevor hissed.

'I need to speak to Chris.'

'You've got no right to be here, none at all,' Trevor croaked.

'Who is it, Dad?' Chris called from upstairs.

'Nothing to worry about, son,' Trevor replied. 'Just someone at the wrong house.'

'Chris, get the fuck down here!' Andrew shouted.

Silence hung in the air for a couple of seconds, and Andrew's ragged breaths stopped. He heard a door slam shut loudly upstairs and footsteps stomped across the landing. He knew what was coming. It's what he'd gone there for.

Chris launched himself down the stairs, and Andrew braced himself.

No matter what, though, he wasn't going to back down. He wasn't going to take a backward step. Not a chance. As Chris stormed out of the front door and stood directly in front of his dad, eyeball to eyeball with Andrew, their noses almost touched.

Andrew could smell Chris' breath, and it was rancid. Alcohol. A shit diet. Andrew saw the white speckles of foam that were forming on the outermost creases of Chris' mouth, a froth borne of the wild anger that ran roughshod from his wide, bloodshot eyes.

The weeks of hatred, turbulence, grief and tumult smouldered from Chris, and it singed Andrew from such close quarters. He blinked first, and stumbled backwards.

'You ever go near my daughter again—' Andrew began.

'Your daughter is still alive, you fucking prick!' Chris screamed, stopping Andrew dead in his tracks. 'You killed my boy and you fucking know it.'

Andrew knew what was coming and, as Chris threw

himself forward, wrapping his arms around his midriff and tackling him just like he had countless times on the rugby pitch, they both tumbled to the floor. Chris' fingers dug into Andrew's skin so tightly that the bruises were formed in an instant. Sitting astride his writhing torso, his legs pinned to the floor.

Andrew could do nothing. His muscle advantage didn't mean a jot. Not when compared with an erupting volcano of grief and anger.

'What about the fucking DNA!' Chris screamed, raising his right hand, his fist clenched tightly.

Andrew got in first with the jab, though. A gut shot, no less. Winded, Chris' momentum stalled and Andrew tossed him aside like a ragdoll. They both rose to their feet and, as they dusted themselves down, their eyes met once more.

'Pack it in, you two,' Trevor rasped from the doorway. His words fell on deaf ears, as they closed in on each other until they were within spitting range.

'There's nothing to fucking say about any DNA,' Andrew hissed, as he jabbed Chris' cheek with his finger. 'If you want to have it then let's go, right now.'

Groups of neighbours began congregating on the street, summoned from their homes by the burning fuse that had been lit in their neighbourhood.

'Right fucking now,' Chris spat back.

Trevor stood in the doorway, rooted to the spot and gripped by anxiety, but Andrew barely noticed him. He was zeroed in on the bloke in front of him, the one who'd made his little girl wet herself at school.

'Chris, come back inside,' Trevor rasped. His breathing was laboured.

'Nah, let's get this sorted,' Andrew said, still staring down his foe. A few drops of rain landed on his head, mixing with the beads of sweat that had formed on his skin.

Chris and Andrew circled each other on the lawn, each of them aching from a pain that was ready to explode into action.

'I'm not going to give up without knowing what happened,' Chris said, staring far beyond Andrew's eyes. 'Never.'

More rain fell, but it didn't douse the flames.

'There's. Nothing. To. Know.' Andrew said, each word deliberate, each syllable exaggerated.

'Chris, please,' Trevor begged, the stress in his voice bouncing off the two alphas.

'Oh I don't know,' Chris taunted. 'I think Maria's got something else she wants to say, don't you?'

Andrew stopped circling. His shoulders grew tense. Now, he didn't need his eyes to close to hear Joe.

ANGE!

'Maybe if you'd been there for Joe a bit more, then this wouldn't have happened,' Andrew shouted, plunging a verbal knife into Chris' heart and twisting it with every bit of spite he could muster.

'Chris,' Trevor pleaded. It was no longer stress in his voice. It was distress.

'It should've been Maria who died, you rabid CUNT!' Chris screamed.

Andrew's words had done it. It wasn't so much a red rag to a bull, more a cattle prod. The two men rushed at each other. They met head-on, throwing punches, grabbing, gouging snarling and spitting venom at each other. They fell to the floor, clinched together in combat.

Trevor could watch no more. His heart pounded as a vice

297

tightened its grip on his chest. His breathing was shallow and his steps faltering, but he couldn't just stand by while this was happening. He needed to do something. Anything. He staggered towards the scrapping men, his feet entirely out of sync with the instructions his brain was giving them, and tried to pull them apart but he just couldn't do it. He didn't have the strength. Once upon a time, he'd been the man who could've driven them apart. Not now, though. Now, he'd been living on borrowed time for long enough, and the debt was being called in.

He couldn't do any more. His chest was painful. Breathing was just too hard. He staggered backwards, gasping for air, before crashing to the floor. Lying face up, the lashing rain stung his cheeks and diluted the salt that ran from his eyes as he thought of his life, of the wasted years without Chris. To his last breath, he would grieve for the daughter-in-law and grandson who he had never met.

'Dad?' Chris cried out.

Andrew shoved Chris away from him, ready for more, but his opponent had tapped out.

'Where the fuck are you going?' Andrew snarled, struggling to channel his vision through the red mist that blinkered him so.

He stalked Chris' footsteps for two paces, until he stopped.

'Shit,' he muttered. The rain was teeming down, splashing all around them and soaking them wet through, but he didn't notice any of it. All he saw was Chris, on his knees, cradling the old man in his arms.

'Someone, get an ambulance!' Chris screamed. 'Come on, Dad,' Chris begged. 'Not now.'

Andrew watched as Chris thudded his dad's chest, and a knot formed in his throat. Should he help, he wondered?

He looked around, and crowds of neighbours had clumped together in groups and were watching him. Staring. Here and there, people held smart phones taking pictures. Videos.

'DAD!' Chris screamed as, in the far distance, Andrew heard the first siren softly wailing in the air.

'Sorry,' he whispered, far too softly for it to be heard. He looked at Chris, swallowed hard, and turned around.

And ran like he'd never run before.

Chapter 40

SOPHIE

Thirty-six Days After

She stared from her bedroom window, as the rain lashed down. It bounced off her car bonnet on the driveway, eventually forming little pools on the ground around it. The storm had come out of nowhere, the type of biblical rain that causes flash flooding up and down the country.

Headlights.

She looked on expectantly. Hopefully. Then, as the car drove past, forlornly.

'Come home,' she whispered.

Family comes first.

It did. It really, really did.

She walked into Maria's room, silently leaping over the floorboard that seemed to have begun creaking from nowhere, and kneeled over her daughter.

'Mummy loves you,' she whispered.

Though the lullabies in the background played their melodic harmonies, Maria's sleep was fractured. All it took to rouse her was Sophie's near-silent words.

'Sleep, sweetheart,' Sophie whispered.

'Can't,' Maria replied, raising her thumb to her mouth and sucking it.

Sophie climbed under the duvet, and gently pulled Maria's head into her shoulder.

'You okay, sweetheart?' she asked, running her fingers through her baby girl's silky hair.

'Mmmm,' Maria replied.

'You know what we need to do,' Sophie whispered. 'We need one of our mummy daughter days.'

Maria sat up, and her thumb dropped to her side.

'Like we used to?' she asked.

'It's not been that long,' Sophie said, pushing her worries about Andrew to one side and smiling.

'Has,' Maria replied.

Her little girl's face was just a picture of confusion, worry and angst. Sophie could've cried.

'We'll get it sorted,' she said, 'I promise. School holidays are around the corner. Our secret though, yeah, don't want Daddy intruding.'

'I can keep a secret,' Maria replied.

'I'm sure you can,' Sophie said. Downstairs, she heard the front door open, then close quietly. She breathed heavily, as a sigh of relief escaped her lips.

She kissed Maria on the head and lay with her, listening as Andrew's muffled footsteps paced the kitchen floor beneath them. It was a constant tap, tap, tapping, but it almost complemented the lullabies, the gentle beating of a drum as Maria drifted away once more.

She pulled the door shut and ghosted down the stairs. In the kitchen, she found Andrew standing in the dark and peering out of a crack in the blinds into the rainy night.

'What the hell...' she said, looking at him.

He was soaking wet and his arms were shaking, but that wasn't the worst of it. Not by a long shot.

'What's happened to your clothes?' Sophie asked, marching over to him and touching the mud and the rips that were all over him. 'Your face…' she whispered, running her finger over the scratches and bruises that were already forming. 'What the hell happened?'

'It all went wrong,' Andrew said, holding his head in his hands. Drips of rain fell from his hair onto the floor. 'I don't know what happened. We argued, then we were fighting, then his dad went over.'

'His dad?' Sophie asked.

'I saw him at the funeral,' Andrew replied, 'I only realised who he was tonight. He was shouting at us to stop and then he went down.'

Sophie could see him grasping for words to convey to her exactly what had happened, but she knew he couldn't find them.

'I think he's dead,' was all he could murmur.

'What do you mean?' Sophie asked.

'Exactly that,' Andrew replied, pacing the kitchen once more. 'He fell over and his face was… gone.'

'Jesus,' Sophie whispered.

Andrew's footsteps were constant. Hearing them while laying with Maria, they'd been almost melodic, soothing. Now, they were like a dripping tap. Unrelenting, grating on her ears.

'Will you sit down!' she muttered.

Andrew obliged without argument, sitting heavily on one of the chairs at the kitchen table.

Sophie looked at him, as her oft thought words of recent days once again swam through her mind.

Family comes first.

'Go and get out of those clothes,' she said, 'and get a bath on.'

It wasn't shell-shock that she could see on his face, more cavernous shock. Again, he took instruction without question.

'And quietly,' she said, as he trudged from the kitchen. There was no refrain, none of the usual 'I know, I know' that she would've expected him to come back with. This one ran deep.

As she listened to him moving around upstairs, she flicked the kettle on and got ready to make two cups of tea. It was all the stuff she was expected to do, the dutiful wife looking after her husband in times of strife as he would for her if roles were reversed. And yet… And yet what, she wondered? She didn't know.

She walked into the hallway with a steaming mug in each hand and looked at herself in the mirror.

'Shit,' she muttered, as her hand twitched and a drip of hot tea fell onto her maternity leggings, right over where Baby Wicks was laying. 'Sorry, love,' she whispered to her bump.

Again, she looked in the mirror, before looking upstairs and back at herself once more. Her mind was playing cartwheels with her emotions. She was still navigating her own, private burdens. Andrew. Joe. Linda. How to make head or tail of it all, to resolve everything in her own mind?

Now, this. In the before, Andrew had always been her rock. Now? She barely recognised him.

She didn't know what was going to follow. Was there about to be a knock on the door, some police officers arriving to cart Andrew off? And would they even knock? Or would they smash the door from its hinges, as they swarmed the house looking for him? And how long would they take him for? What would she do? And Maria? Baby Wicks? How would they cope? How would they survive? Money? It was a hogwash of unanswered questions that spun around and around in her head until she could look in the mirror no longer.

She shook her head, trying but failing to dispel the demons that were gathering, and traipsed upstairs to where her little girl slept and her husband bathed, all while cradling the ever-growing bump.

Chapter 41

CHRIS

Thirty-six Days After

Chris sat in the back of a police car, plastered in mud. Where before it had been bedlam in his street, there was now just a melancholy gloom.

The ambulance had been, scooped Trevor up, and gone. Chris had watched the paramedics work on his dad. He knew the little gestures to look for. The almost imperceptible shaking of a head, the decrease in effort with CPR, the sense of going through the motions just so they could say that they had tried everything. Hope had gone, and he hadn't even been able to be by his side, to hold his hand, to stroke his forehead and clear the rain from his eyes.

'So what happened?' a police officer asked.

In the background, Chris could see various coppers knocking on doors up and down the road. From the grim look on their faces as they walked down each and every driveway, he knew that they were coming up empty in their search for witnesses. No one liked a grass, particularly in a close-knit neighbourhood.

'My dad fell,' he said quietly. He recognised the police

305

officer, but didn't know him well. 'You know who I am, don't you?'

'Yeah I do,' the police officer replied, his voice softening as he spoke. 'Tell me what happened, we might be able to help out.'

Chris thought long and hard about what he was willing to say. From a purely legal perspective, he'd done something he'd vowed not to. He'd committed a crime. Fighting in public? An affray, and it was something that he'd sent plenty of people to court for over the years. He'd been so bloody careful when he'd been at the school to minimise his chances of landing up in court. That had all gone up in smoke, potentially.

Stalling for time was his best option, but time wasn't something that he had a lot of. He just needed to be out of handcuffs and by his dad's side, and every second was of the essence.

'My sergeant has been helping me a lot through all this,' he said. 'Do you think you might be able to get him here? It's Sergeant Mike Adams.'

'I'll see what I can do,' the police officer said, nodding at Chris.

Mike arrived half an hour later, dressed in jeans and a t-shirt. He walked into Chris' house then emerged about five minutes later. Chris saw him talking with the police officer whose handcuffs he was still wearing behind his back, but – from inside the police car – couldn't hear what was being said. Mike's gesturing hands and animated arms didn't give him many clues about which side of the fence he fell on. Mike eventually stomped over to the police car and opened the door. He had a face like thunder, although Chris didn't know where the storm clouds were heading.

'Why is he still wearing bracelets?' Mike barked at the police officer. 'Get them off him, now,' he instructed.

The police officer fumbled for his handcuff key as Chris bent forward slightly to present his hands for extrication. His hands were free, and with the wounds of earlier in the day reopened, lightning rods of pain flooded up his arms. Being roughly handcuffed twice in one day hurt, a lot.

'I'll deal with this from here,' Mike said, ushering Chris towards his front door. They both entered the house and Mike closed the front door behind them.

'In there,' Mike said.

Chris walked in and saw DS Willmott sitting on the sofa. He hadn't seen her arrive, but she let him know she was very much present by the look on her face.

'Sit down,' she said. It was an instruction, not a request, and Chris complied without questioning it.

'Listen, I—'

'No, you listen, Chris,' she began. 'Before we start, you're going to tell me the truth. Mike has promised that he'll arrest you himself if you don't. You're lucky you're not in a cell already. Do you understand?'

Chris looked at the floor. 'Yeah,' he replied.

'Right then,' DS Willmott continued. 'Did Andrew come here?'

'Yeah,' Chris replied quietly. 'He came to have it out with me about what happened at the school.'

'And did you have a fight?' DS Willmott asked.

'I wouldn't call it a fight,' Chris replied, taking time to choose his words carefully. He didn't want to lie. 'Just a difference of opinion. It might've got a bit out of hand.' He didn't really care about any of that, though. Just one thing

307

was occupying his thoughts. 'Has there been any update on my dad?' he asked.

'They were still working on him a few minutes ago,' Mike said. 'I'll go and see if I can get an update.'

He got up and walked out of the house to speak to one of the patrols who were still at the scene, conducting house to house enquiries.

'That's why I'm here,' DS Willmott said to Chris. 'What happened with your dad?' she asked.

Again, Chris thought about his response before answering.

'I don't really know,' he replied. He'd been vaguely aware of his dad calling out to him and Andrew to stop, but it was peripheral noise. 'He just went down. You know he's terminal, don't you?'

'I do,' DS Willmott said. 'I think you know what I'm asking, though, Chris. Did he get in the middle of you and Andrew? Did he get a whack on the head or something?'

'No,' Chris replied.

'You know I've got to ask,' DS Willmott said.

Chris nodded. Of course he did, and he knew where it was all leading.

'He wasn't assaulted,' he said, coldly. Blankly. He knew the law.

Mike walked back into the room. Chris tried to read his face, but there was no story to tell.

'Witness says Chris' dad just went down on his own,' Mike said. 'Off the bloody record, of course.'

'Like I said,' Chris mouthed.

'Also said you guys were fighting like a couple of hoodrats,' Mike added.

Chris remained silent.

'That right?' DS Willmott asked.

'Just take me to my dad,' Chris replied, quietly.

DS Willmott stood up, and looked at Mike, beckoning him to join her in the hallway. Chris saw her eyes narrow as she turned to him.

'CID don't deal with shitty fights in the street, Chris,' she said, 'but your sergeant might want to.'

He watched as she walked out of the room, followed by Mike. They pulled the door to, but he heard what they were saying. He guessed that it was for his benefit, in any case.

'I'll write this one up,' DS Willmott said. 'Take him to see his dad. You've got to tell him, though, Mike. This isn't on... And it can't go on.'

'I'm on it,' Mike replied.

And on it, Mike was. As Chris sat in the passenger seat, gently rubbing his wrists and wincing in pain, his sergeant let him have it with both barrels.

'You know you should be in a cell right now, don't you?' he growled. 'This is the last straw, Chris. I promise you that if something like this happens again, I won't be there to bail you out. Honestly, mate, I'm there for you, but you've got to remember that I'm a copper, first and foremost.'

His words were like white noise to Chris. He heard them, but he didn't listen. In one ear, and straight out of the other. Instead, two things were racing through his mind. First, his dad. He had to get to him. He had to be by his side, to speak to him, to be there for him. That need was all-consuming.

And secondly, Andrew.

He was the architect of all this. It was him who had turned up on his doorstep. It was him who had poked the bear. It was him who had set in motion the chain of events that had led to his dad's collapse. Sure, the law might not say it was his fault, but that was irrelevant. Redundant. Horse shit.

Andrew.

Directly responsible for Joe's death. That, in turn, causing Linda's suicide.

Andrew. He'd decimated his family.

Andrew. Andrew. Andrew. It rang through his head until he could hear and think of nothing else.

'We're here,' Mike said.

Chris didn't respond. External noise had been shut out while Andrew plagued his every thought.

'Chris?' Mike said, louder now.

He gently bumped Chris' arm with his elbow, jolting his passenger back into the present. Chris looked out of the window and saw the familiar surroundings of A&E. He shook his head, trying to dispel the silhouettes of Andrew that pirouetted in every corner of his subconscious, and to focus on what really mattered. Where he really wanted to be. Who he really wanted to concentrate all his efforts on. His dad was in there and, whether he was gravely ill or sitting up in bed joking, he needed to be with him.

They made their way inside and Mike went to speak with the receptionist while Chris stood in the waiting room.

'Through here, Chris,' Mike called out to him, gesturing towards the side door. Chris stopped and stared at the door, his mind rushing back to the last time he'd crossed that particular threshold. It had been weeks before when he had been searching for answers about Joe. A grim sense of déjà vu swept over him as he barged his way into the inner sanctum of the A&E department, where he was directed to the family room. He had been in there countless times before through work. It wasn't a good sign. He knew why people were sent there. It was the room of a thousand shattered families.

'The doctor will be in soon,' Mike said more than once, as they waited for news.

Chris wasn't in the mood to talk. Eventually, a doctor came into the room. With arms by her side, and a face that exuded the calm confidence of a doctor who had been there, seen it and done it, Chris couldn't help but notice a few spots of blood on the thigh of her scrubs. He looked further, and his eyes found a bit of mud under her fingernails. Her sleeves were damp, a mix of sweat and Trevor's wet body. She'd clearly tried her best. Her voice was rational, composed even, but she only managed a few words.

'I'm really sorry, we tried everything we could…' was all that Chris needed to hear, although he hadn't really needed to hear them at all. Her face had told him all that he needed to know. He turned around and left the room, snaking his way through the web of A&E corridors until he reached the exit, with Mike in quick pursuit.

'I'm really sorry, pal,' Mike said. He had nothing else to say. Words were pointless.

'Take me home, please,' Chris said quietly. He had felt grief at the loss of Joe. He had felt tormented at the loss of Linda. Now, he felt something altogether more insidious at the loss of his dad.

Everything that had been good in his life had been taken from him. Ripped from his grasp. Stolen. From the highs of life, he had plummeted to the bowels of death, and that couldn't go unanswered. No way. No chance. Over his dead body, would it.

Chapter 42

ANDREW

Sixty-five Days After

Andrew expected a van-load of coppers to pound at his door, but they never came. He expected a call from DS Willmott, inviting him in for a quick 'chat', but the phone never rang. He expected something, anything, but nothing happened. Google had informed him that having a fight in public was actually something quite serious. Something you could end up in court for. Something that, occasionally, people did time for.

Still, the knock on the door didn't materialise. Still, the phone remained silent. And yet, as much as he tried to put it out of his mind, Joe's voice still haunted him. Linda's presence still stalked him. Put it out of his mind? Thoughts of time healing? They were always there – and time, it marched on relentlessly.

'Alright, love?' Andrew asked, as he walked into the kitchen.

He walked over to Sophie, and rubbed his hand on her tummy. 'And how are you, Little Legs?' he asked, talking to h___ _lly.

'I'm alright, Daddy,' Maria said, staring at her cereal while she ate at the kitchen table.

It may have been weary, but it was still a smile that crossed his face. Maria was getting there. Slowly, but surely, she was on the mend.

As Sophie moved away from him, though, his smile dropped. He knew this was hard for her. No. You say something is hard for a child when their hamster has died. She'd told him everything was fine, but he knew his wife. Or, at least, he thought he did. She was keeping up appearances. Of that much, he was sure. But what was going through her mind, her heart, he didn't have a clue. It was as if she'd bolted everything that happened away in a little box, hiding it in the shadows while she searched for the light.

'Upstairs to get ready,' she said, kissing Maria on the head. Andrew watched as she walked past their daughter and tugged at the sleeves of her pyjamas. They were getting too small for the growing girl who filled them.

'Okay, Mummy,' Maria replied.

Andrew and Sophie looked at each other. At least when it came to matters surrounding Maria, they were in lockstep with each other, he thought.

Her regression to the innocence of childhood had endured as the weeks had passed by. Was it a side effect, Andrew had wondered, a retreat to a younger time in her mind? What would psychologists have said? Sophie had suggested a doctor, just to be on the safe side, but he'd resisted.

He didn't want her remembering a thing.

'You feeling alright, princess?' Andrew asked.

'Yes, Daddy,' Maria replied, as she scooted out of the kitchen and up the stairs.

Maria had gone back to school with no obvious issues.

It was like she had never been away, and she appeared to be suffering no ill effects from Chris' intrusion onto the school grounds. Security measures at the school had been ramped up and, in an effort to placate Andrew and Sophie, the headteacher had agreed that a dedicated member of staff would be responsible for monitoring Maria at a discreet distance for the foreseeable future. It had been one weight shifted from his mind, but a litany of others still remained.

The bruises on his face that Chris had inflicted may have healed but, like Sophie, the wounds within were taking a whole lot longer to mend. The recent past had been nothing but dark clouds, stretching as far as the eye could see. The black dog that had sat on his shoulders over the weeks and months was a part of his penance, and he had no inclination to do anything about it. Instead, he just let it weigh him down, with an occasional bark and the odd nip of the skin here and there. If it was self-flagellation, then so be it. It was something he felt he deserved.

It wasn't just what had come before that occupied his thoughts, though. It was what was yet to come. As Sophie disappeared from the house with Maria, the school run entirely her domain as it had been for weeks, he dealt with the post. As the days passed, and turned into weeks gone by, it was stacking up. The fonts weren't just bold, now, they were underlined too. The red ink wasn't subtle, either, it was deep and angry. Those letters barked at him, warning him that these weren't the final notices. They'd long been and gone. Now, it was time to shape up or ship out.

Andrew sat alone in the kitchen, as those little paper bombs littered the table around him. Soon, the taxman come knocking as well. He puffed his cheeks as he tried to work out what needed paying first, but they were out of money. Out of time. Something had to give, and quick.

His phone rang and, as he stared at the sea of red that dominated the table, he answered it without even looking.

'Mr Wicks?' the voice on the other end said.

'Speaking,' Andrew replied, gazing vacantly into the financial abyss that was surrounding him.

'It's Jodie from Allcroft Property Management,' the voice said. 'Are you still looking for work? I've got a client who needs quite a big job doing. They've asked for you.'

She had Andrew's full attention and, as the phone call went on, his frown turned to a smile. Finally, those bills would be paid.

'Are you able to come and quote for us, say, this afternoon?' Jodie asked.

'Of course,' Andrew replied, trying not to sound too keen. In his mind, though, he'd already quoted, had it accepted and had spent the first instalment.

Hanging the phone up, he breathed deeply, letting the news sink in and liven his senses before he composed a WhatsApp to Sophie. His wife. His beautiful wife. Was this the start, he wondered? She'd be able to stay at home still, to look after the kids. It's what she was best at, and what she loved to do. She'd half joked about doing some cash-in-hand work, but no. He was the provider, and he was going to provide again.

Family comes first.

'You're damn right,' he whispered to himself.

'Hi love, just had a phone call. Good news. Long term gig, renovation. Six months, they reckon. Then might lead to more after. Absolutely made up! Xxx'

Her reply came seconds later.

'Great, well done x'

One kiss, he thought. Progress.

The afternoon couldn't come soon enough and, as he pulled up outside the property, he couldn't help but smile.

It was a beautifully sized house, set in its own grounds, but everything about it screamed that it was unloved. Unkempt. From a builder's perspective, it was manna from heaven.

'Andrew?' Jodie asked, as he got out of his car and walked towards the front door.

'Yeah,' he nodded, shaking her hand.

'Come on in,' she said. 'There's a whole lot of work that needs quoting for.'

Chapter 43

MIKE

Sixty-seven Days After

As the weeks joined together as a month gone by, Mike's unease grew. There were only so many emails from those above him, chasing an update, that he could respond to with some kind of vague answer.

'He just needs time,' he'd said to his boss.

'I'm trying to help him,' he'd said to his even bigger boss.

'I'm trying,' he'd said to his team on so many occasions, 'I'm really, really trying.'

And he was. The trouble, though, was that there was only so much he could do before the patience of those bosses began to wear thin. The emails started to build up, from Welfare all the way through to the biggest of bosses. It may have been Chris who was in the spotlight, but it was Mike who felt the burn of the bulb.

Mike was on earlies. His sleep the night before had been broken, a product of shift working and his ever-growing concerns over Chris. Add in the stress of an impending move back to the firearms team from where he'd been promoted all those months before, and it was all getting too much for him.

They'd come looking for him, the firearms bosses. Poaching the best talent from response teams was normal for those central, sought-after roles. Under normal circumstances, he'd have been flattered. Normal times, though, these were not.

The morning briefing completed, he walked into Inspector Sullivan's office, where his boss offered him a seat.

'What's the plan then?' Inspector Sullivan asked.

'I've got to speak to him,' Mike replied, 'it's been weeks.'

'Enough to force entry?' Inspector Sullivan asked.

'More than, I reckon,' Mike replied. 'Not seen for weeks, questions over mental health, not returning phone calls, post building up inside... I've twatted doors down for much less.'

Their faces were uniformly grim. The last thing Mike wanted to do was to break Chris' door down and intrude on his grieving, but what choice did he have? Anything could have happened to Chris behind those walls. For all Mike knew, he could have... No, that wasn't something he even wanted to contemplate.

The briefing room hadn't been the same since Chris had last been there. Back then, it had been brighter. The chat had been freer. The banter had flowed. Now, though, it was just business. Crewings were given, briefing slides were flicked through and the team went about their work. Mike knew it, but he didn't have a magic pill that could boost morale. Way back when, the banter would have been about him abandoning his team, going back to the enviable role on firearms. The younger members of the relief might have even sidled up to him, asking for him to put in a good word for them. Not now, though. Not after everything that had happened. It was just business as usual, without the heart, without the soul.

'Tash, Jim,' he said, as the others filtered out, 'I need you with me first thing, off comms.'

As Mike spoke, they filled the lines of their pocket notebooks with points of law. With justifications. With the authorisation of what was to come. How it was proportionate. Why it was necessary.

Section 17, Police and Criminal Evidence Act.
Power to force entry.
Saving life and limb.
Subject: Christian JAMIESON.
Concern for welfare.

'Has it honestly come to this?' Tasha whispered, crestfallen. Mike nodded, lips pursed.

They drove the twenty-minute journey in convoy, Mike leading the way in the sergeant's car and Tasha and Jim following behind.

What would they find, Mike wondered? He'd not seen Chris since dropping him home from the hospital with his dad's death fresh on his mind. The lack of contact was understandable, perhaps expected, but it needed to be addressed. His phone rang, and he looked down. It was the firearms team governor.

'Mike, it's Jack. Got a start date for you over here. Two weeks Monday.'

As he hung up after a conversation full of faux interest, he sighed. Whatever was going on with Chris, he needed to get it sorted.

He slowly pulled into Chris' road. A few weeks before, chaos had reigned on that very street. Now, it was calm but, still, the neighbours' curtains twitched. One police car in a quiet, residential street could be passed off as general patrolling. Two police cars, in convoy? Something else was happening.

Both police cars came to a stop directly outside Chris' house. The blinds and curtains remained in the same position they had been for weeks, allowing no light in and letting no signs of life out.

'Alright, guys?' Mike asked, as they assembled on the pavement.

Tasha and Jim both nodded.

Mike led them up the path. He removed his extendable baton and rapped the butt of it on the heavy wood-panelled front door. He placed his ear to the door and heard the echoes reverberating inside. No response came. He repeated the process, only louder. Still, there was no response. He pushed open the letter box and propped it up with his baton, peering inside as light penetrated the gloom. Letters and mail cluttered the floor just the other side of the door.

'Go and get the enforcer, Jim,' he said quietly.

Jim went to his police car and returned moments later with a big, red lump of metal, shaped like a battering ram.

'Chris,' Mike called through the letter box, 'if you're in there then please open the door. We're going to force it if not.' His words weren't answered. 'Last chance,' Mike pleaded but, still, there was nothing forthcoming by way of a reply.

Mike moved out of the way and, with the flick of a hand and the nod of his head, beckoned Jim forward. The door may have been heavy, but the hinges were weak. It took just two, punishing swings from Jim with the enforcer to leave it lying on the floor, in tatters. Mike led them into the house, gently pushing the mail aside with his boots.

'Carefully, guys,' he said. 'Slow and steady wins the race.'

Mike had been dreading crossing the threshold into the

house. Any copper with a few years on the job knew that their nose would dictate what was to come. To his relief, the scent of death wasn't in the air. What was, however, was the stench of bleach and methylated spirits, to the point that it was almost overpowering. Mike pinched his nose, trying to keep the vapours from creeping inside, but it only meant that his throat burned when he breathed through his mouth. He made his way into the lounge, where the smell of cleaning products only grew stronger. Everything was clean. Every surface had been wiped once, twice, then once again. Though the light had been shut out, it presented as if in truly showroom condition. In the kitchen, the tang in the air was stronger still, as if concentrated antiseptic had been thrown on every single surface.

'Chris?' Mike called, walking back into the hallway and holding his forearms across his nose and mouth. 'It's Mike, I just need to know if you're okay.' Again, no response.

Any sign that this had once been a thriving, family home were gone. There were no stains on the carpet, no clutter of toys to trip over or pictures adorning walls. Everything was sterile. Hollow. Without soul. Mike climbed the stairs, letting his hand trail across the shiny banister, without so much as a smear or stain anywhere on it. Reaching the top of the stairs, he looked behind him. Tasha and Jim stood, poised for anything, and the three of them nodded gently at each other.

'Chris,' Mike called gently, tasting peroxide on his palette, 'it's Mike.' Once more, there was no response.

There were four doors leading into different rooms. Two were open and two were closed. Mike peered around the two open doors, finding first a bathroom that, if he didn't know better, had never been used before, and secondly, a spare bedroom with only a scrubbed carpet on the floor. A cursory check of them revealed nothing, apart from the same, intoxicating stench of something antiseptic. Mike knocked gently on one of the closed doors and then opened it slowly. The hinges were silent.

It was a world apart from the rest of the house.

A child's bedroom. Immaculate. Almost like stepping back in time, to when this specific room was full of love, laughter and life. It was Joe's room, preserved in exactly the way that Linda had left it. In there, light prevailed. Beyond that door, there was hope. It wasn't cleansed, sterile or decontaminated. Instead, it was a totally different kind of pure. Mike felt like an intruder, trespassing in a sacred shrine, and he quickly closed the door and took a step back. He wasn't there for that. He was there for Chris.

'Alright, Sarge?' Jim asked. He had joined Mike on the landing as Tasha watched on from the top of the stairs.

'Yeah, mate,' Mike replied. 'Just this one to go,' he said, pointing to the other closed door.

'Who's up there?' a voice shouted from downstairs.

The voice may have been loud and the tone harsh, but the three police officers knew immediately who it was.

'Chris, it's me,' Mike called. 'I'm here with Jim and Tash. We're coming down.'

They made their way down the stairs and, as they retraced their steps, Mike winced as he looked at the carpets underfoot. They'd been hoovered to within an inch of their existence, yet three, plodding coppers had left them covered in dirt and muck of every variety.

'Chris?' he asked.

Superficially, it was. Of course it was. He was wearing the same skin, clean-shaven and presentable, and sporting Chris' clothes. He had Chris' hair, groomed, washed, and brushed. He wore Chris' aftershave and Chris' wedding ring.

He didn't have Chris' eyes, though. The gateways to his soul had been blackened by what had befallen him and his family. He didn't have Chris' voice. Where it had once upon a time been benevolent, often kind, it was now made of gravel, as though the salty, coastal air had wreaked havoc on his vocal chords.

'What's going on?' Chris asked.

'We've been worried about you, mate,' Mike said, trying to ratchet down the tension that was building between them. 'I haven't heard from you for weeks now, I just needed to know how you're doing.'

'I'm doing fine,' Chris snapped back.

'Listen, mate, I'm worried about you,' Mike said placidly, looking beyond Chris and seeing that the back door was ajar. It had been locked when they had gone upstairs. He really didn't want to turn the situation into an argument. 'Is there anything we can do for you? How about a cup of tea or something?'

'I don't need anything,' Chris snapped.

'Mate, what's with the bleach everywhere?' Mike asked. 'It can't be good for your lungs.'

'It's clean, how Linda liked it,' Chris bit back, 'and who the fuck is anyone to say how I decide to live?'

'Alright, bud,' Mike said, 'just wanted to check in, to see you were alright.'

'I'll deal with things my own way and at my own pace,' Chris muttered. 'Now who's going to fix my door?'

Mike sighed, and held his hands up. The man who stood before him was a good one, but what could he do? Chris was alive. He was coherent. He was cognitively aware.

From a policing point of view, that was about it. On a personal level, Chris didn't want to know. That much was obvious.

'I'll get it arranged,' Mike said. 'If you need anything, you know where I am.'

'If you ain't gonna sort it, I will,' Chris said, as he stormed up the stairs.

A bedroom door slammed after a few seconds.

'Let's go, guys,' Mike said, turning to Jim and Tasha.

Both of them had tears falling down their cheeks.

It was a slow journey to Beachbrook nick, where Mike stumbled into Sue's office. He found himself barely able to tell her just how far gone Chris was.

'You're kidding,' Sue said.

Mike wasn't a crying man, but he felt close to the edge.

'Wish I was,' he replied.

'That bad?' she asked.

'Worse,' Mike said. 'It wasn't him. It wasn't… Chris. You know what I mean. Copper's nose. He's…'

They both sat in silence, and he looked at her. They may have been the same rank, but it was clear who was in charge.

'You've done your best for him,' she said, 'but it's time for Welfare to take over.'

He knew she was right. Of course she was. Procedurally, it hadn't been a hard decision. Far from it. Emotionally, though… Well, that was a whole other story. As he lifted the receiver and struck the numbers on the keypad, the dialling tone rang harshly in his ear.

'Welfare,' the voice on the other end said.

'Sergeant Adams here,' Mike replied, 'over at Havington. I need to refer one of mine to you.'

As he spoke, she never broke eye contact with him. A little

nod here. A conciliatory smile there. It was the little things, he knew, that meant the most.

'Alright?' Sue asked, as he hung up the phone.

'Not really,' he replied. 'It is what it is, though.'

No matter just how much Mike tried to take his mind away from Chris, he couldn't do it.

Pride? Maybe.

Compassion? Perhaps.

Guilt? Definitely.

Chapter 44

ANDREW

Eighty Days After

'Good day?' Sophie asked, as Andrew walked into the kitchen.

'Good day,' he replied.

He eyed the stack of letters that he'd left at the side of the kitchen table. It might take a while, but he was going to get them all sorted.

The renovation was, without cliché, the job of his dreams. As the days passed, and he got stuck into it, he realised just how much there was to do. A total facelift, he'd been instructed. Do what it takes to get it up to spec. With the promise of more work to come from the agents, he settled in. He'd got his family into a financial mess, and it was his responsibility to dig them out.

That was one part sorted. No issues on that front, anymore. What he hadn't found, though, was the means of dealing with the demons that plagued him whenever he closed his eyes, whenever he slept. When darkness came, the ghosts came to life.

ANGE!

It was usually enough to bring him back from the darkest moments of slumber, but not now.

The waves pummelled the little boy, the little girl, and him. He tried his best to tread water, but the weight of both kids sent him under. It was too much. Water filled his mouth with the salty brine that he'd tasted all those years before, and panic set in.

DADDY!

ANGE, PLEASE! MARIA, DON'T!

He woke, with a jolt, sitting up so quickly that the muscles in his back twinged. Cold beads of sweat dribbled down his forehead, dripping off his nose and dampening the duvet beneath him. He looked around, but Sophie's space in the bed was empty. For once, he hadn't heard her get up.

He crept out of the room, his feet like feathers as he glided across the landing. He knew the route to take, what floorboards to avoid. He tip-toed down the stairs, rubbing his eyes in the darkness and guided by autopilot. In the lounge, he heard movement. A rustle on the sofa. He walked in, and found Sophie staring at her phone.

'Alright, love?' he asked.

She flinched, and fumbled at the screen, trying to make Linda's face on the contact page disappear.

'It's alright,' he continued, quietly.

Sophie looked at him, then back at her phone. Her face was lit up by the screen, but her features were broken.

'It's alright, Soph,' he continued.

He watched, as she pressed Linda's phone number, then hit the speaker button.

'This number is no longer in service. Please check and try again. This number is no longer in service. Please check and try again.'

'She's gone,' Sophie whispered, as a long beeping sound followed the automated message.

Andrew sat down next to her, and took hold of the phone. He killed the screen, plunging them into a darkness that was only softened by the red, standby lights on the television and Sky box. He could hear her shaking breaths, and took hold of her hand.

'We'll get through this, love,' he whispered.

'Will we?' she replied, in a flash.

'Course we will,' he said.

He squeezed her fingers, but they lay limp in his palm.

'We've got to,' he continued, 'just got to.'

He stroked her tummy.

'Come on,' he said, standing up and giving her a gentle tug, 'let's get you upstairs. You need sleep, for you and Little Legs.'

She climbed to her feet and followed as Andrew led her upstairs. Before long, they were lying in the same space, yet facing different directions and worlds apart.

He didn't sleep. Joe had already visited him once that night, and it was more than enough for him. Instead, he lay there and listened as, eventually, Sophie fell asleep. He didn't dare move, lest he wake her. Her twitches told him that she was dreaming. What about, he wondered? Did Joe visit her, as he did him? Did Linda haunt her as well?

The load she'd been carrying wasn't just a mental thing, either. He knew that. Baby Wicks was blooming by the day, and he couldn't even begin to imagine how it was all coming to a head in her mind. Loss. Grief. Hormones. Pregnancy. She was a powder keg, waiting to explode, and he had to step up.

And so it was that, the next morning, and for the first

time since… it… had happened, Andrew began his day volunteering to do the school run. The holidays had been and gone in a flash, and a new school year had meant a new start for Maria.

'There's a chill in the air,' he said, as he wrapped Maria in a warmer coat. 'Come on, miss, we've got to get going.'

At his request, Sophie had stayed in bed. She may not have been sleeping, but she was resting. It's what she needed, he'd reasoned, a peaceful start to her day, for once free of the usual rigmarole of breakfasts and traffic.

'Let's get this show on the road, kiddo,' he said, as he opened the front door. 'Say bye to Mum.'

'Bye Mummy,' Maria shouted up the stairs.

'See you later, sweetheart,' Sophie replied.

'See you, love,' Andrew called out.

'See you,' she replied.

He closed the door, and Maria skipped towards the car, jumping in as soon as he clicked it open on his key fob. He climbed in and, as he slowly reversed off the driveway, he looked in his mirror at Maria. For a few, fleeting moments, it was gloriously normal. It was stunningly ordinary. It was how things were meant to be. Beyond then, though, he felt a sense of foreboding. He knew what was coming. The school gates, and the hushed voices that he knew would announce his welcome. The eyes, that would burn him as other parents did their darndest to fail not to stare at him. The shade, that he knew was coming his way. He'd ignored it all as best he could, but he knew the papers had said their bit. He knew that social media had slammed him. It was all a part of his penance, but now he had to run the gauntlet.

'Shit,' he said, as he stamped on his brakes, barely avoiding an oncoming car that beeped at him.

'That's a swear word,' Maria said.

Andrew looked at her in his mirror. She was smiling at him.

'Sorry,' he said.

'Swearing's bad,' she said.

'Definitely is,' he replied.

'It's alright,' she said, 'I won't tell Mummy.'

'Our secret,' Andrew said, returning her smile.

'I'm good at keeping secrets,' she said.

'That's good, princess,' he replied. He looked at her in the mirror.

'Chris said that swear word to me,' she said. 'In the playground.'

The smile vanished, and she closed her eyes. A look of fear spread across her face as Andrew signalled left and pulled over to the side of the road. He knew that look. He'd worn it on his own face enough times when thoughts of Joe came to visit him in his mind.

'Daddy…' she said, opening her eyes wide.

Andrew jumped from his seat into the back, and sat where Joe's booster seat used to be.

'It's alright, princess,' he said, cradling his little girl in his arms.

'What happened in the sea, Daddy,' she whispered. 'I can remember it.'

'Don't,' he said, taking hold of her cheeks and looking into her eyes. 'Just try to forget.'

He stroked her arm and continued to stare deep into her eyes, radiating as much calm as he could muster.

'I can't forget it, Daddy,' she said.

'Me neither,' Andrew replied, 'but it'll just have to be our secret, okay? Just me and you. And you're good at keeping secrets, aren't you?'

Maria nodded with earnest.

'Can you promise me, sweetheart?' he asked, his eyes pleading. 'Can you pinkie promise that you'll never tell anyone what happened out there?'

'Pinkie promise, Daddy,' she said, hooking her little finger around his. He could only hope that the promise would hold.

'Daddy loves you, kiddo,' he said. 'You know that, right?'

'Love you too, Daddy,' she replied.

Chapter 45

SOPHIE

Eighty Days After

As soon as Sophie heard the door shut, she was out of bed and into the bathroom. A long, warm shower couldn't wash away the fog of the night before, but it could reduce it to a haze. She watched, as drops of water tumbled down her chest before reaching a Baby Wicks barrier. Whereas before those vey drops would have just fallen to her feet, now there was a blockade in their way. To make progress, they had an obstacle to navigate.

So, too, did she.

'Not long now,' she said, stroking her belly. The kicks in her womb were getting stronger as the weeks passed by. Now, she could almost make out a footprint on the underside of her skin.

She got dressed, but even her maternity leggings were getting too tight for her. On the one hand, time was passing by at a snail's pace. On the other, it was flying. The last time she'd pulled them on, they'd been snug. Now, they were claustrophobic. Ever the problem solver, though, she pulled out a pair of scissors and made a little nick in the top of the stretchy fabric that felt so restrictive. Straight away, it relieved the pressure, like loosening a belt that was too tight.

'Mummy's still got it,' she whispered.

As she climbed into her car, Baby Wicks lay silent.

'You like a car ride, don't you?' she said.

She drove under a canopy of light cloud. It was neither too hot nor too cold, but one of those perfect days where the wind was a mere breath. She pulled her window down, and let the outside world in. As she meandered along the coastal road, driving at leisure and without urgency, she let her mind drift. To Joe. To Linda. To everything that had gone before.

But this time, she was letting them in, inviting them to a party in her head. They weren't banging down the door, unwanted intruders who had black eyes and grey souls. They were the version of mummy and son that she held in her heart, in that box that she had tried to keep locked. *They* were the ones she was dancing with in her mind.

She rolled to a stop, not ten feet from where Linda had abandoned her car one last time all those weeks before. She climbed out, still clinging to Baby Wicks as she walked towards the top of the slope that led down to the beach. She hadn't been there since that day. It felt like a lifetime ago.

Beyond her, the sea was gentle. It lapped into shore so gently that it wouldn't have woken a baby sleeping at its edge. There were no waves, no chaos, no foaming rolls. Today, the beast was dormant.

She looked down at the memorial that still lay at the top of the slope. The teddy bears had suffered from the elements, their colours dulled as nature had its way with them. The cards had lost the ink that had been inscribed inside, the rains having erased them from existence. Flowers, too, had wilted, their shelf life more than having expired. In the middle, though, was a bunch of roses. Fresh ones. Red. Just like Linda had loved. She picked one out, and held it to her nose.

The bloom infused with the salt of the sea as she inhaled, and she closed her eyes. Sweet met bitter. Life met death. Her senses were alive, as she opened her eyes and stared out to sea.

'Sorry, Joe,' she whispered.

With the rose in one hand and the other firmly attached to her tummy, she began walking with the sea on her left. It was flat for a few metres, but then the incline came.

They were the steps that Linda had trodden in her last moments.

Up, she went. Higher and higher.

'Where was it, Lin?' she asked. 'Where did you go?'

She kept walking, looking for clues, searching for anything. On and on she went until, about fifty metres along the cliff path, she stopped suddenly. She'd never seen out over the bay from there before. Something, though, told her to stay put. Something within her. Something deep.

'Was this it, Lin?' she whispered.

She looked out to sea. It was so calm, so peaceful. The wind had disappeared and there wasn't a noise to be heard anywhere. This was it. She knew it.

'Hi, Lin,' she said, clinging to the stem of the rose with a grip she didn't knew she possessed.

She closed her eyes, and a blanket of peace wrapped itself around her.

'I'm so sorry, love,' she whispered. 'Sorry for Joe. Sorry? It doesn't cut it, does it? Without another word that reaches where I want it to, that'll have to do though.'

She stroked her tummy. From one mother to another, these were the words that she needed to say, sentences that Andrew could never understand.

'Andrew told me, you know?' she continued. 'That he just couldn't save Joe. That he tried, and by God I bet he did, but he just couldn't do it. And I'm struggling with it, Lin, I'm really struggling with it. It's the kind of thing where you're the only one I can talk to about it, but I can't, and that's just not fair.'

She opened her eyes and allowed the tears to fall.

'Because you should be here still,' she cried, 'and so should Joe. And there's nothing I can do or say to change it, and it's just not fair. It's just not fair.'

She inched closer to the edge of the cliff, and peered over.

'This was it, wasn't it, love?' she said. 'This is where you went. I get it. I get why you did it. If that'd been me...'

She looked out to sea. The sun was trying to poke its head through and, as it did, the shards of a million diamonds sparkled on the surface. It was serenity. Perfection.

With the flick of an arm, she threw the rose in the air. As it fell over the cliff, she stood back from the precipice.

'I'll never forget you, Lin,' she whispered, 'or Joe. Sleep peacefully, both of you.'

She edged back down the cliff path, her centre of gravity out of kilter with Baby Wicks in tow. It wasn't a weight that had been lifted, not by any stretch of the imagination, but she'd confronted something that she knew was necessary. It was a start. That was all. Now, the day was her own.

The High Street in Beachbrook was in a state of transition. Once upon a time, it had been a place where the household names had resided. Woolworths. Our Price. HMV. Now, it was for the artisans. Indie shops, non-chain restaurants, local taphouses, and resident crafters. From the brinks of despair when all had seemed lost, the High Street had risen from the ashes.

It was a salon she'd never used before, but it looked welcoming enough.

'What do you reckon?' she asked, stroking Baby Wicks.

As she opened the door and walked in, she smiled nervously, and the nail technician smiled back. The smell of sweet perfume filled the air, and the radio played soft modern tunes in the background. Good enough, Sophie thought, as she sat down. Good enough. The talk was small as the technician set to work, just the usual chit-chat.

'Up to much today?'

'When are you due?'

It was nothing, but it was everything. An interaction with another human being, just two women together, chewing the fat with bubble-gum conversation. Sophie looked around as the nail file made light work of the jagged edges that had once been pristinely manicured, and with every passing stroke, it felt like life might be just a little bit more normal. In the mirrors on the wall beyond the technician, she could see herself and, behind her, the world passed by.

A woman, with a pram. An elderly couple, hand in hand. A couple of kids, bunking off school.

And a figure stalking the shadows on the far side of the street.

Sophie squinted as her every sense overloaded, sending shockwaves to her every extremity.

'Are you alright?' the technician asked, as something akin to rigor mortis froze Sophie's fingers solid, but no answer came.

'Love?' the technician asked, as the fingers in her care tremored.

It was him. It was Chris. And in the blink of an eye, the shade that he'd crept in was empty. He had gone.

'I'm alright,' Sophie whispered. 'Just a cramp.' She nodded down to her tummy. 'I'm alright now.'

'I feel ya,' the technician said, her eyes once more focussed on Sophie's nails and her file scraping away at the edges, 'had my first last year. Every twinge felt like she was gonna make an early entrance.'

Sophie's eyes remained fixed on the mirror, on the world outside the salon. The sun may have shone, but it was the shadows that she watched, waiting for something. Anything. The small talk in the four walls around her ran silent as her answers to those mundane questions became mumbled, one-worded ripostes. She wanted out of there, now.

'Thank you,' she said, offering two twenty-pound notes and not waiting for any change as she stood with freshly gelled, blue nails.

'You sure?' the technician asked, but Sophie had already stolen a march towards the salon door.

The jingling bell announced to the world that she was coming, and it sent a chill down her spine.

'Breathe,' she whispered, as she felt a kick from inside, 'just breathe.'

Another kick. And another. One more, and levity was nearly restored in her mind. Coincidences happen. And was this even that? They lived in the same town. At some point it would have been inevitable.

Inevitable. Same town. Inevitable. Same town. Inevitable. Same town.

The hand on her arm made her jump out of her skin.

'Love,' the technician said, 'you left your bags. Glad I caught you.'

'Thank you,' Sophie whispered. She stepped back into the salon.

As she took the carrier bags, she glanced in the mirror.

He was there, again.

Once was a coincidence. Twice wasn't. His head twitching as he chewed his gums. He was dressed as Chris always did. Denim, t-shirt. One of those old brands that they'd always joked hadn't been in fashion even back then. His hair was a bit longer than normal, but combed. He was thinner than when she'd last seen him. Of course he would be. He carried a rucksack. On the surface, nothing was out of place. But something was different. A malevolence. She'd seen it in his eyes when she'd knocked on his door with the roses all that time ago, and she saw it again now.

She took her phone out of her bag, but she had to wait for her arms to stop shaking before she could unlock it and dial Andrew's number.

'I've just seen Chris,' she said, her voice shaking. 'Can you come and get me?'

'Ten minutes,' he replied.

Eight minutes later, Andrew took hold of her hands and pulled her into a tight clinch, manoeuvring his body to accommodate her bump. Her shaky limbs only prompted him to hold her even tighter.

'Come on, love, let's get you out of here,' he said quietly.

She clung to his hand as if holding on for dear life as he led her from the shop, hugging the building line as he acted as a moving sentry for her, for Baby Wicks. They were the same shadows that Chris had been stalking, only minutes before.

And yet, while they were hiding in plain sight, Sophie couldn't shake the feeling that they were locked into cross hairs that tracked them from a distance.

Chapter 46

MIKE

One Hundred Days After

Life moved on. So too did work.

One constant in the police, Mike knew, was that nothing stayed the same forever. He'd said his goodbyes to his old team at Havington nick, having left them in the hands of a new sergeant. They'd returned to full strength, Chris' name having been scratched from the duties list and new ones added. As the weeks had drifted by, the spectre of Chris that had loomed large in every nook and cranny of Havington Police Station had slowly been exorcised. In the briefing room, the banter returned. In the offices, the gossip mill turned once more.

Mike had dwelled on his decision to leave, but it had been cemented in his mind on one of his last days when he had walked into the briefing room and seen Chris' seat occupied by one of the new guards. It had been a painful reminder of the depths he'd navigated with Chris, of the valleys he'd tried to guide him through. It had left a mark on him, and wasn't one that could be shifted with the flick of a switch.

He'd tried so hard with Chris. So hard. And as he moved on to old pastures in a new role, he couldn't help but feel that he'd failed him.

His transition onto the firearms team was about as easy as it could have been. When he'd left, he'd been one of the troops. Now, he was welcomed back into the fold as the boss, the one with stripes who made the decisions. On those units, people only left for promotion. Once you got there, you were there for life. So it was, that Mike's team was made up of the very personnel that he'd patrolled with so many times before. It was a home from home, in so many ways, and he slipped back into it like he'd never been away.

And because he was the skipper, he had free reign of the whole policing area.

Welfare may have been dealing with Chris, but it didn't mean that he wasn't going to take an unofficial interest. He got stick from the officers under his command for the number of times that he commandeered the unmarked firearms vehicle, the one that everyone wanted because it meant that they didn't get flagged down for the run-of-the-mill, everyday stuff.

'Earn your stripes,' Mike would say, 'and then you can have it.'

'Fair point,' was the general reply.

And as time drifted by, he'd sit outside Chris' house on occasion, hoping to see him emerge. Hoping to see a crack in the blinds. Hoping for... Anything. Just anything.

The cars on the driveway didn't move. Not once. He'd even left a stone on the front tyre of Chris and Linda's vehicles, yet each time he came back, those stones were still in place, untouched. An old copper's trick for sure.

And time, it marched on. No matter how many clandestine visits Mike made, everything remained exactly the same.

Blinds pulled.

House dark.

Ghosts lurking.

Chapter 47

SOPHIE

One Hundred and Twelve Days After

'Is this a good Sunday?' Sophie asked.

Maria was too busy shovelling spoonful after spoonful of chocolate ice cream into her chops to answer. Instead, it was a soft grunt that gave affirmation.

'Don't make too much of a mess,' Sophie said, laughing and reaching for Maria's cheeks with a bit of spit on a tissue.

'Mummy,' Maria said, her words muffled by a full mouth as flecks of brown goo cascaded from her lips, 'that's disgusting!'

'Never did me any harm,' Sophie replied, smiling.

Maria brushed her hand away, and Sophie rolled her eyes. Was the daughter of old emerging from the ashes of what had come before, she wondered?

'Come on, miss,' Sophie continued, 'let's go and get some bits for your little brother or sister.'

'Can I choose something?' Maria asked, wiping her face clean with the sleeve of her jacket.

'Course you can,' Sophie replied.

She took hold of her baby girl's hand as they headed

towards the High Street. It was only a hop, skip and a jump from the sea-front ice cream parlour and, though they passed the little memorial at the top of the slope that led down to the beach, Sophie didn't look over. She'd done what she needed to do and said what she needed to say all those weeks before.

Family comes first.

This was what mattered, she knew. This. Moments with Maria. Precious time, that she'd never get back. She had a baby on the way, and it was about time she prepared for it.

A full afternoon spent buying bits and pieces with her little girl, getting ready for the arrival of the next one. It was cleansing for the soul.

'How about this one?' Maria asked, holding up a pink sleepsuit.

'Yellows,' Sophie replied, 'got to be yellows.'

'She's a girl,' Maria said, stroking Sophie's tummy.

'Not knowing is all part of the fun,' Sophie replied.

Afternoon melted into evening and, as they sorted everything out into piles of what they had, and Sophie dictated for Maria to scribe what they still needed, Andrew walked in to find them.

'Jesus,' he said.

'Haven't finished yet,' Sophie replied, 'got loads more to get.'

'Bugger my wallet,' Andrew said, walking out.

Sophie smiled at Maria and ruffled her hair, her hair shining blonde under the glow of the lounge lights.

'Bed time soon, poppet,' she said. 'School in the morning.'

'Okay, Mummy,' Maria said, nestling in for a cuddle.

'Good day?' Sophie asked.

'Best ever,' Maria replied. 'Best ever EVER.'

Chapter 48

CHRIS

One Hundred and Twelve Days After

The blinds and curtains kept out the light, and that's just how Chris liked it. He'd grown used to the dark. As he walked into the lounge, a sliver of sunshine burst through the merest crack in the drapes that ran from ceiling to floor. In the blinding light, he could see dust flying through the air, polluting the room all around him. He screwed his eyes shut, feeling his way forward until he felt the thick, heavy fabric in his hands. He yanked them across each other, bringing night to daytime.

Better. It was much, much better.

He stopped on the landing and stood outside Joe's room. He pursed his lips, and opened the door. There were no creaks from the hinges. He'd seen to that. It was the one room where light was allowed, where it didn't burn him to the core, and it shone in through the window. Though the wind was blowing outside, there was no whistling through the glass. It had been another job done. Another thing ticked off.

He took his shoes off and stepped inside. Looking in front of him, he saw Linda reading. He saw Joe lying on her tummy, listening. He could hear her. He could hear Joe asking for more. More. More.

Just one more, Mummy, please.

He looked to the corner of the room, where a football lay with a pair of goalkeeping gloves. Joe's voice spoke to him again.

Please, Daddy, come on, let's go and play.

He heard himself, replying. 'Blooming football, let's get the rugby ball out.'

Joe's face was sad. He'd made his boy sad.

He closed the door and bathed in the darkness until the sun rose.

There was a fresh, autumnal dawn down over Beachbrook. It was Monday, and he hated being in and amongst the crowds. The school run, especially. Fuck that. Fuck them. He waited until mid-morning and hid behind his sunglasses as he emerged from the dark. Still he squinted. Still, it was too bright, even behind the darkest lenses that money could buy.

More supplies were needed, and he knew their routines well enough to know that he wasn't going to miss anything. Sophie's next 'appointment' wasn't until the afternoon. He had it committed to memory, after all.

It was a journey that he'd taken countless times that week as his resources ran dry time after time and, as he roamed the High Street, flitting from shop to shop, his vision was tunnelled. His focus was laser-like.

He was a man on a mission.

Chapter 49

SOPHIE

One Hundred and Thirteen Days After

She'd sat in a coffee shop sipping on a decaf latte but, in truth, it was the ambience that she'd been drinking in as much as anything else. She had just kicked back and watched the world passing her by, finding comfort in the cloak of anonymity that seemed to have settled over her shoulders since that day when she'd seen Chris. It had been a coincidence, she'd told herself over and over again until, eventually, it had stuck.

She looked at her watch, and drank the last mouthful of her drink. Other expectant mothers had been gathering on the tables around her and, with smiles all around, they filed out of the coffee shop and into the building next door.

'Hi, Sophie,' the lady with the register said, ticking her off.

'Afternoon, Sarah,' Sophie said, walking into the hall and taking a seat.

She smiled at some of the other expectant mothers, greetings that were returned. The media circus had long since left town and, though she was sure that Beachbrook wouldn't forget what had happened, she had grown to believe in people's capacity for forgiveness.

'Hiya,' she squeaked, as one of those mothers made the effort to walk over and sit next to her.

'Hi, love,' the lady said, 'I'm Josie.'

'Sophie,' she replied.

Baby Wicks booted her insides, buoyed by the jolt of adrenaline that coursed through the lining of her womb and into their veins.

'How long have you got left?' Josie asked, looking at Sophie's tummy.

'Too long,' Sophie replied, laughing. It was small talk, inane chat, mother to mother but, just like it had been in the nail salon, it was everything.

'Tell me about it,' Josie said, 'eight weeks left for me and it feels like he needs to come out, like, right now.'

'I know, I'm the same,' Sophie said.

'Do you know what you're having?' Josie asked.

'Not this time,' Sophie said shaking her head.

'Aaaaah,' Josie said, 'you're a pro at this then. How many have you got?'

'Just one,' Sophie replied. 'Maria.'

She reached for her bag to grab her phone, to show off her baby girl. As she reached in, it wasn't there. She picked the bag up and rummaged, but she came up empty.

'Shit,' she muttered.

'You alright?' Josie asked.

'What if something happens?' Sophie whispered to herself, as she poured the contents of her bag onto the table next to her.

It wasn't Baby Wicks doing cartwheels in her tummy, now. No, it was the fear of the unknown. What if something happened to Maria at school? What if she needed her mummy? What if she was crying, and they couldn't get hold of her parents? What if, what if, what if?

Her mind exploded as the gripping fear of the past few months set about her. The rational Sophie would have laughed it off, a few hours without a phone being a Godsend.

Now, though? After everything that had happened? Her phone was her lifeboat, and she was rudderless without it. She'd left it on the kitchen table, she was sure of it.

'I've got to go,' she said, jumping to her feet and running from the hall.

Chapter 50

CHRIS

One Hundred and Thirteen Days After

Normality? Routine? Lies unchallenged? How fucking dare they?

He'd watched, and waited, comforted only by the knowledge that their time was coming. Soon, it would all come to fruition.

He'd looked at the clock on the car as he waited a few streets away. Morning had just turned to afternoon and, like clockwork, he saw her car turn from their road. He followed, his eyes drawn as they always did to the 'baby on board' sticker that rode on the back window.

'Cunt,' he'd muttered to himself.

At least she was gone, though. Earlier than expected, as well. Her ante-natal class wasn't for a while yet, but it didn't matter. It just gave him a bigger window of opportunity.

Now was the time.

Now it was perfect.

In.

Done.

Time to get out, before she got home. He looked at his watch. She wasn't due for another half hour. He had time on his side.

'Fucking masterpiece,' he whispered.

Chapter 51

SOPHIE

One Hundred and Thirteen Days After

'Shit,' she shouted, as she sped home, 'shit shit shit!'

She drove faster than she knew was right, but her stomach was in knots.

She tried to regulate her breathing, but it was no use. Something inside her was broken. An internal barometer that would have informed her that this was a massively irrational overreaction, something entirely out of kilter. Hormones? No, it was something so much more intrinsic, something borne of everything that she had gone through over the months gone by.

She hadn't even checked the car before she'd sped away and, as the chimes of a text message drifted from under the passenger seat, where her phone had fallen from her bag and hidden itself on the journey to the ante-natal class, she indicated to the side of the road. She slowed to a stop and closed her eyes.

'What the hell?' she asked herself.

Tears filled her eyes as she opened them.

'What the actual hell?' she repeated, as she leaned over with great difficulty and reached for her phone.

That was it. One message from Andrew. No others, no message from the school, no warnings of bad things having happened, nothing. It was bittersweet.

And now? She'd run from the class with such gusto, there was no way she could go back. Not now. Maybe another time. Instead, she indicated back into the carriageway and crawled along the roads, homeward bound.

She found the front door unlocked.

She'd locked it, hadn't she? Of course she had. Or had she? Was her baby brain fogging her memory?

She reached for her phone, and dialled Andrew's number. Maybe he'd been home and forgotten to lock it. As she walked in and waited for Andrew to pick up, the door hinges creaked a warning that she simply couldn't decipher.

When she saw him, she dropped her phone.

'Hello, Sophie,' Chris growled.

Chapter 52

ANDREW

One Hundred and Thirteen Days After

Andrew hadn't taken the time to admire the size and scale of the property that he had been working on, nor the generously sized grounds in which it was situated. He surveyed the gardens, with various derelict outbuildings plotted about and masses of overgrown weeds and foliage. There was so much potential, all of it untapped. For a builder with vision, the possibilities were endless.

His phone vibrated in his pocket. Sophie.

'Hi, love,' he said.

On the other end, silence.

'You there?' he asked.

A mighty cracking sound vibrated in his ear. Then, in the background, a voice. Gravelly. Grim.

'Hello, Sophie.'

Andrew's blood ran cold, freezing him to the spot.

'Get out of our house,' Sophie said. Her voice quivered.

That was it. Sophie had told him where he needed to be. In a flash, he was out of the door and in his car.

Red lights? Fuck off. His phone connected to his car, and

Sophie and Chris' exchanges played out through the speakers all around him.

'What are you doing here?' she asked.

'Just a reminder,' his voice was cold. Calculated. Blood-curdling.

'Get out,' she whispered. Defiant. Brave.

'Don't think so,' he replied. Insolent. Brazen.

'CHRIS!' Andrew screamed, but he knew his voice was barely a whisper as it arrived in his house. 'GET OUT!' It was no use. Sophie didn't have him on speaker.

Impervious to the beeps of other motorists as he cut them up, barged between them and forced them out of his path, he was a man on a mission. More than once, he scraped against another car. It didn't matter, though. Nothing did.

As he screeched around the final corners, straightening them out like chicanes on a racetrack, his engine grumbled and smoked. His brakes screamed as he skidded to a halt outside his house.

The front door was ajar, and he shouldered it open.

'SOPHIE!' he shouted.

'ANDREW!' Her screams carried through the air.

He ran into the lounge where Chris stood, on the far side, stony faced and wild-eyed. Sophie was rooted to the spot, her face paralysed with fear.

'The fuck are you doing!?' Andrew barked, pulling his wife close to him.

Chris stared at them. His pupils were fixed, his glare foreboding.

'You'll see,' he muttered.

Andrew reached into his pocket, and clicked a button on his phone five times in quick succession. The mild vibrations told him it had worked. He'd read somewhere that pocket dialling the emergency services was one of their biggest time-wasters. Now, he prayed the operator didn't hang up – the phone was their lifeline.

'Get out of my FUCKING HOUSE!' he shouted.

His pocket spoke to him. The operator was talking, and he needed to reply.

'It's all gonna come out,' Chris murmured.

'You've broken into our house, Chris! This is where *the WICKS* live, not you,' Andrew shouted.

Chris' eyes narrowed.

'What are you doing?' he asked.

Andrew pulled Sophie in tighter still, and inched backwards towards the lounge door.

'Ready, love?' he whispered.

Andrew looked at Chris, who in turn stared back at him. He had one hand still wrapped around Sophie, and the other fiddling in his pocket as he tried to ensure the microphone on his mobile was transmitting as much of what was going on in the house as it could. Andrew watched as Chris looked downwards. The tip of his phone was poking out of his pocket, and he knew that Chris could see it.

Chris lurched towards them and, for the first time, Andrew caught sight of a blade glinting in the sunlight and sending reflected shards around the room.

'You mother fu—'

'HE'S GOT A KNIFE. GO!' Andrew shouted, dragging Sophie from the lounge, into the hallway and out of the front door, down the driveway and into his car where the engine was still running. Slamming the doors behind them, and locking them, Andrew's hands shook violently as he put the car into drive, and he sat, waiting.

'Go,' Sophie cried.

Andrew waited. He could hear distant sirens starting to draw closer.

'Please,' Sophie shouted. 'Drive!'

'It's alright,' Andrew replied, his eyes fixed on the front door.

'Why aren't you going?' Sophie whimpered, as those wails in the air grew stronger.

'They're coming,' Andrew whispered, pointing outside. 'He ain't getting away with this, not this fucking time.'

He braced himself for a madman to come sprinting from the front door, blade in hand, with murder on his mind. His foot touched the accelerator, and the engine revved more. He was ready to go, poised. Prepared. But over his dead fucking body was Chris going to slip out the front, unnoticed.

He reached across and felt Sophie's hand. Clammy. Trembling. Cold. He pulled down his window just an inch, to let the sirens in. To make them louder. To use their harsh tones as a comforting blanket.

The sudden shattering of glass tore through the air. It had come from their house, no doubt. It had been something substantial. Something strong. Andrew looked at Sophie, and they both knew.

'He's smashed the bifolds,' Andrew whispered.

'FRONT ROOM, CLEAR.'

The copper's shouts from inside the house carried outside to where Andrew and Sophie stood on the pavement next to a line of abandoned police cars.

'DINING ROOM, CLEAR.'

'KITCHEN... WHAT THE F... CLEAR.'

Andrew squeezed Sophie's hand, but she didn't respond to it.

'BEDROOM, CLEAR.'

The deeper they went into the house, the quieter the shouts sounded.

'KID'S BEDROOM, CLEAR.'

'BATHROOM, CLEAR.'

It was systematic, and thorough.

'HOUSE, CLEAR.'

Six police officers emerged, each of them still wielding their extendable batons and with their eyes darting in all directions. All they knew was that, somewhere, there was a madman with a blade, and they had yet to find him. One of them was wearing stripes. Andrew knew what that meant, now. She was the one in charge, the sergeant, and it was her who approached him and Sophie while speaking feverishly into her radio.

'Get patrols to the rear and fan them out,' she said, without waiting for acknowledgement. 'He's likely on foot and garden-hopping. Any update on the helicopter?'

'Negative,' came the reply. 'Helicopter already deployed elsewhere to a high-risk Misper.'

'Always the way,' she muttered.

'No sign?' Andrew asked, as she stood in front of them, his eyes pleading for an answer that he knew he wasn't going to get.

'Nope,' she replied, 'he's put a chair through your bifolds and hoofed it out back by the looks of it.'

'Fuck,' Andrew whispered.

'There's something else,' the sergeant said. 'I think you need to see it yourself.'

Now, Sophie squeezed Andrew's hand.

'Okay...' he replied, and followed as the sergeant led them back up the driveway and through the front door into their house. Their dwelling. Their tarnished family home.

'Just in there,' the sergeant said, pointing into the kitchen.

Andrew and Sophie stood in the doorway with feet like concrete, and stared. It's all they could do.

This was why Chris had been there.

Photos and newspapers, emblazoned on the back kitchen wall. Linda and Joe staring at him, their eyes cutting through his skin and scorching his soul. School photos. Family photos. Clippings and cuttings relating to their deaths. The words jumped out at him, in bold, in capitals.

DEATH. SUSPICION. LOCAL MAN. ARRESTED. VICTIMS. NEGLECT.

It was a morbid mosaic, dedicated to a departed mother and son, and it dominated every inch of the kitchen. Circular in design, it had been deliberately placed to strike fear in the hearts of Andrew and Sophie. Only months before, Joe had eaten breakfast in that very room. He'd dribbled milk down his chin onto the table in front of where his face now stared upon them from various snapshots of the past.

'Madness,' the sergeant said, shaking her head and staring directly at Andrew.

'Please can you call DS Willmott?' he asked, quietly. 'She knows all about it.'

The sergeant walked out, as Andrew and Sophie stood and took it all in.

'What the fuck?' Sophie whispered.

'Dunno, love,' Andrew muttered. 'Just don't know.'

'I've got to get out of here,' Sophie said, turning and following the sergeant out of the front door.

Andrew heard her footsteps retreating, but all he could do was stand and stare, as more and more headlines jumped out at him.

GRIEF. LOCAL ANGER. COMMUNITY DEVASTATED. TRAGEDY. DEATH. DEATH. DEATH. SUSPICION. DEATH.

And the photos. Oh, the photos. Joe, in that Arsenal kit that he seemed to live in. Joe, on the beach. Joe, in school uniform. Joe, Joe, Joe. And Linda. In her wedding dress, holding a bouquet of red roses. Linda, in her paramedic uniform, looking knackered but proud. Linda, holding baby Joe. Holding toddler Joe. Holding nursery aged Joe. Holding him on his first day of school.

He couldn't breathe. He couldn't look any longer. He turned on his heels and walked away, his feet dragging as if churning through mud. Everything felt stained, corrupted. The carpet under his feet, soiled by Chris' footsteps. The family photos in the lounge, tainted by what they had witnessed. Hell, even the air all around him, polluted by Chris having breathed it.

He burst from the front door and aerated his lungs with the autumnal breeze that blew around him. It wasn't enough to get rid of the bitter taste that had soured his palette, though. He spat a mouthful of saliva onto his driveway, rousing a look of disgust from a nearby copper.

'Sorry,' he mumbled, as he marched towards his car.

Sophie was sitting in the passenger seat, her hands planted firmly on Baby Wicks and her cheeks raw from the streaks of tears that had tracked down them. Andrew climbed into the driver's seat and shut the door. He reached for her knee and held it firmly, trying to ease her tremors.

'It's never going to go away, is it?' she asked.

What could he say? He couldn't find the words. Instead, he squeezed her leg.

'We can't go on like this,' she said.

'Police will sort it,' Andrew said.

'Will they?' Sophie asked.

'They'll have to,' he replied.

Chapter 53

MIKE

One Hundred and Thirteen Days After

'Sue?' he said. He looked around his shiny new office, with a lump in his throat as he held his phone to his ear. Any calls she'd made to him recently hadn't exactly been bearing good news.

'Mike, we've got a problem,' she said.

'Where am I going?' he asked.

'Andrew's house,' she said. 'Get on hands-free and I'll fill you in on the way.'

It was a longer journey from Central Headquarters than it would have been if he'd still been in the Havington District, but the urgency in her voice told him that blue lights and sirens were needed. He arrived about fifteen minutes after her, suitably briefed but barely believing what he'd been told. He climbed from his car, and walked towards the front driveway of Andrew and Sophie's house where DS Willmott was standing, waiting for him.

'It's…' DS Willmott began to say. 'It's…' Mike got it. She didn't have to say the words. 'I take it you've heard nothing from him since you passed him off to Welfare?' she asked.

'Nothing,' Mike replied.

'How fucked up is he?' DS Willmott asked.

Mike raised his eyebrows, but didn't answer her. He didn't need to.

'So what are you going to do about all this?' Andrew asked.

Mike looked around, as Andrew approached them from his car. He looked beyond the man with thunder on his face, and saw Sophie sitting in the passenger seat of the vehicle, staring straight ahead of her. She'd been spooked, alright.

'Got to work out what we're looking at first,' DS Willmott said.

Mike stood square on to Andrew, and saw the look on his face as he got a glimpse of the sidearm that was holstered to his hip. Andrew checked his progress up the driveway. Guns tended to do that to people.

'Come on then, let's go and see it for ourselves,' DS Willmott said. 'Sorry, Andrew, you'll have to wait here.'

Mike nodded, and followed as they walked away from him and up the driveway. Crime scene tape had been placed across the front door of the property and a police officer stood guard across the entrance, sternly guarding his scene. DS Willmott and Mike inspected the front door. No signs of forced entry, she noted in her day book. They stepped inside the house and walked into the kitchen. They stood, cemented to the exact same spot that Sophie and Andrew had found roots only an hour or so before, with their mouths agape. It was a harsh clash between photos that radiated life, and news articles that screamed death. Colourful pictures of Joe and Linda in the prime of life interspersed with bold, ravaging headlines announcing their demise. It took them a few minutes to appreciate the scale of effort that had gone into collating this and erecting it.

'Shitting hell,' Mike whispered.

'Amen,' DS Willmott murmured.

They each took baby steps towards the wall, drinking in the full extent of the macabre project that had been undertaken in that very room.

'Can we get CSI here, please,' DS Willmott said to a uniformed officer who was standing in the kitchen, writing in her pocket notebook. 'If they can't get some fingerprints or DNA off that lot then they're in the wrong job.'

'What the hell are you going to do?' Mike asked. 'I mean… Look at it.'

'Statements from Andrew and Sophie,' DS Willmott replied. 'Then… Well, you're going to have to find him I guess.'

'I'll sort out a team,' Mike said. 'Bell me when you've got an update.'

They nodded at each other, and left the property together, each of them going their own way with their own tasks to carry out.

Mike's first job was a simple one. He still had Tasha's phone number on speed dial and, even though his old team weren't due to start work for another hour or so, she answered within a couple of rings. If Chris was going to be nicked, then he was going to have some familiar faces doing the deed. They owed him that much.

'Sarge?' she said.

'Tash,' he replied, 'can you get Jim, get kitted up and meet me at Chris' house ASAP. Don't park outside, meet me on the main road into the estate. I'll fill you in when you get there.'

'Okay,' she replied quietly.

Mike was there and waiting long before Tasha and Jim arrived, and it gave him time to reflect on everything that had happened. However dispassionately he tried to, though, he just couldn't look at it through a cool, unbiased lens. Through his own eyes, he'd watched Chris descend to the pits where he'd now taken residence. Could he have done more, he wondered?

Chris had fallen apart on his watch, and he couldn't see past it. Over and over, he revisited the events of the months gone by, each wounding him in its own little way. Death by a thousand cuts? Definitely. It took his phone ringing to rouse him from his internal wranglings.

'Sue,' he said, answering the call, 'what's the plan?'

'He let himself in to their house,' she said, 'he had a key from before all this happened.'

'Okay,' Mike said.

'He had a knife as well,' she blurted out.

'Fuck's sake,' Mike sighed. 'What are we looking at?'

'Harassment as a minimum at the moment,' DS Willmott said. 'Burglary, threats to kill, affray, take your pick.'

'Okay,' he replied, as Tasha and Jim pulled up in front of him. 'I'll brief the guys and then we'll go and put his door in, I guess.'

He hung up and climbed from his car where he met his two colleagues on the roadside. He sucked his cheeks as he looked each of them in the eye. There was no banter now, no mention from Jim of Mike abandoning them for a better role, nor any dig at the skipper for having to carry a sidearm for protection.

As Mike briefed them, he watched their faces drop. None of them could quite believe how far he had fallen, and what was now to follow.

'Remember, he's still one of us,' Mike said, 'but he's gone way off the rails.'

It felt like déjà vu as Mike led Jim and Tasha to Chris' front door. They had trodden this path before, but then it had been to check on Chris' welfare. Now, they were there to put him on a one-way journey through the criminal justice system. Still, they had to do it. He had to do it. He'd sworn an oath all those years before, and Chris was now well and truly on the other side of the fence.

The curtains and blinds still hadn't moved an inch. A new front door had been installed, courtesy of Beachbrook Police, but it was cheap and flimsy. If the old one hadn't offered much resistance to the enforcer, this one looked as if the spine of a feather could make short work of it. The cars were still on the driveway. Chris must be there, Mike thought. He banged on the door with the butt of his baton. No reply came.

'Chris, we need to talk!' he shouted through the letter box, listening as his knocks echoed inside.

Again, there was no reply, as his words were swallowed up by the darkness inside. Mike stood away from the door, then turned to Jim. 'Same as before, mate,' he said quietly.

It took one, half-hearted swing and the new front door lay in shattered pieces on the floor. Mike led them as they made their way into the house. Last time, the risks posed upon entry had seemed lower. Then, it had just been a welfare check. Something in Chris' best interests. Even though they'd been there for him, he'd acted the part of the aggrieved. Now, Chris was wanted for criminal offences. The stakes had risen markedly, and Mike welcomed the cold, protective presence of his extendable metal baton that moulded around his palm.

The sterile cloak of bleaching agent that had welcomed them previously had intensified in both odour and strength. It hit all three of them like a wall as they crossed the boundary from public place into private dwelling.

'Why the bleach?' Jim whispered, stifling a cough.

'It's what Linda did,' Mike muttered, 'she always like it clean. He's just... I dunno, taken it to the nth degree.'

They searched downstairs but there was no sign of life. Nor, it seemed, was there any evidence of living. Of family. Of joy, of intimacy. As Mike walked into the lounge, and held his cuff to his mouth to prevent the vapours from burning the back of his nose, what had once been a lounge filled with the energy of existence had been reduced to a shell. The photos had gone. The canvases on the wall had been removed. Every surface was spit-and-polish shiny, but the room had no soul. It was eerie. Creepy. Spine-chilling. Mike exited as quickly as he had entered.

'Chris, if you're upstairs then come out,' Mike called. 'We're coming up.'

His feet were light as he breezed up the stairs. In his head, he counted them down. *Thirteen, twelve, eleven, ten.*

The upstairs was exactly as it had been the last time. The bathroom, seemingly unused, so pristine and sparkling. The spare room, devoid of feature or character.

Joe's bedroom door was shut and, though it pained him to break the seal between light and dark, he had a job to do. He had to clear the room, to check that Chris wasn't lurking inside. He pushed the door open. A dizzying brightness shone from the boy's room. Mike stood, mouth agog, as the haven of peace beckoned him in. It was in such stark contrast to how the rest of the house presented. Untouched. Untainted. Unpolluted by the sterilisation that everything else had been subject to. It was... Just perfect. A room, trapped in time, Joe's little haven in a house gone mad.

Mike felt a little tug of sympathy, but he put it to one side. He had to. Time had passed, and lines had been crossed. He gently shut the door, preserving what he could of what had once been.

Only one room remained unchecked. Chris' bedroom. He gestured to Jim and Tasha that he was going to enter.

'Get ready,' he mouthed.

All three of them stood, poised, with heart rates climbing as Mike quickly opened the door and pushed it with his baton.

'Chris, are you in there?' he said, his voice trembling.

Silence. Grievous silence.

His hands dropped to his side as he stood with his mouth wide open and his brain barely believing what his eyes were disclosing.

'Oh my God,' Tasha whispered next to him.

'Fuck's sake,' Jim said.

Mike pulled out his phone and dialled DS Willmott. She answered on the first ring.

'Sue, you've got to get to Chris' house,' he mumbled. 'You've got to see this.'

She arrived at Chris' house a little over fifteen minutes later and was met in the front garden by Mike, Jim and Tasha.

'So what's going on?' DS Willmott asked.

'He's not here,' Mike replied, before pausing. 'But there's something you need to see upstairs. We haven't touched anything.'

She followed Mike into the house. They both pinched

their noses as he led her upstairs, lest the dizzying aroma of bleach overtake their senses. Mike had closed all of the doors upstairs, and slowly opened the one leading into Chris' bedroom. DS Willmott stared at the scene before her.

'Fuck…' she murmured. It was all she could muster.

Not an inch of wall space had been spared. Every available surface was plastered with an array of photos, newspaper clippings, and scrawled messages. The scale of it made the assembled collection of similar items placed at Andrew and Sophie's house look like a paddleboat in an ocean.

Mike stepped into the room and DS Willmott followed, mindful of the need to preserve evidence but drawn like a magnet to the sheer volume of material present. As a shrine, it was entirely macabre. How long must it have taken Chris to assemble this? Why had he done it? They delved further into the room, taking the time to look at some of the photos. Joe as a baby. Linda on their wedding day. Holiday photos. Family photos. School photos. Blown-up newspaper clippings brought context to the photos, most of it from local media but some that the national tabloids had run in the initial, chaotic stages of the investigation, then those that had followed when Linda had taken her life. Thick, red, permanent ink stained many of the articles and photos. Words jumped out at her as, with every flit of an eye, there was something new. Something morbid. Something foreboding.

'Jesus fucking Christ,' DS Willmott whispered as her eyes scanned from floor to ceiling.

'I know,' Mike replied.

The bedroom was the manifestation of so many of the emotions that had been plaguing Chris. Grief. Anger. Pain. Fury. Wrath. Utter, total wrath.

Mike walked to the far wall, drawn by photos of a different nature. These weren't of Linda and Joe.

'Sue...' he called, unaware that she was standing behind him, looking at the same thing.

A whole portion of wall space, dedicated to photos of Andrew, Sophie and Maria. But not normal photos. These weren't from photo albums, and weren't of nice, family days out.

These were surveillance photos, taken without the knowledge or consent of the subjects, and scrawled on some of them in the same, red ink, were words that sent DS Willmott's blood cold.

MURDERER. BURN. ROT IN HELL.

And there were masses of them. Maria at school. Andrew in his car. Sophie in the High Street. Various photos of the Wicks' house, both by day and night. Images of the bedroom windows and front door. And, pinned to the plasterboard wall with a small but deadly hunting knife, a written itinerary detailing a typical day for Andrew. For Sophie. Times he left for the school run, and arrived home. Details of her attendance at ante-natal appointments. He had been stalking them, and knew to the minute how their days were structured.

'What the...?' Mike said.

'Have we got any idea where he is?' DS Willmott asked.

'No,' Mike replied. He didn't have anything else to offer, his mind running at a million miles an hour as any semblance of composure deserted him. Chris and Linda's cars were still on the driveway. He had no family in the area. He had nowhere else to go. They both walked out of the bedroom, shutting the door behind them.

'No one goes in there until Forensics have done their

thing,' DS Willmott said to Jim and Tasha, who were waiting for them at the top of the stairs. 'As of now, this is a crime scene. Everyone, out, please, and get a scene log started.'

Mike was the last out of the house and, as he looked back at the wrecked frame where the front door had once stood, he felt weak in the legs. Beyond that threshold, madness had reigned. In there, a seriously unwell, mentally unstable man had spent his days, descending into mania while plotting, planning, scheming.

His colleague.

His friend.

It was a man who knew how the police played the game. A man in the wind. A man who was too far gone.

And a man with the most serious kind of scores to settle.

Chapter 54

DS SUE WILLMOTT

One Hundred and Thirteen Days After

She was normally unflappable, entirely impervious to everything that being a copper threw at her. Not now, though.

The mid-afternoon sun shone in her eyes as she climbed from her car. Autumn may have fully established itself, but the nights hadn't fully drawn in yet. As she walked up Andrew and Sophie's driveway, she found the front door open and a copper standing just beyond the threshold. She nodded at them, then walked inside, finding Andrew holding court in the hallway.

'Andrew,' she said, nodding.

He didn't have time for small talk.

'He had a knife, and he was standing right there' he growled, pointing towards the lounge from the hallway where they were standing.

DS Willmott held her hands up.

'There's more to it than that,' she said. 'We have evidence that he's been stalking you and your family.' She leaned in closer to Andrew and lowered her voice further still. 'It's serious, Andrew. Very serious. I don't use the word obsessed lightly, but he's fixated on you all.'

'And have you found him yet?' Andrew murmured.

Her words had hit him like a ton of bricks. She got it. She understood.

'No,' DS Willmott replied. 'We don't know where he is.'

'You must have a plan though, right?' Andrew said, as his stomach grew tight. He was almost begging for DS Willmott to provide him with some comfort, a strategy to show that something – anything – could be done.

'That's what we're here to discuss,' she replied. 'I appreciate how scary this must feel, but threats of harm aren't uncommon to the police and there are a range of things that we do to deal with them. Someone from our technical team will be coming here to install a panic alarm that links directly to our control room. Until that's done, a patrol will be parked outside permanently. After it's done, your house will be a priority tasking for high visibility patrolling. In the meantime, we'll be doing everything we can to find Chris.'

'My family,' Andrew whispered, taking hold of DS Willmott's arm.

'I get it,' she replied, 'I really do.'

She'd overloaded him, and she knew it. So much information, so terrifyingly close to home.

Stalking. Obsessed. Fixation. Panic buttons. Priority tasking.

It would have hit him like a bolt out of the blue.

'Daddy,' Maria said, running up to Andrew and cuddling his leg.

'Princess,' Andrew replied, looking down at his little girl.

'Hi, Maria,' DS Willmott said, bending down and facing

her. 'How are you doing? Did you enjoy the ride home from school in the police car?'

'You're not going to take my daddy away again, are you?' Maria asked.

'Of course not,' DS Willmott replied.

She smiled, but it was a mask that concealed a growing sadness in her. There were blurred lines everywhere, and she couldn't differentiate one from the other. In Maria, she saw Lottie, much as she had in Joe.

Kids. They were all just kids. And the one standing in front of her was petrified.

She stood up, and walked to the police officer standing by the front door.

'Stay here until the tech team have been and done their bits,' she instructed, before turning to Andrew and looking him in the eye. 'We'll get this sorted,' she said, as she turned around and marched from his house.

Torn? Conflicted? DS Willmott was both, and then some. Where was the tipping point, she wondered, between what Andrew had done, and how Chris had retaliated? One thing was for sure; it was her job to see justice done – no one else's responsibility, certainly not Chris'. It had been her job from the start, and it still rang true all those weeks and months down the line. First, though, she had to find Chris.

Coppers up and down the country knew all the tools in their armoury to locate wanted people. The problem was that Chris knew all the tricks of the trade, and he knew just how they'd be trying to get hold of him. In a game of cat and mouse, the hunted was four steps ahead before the game had even begun.

DS Willmott rubbed her temples as she sat in her office

and took stock of what she needed to do next. She scribbled in her day book, logging actions and making sure that she'd covered all bases. Chris' phone was off, and hadn't shown any signs of activity for a while. He didn't use social media. His and Linda's vehicles were on his driveway and hadn't been moved. His bank cards hadn't been used in weeks. Put simply, he had vanished, and left no trace.

One thing was obvious. There was no coming back from this, and his career was over. DS Willmott sighed. That was the least of his problems. Even so, she felt a personal obligation to him. Given the circumstances, given everything that he had been through, how could she not? She'd circulated him as a wanted person, but it was as much for his own sake as for anything else.

Mike sat opposite her, both of them nursing cups of coffee that had long since lost their steam. Each of them wrestled with their own, inner reflections. Could they have done more? Could they have done things differently?

'Can we get a plain clothes patrol sitting up on Chris' house?' Mike asked. 'At least then we can see if he comes back and nick him before anything else happens.'

'Already in hand,' DS Willmott replied. 'I'm just waiting for the superintendent to sign the surveillance authority.'

They both sat in silence as day turned to dusk. Words weren't needed. It was an unmitigated disaster, and it was far from over. The sun had long disappeared over the horizon, and the dark of night was well on the way.

'Superintendent has signed the authority, Sarge,' DC Harris said as he walked into DS Willmott's office, waving a piece of paper.

'Right, let's get moving then,' DS Willmott replied. 'You're up first, Tom. One of you at the front and one of you at the back. Keep it nice and tight please, and report anything out of the ordinary.'

'On it, Skip,' Tom replied. He marched from the office, leaving DS Willmott and Mike alone once more.

Again, there was silence.

'What are we missing, Sue?' Mike asked.

It was the very question that she was asking herself, over and over. For the umpteenth time since she'd sat down at her desk, she leafed through the pages and pages of documents relating to the case. She knew them all by heart, but it didn't stop her doing it once more.

'How messed up is that?' she whispered to herself, as she looked at a picture she'd taken on her phone of the mosaic of photos from Chris' bedroom, those where he'd surveilled the Wicks family.

'What's that?' Mike asked, but DS Willmott held a finger up to him.

Her mind was ticking, as she zoomed in on each of the photos. Maria, at school. Sophie, doing the drop off. Andrew, in wholesalers. Sophie, walking into ante-natal classes. Maria, eating ice cream. Andrew, in his car. Sophie, in her car. Maria, in the back of both of their cars. Photos, recent ones, taken from the driver's seat of another car.

'Mike...' she said, trying to arrange the words in her own mind. 'You said that the cars on Chris' driveway haven't been moved for weeks?'

'Nope,' Mike replied, 'I put a stone on the front tyres weeks ago, they haven't moved. Old copper's trick.'

DS Willmott sighed.

'Trouble with old copper's tricks,' she muttered, 'is that old coppers know them.'

Mike looked at her, perplexed, as she beckoned him over and showed him the photos on her phone.

'He's mobile,' she said. 'Not in his car, maybe, but he's definitely using one.'

'But his bank cards are all clean,' Mike said. 'Haven't been used for weeks.'

'Tell me something I don't know,' DS Willmott replied.

Chapter 55

ANDREW

One Hundred and Thirteen Days After

'Where are they going?' Sophie whispered, as she watched the patrol car slowly drive away.

'DS Willmott said they'd pay passing attention or something,' Andrew said.

In his hand, he grasped the panic alarm that had been left with them by the technical installation officer. It wasn't rocket science, he'd been told. Press the big red button, and the cavalry would be en route.

'And that's it?' Sophie murmured.

Andrew nodded.

'That's it,' he replied.

'So we're on our own?'

'Go and lie down,' Andrew said, trying but failing to assert some level of control. It was all he could do. As he looked his wife up and down, the bump was like a bomb waiting to go off. The fuse had been lit, and time was ticking by.

Sophie was about to protest, but the fatigue of being so close to full term hit her in every way possible.

'You'll be alright?' she asked.

He held the panic alarm aloft, and nodded, as Sophie lumbered heavily up the stairs.

Andrew slumped into a kitchen chair, before jumping straight back to his feet as if razor blades had been affixed to the fabric under his backside. It was his house. Upstairs, it was his family. It was time to make it a fortress, to make them safe. DS Willmott's assurance that every effort was being expended to locate and arrest Chris hadn't satisfied him and, now without overt protection, Andrew felt exposed. Vulnerable. Open to attack. He rushed to the front door and double-locked it, leaving a key in from the inside lest Chris try to use his to get in, then walked around the house checking that all of the windows were secure. Finally, he locked the back door and bolted it top and bottom. No chances were being taken at all.

He sat in the kitchen looking out of the window, not able to look at the wall behind him. Though Chris' mosaic had been removed, evidence in the case that was being built against him, the mental stain that it had left behind would forever taint their family home.

Night had fallen, and darkness was all around. What was he looking for, he wondered? What would be the signs that something bad was about to happen? What was something out of the ordinary? A screech of tyres? A dog barking into the night? For someone looking for threats, they could be found anywhere. Every passing car provoked panic, every noise aggravated his senses. Chris may have been just a ghost in the black of night, but his presence loomed large.

He didn't move from his seat, a captain manning his sentry post and protecting his troops. His eyes felt heavy, but he couldn't close them. Sleeping on the job wasn't allowed, not when there was a threat to his family.

He looked at the clock on the oven. 10.38 p.m. His tour of duty had barely started.

Chapter 56

DS SUE WILLMOTT

One Hundred and Thirteen Days After

No matter how many times DS Willmott or Mike ran their fingers over every line of every document in the case file, they couldn't put together in their minds what their instincts were telling them. As the clocks ticked forward, their searching yielded yet more dead ends. Sleep? It wasn't on their radar. Not while Chris remained in the wind.

11.59 p.m. turned to midnight, and a little clock on DS Willmott's desk chimed. She looked at it, and picked up her police radio.

'DS Willmott to Amy or Tom,' she said, pressing down the transmit button as she spoke.

'Go ahead, Sarge,' Amy whispered.

'Anything there?' DS Willmott asked.

'All quiet at the mo,' Amy replied.

'Same at the front,' Tom added.

'You both okay?' DS Willmott asked.

'All good,' Amy replied.

'Same,' Tom added.

DS Willmott dropped the radio down onto her desk,

and stared at her computer screen, at the arrest package that she was compiling with Chris' face emblazoned in the centre. The bright, artificial light that glared back at her bore through her eyes and into her brain. She could feel one of those tension headaches slowly announcing its arrival.

'Alright, Sue?' Mike asked.

'Not massively,' she replied.

'Same,' Mike said.

They sat in silence, as the clock slowly ticked over. 12.01 a.m. became 12.02 a.m., and beyond.

It was going to be a long night.

Chapter 57

ANDREW

One Hundred and Fourteen Days After

Andrew woke, his eyes stinging and his mind disorientated by the screaming noise that filled his ears. He looked at the clock on the oven. It was 1.15 a.m., but he could barely make out the time through the thick fog of smoke that rode heavy in the air. The screeching sound of the smoke alarm coming from the hallway brought clarity.

Fire.

Danger.

The threat was now, and it was real.

'SOPHIE, MARIA!' he screamed.

Smoke filled his lungs, choking the life out of him. He beat his hand down on the panic alarm, before running from the kitchen with his arm raised to his mouth. In the hallway, flames licked the front door and climbed the walls all around him, beating him back with their intense, suffocating heat. The blanket of smoke was denser in the hallway, and panic made him suck more of it in. Fumes came in waves, rolling in and smothering him.

Holding his throat and beaten to his knees, he crawled

and scraped his way into the front room where he slammed the door shut. There was less smoke, but still too much, and his rasping breaths only filled his lungs with yet more deadly vapours.

He needed air. He needed the oxygen it provided. He picked up a vase from a table, tipping the dead roses from within and threw it at the window. The simultaneous shattering of glass and pottery afforded him a means of cleansing his lungs and ridding them of the poisons that had engulfed his insides. He hung his head between the broken shards, feeling one of them nick the skin of his neck and draw blood. He drank in the night air, forcing it in his mouth and down his throat as quickly as he could. A few deep breaths and a few explosive coughs were all he needed to turn around and face fire with fire. Time mattered. Every second counted. He wasn't leaving without his wife and daughter.

No doubt his panic alarm would have sent the balloon up, but there was no way anyone would get to them in time. Not with the way the fire spreading, with how the smoke was slithering all around him. He was entirely on his own. He pulled off his jumper and held it to his mouth, but all he sucked in was the fetid smoke that clung heavily to it. He pulled off his t-shirt, now naked on his top half, and used that instead. Better. Much better. Then, back into the fray.

'SOPHIE, MARIA!' he screamed as he ran back into the hallway, his words muffled from behind the fabric. The fire around the front door had intensified and was taking hold in the hallway itself. With every second that passed, the bowels of hell grew closer. With every step he took, the cloak of death loomed larger.

He tripped on one of the stairs as he bounded up them, placing his spare hand onto the banister to steady himself and feeling it singe on the gloss paint that bubbled in the heat. There was no time for pain. He had to get to his wife, his daughter, his unborn child.

'SOPHIE, MARIA!'

What had been a screeching noise downstairs was strangled by the shroud of smoke upstairs, and the alarm barely registered above Andrew's screams. Maria's door was shut and he charged through it, screaming as he did. He'd got there before the fire, but the smoke had crept in silently, its intent insidious. It was spreading without remorse, without conscience, enveloping Maria's room with its lethal toxins.

'SOPHIE, MARIA,' he repeated, choking as the smoke bit his throat with venom.

His two girls sat bolt upright in Maria's bed, shaken to consciousness by Andrew's arrival with a look of collective terror spread over their faces.

'There's a fire!' Andrew shouted, as the smoke that had clung to him billowed from his skin. 'Let's go.'

He grabbed the first thing that he could find on the floor, a towel that Sophie had used to dry Maria after a bath earlier in the evening. He wrapped it around Maria's head, covering her mouth and nose. It was still damp. Perfect. He thrust his t-shirt into Sophie's hands, gesturing for her to cover her mouth face with it, as he scooped Maria up in his arms. He didn't need a mask. He was fuelled by paternal instinct, driven by the crushing need to get his daughter out. His hands were full, and his mission simple.

'We're going NOW!' he shouted to Sophie. He could hear the lick of the flames taking hold downstairs. 'Hold on to my belt,' he called, and felt Sophie tugging at his midriff.

He took a suffocating breath in and moved quickly. The flames were engulfing the stairs, but his steps were steady, his stride deliberate. He could feel Sophie's grip loosen every time he tried to move faster, her bump slowing her down and checking her progress. If he lost her now, he doubted he'd get her back. He could feel and smell the hairs on his back fizzing as flames kissed his skin. The heat intensified on each step down the stairs until it was almost unbearable at the bottom.

Still, he fought on. His arms tightened around Maria as he willed the inferno to scald him and not her. His lungs were empty. He needed to breathe. He turned and marched quickly down the hallway away from the front door, arriving at the back of the house, setting Maria down and blindly unbolting and unlocking the back door. Sophie still clung to his belt, a passenger who had navigated hell's furnace. Andrew pulled her out first, before reaching for Maria and throwing her across the divide.

Then, it was his turn. Fresh air hit him, and he devoured it.

The wailing of sirens in the distance barely registered under the shrill blast of the alarm from inside the house. The cavalry would never have made it in time.

Andrew unwrapped Maria's towel and pulled Sophie in close to him as he embraced his family while still choking on the smoke that had ravaged him.

Behind them, ashes filled the air as their home burned.

Chapter 58

DS SUE WILLMOTT

One Hundred and Fourteen Days After

On Mike's radio, the usual calls were being broadcast. A domestic. An RTC. Then, as DS Willmott looked at the clock and wondered where the hours had gone, the radio operator came on the air once more. Her voice was different to how it had been all night to that point. Tinged with urgency. Laced with gravity.

'Control to any patrol available to attend a panic alarm activation?'

DS Willmott's eyes grew wide. She looked at Mike, and saw in his face the anxiety she felt in her own. There were a few panic alarms out there in the community, but instinct told them both exactly who had pressed the button.

'Control, further calls are coming in from multiple informants of a house fire at the location of that panic alarm.'

'Control from Sergeant Adams,' Mike barked into his radio. 'Who's the occupant at the location of the panic alarm?'

'An Andrew Wicks,' came the reply.

'Christ,' DS Willmott said, exasperated, as she jumped to her feet. She grabbed hold of her own radio and ran

386

from her desk, following Mike who had got the jump on her. They sprinted down to the rear yard where they both climbed into his unmarked firearms car.

The airwaves were alive as patrols rushed to the scene, the sirens in the air screaming and waking Beachbrook from its slumber. Mike's right foot was heavy as they screeched out of the gates, and DS Willmott fumbled for her seatbelt.

'Control from DS Willmott,' she yelled into the car radio set, seizing on a momentary lull in airwave traffic, 'is there an update on the occupants at the scene? Accounted for? Injuries?'

'Negative,' came the reply.

'Fuck's sake,' she muttered, slamming the transmitter mic back into its cradle.

She picked up her own radio, which was still tuned into the frequency that Tom and Amy were transmitting on, and spoke with urgency.

'Tom, Amy, you receiving?' she said.

'Go ahead, Sarge,' Tom whispered.

'It's all going off,' DS Willmott said. 'Fire at the Wicks'. Keep your eyes peeled and your wits about you.'

'Shit...' Amy replied.

'Christ,' Tom chimed in.

'Chris is out there, somewhere,' DS Willmott said. 'If he comes your way then just hit your emergency button.'

'Received,' Tom said.

'Got it,' Amy added.

DS Willmott dropped the radio into her lap, and looked at Mike, as he threw the car around a corner.

'He's...' she began to say.

'Gone in the head,' Mike said, finishing her sentence for her.

'Yeah,' she muttered.

As they arrived at the Wicks' house, the fire still raged as blue lights shimmered from every direction. Emergency service personnel were running from pillar to post, doing their best to restore order amidst the chaos. Crowds were gathering and being marshalled by police officers and, at the side of the road, there were two ambulances, both with doors ajar. Head bowed, DS Willmott made her way in their direction. She knew she owed the Wicks' something. An explanation, maybe? The trouble was, there wasn't a lot she could say.

She peered around the rear door of the first ambulance but found only an empty cabin. She pulled the door shut, and made her way to the second ambulance. From inside, she heard raised voices but they weren't angry, more fretful. They weren't words of fury, but bellows of concern. She pulled open the door and stood, wide-eyed, as she surveyed the scene that presented itself to her. It was a regular-sized ambulance, but was crowded with people. Maria was sitting in one of the passenger chairs with a seatbelt over her lap, looking physically unharmed but with a vacant look on her face. Andrew was standing over Sophie, who was lying on the trolley while a paramedic placed straps above and below the unborn baby in her tummy. That bump was so low that it couldn't fall much further. She was conscious but her mouth was covered by an oxygen mask. Even so, DS Willmott could see the pain beneath. She was a mother. She'd been there. She recognised it.

'What's going on?' DS Willmott said. Her voice floated in the air, but wasn't heard by anyone in the ambulance.

'Andrew?' she called, her voice louder this time.

Andrew looked in her direction. His eyes glowered.

'You call this protecting us?' he shouted, his voice laced with a special kind of potency.

'Andrew!' Sophie called from the trolley, pulling the oxygen mask away from her face to get his attention. 'It's coming, I can feel it coming.'

'Excuse me, love,' one of the paramedics said to DS Willmott. 'Can you shut the door? A bit of privacy, if you don't mind.'

'I'm a police officer,' DS Willmott said, showing her warrant card.

'I don't care if you're the chief constable,' the paramedic replied. 'If we don't get her to hospital soon then the baby will be born in here. Now move, please.'

DS Willmott held up her hands before stepping back and shutting the ambulance door. The air was still thick with smoke. It was no place for a baby to be born.

A knot grew in her stomach as she looked around her. It was mayhem. The criminal investigation would come, of course. She intended to be at the front of the queue to be in charge of that. In the back of her mind she knew that a parallel investigation would soon begin as well, one that would be conducted by the Professional Standards Department and that would examine if every possible step had been taken to prevent this from happening. A serving police officer had likely committed some of the most serious offences possible and was still at large. There would be a day of reckoning, that was for sure. The ramifications would be immense, and she would be at the heart of it.

The ambulance moved slowly away from her, navigating a tricky path around emergency service vehicles and personnel. DS Willmott hadn't established if the baby was at risk or if Sophie was in a natural labour.

'Fuck,' she whispered, as it dawned on her that the gravity of the crime could escalate dramatically if a baby's life was in danger.

'Mike,' she shouted, 'I've got to get to the hospital.'

She needed to be there, and she needed to be there now.

They arrived at A&E in good time.

'I'll leave you here, Sue,' Mike said, as she jumped from the car, 'I'm gonna make a start on finding where the hell Chris is at.'

DS Willmott burst through the doors and approached the receptionist.

'Sophie Wicks, I need to check on her,' DS Willmott said breathlessly, again flashing her warrant card.

The receptionist tapped on her computer. 'No-one here by that name,' she said.

'She must be,' DS Willmott replied. 'They've just brought her in. She's having a baby.'

The receptionist flashed half a smile. 'Then she'll be in the maternity unit, love,' she said.

'For fuck's sake,' DS Willmott muttered.

The maternity unit was on the other side of the hospital. She didn't acknowledge her mistake, just turned around and ran back out of the A&E doors. She knew where the maternity unit was. Every mother did.

It took her ten minutes to navigate the dark and empty corridors of the hospital. At night it was solemn and quiet, like something from a horror movie. Every step echoed into the distance, every sterile corridor awash with only the light of the moon that had poked its head out from behind the clouds. She didn't have time to fear it, though. As she marched through the labyrinth and conquered the maze, she emerged from the main hospital and jogged to the maternity doors.

The maternity unit was a ward where the clock didn't matter. It was fully operational twenty-four hours a day. As DS Willmott was buzzed in, it was alive with activity. She approached a receptionist who looked tired and stressed.

'I'm here for Sophie Wicks—'

'Visiting begins at 10 a.m.,' the receptionist said.

'I'm a police officer,' DS Willmott replied. 'She's been brought in by ambulance and I'm here to check on her welfare. Now, where is she?'

The receptionist rolled her eyes and looked at her computer. 'She's in delivery,' she said. 'You can't see her.'

'And her husband?' DS Willmott asked. 'Where is he? They came in with their daughter.' Her patience was wearing thin.

'If he's not in delivery then try the family room,' the receptionist said, pointing down the corridor. She turned on her chair and started reading through a pile of paperwork in front of her. The conversation was over.

DS Willmott made her way to the family room and gently held her ear to the closed door. She heard Andrew, talking in hushed tones. She quietly knocked on the door and pushed it open. Andrew was sitting on a chair with Maria straddled on him, her head nestled over his shoulder.

DS Willmott tiptoed across the floor and sat next to him, shrugging off his glares.

'I've just got her off,' he said, his voice calm and soothing but his face etched with rage.

'I'm so sorry about what happened,' DS Willmott whispered.

Andrew's face wore a grimace of anger, but he couldn't

let it out. Maria was there. She was asleep. Instead, his lip twitched as he kept it all under lock and key.

'How's Sophie doing?' DS Willmott asked. 'I need to ask you and the doctors some questions about what brought on the labour, once Sophie's okay, of course.'

'I don't know,' Andrew whispered. 'There's no way I was going to leave Maria on her own.'

DS Willmott looked at him, and shook her head.

'What an awful decision to make,' she mumbled. Choosing to leave his wife in the worst kind of distress, in order to look after his child. It didn't bear thinking about.

'I'd choose my kid, every time,' Andrew replied, quietly.

He stared at her, and she at him. Their eyes locked on each other's, and didn't move.

'What does that mean?' she asked.

'Exactly what I say,' Andrew replied. 'My family come first, every single time.'

His eyes burned into her, to the point where it was uncomfortable. For the first time in a long career of policing, she blinked first.

'And right now, Sophie needs you,' she said. 'Go on, I'll stay with Maria.'

'You sure?' he whispered. 'What if it takes a while?'

DS Willmott smiled, nodding towards the door.

'Go on, I'll be here,' she said.

Andrew gently lifted Maria and manoeuvred her onto the sofa that sat on the opposite side of the room. Her sleep was heavy, and she didn't wake.

'Thanks,' he murmured.

DS Willmott looked at him and saw something she'd seldom seen in Andrew. A vulnerability. A father. A man, doing what he could to protect his family.

'My pleasure,' she replied, sitting next to Maria and stroking her hair just as she would with Lottie.

The room was warm. The hour was late. She looked at her phone before looking at the sleeping girl, and flicked it to silent. She set it down on the seat next to her, face up so she could see it light up if it rang.

There must be soundproofing on the walls, she thought, as the hustle and bustle of a busy maternity ward seemed muffled to near silence in that cocoon of tranquillity. She looked at Maria. So very, very peaceful.

DS Willmott's eyes closed, as she drifted off to her own, private dreams.

Chapter 59

MIKE

One Hundred and Fourteen Days After

Mike sat alone in DS Willmott's chair, leafing through the case file once more. The radio crackled in the background, but that was a mop-up operation, with bosses and bigger bosses working out how to manage the logistics of a resource-intensive crime scene.

Mike's focus, on the other hand, was on two things.

To find Chris.

Then, to bring him in.

Joe's photo stared up at him from the front of the bundle of papers that lay in front of him, and it hurt his soul. What Chris had been through... Well, it would have broken any man.

He pulled Joe's photo to one side, and stared back at it.

'Where's your dad at?' he asked.

Joe's grin was fixed. Permanent. Stuck in time.

Mike put the picture back, as gently as his weary fingers could manage, and picked up the photos of Linda and Trevor that DS Willmott had added to the case file as those particular dominoes had dropped.

'Chris, where are you, mate?' Mike whispered, as the ghosts of those departed circled around him.

He looked at Linda. Beautiful. Radiant. Taken in a time when life may have been hard but it was care-free. Again, he set it down, ever so softly.

Then, Trevor. In the absence of a photo of him living, the file photo was of him lying on the slab just before his post-mortem. In death, he looked more peaceful than in life.

Mike's mind rewound to the first time they'd met, all those weeks before, at a house that had been about as run down and unkempt as the man who had answered the door. It had been a real shithole, alright. What had become of it, now that the old man was dead, Mike wondered.

'Shit,' he gasped, as his synapses fired.

He reached for the phone, plucking it from the receiver and dialling a number in one, seamless action.

'Intel on-call DC,' came the reply.

'Sergeant Adams,' Mike said, breathlessly, 'I need some urgent financial checks done.'

'What you got?' the on-call DC asked.

'Need to check if a bank account has been used recently,' Mike replied, 'the subject is deceased, but...'

His voice trailed away, as the pieces of the jigsaw slowly fell into place.

Chapter 60

DS SUE WILLMOTT

One Hundred and Fourteen Days After

DS Willmott opened her eyes, and found herself in that bewildering, confusing space between sleep and consciousness where her surroundings were starkly unfamiliar. Her eyes darted all around as her senses came alive.

Bright lights.

The smell of smoke.

Muffled sounds, outside the room.

And then, she remembered. The bright lights were in the family room. The smoke was from her clothes. Those muffled sounds, the chatter and constant noise that came with a maternity ward.

She looked at her watch, and yawned. Forty-five minutes had passed in the blink of an eye or, more appropriately, in the closing of both eyes.

'Bugger,' she whispered to herself, as she checked her phone. A few missed calls. Two from Mike. The most recent, only ten minutes before. With it, an answerphone message.

'Sue, I'm on my way to you, I know how he's been getting about.'

She may have stolen only a couple of hours' sleep, but Mike's words sent a shot of adrenaline through her. Suddenly, she was awake. Suddenly, she was ready to go.

She stood from the sofa, and looked at the space next to her, where Maria had been sleeping.

And where Maria wasn't sleeping now.

Her eyes darted around the room as, outside the room, she heard movement. The door cracked open, and Andrew poked his head through the gap. He wore a smile reserved for those who had just witnessed a miracle yet, as he looked in, and his eyes searched the room, it disappeared as soon as it had broken out.

'Where's Maria?' he asked.

'She's not with you?' DS Willmott replied.

Andrew stared at her, before barging through the door and turning over every piece of furniture in the room. No matter how improbable it was that she was under the sofa, no matter that it was impossible that she was under the table, he lifted it all and discarded it when he was left wanting.

'Where the hell is she?' he yelled.

DS Willmott's knees nearly buckled under her. Maria had been in her care, under her watch. With a stumble and a trip, she walked from the family room and back along the corridor to the reception.

'The girl,' she mumbled. 'Did you see the girl go?'

'Yeah,' the receptionist replied. 'The police officer took her.'

DS Willmott's eyes had been wide, and they grew wider still. She looked above the reception desk at the camera that was pointed squarely in her direction, and flashed her warrant card.

'I need to see your CCTV video, now,' she whispered.

'Sue,' Mike said, marching in from the entrance door and joining her at the desk.

She shook her head at him, as Andrew came running along the corridor.

'Where the fuck is she!?' Andrew screamed.

'Tell me what the police officer said,' DS Willmott whispered.

'He came in, said he was doing a welfare check on the mum, then walked out with the girl a few minutes later. He said he'd take her home,' the receptionist said. 'He was a family friend. Knew her name, and the parents, where they live and everything.'

'And you let him take her?' DS Willmott asked.

'He was a copper,' the receptionist replied, with a look of confusion on her face.

'Sue, what the hell's going on?' Mike asked, as Andrew paced the floor behind them, cursing under his breath and holding his head in his hands.

'It's him, isn't it,' Andrew said. 'It's fucking him.'

It took a mere second of viewing for DS Willmott to confirm it. Chris. Walking in, his uniform hanging from his gaunt, wasted body, then two minutes later walking out with a sleeping Maria over his shoulder.

DS Willmott marched outside the entrance, into the night air. The sun was on its way, but it hadn't crept across the horizon just yet.

'You didn't hear him?' Mike asked.

'I...' DS Willmott said.

'You FUCKING what!?' Andrew screamed.

'I didn't hear a thing,' she mouthed. Her lips parted, but her voice was absent. It may have been dark still, but her face was ghostly white.

'Sue, we've got to get this broadcast,' Mike said.

'Right now,' she agreed.

Mike reached for his radio, and the battery grunted at him that it was near the end of its life. It died as soon as he hit the transmit button, and he beckoned DS Willmott to follow him to his vehicle. She walked beside him, with Andrew barely a footstep behind.

'You've got to find her,' Andrew whispered.

DS Willmott and Mike lengthened their strides, and quickened their pace.

'You hear me?' Andrew shouted, grabbing hold of Mike by the shoulder and spinning him around so roughly that he nearly lost his footing. 'You've got to find her, you've GOT to!'

Mike took hold of Andrew's arm, but it wasn't a restraint. He wasn't trying to do any funny police moves on him. Instead, it was placatory, a soothing caress for a wounded animal.

'Let us do what we need to do,' Mike said.

'Control from DS Willmott,' she said, as they reached the car and she summoned the resolve to share what had happened on her watch. 'Urgent message. We've got an active kidnapping. Repeat, active kidnapping.'

Her mind was a quagmire of activity, as her heart did battle with her head. In normal times, she could put aside emotion and deal with process. It's what she did, what she'd always done. Strip away the sentiment and work through lines of enquiry and actions judiciously. Now, though? It ripped through her as if it were Lottie who had been snatched. And it had been her fault.

'Control to DS Willmott,' came the reply. 'We're still bringing patrols across from all over the county for everything else that's going on. Standby.'

She looked at Mike.

'We've got to find them,' she said, her voice brimming with guilt. 'You said you know how he's been getting about?'

'Oh Christ, yeah, he's been using his dad's bank cards,' Mike said. 'Rental car, food, drink, the lot. Should've seen it earlier.'

'Oh God,' DS Willmott replied. 'Of course.'

So obvious. Too obvious. Hidden, in plain sight. An only child, the sole beneficiary of an estate. How hadn't they seen it? How hadn't she seen it?

'Mike, what's the dad's address?' DS Willmott asked. 'He's got to be there, right?'

'The Glades,' Mike replied, 'Hillside Approach. I went there when Linda d—'

'Sorry, what was that?' Andrew asked.

'His dad's address,' Mike replied.

'What address, I meant,' Andrew asked.

'The Glades, Hillside Approach,' Mike said.

Andrew stumbled backwards, mumbling incoherently.

'You alright?' Mike asked.

'That's where I've been working for weeks, renovating it,' Andrew whispered.

Chapter 61

ANDREW

One Hundred and Fourteen Days After

From the euphoric highs of having been witness to the miracle of creation as baby Lewis was born just moments before, to the crashing lows of the hell that now befell him, Andrew's lips twitched involuntarily.

'I'm coming with you to find her,' he said. He was resolute. The only way they were going to drag him from the back seat of Mike's car was by arresting him and, even then, he wouldn't go without a fight.

On the car radio set, confusion reigned. A house fire to manage and, now, an active kidnapping. It may have been the small hours, but the nightmare over Beachbrook loomed large.

'What about the baby?' Mike asked. 'What about Sophie?'

'Lewis is safe with her,' Andrew replied, digging in. 'Maria needs me.'

'You can't come with us,' Mike said, pleading for Andrew to get out of the vehicle so that they could make tracks and do what needed to be done.

'I'm not getting out,' Andrew repeated. He closed the

door and locked it from the inside. It didn't matter that there were child locks already in place, nor that Mike could have just zapped it open with the key fob, it was the intent that mattered, and time was of the essence.

'Fuck it,' DS Willmott said, climbing into the front seat of the car.

Mike followed suit and, within seconds, they were skidding away from the maternity ward and back onto the wide, empty streets of Beachbrook.

Andrew stared forward, his gaze on the road but his focus lost in the fog of his emotions. From the euphoric high of a new arrival, to the bowel-numbing hell that now crippled him, he felt every muscle twitch and every nerve jangle. Bumps in the road caused physical pain to his every extremity.

In the front, DS Willmott had tears streaking down her cheeks, but it didn't register with Andrew. He was running on fumes, dressed in yet more hospital clothes but with the smell of smoke still stagnant in his hair. That Mike opened a window made no odds. The fire at Andrew's house was still releasing vapours into the Beachbrook air, and it just threw more of the stench into the mix.

'It's his dad's house,' Mike mumbled, shaking his head as his mind wandered.

It's Jodie from Allcroft Property Management.

Are you still looking for work?

I've got a client who needs quite a big job doing.

They've asked for you.

He'd needed the work so much, he'd never asked who, or why. He felt sick. Not nauseous. Sick, to the very depths of his being, as DS Willmott's words from the day before rung in his ears.

He's been stalking you and your family.
He's fixated on you all.

Chris had lured him in, and kept him busy while he'd been out stalking. And had he been watching him while he worked? Keeping tabs, while Andrew picked his nose, sang at the top of his voice, spoke to himself about life, all in what he thought was safe privacy? Had he sat silently upstairs, or peered in through the windows? Had he revelled in the power, knowing that he'd placed Andrew there, exactly where he wanted him, and had him dancing to his wicked tune? Andrew retched, but brought up nothing other than the foul stench of fetid smoke from his wheezing lungs.

'We've got to find her,' he whispered.

Mike's driving was suddenly meek and mild, lest they announce their arrival with the squealing of tyres and the screeching of brakes. Silence was needed. A covert approach. As he made the final turn, the engine barely idling over, they drove past the street nameplate. They'd arrived. Hillside Approach. Andrew looked at it, like he had done the first time that he had turned up for work, and on all the days and weeks since. It had been a Godsend, a job sent from the heavens. How was he to know that it had been the Grim Reaper's work after all?

'You've got to stay in the car,' Mike said, as he slowed gently to a stop behind a car that was parked, half on the verge and half on the road, outside The Glades. His words were for Andrew, but his eyes were on the abandoned car.

'That's it,' Mike muttered, looking at the vehicle registration and cross referencing with his pocket notebook, 'that's the motor he's been using.'

Andrew said nothing but, as he reached for his door handle, this time the child locks worked against him.

403

'If you don't let me out,' he said, 'I'm going to fucking scream.' His voice was calm. Controlled. And deadly serious.

Andrew looked at Mike man to man, and watched as the sergeant turned his gaze to DS Willmott. She didn't look back. She was a shattered, shell of a person, wrecked by what had come before.

'Let me out,' Andrew instructed, his voice rising with every syllable.

The sky was still dark, the hour still early. The sun was on its way, but was yet to poke its nose above the horizon. For them, stealth was all they had, the element of surprise should Chris be there. A screaming, shouting Andrew would have telegraphed their arrival.

'Let him out,' DS Willmott said quietly, as she climbed from the front seat.

'Sue, we've got to call in backup,' Mike replied, from the driver's seat. He'd been awake for nearly twenty-four hours. His tour of duty had started nearly that long ago, too, and it wasn't over yet.

Andrew could see him squinting as he fought to think with clarity, with precision.

'Control from Sergeant Adams,' he said, holding the car transmitter to his mouth. 'Urgent assistance required at The Glades, Hillside Approach. Suspect vehicle at location.'

The radio came alive with respondents.

'Let me out,' Andrew repeated, once more, louder still.

'Fuck's sake,' Mike muttered, as he climbed from the car and opened the back door.

Andrew bolted from the rear of the car like the lightning that had chased them across the sea, all those months before. The air was still, though the smell of smoke still lingered. Those fires, they'd spread their fumes everywhere. Under the

404

light of the moon, he ran past the weeds in the front garden that fought with wild flowers for space. He was halfway up the path when Mike's voice caught up with him.

'Wait,' Mike hissed. 'Think of Maria.'

Andrew stopped dead in his tracks, those words cutting through him like a scalding knife through warm butter.

Mike overtook him in a flash.

'You, don't you DARE run off like that,' Mike said, his voice sizzling with authority.

'Go on then,' Andrew muttered.

'We've got to wait for backup,' Mike barked.

'Fuck that,' Andrew replied. 'That's my baby girl. You can wait, I'm going in.'

'Don't make me handcuff you,' Mike said.

Andrew tensed his arms. He might've lost some mass over the weeks and months, but no copper was a match for a parent separated from their child.

'Just you fucking try it...' he muttered. He strained his ears, but the only noise he heard was the early call of the seagulls. Sirens? The screeching of tyres as the cavalry came to their aid? That was distinctly absent.

'Listen,' Andrew said, 'you do what you've got to do. Me? I'm doing what I've got to.'

'Christ's sake,' Mike replied. 'Take this, Sue,' he said, handing DS Willmott the canister of incapacitant spray from his kit belt as she marched up behind them.

Andrew stood behind the two sergeants as Mike racked his extendable baton. Footstep by silent footstep, the three of them moved towards the front door in tandem.

'Unlocked,' Mike whispered as he tried the handle.

'I didn't lock it yesterday,' Andrew muttered. 'Chris, Sophie, my house, remember?'

The hinges groaned and creaked as Mike pushed it open, and the three of them winced as one. So much for the element of surprise. Mike grabbed the door, trying to silence it, but it was too late. He might as well have just smacked the heavy, metal knocker a few times.

'CHRIS,' Mike shouted, 'it's Mike. If you're in here, let me know where you are.'

Those words echoed all around, bouncing off half plastered walls and lifted floorboards. They returned to him, without response.

'Chris,' Mike repeated, 'we need to check you're okay, and Maria too.'

Andrew couldn't keep his feet still and, as Mike crossed the threshold, with DS Willmott holding tightly to his belt, he inched forward behind them. His eyes darted all over, from side to side, up and down. He didn't need an extendable baton, or some pepper spray. No, his weapon was something much rawer, much more instinctive. It was paternal rage. He knew the layout, better than anyone and, as the faintest hum of sirens trickled into his ears, and they inched further down the hallway and past a window that looked out into the garden and the grounds beyond, he saw something he'd never seen before.

A murky, dull light, shining around the cracks of a newspaper-covered window, in one of the outbuildings. He may have spent a lot of time renovating the main house, but those buildings in the grounds beyond had always been locked with deadbolts.

Now, it was clear why.

Chapter 62

MIKE

One Hundred and Fourteen Days After

'Wait,' Mike shouted.

It was too late. Before either he or DS Willmott had the time to process Andrew making a sprint for it, he had got to the end of the hallway and was out of the back door and running. By the time that the smoky air hit Mike, as he ran through the very same door, Andrew was halfway across the grounds and running in a direct line for the outbuildings.

'For Christ's sake!' DS Willmott shouted as, in Mike's ear, the sirens grew slightly louder.

The cavalry may have been on their way, but this was here. This was now. Backup? It might as well have been coming from Mars.

The moon shone a spotlight over Mike and, as he sprung after Andrew, his work boots became entangled in the heavy grass that clumped around them. It was like quicksand and, the faster he churned through it, the more his progress seemed stunted.

He looked up. Andrew seemed light of foot, like he was

gliding across the terrain. In an instant, he was at the door to the outbuilding and had disappeared inside.

Mike's calf muscles growled at him as he forced his legs up and down, but he ploughed on. Those sirens were getting closer, but they were still too far away.

'You with me, Sue?' he shouted.

'Right here,' she called from just behind him.

They reached the outbuilding together. It was brick-built, with a decent roof and windows that were lined with a couple of layers of newspapers. To keep the light out, Mike wondered, or to keep whatever was behind the walls in? The door was still ajar, and a dull glow shone out through it, the type of mood light that a bedside lamp would have given off. Mike pushed it open with his extendable baton and walked across the threshold.

In the room that greeted them was a scene they'd seen before.

Newspaper clippings. Photos of Joe and Linda. Every surface covered.

More photos of Sophie, Andrew and Maria. On these ones, though, faces had been scratched out. Gouged. As if done by a school compass, or a scalpel.

Mike stumbled inside, drawn towards a desk that stood on the left-hand side of the room. On top of it sat piles and piles of photos, camera equipment, newspaper clippings, tape, glue, all the tools of Chris' trade. Next to them, a stack of letters, all addressed to Trevor Jamieson, but with Royal Mail redirection stickers on them, bearing Chris' address.

'LET GO OF HER!' Andrew screamed.

Mike looked up. There was another door that led to an adjoining room. He walked straight towards it, and into whatever danger lurked beyond, without a moment's hesitation. Those seconds... right now, they mattered.

'Chris,' he said quietly, as he walked through the door, baton raised.

The second room was smaller. More intimate. More homely. It was, in many ways, a living space. Tins and tins of food, and gallons of water. Enough to live on for a long time. More surveillance equipment. A bed, the dividing barrier between one half of the room and the other. On the bed, a mattress. On the mattress, a duvet. And on that duvet, a heavily thumbed picture book, with battered and frayed edges, one that had been read and read and read to death, most recently at a funeral parlour in the middle of town.

In the middle of the room, Chris stood with Maria gripped tightly with one hand, and the other holding a knife next to her head.

Mike glanced to his left, where Andrew stood at the side of the doorway with his hands in the air and sheer terror etched on his face. Next to him, DS Willmott was rooted to the spot. As he turned his head straight, his attention was drawn to the blade. It hadn't come from a kitchen set, that was for sure. It was twelve inches of shiny, semi-serrated steel, not quite a machete but, still, a tool that had been forged with only malice in mind.

'Chris,' Mike said, lowering his arm with the baton down to his side. His fingers brushed over his sidearm as he did. 'Come on, mate, you haven't got to do this.'

Chris' grip around Maria's neck tightened, as the tip of the knife dug in a bit more exaggerating the dimple on her cheek.

'Please,' Andrew stuttered. 'Please, Chris. She's just a kid.'

'JOE WAS JUST A KID!' Chris screamed, as flecks of white, stringy spittle from his lips showered Maria.

'Chris,' Mike said, 'you're a better man than this. Come on, mate, remember that man, the decent one that you are, remember him.'

'Am I?' Chris asked.

Mike stared at him, his hands twitching. Chris' eyes were black now. His police uniform, once filled by a man of honour, of integrity, was now occupied by something else entirely. His every fibre screamed at him to stay calm, to speak placidly, to try to reanimate the Chris he knew from the shell of a person who was standing before him. As he stared into Chris' broken eyes, though, one thing was clear; one wrong move would spell utter disaster.

'You did this,' Chris mumbled, turning his eyes to Andrew. 'This is all on you.'

'She's a kid,' Andrew repeated. 'Just a kid, Chris.'

'What happened to my kid?' Chris growled.

'I don't...' Andrew replied.

'Not talking to you,' Chris muttered, 'I'm talking to Maria. What happened to my Joe, Maria?'

Mike watched, as Chris looked down to the little girl who was helpless in his grip. Maria's face screwed up in terror as the tip of the knife pierced her cheek. Her whimpering seemed to do nothing to placate the madman, though.

'SPEAK!' Chris snarled, as more white specks of spittle sprayed from his lips.

'My daddy,' Maria sobbed. 'He said it was an accident.'

'WHAT WAS!?' Chris screamed.

'In the sea,' Maria cried, 'I didn't mean it.'

'MEAN WHAT!?' Chris shouted.

'To make Joe a star—' Maria whispered.

'ENOUGH!' Andrew screamed. 'That's enough! You've

made your point, Chris, you've fucking made it, alright, now just let her go!'

Mike twitched, as his eyes tracked Chris' hand with the knife. It was shaking, and the tip of the blade was bouncing off her skin.

'And you've had another, haven't you,' Chris growled, looking back up at Andrew.

Mike's hands fidgeted, as Andrew left Chris' question unanswered.

'I SAID YOU'VE HAD ANOTHER ONE, HAVEN'T YOU!?' Chris bellowed.

'Yeah,' Andrew whispered.

'Boy or girl?' Chris asked.

'Boy,' Andrew mouthed.

'Name?' Chris asked.

'We were thinking Lewis,' Andrew said, his voice cracking.

'Lewis Wicks,' Chris mumbled. 'Lewis, Lewis Wicks.'

'Please, please let her go,' Andrew begged.

'Lewis Wicks,' Chris repeated. 'Little L W, Lewis Wicks.'

'Come on, Chris,' Mike said, 'this ain't you.'

'Lewis Wicks,' Chris said again, 'Lewis Lewis Wicks.'

He closed his eyes, and took a deep, lingering breath, before raising his knife-wielding hand stiffly into the air, with the tip of the blade pointing down at Maria's head.

'An eye for an eye balances the books,' he whispered.

'NO!' Andrew screamed, as he tracked the three metres across the room towards Chris. Towards Maria. Towards the blade that was about to come thundering down.

Instinct took over. Mike had played out this scene so many times before, but never in the field of play. It had always been a simulation, a role play. It happened both in the blink of an eye, and in slow motion.

411

Threat to life, immediate.

Negotiations, failed.

Sidearm, drawn.

Aim.

Fire.

And, as the sirens drowned out the echoes of his smoking gun, the two men in front of him fell silently to the floor, locked together, with arms entangled.

Chapter 63

Six Months After

The frost and bite of the bleak midwinter had given way to the promise of a new season.

A new dawn.

A new start.

It may have been new roots that were sought, but the shoots wouldn't grow without closure. As Sophie drove, and the air grew fresher as the coast drew closer, she ticked off the hours in her head. Four to go. Then three. Two. One.

Then, into minutes. Fifty. Forty. Twenty. Past Havington, and on the final stretch. She looked to her left as she navigated the coastal road, watching as the sea sent shards of sunlight glistening in every direction. It had been days like that when she had loved it so.

'Alright back there?' she asked.

'All good, Mum,' Maria replied.

'And Lewis?' she asked.

'He's good,' Maria said.

'Nearly there, now,' Sophie said. 'Nearly there.'

She looked ahead, but the roads were empty. Beachbrook was still lying dormant, without the tourists. Summer, though, was on its way. Soon, those very roads would be gridlocked.

She drove towards the town centre, but turned off before

she got caught in the ring road. She knew a short cut. All the locals did.

The driveway was long and winding, with towering oaks lining the way. Apart from the gentle revs of her engine, it was silent. But then, that's how crematoriums and their grounds were supposed to be.

She rolled to a stop in the car park, one of only two vehicles there. No funerals on a Saturday. That's why she'd chosen that day, after all. Climbing from the vehicle, she looked in at the kids.

Then, to Andrew.

'You ready?' she asked.

He nodded.

'Go for it,' she said.

He climbed from the car. It may have taken a minute, but he did it on his own. No help. Small wins. She watched as he shuffled forward, his faltering steps a result of both his physical ailments and his proximity to the very thing that had reaped them on him.

The graves were only kicking distance from the car, arranged in such a way that Sophie could see them while still watching the kids in the car. There was no way that she was letting them out of her view. None at all.

Andrew's footsteps grew more ragged still, but he kept his chin up. He kept his shoulders back. He pressed on, regardless, until he was in front of them once more. The boy, he'd loved. The woman, a person with whom his wife had been thick as thieves. And the man, who'd once been like a brother.

A modest stone. Granite. And a simple engraving.

Christian, Linda and Joe Jamieson.

Now together, in eternal peace.

Red roses sat in a plastic vase next to them. They'd been there a while, and the petals were falling from them. Andrew looked around, craning his neck as best he could manage. Whoever had been tending to the graves certainly wasn't there now.

'Hi, guys,' he croaked. He'd still not yet got used to the fact that his voice had changed, much like every other part of him.

He stopped, and waited, looking for a sign. A gust of wind, maybe? A rustle of leaves, perhaps? But no, there was nothing. The floor was his.

'Soph and I, we've driven down from our new digs,' he continued, 'because I needed to see you all. What do they call it? Closure? I dunno. I just... I guess I needed to be here, to see it with my own eyes.'

He looked behind him. Sophie was still there, still watching.

'She's been a rock, you know?' he continued. 'Don't know how she does it. Family comes first, she says, and I guess that was true for you guys as well, right?'

He breathed in and out, tasting the salty, sweet air that is only found in a coastal town.

'I'm sorry,' he whispered. 'Sorry to you all. Just know that, whatever is said or done, I get it. I understand.'

He closed his eyes.

ANGE!

'I deserved it,' he muttered.

He turned around, and hobbled back to Sophie as, behind them, another car drove slowly into the car park. They watched as, the door opened, and DS Willmott climbed out, with a fresh bunch of red roses in her hand.

'Andrew?' she said. Her chin didn't hit the floor, but it might as well have.

'Yeah,' he croaked.

She walked over to them, her feet crunching on the loose gravel underfoot.

'What are you doing here?' she asked.

'Had to see them,' he replied.

'Why?' she asked.

He shook his head. Good question.

'Closure, I guess,' he replied.

She looked at him, and paused.

'Did you get it?' she asked, quietly.

Andrew looked at her. He wasn't the only one with something missing behind their eyes.

'Don't think I ever will,' he said.

They stood in silence. It wasn't peace that permeated in the air all around them, but it wasn't discord, either. It was just... A consensus. Things had happened. Lives had been ruined. People had been lost. For those still standing, there were barriers yet to overcome.

'Why are you here?' Andrew asked.

DS Willmott paused before answering.

'Don't know, really,' she replied. 'Just to keep it tidy, I guess. They didn't have anyone else, did they?'

'You've been laying the flowers?' Sophie whispered.

'Yeah,' DS Willmott replied.

'She loved red roses,' Sophie said, wiping a tear from her cheek.

For a moment, there was silence. Peace. Tranquillity.

'What happened, Andrew?' DS Willmott asked, quietly. 'What happened in the sea?'

Andrew looked at her, through the mist in her eyes, and shook his head.

He'd made a promise to his daughter. The truth wasn't for sharing.

'The things we do for our kids, eh?' he replied.

Epilogue

JOE

'TAG!' Joe shouted.

For once in his life, he'd caught up with her.

'Doesn't count,' Maria replied. 'I was trying to get the kite open.'

'Does too,' Joe said. 'Tag, tag, TAG!'

He tapped her again and again. In a world where Maria always won, this was his time. It was his turn.

'Stop it,' she said, pushing his hand away.

Joe smiled at her, but only received a pout in return.

They both looked out to sea, as the surf rolled towards the shore with a roar.

'Those waves...' Maria said.

'Ginormous,' Joe replied.

'REALLY ginormous,' Maria said.

They looked at each other. Now, there was a smile on her face.

'Come on,' she said, racing back to the beach hut. This time, there was no catching her. Joe tried, but she was up the ladder and onto the promenade with him trailing in her wake.

'Don't even think about it,' Andrew said, but Joe knew

how the conversation was going to end. He might only be a kid, but he'd heard it enough times.

'I'll tell you what,' Andrew eventually said, after Maria's arguments had been put across, 'you can go in the little sea. That's what's called a compromise.'

Joe looked out to sea. The waves might have been ginormous, but it didn't look fun. Still the little sea would be alright. Anything for Maria.

'You don't have to go if you don't want to, mate,' Andrew whispered to him.

Joe forced a smile. 'Maria wants to play so I'll go with her to make sure she's okay,' he said.

Maria was first down the ladder, with Joe in hot pursuit. He felt the drizzle in the air stinging his cheeks, but he ignored it. He'd soon be wet, anyway.

Maria was the first into the little sea, diving onto her tummy. The water barely covered half her body, though. Joe splashed down next to her, covering the back of her orange wetsuit with a sludge of watery sand.

'Joe!' she said.

He smiled, and used his hands to cup some more over her.

'Stop it,' she said, smiling as she splashed him back, the sea water from her hands hitting him in the neck and trickling down the inside of his wetsuit.

'COLD!' Joe shouted.

It only prompted Maria to do it again. They both jumped to their feet, and kicked water at each other, giggling as it rained down on their adversary. Their opponent. Their best friend.

'TEN MINUTES!' Andrew shouted.

Joe looked up, and Maria scowled.

'Nah,' she muttered.

Joe smiled, as he splashed Maria again, but she was

losing interest. As he kicked more and more water over her, she was looking far beyond him. The air may have been misty, with sea spray and mizzle, but Joe knew what she was staring at, and he looked too.

'Ginormous,' she whispered.

'REALLY ginormous,' he replied.

A knot grew in his tummy, but he didn't know why.

'Five minutes!' Andrew bellowed, from way behind them at the beach hut.

'Alright, five minutes,' Maria shouted back.

The winds may have been strong but, as they inched away from the little sea, the rumble of thunder that bellowed overhead filled their ears.

'Cool,' Maria said, smiling.

'Really cool,' Joe replied, not replicating her smile.

'Can't catch me!' Maria said, springing away from him.

'Can too!' Joe replied.

Behind him, he heard a dog barking and someone shouting, but that didn't matter. He'd already tagged Maria once that morning, and now he was going to do it again.

She had a head start on him, but the challenge had been laid down.

'Gonna get you,' he shouted, as she ran through the thick, clogging sands.

As he gained ground, she looked behind him.

'You're cheating,' she shouted back, upping her pace.

'Gonna get you!' he repeated, feeling a surge of adrenaline as he realised that he really was catching up with her.

She was normally quicker than him, but his little legs cycled and cycled like they never had before. He could still hear the dog barking, but it didn't matter. Nothing did. As

Maria changed direction, and darted towards the sea, he was actually going to win. He was sure of it.

'Stop cheating!' she shouted.

He knew he wasn't. He was blind to her path, just chasing the sand that she was digging up with her heels as he got even closer. Five paces away. Four. Three became two, then one. As she splashed into the big sea, he caught her. He tagged her. For the second time that morning, he'd won.

'I GOT YOU!' he shouted, euphoric.

Her face was like thunder as waves crashed all around them. They may have only been a few metres in, but the water crashed into their thighs.

'No,' she shouted.

'I did, I did,' he said.

'NO,' she screamed, but her words were swallowed by the waves.

Then, she pushed him.

He stumbled backwards, and fell, disappearing into a breaking wave.

'Joe?' he heard Maria say, but she sounded far away. The wave had gone over his head and he couldn't find where the ground was beneath his feet in order to stand up again.

'Joe?' Maria shouted, much louder this time, but she sounded more distant.

He felt himself getting tugged under the water, pulled along.

'MARIA!' he shouted, as the sea sucked him away from shore. That knot in his tummy was tightening, and he was so, so scared.

'JOE!' she screamed, taking a step towards him.

Joe watched as Maria walked straight into the same powerful current that was pulling his whole body. In an instant, they were reunited as Maria slammed into him. He was terrified, but at least Maria was with him now.

Ten metres away from shore. Fifteen. Twenty. They were passengers, yet they clung to each other, refusing to let each other go. Joe kicked like he'd never kicked before, treading the water beneath him, not giving in to the waves that were trying to prise them apart.

'KICK, Maria!' shouted Joe, through mouthfuls of water. They both kicked furiously, faces screwed up as saltwater burned their eyes. It felt like hours had passed and Joe felt his legs getting heavy and harder to move. But still, he kicked.

And then suddenly Andrew was there. Adults could solve anything, Joe thought.

'KIDS,' Andrew shouted, 'climb on me.'

Joe climbed on one shoulder, and Maria the other, but they just pushed him under.

'AGAIN,' Andrew shouted, re-emerging from under the surface. He was stressed, and it scared Joe. Andrew was always the calm one, always the fun one. Now, he wasn't.

Joe buried his face into Andrew's shoulder, but once again, they pushed him under. This time, Andrew shook them both off.

'DADDY!' Maria shouted, sounding panicked.

'ANGE!' Joe screamed.

Andrew scrabbled at the surface, somehow pulling himself up, but his face was like a ghost.

'DADDY!' Maria repeated as she flailed her arms all around.

'ANGE, PLEASE!' Joe repeated. He could feel the tug of the water underneath him. He was kicking as hard as he could but he could feel the waves slapping him on the face, and it hurt.

Maria was getting pulled along next to him. She reached out for her dad, but both her and Joe had drifted too far from him. Her little arms stretched, but it was no good. Joe, though… Well, he was within her reach.

'MARIA, DON'T!' he screamed, as she grabbed him. This time, it wasn't for support, this time it was for buoyancy.

'Maria, come to me!' Andrew shouted from somewhere.

'Can't!' she replied, gripping Joe's shoulders tightly.

Joe's mouth filled with water as he struggled to stay afloat. Maria was pushing him down as she fought to keep her head above the water.

'MARIA, DON'T!' he repeated, as that water swamped down his throat. He tried to pry her hands from his shoulders but his fingers were numb and her grip was so strong.

'Maria, you've got to come to me, LET HIM UP, NOW!' Andrew screamed.

But Joe felt Maria's full weight holding him under as her panic rose. He felt her hands slip from his shoulders, but in an instant she grabbed hold again. Tighter, now. It was as if he was giving her a piggyback, and she wrapped her arms around his neck as she sucked down the air that he was being denied. He tried to thrash his arms, but under the surface they just floundered gently. He tried to kick his legs, but they felt heavy and stiff, and he struggled to move them.

'Maria, let him up!' Andrew cried. It was a muffle in Joe's ears, and it was too late anyway.

Joe's limbs went still.

He thought of his daddy.

He thought of his mummy.

Then, darkness.

Acknowledgements

After The Storm was conceived way back in 2021. While a few speedbumps were hit along the road to getting published, it's been a thoroughly enjoyable ride.

To my agent, Nicky Lovick at WGM, thank you so much for taking a punt on me, for your friendship, your work in the editorial trenches, and for the hours spent chewing the literary fat together. It's been fun, hasn't it!

To my editor, Rachel Hart, your vision is second to none. Let me say that again. Your vision is second to absolutely, totally, entirely, none. The instant that I clamped eyes on the first structural pass that you completed, it was like your views on how *After The Storm* could be a more complete package were aligned entirely with my own. Your work has strengthened it, has bolstered it, and has breathed renewed life into Beachbrook.

To all the team who have worked so hard on this book, my heartfelt thanks. To Raphaella Demetris, for all the editorial work you have done with Rachel. To Anna Nightingale, who did such a stellar job on the copyedits. To Rachel Sargeant on the proofread. To Maddie Dunne-Kirby who manages the marketing. To Holly Macdonald who designed the cover. To Katie Buckley, who gets the book 'out there'. To Amanda Percival who sells it to the rest of the world. To Emily Gerbner,

Jean-Marie Kelly and Sophia Wilhelm, who are in charge of the US side of things. And to the rest of 'Team Avon' – Helen Huthwaite, Sarah Bauer, Amy Baxter, Elisha Lundin and Ella Young. Thank you, thank you, thank you all. That's one heck of a list of names, and it shows just how much goes into publishing a book, and just what a collaborative process it is.

To my publicist, Laura Sherlock, thanks so much for everything you've done. It's been a joy, an honour and a privilege to work with you.

To my friend Kimberley Dadds who I've known since we were just three years old, thanks so much for your time, your support, and your encouragement (and your contacts!). Your turn next.

To James Kermack, my wonderful friend and regular collaborator on all things film/TV, thank you so much for taking a punt on a self-published, little-known novel that you picked up at my cafe. That's still one of my favourite stories from this whole process! To you, Julien Loeffler, Meredith Coral and all at Featuristic Films, my heartfelt gratitude.

To my sisters, Claire and Nicki, your support has been unwavering and your love unconditional. Thanks for everything, from all the happy memories we've got from growing up, to all the ones we've got left to make in the future. None of my early drafts would have been the same without Nicki's yellow highlighter pointing out inconsistencies and spelling/grammar mistakes. It's like being back at school all over again!

To my parents... What words can I possibly write!? You are both, quite simply, the best. Mum, for never saying 'no' to any of us, even when you probably should sometimes. Dad, for always buying the coffee and for being the BEST proofreader who ever proofread! You've supported me and the girls through everything and I think I speak for all of us when I say that, while we can't repay you, we can choose you a bloody good nursing home. That's a joke, by the way (Claire will put you up).

To my wife, Naomi, who just so happens to be the best mummy to our babies, as well as being a pretty, special wife (double meaning – commas are great)... Thanks for allowing me the time and space to get on with getting on. I'm under no illusions that, without you being the greatest pillar of support I could ever have wished for, these words would never have made it to paper. You're my best friend as well as my wife, and I'm very lucky to have you. Love you, wifey.

To my babies... To Florence and Sully. Thanks for keeping me on my toes, for being the best kiddies that a parent could ever ask for, and for giving the best cuddles. You're both amazing, you try so hard at everything you do, and I couldn't be a prouder daddy. I love you both more than chicken nuggets.

And finally, to everyone who has bought or read this book. Writing it was both life-changing and life-affirming. If you've ever been tempted to take the plunge and put pen to paper, I couldn't recommend it more. Everyone has a book in them. You've just read mine, and I really, really hope you liked it.

Until next time, much love.

Gaz

Content Warning:

This novel contains themes that some may find upsetting, including: child death and bereavement, suicide, mental illness, death at sea and violence.